the FAMILIAR STRANGER

CHRISTINA BERRY

MOODY PUBLISHERS
CHICAGO

Editor: Pam Pugh
Interior Design: Ragont Design
Cover Design: The Design Works Group
Cover Image: Corbis

Library of Congress Cataloging-in-Publication Data

Berry, Christina, 1977-
The familiar stranger / Christina Berry.
p. cm.
ISBN 978-0-8024-4731-9
1. Married people—Fiction. 2. Amnesia—Fiction. 3. Family secrets—Fiction. 4. Domestic fiction. I. Title.

PS3602.E76364F36 2009
813'.6—dc22

2009014650

We hope you enjoy this book from Moody Publishers. Our goal is to provide high-quality, thought-provoking books and products that connect truth to your real needs and challenges. For more information on other books and products written and produced from a biblical perspective, go to www.moodypublishers.com or write to:

Moody Publishers
820 N. LaSalle Boulevard
Chicago, IL 60610

1 3 5 7 9 10 8 6 4 2
Printed in the United States of America

"Christina Berry's stories are wonderfully told, rich in detail, exact in dialogue, and exciting from the moment you begin reading!"

—Eva Marie Everson
author of The Potluck Club series

"As readers discover Christina's writing and realize how friendly and approachable she is, they won't be disappointed."

—Donna Fleisher
author of the Homeland Heroes series

"Christina Berry is a woman who really understands how men think. *The Familiar Stranger* had me from the very first sentence, and it kept me flipping pages right through to the end. It's a terrific debut novel and I'll be watching eagerly for her next one."

—Randy Ingermanson
Christy award-winning author of *Oxygen*

"Christina Berry writes with language that stimulates the senses while challenging our thoughts. She ties mystery with inspiration, giving us good stories well told."

—Jane Kirkpatrick
author of *All Together in One Place, A Clearing in the Wild,* and *A Name of Her Own*

"*The Familiar Stranger* is a great ride. From the opening page to the very last I had to know more. Christina Berry's original voice and her ability to raise uncertainty drives the reader forward to a surprising ending. A wonderful first book!"

—Bonnie Leon
author of the Sydney Cove series

"*The Familiar Stranger* crackles with energy and intrigue. The characters gripped me; the situation haunted me. I didn't want to put it down."

—Jill Elizabeth Nelson
author of the To Catch a Thief series

. . . to Mom and Dad, who were the first to believe.

. . . to all those in hurting marriages. May God grant you a measure of hope through this story.

. . . and to the One who captured my heart with His words of Truth. My life is Yours.

Chapter One

His

I WRAPPED A TOWEL AROUND my waist as Denise stalked into the bathroom. Avoiding her eyes, I wiped a clear spot on the steamy mirror and studied my reflection. A caged man, a Houdini, stared back at me. Bound inside a straitjacket, locked in chains, submerged in a tank, I could taste the metallic tang of the key hidden in my mouth. If I held my breath a little longer and waited for the right time to rip my shoulder from its socket, I would escape my stifling life.

"Did you wipe down the shower, Craig?"

What harm would happen if once, just once, I left droplets on the glass doors? I bit back my retort. "Of course, honey."

"Good." She peered into the brushed-silver mirror hanging above the white marble countertop—a bathroom that had cost me a month's wages—and added another layer to her lipstick. "Need to hurry if we're going to be on time."

"I'm not going." I said it as if I didn't care one way or the other what she thought of my bombshell.

"What are you talking about?" Her shoulders tightened into unnatural stillness.

I rubbed the scruff of my neck and scrutinized my image. A few wrinkles around the eyes. Two slight recessions on either side of the hairline. Not bad for a guy of forty-six.

"Craig, the deacons' meeting is right after the service and you've missed the last two. Are you trying to sabotage your position?" Her reflected hazel eyes drilled into me.

For a second I thought of giving it all up, going to church with her and the kids, acting as though that was all I had planned for the day. Then the image faded and a pair of deep brown eyes replaced hers. No, I wouldn't be setting foot in a house of worship this Sunday, or ever again.

She wouldn't turn away without some kind of explanation.

"Denise, every day of the week I'm looking into people's mouths. Different teeth, different breath, same office, same chair. Same mindless, indecipherable banter. This is my one day off and I'm not going to waste it sitting in a pew with a bunch of pretenders."

"Pretenders?" Her lipstick tube tumbled to the counter, leaving a blood-red slash against its starkness. "Sometimes I don't understand you at all." As she rubbed a tissue over the spot, the red smeared across the dead veins in the rock, veins that merged and parted, crossed and died, without purpose or pattern.

Had I pushed too hard? The last thing I needed this morning was an interrogation built on suspicion.

I'd planned this day for too long to blow it now.

I turned and put my arms around her. "I'm going crazy. Call it a midlife crisis if you will, but I can't put on a tie and sing a happy little hymn. I'm going hiking."

Relaxing into my embrace, she fingered my jawline. "Hiking, huh? Along the trails in Washington Park?"

Why do you always have to make a suggestion so it still seems as if I'm doing what you want? It was her fault I had to carry out my plan.

Yet I had to feign tenderness, feign caring. I tried to smile. "No, to Multnomah Falls. The weather's supposed to be great in the gorge."

Denise stiffened again and moved away from me, heading into the bedroom. "The Columbia Gorge is kind of a long drive for a spur-of-the-moment thing, don't you think?"

Trailing after her, I recalled all the weekends I'd spent following her from one of the kids' soccer games to her friends' barbeques after work on Saturday. Waking the next day to the usual church service, out for lunch with another of her friends—the husband and I pretending camaraderie even though we knew nothing more about each other than our favorite football teams. Back to church for the evening meeting. Finally dropping into bed, dreading the idea of telling people to floss more, brush with softer bristles, lay off the self-whitening strips for a while, and all the other advice I dispensed only to have it ignored.

I slipped on a pair of loose jogging shorts and a T-shirt over my head. "Give me today, and I'll do whatever you want next Sunday."

"Fine." She sighed. "Your mind's made up anyway. I'll figure out something to tell everyone."

"Say a dental emergency came up. A root canal."

She touched the edge of the dresser and balanced on one foot while she slid on a new shoe, a beaded red high heel. I'm sure it set me back a pretty penny. Dyed honey-blonde hair hung over her face as she leaned over to put the other shoe on, calf flexing. I was surprised at how young and attractive she looked. Apparently our physical connection still flowed deep, like the veins in the marble, but my heart sat cold and dense.

What was I doing? Maybe I could—

No. I steeled myself, kissed her forehead for the last time, and wandered down the hallway in search of the boys. I found them in the bonus room, sprawled on the couch, playing a shoot-'em-up video game. Nicolas, fifteen, had gelled his hair into a conservative style and wore a blue oxford. Twelve-year-old Jamie's hair stuck up in blond-tipped spikes. His orange shirt, black flames blazing across the front, shouted, "Look at me!" But the shirt was a button-up, so technically it met Denise's church dress code.

"Guys?" I cleared my throat. "Guys."

They turned their attention from the TV screen.

"Want to skip church and go for a hike?" I held my breath.

Jamie cocked his head back. "Are you serious?"

My heart stopped for a second. I'd been so sure they wouldn't take me up on my invitation. Asking them, and getting turned down—that was what I had counted on.

Nick paused the game and shook his head. "I'm helping with children's church."

Laughing, Jamie jabbed Nick's shoulder. "What he means is that he's helping Heather McCallister with children's church." He turned his attention back to me. "Mom's letting you play hooky?"

I nodded, ignoring the insinuation that Denise arranged my days.

"Man." He kicked at the coffee table. "I'm skateboarding with some friends at the park after lunch. But I can ditch them and come with you, if you want."

"No, no. You do what you've planned."

Nicolas unpaused the game and they went back to shooting each other.

It struck me as an odd pastime to pursue before a sermon. I stood for a moment, gazing at my boys. Almost men. Would they miss me if I weren't around? Denise did everything for them, though I financed it all. I could still do that, fulfill my financial role, even if . . .

My heart thumped, sped up, grew louder, drowned out the sound effects of the guns. Blackness crept into the sides of the room, and I feared I would pass out right in front of the boys. Closing my eyes, I focused on breathing in and out slowly.

The episode passed.

I wanted one last contact with my sons as well. I squeezed the back of Jamie's neck and pulled on Nick's ear before I left the room.

Denise walked past me, positioning her body so we wouldn't accidentally touch. "Boys, time to turn off the game and get into the car."

The boys yelled their good-byes and clattered down the stairs and out to the garage. Denise followed. A mechanical drone signaled the garage door's opening; another, its closing.

I was left standing in the hall directly in front of the family portrait we'd ordered after Jamie's birth. Denise's face glowed, her arms wrapped around the baby. I stared at my image, a three-year-old Nicolas perched on my lap.

Would I have a different life if I'd been a different father, a different husband?

Probably not. No matter how intently I inspected the photo, I couldn't read anything but satisfaction in my expression. Had I really been happy? Or had I been more willing to fake it then?

"No longer." I rubbed sweaty palms over the front of my shirt and glanced down at the wet streaks. Without thinking, I'd put on a white shirt. Denise had to know I was wearing black shorts with a blue shirt. It was critical to the plan. Nervous energy surged through my body.

Should I call her? Say I've changed my shirt?

And have her think I'd completely lost my mind? I pantomimed holding a phone. "Hi, honey. I know you've just left the house, but I'm wearing a blue shirt now. It matches my eyes better." Yeah, right.

A reason. All I needed was a reason. I hustled to the kitchen, smeared some ketchup—she knew I loved scrambled eggs with ketchup for breakfast—on the sleeve as if I'd wiped my mouth on my arm. Upstairs, I threw it in the hamper and found the blue shirt I needed to wear.

"The devil's in the details." My father's voice echoed in my mind, vibrating like my childhood house after he slammed the door and walked away from our family for the last time.

Hers

THE SHOWER STOPPED and I heard Craig step out. I waited until I was sure he'd covered himself and hurried in to check my makeup. Thinking of the tension between us over the last few months had me biting at my lower lip again. Craig always thought that was so cute when we were dating, but now . . .

I rolled my lips in as I passed him. No sense in giving him the opportunity to ridicule me for a silly bad habit.

When he'd first started picking at me, I took everything personally. All my efforts at self-improvement came to naught. So I started talking. To Craig. To my pastor. Eventually to a counselor. I showed all my emotional cards and begged for some insight in return. Yet the tighter I pulled at him, the harder he fought.

My new tactic, besides constant prayer, was to keep it light and easy, distract with the mundane. "Did you wipe down the shower, Craig?"

He smirked, as if I were a prison warden set on micromanaging his life. "Of course, honey." The endearment demeaned me.

"Good." I ignored his inflection and put on a fresh coat of lipstick to cover my tooth prints. "Need to hurry if we're going to be on time."

He posed in front of the mirror. "I'm not going to church."

"What are you talking about?" I'm sure my eyes asked more questions than just that one. Like, *Why don't I feel like I know you anymore?* or *Why do I hold my breath when you walk into a room and relax when you leave?*

He launched into a tirade, sharp words filled with calm anger. My lipstick slipped through my fingers as I listened, numb. I searched his face, hoping to see some sign of the man who had stood next to me at the altar and pledged to be the spiritual leader of our home. All I perceived was a magic show, a sleight of hand, a transformation into a contained, painfully polite man. He gentled his voice and explained it all away with the phrase "midlife crisis."

I completely agreed with his self-assessment. Midlife crisis was not just some term to cover buying a convertible—which Craig already had—but a full-on assault to the durability of our marriage. According to my therapist, Craig and I were "dealing with major communication issues."

Yet, when he held me, my body betrayed me, practically melting into him. Was I so desperate for his attention, his physical touch, I could ignore his uncaring behavior the instant his arms came around me? The implication rattled my dry soul. I pulled away, left the bathroom, and hunted for a pair of shoes that matched my red and cream suit.

Setting the heels next to the dresser, I remembered the first pair of brand-new shoes I'd bought before Craig's graduation from dental school. I made do with secondhand sandals while he studied and fretted over the baby on the way. Then—like the first beams of sunshine through a wrung-out cloud—he told me to get a new pair of shoes for the commencement ceremony. Soon, he told me, all of our sacrifices were going to pay off. Literally.

Tipping my head so my hair would hide the tears welling in my eyes, I slipped the shoes on. I kept looking at the floor as he kissed my forehead and left the room. Sinking onto the duvet, I couldn't keep the tears from seeping out. When had our joint effort at marriage turned into two Clydesdales pulling in opposite directions?

From the bonus room, I heard Craig ask the boys if they'd like to go hiking with him. A new veil of tears came. Yes, it was the first weekend of summer vacation, but had he even thought to ask if *I* would go with him? After all, he was right. He did work hard every day except Sunday. Surely the Lord wouldn't begrudge him one day of relaxation. A day to soothe the heat of burnout I felt flaming from him.

Was it his job? I'd seen an article once that said dentists had one of the highest rates of suicide for professionals. For Craig, I wasn't sure if the hours, the work, or the demands of his family stressed him more. Whatever the case, he had ceased flirting with me long ago. He used to chase me around the house when the kids were little, catch me by the waist, and tickle me. As soon as the boys laughed, he'd chase after them. When was the last time we had shared a laugh as a family?

I stood, dabbing a tissue at each eyelid. One glance at my watch said my mascara fix would have to wait for a red light on the way.

Craig came out of the bonus room just as I entered the hall. His shoulders filled the doorway. Most people tended to think of dentists as little men, very precise, wearing glasses, with looming nose hair. My husband was nothing like that. He was built like a runner, a true athlete, one whose muscles bulged as he drove his arms forward and yanked his knees up. His fingers were fine and long. Adept at what he did.

One touch of his hand, and I would melt into an emotional mess again. I edged past him, praying he wouldn't reach out. My breath came a little easier once I walked out of range.

Nicolas and Jamie turned off the game the first time I asked. They had always been good at doing what they were told. Must have gotten it from me. Sure as rain deluged our part of Oregon in November, they didn't inherit it from their father.

Stomach clenching at the idea of leaving Craig with such little discussion about his decision, I mustered the determination to let him make his own choices and led the boys to the SUV.

Nicolas called shotgun a millisecond before Jamie, throwing himself into the front seat.

I fumbled to get the key into the ignition.

Jamie leaned forward through the gap in the front seats and punched the garage door opener clamped to the sun visor above my head. "Dad's really not coming?"

"He needs a break." The key slid into the slot.

"You okay with that, Mom?" Nicolas fastened his seat belt .

I patted his knee, grateful for his thoughtfulness. "Sure, I'm fine." My hand shook as I reached for the wheel.

Chapter Two

His

COMPARED TO A USUAL day's traffic, I-5 toward Portland stretched out ahead, full of empty space. A RAV4 zoomed past my Mustang, zigzagged through three lanes of traffic, and followed a ramp off toward Lake Oswego. I was in no hurry. I'd planned this day for so long, timing various routes, considering every eventuality. As long as I took care of the details, nothing could go wrong.

I drifted into the middle lane. Mentally, I drifted back to Denise and the boys, to our last family trip. We'd given Jamie his first surfboard, though Denise made him save up his own money for the wet suit. Which took way too long, until I slipped him the last twenty. Nicolas shuddered at the thought of riding the waves. He would rather sneak around the tide pools, explore the creatures hiding in the still waters.

On that first day, Jamie caught a wave. His skinny form, clad in the black wet suit, wobbled back and forth over the board. He rode it out and shouted with triumph. I liked to think his determination and talent came from me. Anything I ever put my mind to, I'd excelled at. He sure hadn't inherited it from Denise. The only worthwhile thing she'd accomplished the whole time I'd known her was latching on to me.

I veered off the freeway at the next exit, stopped at the light, and lowered the automatic top of the convertible.

A woman in the car next to mine rubbed her full lips together. Catching me staring at her, she traced the outline of her mouth with the edge of her coffee cup.

Grinning, I winked.

She tossed her head and waved with her left hand, highlighting the unadorned ring finger. The light turned green and she accelerated across the intersection.

I'd almost forgotten about the constricting band on my own finger, one of those details I could not afford to overlook. I should have felt something then, some seizing of my heart that I could be cruel enough to leave my family. But I didn't. I pictured my heart, a pea-sized pebble rolling around in the cavity of my chest.

Turning right, I scanned the parking lot of the corner convenience store. A man stood between the two graffitied bathroom doors on the side of the store nearest the Dumpster. I parked in the corner of the empty lot, entered the store, and meandered through the aisles, making sure the security cameras captured plenty of footage of me from different angles. There could never be any doubt I'd been in the store alone.

I bought a pack of Dentyne Ice, two bottles of water, and a bag of sunflower seeds. Denise hated when I spat the shells out on our manicured lawn. The guy behind the counter took my credit card, the one marked "See ID" instead of bearing a signature, swiped it, and gave me the receipt without glancing up. Oh, well. He might not remember me, but there would still be an official record of my purchase when the investigation began. Swinging the plastic bag at my side, I jogged to the convertible and slid into my seat.

As I pulled out of the parking lot, I knew I was choosing to put all my chips in one pot. To risk it all for a slim chance at happiness.

But, because of my brilliant planning, I was fated to win the bet.

Chapter Three

Hers

I SWAYED TO THE RHYTHM of the others in my pew, clapping along with the upbeat worship song. Trying to keep my mind on the words instead of Craig's hike made my head feel blurry, as though the two trains of thought pulled apart the synapses connecting my brain. Each nerve stretched taut, fraying into fuzzy ends before the last cord snapped apart.

Despite the warmth of fellowship in the church, I could not shake a cold feeling of doom. *What,* I asked the Lord, *is doomed?* Just this weekend? This year? My marriage? My life?

I shut my eyes and prayed that I might die to thoughts and questions of self. God's love never failed. That's what really mattered. I sang the rest of the song from memory, trying to focus on my Savior.

The music faded to a close. Taking their seats, the congregation rustled. I scooped my dress underneath me, smoothing it as I sat. Sarah Monroe, one of my closest friends, turned in the pew in front of me and mouthed, "Where's Craig?" Her gorgeous almond-shaped eyes seemed to see right through me.

I shook my head and directed my gaze at the pastor as he climbed the steps to the pulpit. The fragile dam I had erected to keep back the thoughts of Craig breached, and quivering emotions flooded over me once again.

When the pastor dismissed the youngest children, Nicolas rose from my side and headed toward the back of the auditorium. I craned my neck and saw my son greet Sarah's niece, Heather McCallister. They, and several other teens from the youth group, herded the little kids out the door.

"Let's open with a word of prayer." The pastor, our church's first African American leader, bowed his head and his digital image did the same on the two big screens on either side of the platform. Jamie slunk down and propped his feet up on the hymnal holder.

I tried to pay attention, but I think I heard even less of the sermon than Jamie. I pictured Craig driving along in the convertible, sun glinting off his perfect teeth. He embodied money, health, good looks—all attractive things to certain girls. Girls who simpered and flirted, flipped their hair, and begged to be taken care of so they wouldn't mess up their newest manicure.

What if he's with someone else right now? Not hiking at all, but setting up a quick tryst with another woman? The image, full-color and larger than the church's big screen could hold, pierced my heart.

"Search your heart. Cry out to Jesus." Pastor Miles closed his Bible, and the congregation stilled. The sermon done, we bowed our heads as one. A half hour lost to ruminations and fears. Never had I been more grateful to hang my head and hide my face.

Jamie seemed to sense my despair and draped his arm around my shoulder during the closing prayer.

Please, Lord, show me what's going on. Bring my husband back to me and—

My cell phone, in my purse on the floor next to my feet, rang. Why, oh, why, hadn't I remembered to put it on vibrate before the service started? Because I was so caught up in my life. Its loud, musical ring echoed throughout the cavernous room. I grabbed for my purse, but ended up shoving it farther under the seat in front of me. Dropping to my knees, I lunged for the bag. The phone played the tune once more before I could unzip the compartment and open my cell. Mortified, I whispered, "Hello?"

It was Craig's fault that I was sprawled on the carpet of our sanctuary while hundreds of people pretended their prayers had not been interrupted by a ringing phone.

"Denise Littleton?" The unfamiliar voice sounded loud as thunder. I cupped my hand around the phone and tried to turn the volume down.

"Yes?" I hissed. I didn't hear a thing. "Hello?" Still no response. I pulled the phone from my hair. The display was blank. I must have hit the hang-up button when I tried to quiet the voice.

At least I had the presence of mind to hit vibrate before I got off the floor. As I crawled out from under the pew, I caught Jamie with a huge grin on his face.

I smiled back at him with more than a little embarrassment. "I'm going to the lobby," I whispered. I walked up the aisle, feeling as if every squinted eye in the place were on me, though the pastor's prayer continued.

My heels clicked on the tile as I crossed the lobby. The phone rang again, silently vibrating, before I could hide myself between two ficus trees. "Hello, this is Denise Littleton."

"Ma'am, I'm sorry we got disconnected before. To confirm, are you married to Craig Littleton?" The voice was formal, distinctly female, yet it didn't sound like someone calling to tell me she'd just been with my husband in a dirty, by-the-hour motel.

"Yes, I am. To whom am I speaking?"

"This is Tonya with the Multnomah County sheriff's office. Your husband has been involved in a car accident."

My heart rate accelerated. "What? Where is he?" How could I have been conjuring up images of an affair as he lay dying in a smashed car? *Oh, Craig, I'm so sorry.*

"Please don't panic. He's doing fine. I do need you to meet him at St. Andrew's Hospital. Do you know where that is?"

"No. I mean . . . I can't remember." I scrambled over to the table in the lobby and grabbed a bulletin and a pen with the motto of our church printed on it. *Alone, we fall; with Him, we stand.* "How do I get there?"

"Ma'am, please remain calm. Are you at your home address right now?"

"No, I'm at . . ." The name of our church left my mind. I couldn't think of it to save my life . . . or Craig's. I fanned my face with the bulletin. Maybe the circulation of air through my blonde head would help me remember.

The bulletin! "At the Green Valley of Hope Church in Tigard."

"Okay." Computer keys clicked in the background. "You're going to get on I-5 headed north. Take the exit toward I-84 and you'll see the hospital signs."

"I'll be there as soon as I can, but I've got to get my sons and—" Why was I going on and on? She didn't care about my family or who I needed to find before I left.

"Is there someone there at the church who can drive you to the hospital, ma'am?"

"Yes, my friend Sarah." Like she cared about the name. "Thank you."

"You're welcome, ma'am. Just ask at the front desk about your husband and they'll tell you where he is."

The double doors on both sides of me opened and people spilled into the lobby.

My knees collapsed and I fell to the floor, my open phone clattering beside me. I needed to get to Jamie and Nicolas. And I had to find Sarah.

Like an answer to prayer, Sarah appeared at my side, tucking her long straight hair behind her ears and waving others away. "Denise? Are you all right?"

I shook my head and started to explain. A mouthful of my own hair impaired my speech. With both hands, I shoved it back and started over. "Can you take me to the hospital? Craig's been in an accident."

"How badly is he hurt?" Sarah grasped my elbow and pulled me to my feet.

"They say he's fine, but everyone knows that's just what they tell you on the phone." The reality of that truth shot through my heart. "He could be dead and they aren't telling me, just luring me to the hospital first." My voice had risen to a wail.

"Denise, it's okay. Craig's too ornery to die. Which hospital?"

"St. Andrews. I can't even think of where it is. Do you know the way?"

Sarah flagged down Jamie as he came out of the sanctuary. "Jamie, you go get your mother a cup of water and hurry back."

He glanced at my face and hurried across the hall before I could think of a thing to say. "I'm not thirsty, Sarah. I don't want a drink. I want to get to the hospital. Are you going to help me or not?"

"Girl, I'm worried about you. After having two babies there, you know the way to St. Andrews like you know the way to the makeup counter at Macy's." She put her hands on my arms. "Sit down and have a drink of water with Jamie while I find Nicolas."

Jamie pushed through the crowd, holding a cup in front of him. "Here, Mom. What's wrong?"

Sarah patted his shoulder and took off toward the children's wing. Suddenly parched, I reached for the water and downed it before answering. "Your father's hurt. Sarah's going to take us to see him."

Jamie blanched.

"Don't worry," I quavered. "He's going to be just fine."

I heard Sarah's panting breath before I saw her. "Nicolas isn't in the classroom anymore. No one knows where he is. I'll have Ethan bring him to the hospital when he finds him. Give me your keys and let's go."

Planting my feet, I rested one hand against the wall. "I'm not going without both my boys, Sarah. Whatever shape Craig is in, they deserve to be with me. I'll help look for Nicolas."

Sarah blew a puff of air. "If we haven't found him in five minutes, we leave and Ethan takes your car."

What if we got there just in time to hear Craig's dying words? Would Nicolas ever forgive me for leaving him behind? Of course, if we stuck around much longer, we might not make it in time. Oh, why was I being so dramatic? Most likely, he'd broken an arm or sustained a concussion from slipping on the trail. They needed me at the hospital to bring him home when they were done with the X-rays or putting on a cast.

But, no, she had specifically said "car" accident.

Still, I didn't want to separate our family. "No, I'm not going without Nicolas."

Sarah sighed and crooked her head. "Fine. Where do you think he might be?"

I racked my brain. Nicolas was my responsible one. If Jamie were missing, I'd check the skate park, the mini-mart, or his best friend's house. But Nicolas always let me know exactly where he was, whom he was with, and when he'd be home. Usually, he came home with a half hour to spare before curfew.

I didn't like to compare my boys—nothing good could come out of a parent's doing so—but as Jamie began to snicker, I couldn't help thinking Nicolas would never be getting a kick out of anything at a time like this.

"What's so funny, Jamie?" Anger seeped through my careful tone.

"I just figured out how to find him. It's so obvious, it's funny." He glanced at Sarah. "Call Heather's cell and I guarantee you Nicolas will be right beside her."

Sarah rattled off Heather's number while I punched it in. I scooted around the conversational crowd and walked back into the quiet, nearly empty sanctuary.

The phone rang three times before she picked up.

"Heather? This is Mrs. Littleton. Is Nicolas with you?"

"Yep. He's right here." In the background, I heard, "Nick. It's your mom."

Nick? He hated to have his name shortened in any way, which Jamie loved to take advantage of by calling him *Nickname.*

"Hi, Mom."

"Nicolas, where are you?"

"Behind the church at the playground. A couple of the parents said Heather and I could take their kids and work off some of the sugar we fed them in cookies and punch."

I would have scolded him for not asking me before he took the kids, but he was still on the church grounds and, truthfully, any other day I wouldn't have noticed his absence for fifteen minutes more, which I'm sure he was well aware of. "Meet me at the car as fast as you can. Your father's hurt, but we don't know how badly. We've been trying to find you so we can get to the hospital."

"Are you kidding?"

"Would I joke about something like this? Get over here."

"Meet you at the car." He hung up.

I collected my Bible and purse from our pew, rushed back out to the lobby, and declared success to Sarah and Jamie. The sun temporarily blinded me as I stepped outside after the two of them. I pulled my sunglasses out of my purse.

The head deacon, Gage Browning, swooped in. "Denise. Good to see you. The meeting starts in five minutes, and we're wondering where Craig is."

At least I didn't have to use the flimsy lie of an emergency root canal. "The police called me and he's been in an accident. He's at the hospital right now."

The disapproval on Gage's face changed to curious anxiety. "I hope he's okay?"

"We won't know until we see him, but I'm sure he is." I shifted my Bible to the other hand.

Gage touched my arm. "I'll let the others know and we'll pray for him. Give us an update as soon as you can."

"Will do." I spun and ran toward the car as fast as my heels would allow.

Chapter Four

Hers

SARAH DROPPED THE KEYS into my purse, hopped out of the SUV, hurried around, and opened the passenger door for me. She came as high as my shoulder and wore half my size in clothes, but she was the only one big enough to lean on during this crisis.

All the years that Craig and I have been together, Sarah encouraged me through the rough spots and cheered the smooth. Without her at my side, I couldn't have gone into the hospital. But we did.

The boys trailed behind us. During the drive, we'd dissected everything the dispatcher had said, trying to figure out from limited information exactly what had happened. Talking was all I'd done with the boys, not comforting or praying. The sooner I knew how their dad was, the sooner I could help them handle it.

Sarah asked at the desk, explaining our urgency. Somehow she knew I couldn't speak.

"Mr. Littleton is in the critical care unit." The clerk pointed a stubby finger in the direction of the elevators. "Take the elevator to the second floor and check in there."

The very second "critical care" hit my ears, the frail hope that Craig was barely injured fell away. Yet it did not escape my feeble mind that the clerk hadn't told us to go to the morgue.

"Thank you," I mumbled, and we moved as one, like a small herd of caribou wary of predators lurking in the shadows.

We checked in and waited for a doctor to come brief us. Each glance at my watch showed the same time. I stared at the second hand, questioning whether it was truly making a full revolution or not. *Lord, help him be all right. Give everyone here wisdom as they deal with his injuries.*

A small sitting area with the standard fish tank and boxlike, beaded child's toy was tucked into an alcove just past the desk. Jamie coughed twice and walked across the rug to the window. Nicolas raised his eyebrows at me, and I realized I was expected to follow my youngest boy.

"Jamie?" Once I reached him, I touched his shoulder. "Don't worry about Dad. He's a tough guy."

"It's not that." He shrugged my hand away, and I caught sight of a tear at the peak of his well-defined cheekbone. "Dad asked me to go with him, and I didn't."

I swallowed. "You're feeling guilty because you're glad you weren't hurt?"

"You don't understand!" His outburst knocked me back a step. "Maybe if I'd been with him, he'd have driven safer or I could have warned him or something!"

This time he let me rub his back and pull him into a loose hug. He hid his face in the crook of my neck as he swiped at the tear.

"Mrs. Littleton?"

I turned to face the speaker, keeping one arm around Jamie's shoulder. The doctor, who'd probably heard every word between Jamie and me, waited with a clipboard in his hands. "Yes?"

"I'm Dr. Rossing. Before I take you to see your husband, I'd like to give you some information about his injuries."

"How is he? He's still alive, right?" I blurted.

Jamie shuddered, and I wanted to slap myself.

"Yes, but he's lucky to be here at all. Would you like me to explain it to you in private?" He glanced at the boys and Sarah.

"I'd just repeat it to all of them anyway, so go ahead."

Nicolas came to my other side and Sarah stood slightly behind me, as if prepared to catch me mid-faint.

"From what the police have told us, a car hit his vehicle when it was pulled over on the shoulder of the interstate. If he'd been inside with his seat belt on, he might have walked away from the accident. Instead, he was standing in front of the car."

I pictured a car smashing the convertible into Craig, his body bouncing up onto the hood. At the speeds people traveled on the freeway . . .

"Why was he on the side of the freeway? Did he have a flat tire?"

The doctor grimaced. "Mr. Littleton is unable to answer any questions right now. He suffered trauma to the head, among other things. Due to the extent of his injuries, we've placed him in a medically induced coma."

I gasped and stepped back into Sarah's strength as the boys closed in around me.

Jamie coughed again. "Is my dad going to die?"

Nicolas kicked Jamie in the shin. "That's a dumb thing to say right in front of Mom."

"Is he?" I waited for the answer, sure I might collapse if Dr. Rossing said yes.

"At this time, because he's in the coma, he's stable. Putting him to sleep gives his brain less work to do and allows his body to try healing itself more quickly, but we can't say for sure what might happen tomorrow or a week from now. The best thing for him will be to have his family around him, giving him strength. You can help him through this time just by being there." Dr. Rossing cleared his throat and bounced the clipboard against his hip. "Would you like to see him?"

We followed him down the brightly lit hall. I bit my lip again and chided myself. Only heroines in romances bit their lips. I hated to be cliché in such a situation—not to mention that my relationship with Craig would be a hard stretch to fall into the romantic category—but I couldn't help it.

Dr. Rossing stopped at a door, held up his hand for us to wait, and went into the room. He returned without the clipboard a moment later. "I should mention that he's on a ventilator. The coma also ensures he won't try to remove the tube. Only two people at a time, please. Keep your visits to around ten minutes, and then find me at the nurses' station. I'll answer your questions." He jerked his head to the side. "And I think they might have a few for you, too."

I followed the direction of his nod. Two police officers stood in the hall. We'd walked past them and I had not even realized they were there. The female officer raised her chin in acknowledgment of my stare. I waved before I knew what I had done.

The smell of my mother's hospital room came back to me. I sought out Sarah's eyes. "You go first with one of the boys."

"Denise, no. I'm not going in before you." Her incredulous tone reminded me that I needed to explain.

"Hospitals make me sick, truly sick. Besides having the boys, have you ever known me to enter one?" The smell brought back the year before Craig and I married, the year I nursed my mother as she died. Even when we returned home after each round of chemotherapy, a distinct aroma clung to my mother's hair—while she still had hair. Every time she threw up, I did, too. I came to associate vomiting with hospitals. The thought of seeing Craig lying in there with tubes coming out of him made me want to dash right back to the car. "If you go in with Nicolas or Jamie, you can warn me. Prepare me for what to expect."

"I understand." Sarah nervously licked the corner of her mouth and turned to my boys. "Who wants to see your father first?"

Nicolas stepped back. "I'll stay with Mom."

Jamie's nod held a trace of thankfulness and he followed Sarah into the room. Ten minutes later, he came out with tear streaks down his face and stumbled into my arms. Sarah closed the door behind them, shaking her head.

"Is he that bad?" I whispered into his spiked hair.

"I couldn't even tell it was Dad." Jamie sobbed and I stroked his back. He looked like a tough, young preteen to the outside world, but I knew the tender heart that lay within my baby. "I told him I loved him, and he didn't even move."

"Oh, Jamie. Those are the drugs they've got him on. They put him in a coma so he can't move, can't react to any pain, but they believe he can hear us." I rocked from side to side with him.

"Jamie," Sarah said, "you did just what he needed. You were perfect."

Sniffling, he pulled back.

It was my turn to be strong. I took hold of Nicolas's hand and pulled him into the room with me. Craig lay in the single bed. At least, it was supposed to be Craig. The figure on the bed looked nothing like my husband. IVs and various tubes were attached to him, but they disappeared under bandages before entering his body. He was wrapped in white nearly from head to toe, mummy-like. His legs, cast to the knees, lay elevated on pillows. A sheet draped across his middle. The only visible part of his face was his eyes, which were swollen and closed.

Eyes that would remain shut, giving him the appearance of a dead man, until they brought him out of the coma.

Nicolas moved to one side of him and I to the other. Now I could see Craig's familiar, thick eyelashes. Why was he so bandaged? How could every inch of his body be hurt? A fresh wave of tears built up as I imagined the pain he must have been in. Had he screamed in agony as he lay on the road waiting for help to arrive? Or had the intensity of the pain spared him by causing him to lose consciousness?

I sought a patch of skin to touch, for Craig to feel that I was with him. There was none. I leaned toward his head. "Craig, honey? I love you. Nicolas and I are here. Baby, you're going to be fine. I know you are."

As Jamie had said, Craig didn't move. Even the bulge of his eye under the closed lid remained motionless. I kissed my palm and gently pressed it to the side of his bandaged face.

Nicolas stepped closer. "Dad? I . . ." He couldn't find any words to continue.

We stood in silence for a few more minutes, staring down at Craig.

"Should we go talk to the doctor, Mom? I want to know more about what happened."

I pressed another kiss to Craig's covered face and followed Nicolas out the door to where Sarah and Jamie waited down the hall.

Sarah nodded her head toward the door. "The doctor's already in his office."

Dr. Rossing rose as we all funneled in. "Mrs. Littleton, I hope it wasn't too much of a shock to see your husband like that."

I shakily perched on the edge of a chair facing his desk. "Was he burned? Did the car catch on fire?"

"The car did burst into flames." He raised his eyebrows. "Fortunately, your husband was pulled from the wreckage before the fire reached him."

"But his whole body is wrapped up. Why—"

The policewoman walked in and stood in the corner of the room.

I scooted the chair closer to the desk, doing my best to ignore her. "Why is he so bandaged?"

"He was caught beneath the wheel of the car as it was pushed forward. He's got an extremely bad case of road rash over the front of his body. His face, I'm sorry to say, was scraped to the bone in some places."

Sarah put her hand on my shoulder and squeezed, a show of support, but I felt like someone had pulled me out of the audience and cast me in a play. I needed to discover the plot and the correct lines. "Please go on." That sounded like the right thing to say.

"We're treating the lesser abrasions on other parts of his body. His legs, however, were broken when they bounced off the concrete barrier on the edge of the road. His most immediately worrisome injury came from the tire coming to rest on his chest. X-rays show one of his many broken ribs punctured a lung, but we're waiting to see if that will stabilize on its own. Quite often, leaks seal themselves. There is some fluid in his brain, called hydrocephalus—literally 'water on the brain'—that we're keeping an eye on. If it starts to build up, we'll have to put a shunt in. Again, sometimes this fluid can be absorbed as the body heals. All in all, your husband obtained quite a few injuries, but none of them are imminently life threatening."

I nodded, acting as if I heard this kind of talk every day. "His prognosis is good?"

"Physically, he's probably going to make a full recovery. We'll have to wait until he's awake to see if he's retained any permanent mental damage."

"Mental damage?"

"Don't worry about that yet." Dr. Rossing stood. "Officer Rylant would like to speak to you in private. I offered the use of my office." He moved toward the door, and the boys and Sarah left without speaking. If I knew Sarah, though, she'd have a ton of questions for the doctor to answer in the hallway, away from my ears.

Officer Rylant slid into the chair beside me instead of taking the doctor's office chair. For some reason, it lessened my fear.

"I'm sorry, Mrs. Littleton. I wish we could leave you alone right now, but we have some questions that need to be answered, and you're the best person to do so."

Without looking at her, I nodded.

"First of all, do you have the contact information of the man who was with your husband? We were unable to find any identification for him at the scene of the accident."

"Who?"

"The man your husband was talking to at the front of the car. It would be a big help."

Someone else was in front of the car? My shoulders tightened. "How could I help you with that?"

"If you tell us who your husband was with today, we can get ahold of his family."

"He wasn't *with* my husband. You just said they were talking outside the car."

"So he was traveling alone?"

I tucked a strand of hair behind my ear, allowing me to glance at the officer's face without turning toward her. "Yes. Craig was going hiking by himself. He never mentioned anyone else before he left this morning. He was looking for some peaceful time alone."

"There was no other car in the vicinity. Does your husband often pick up hitchhikers?"

"Never." He wouldn't be able to stand the thought of their unwashed bodies on his precious leather.

Officer Rylant fiddled with her badge. "Is it possible that your husband was romantically involved with him?"

My stomach turned and I jerked my head up. "No, Craig's not that kind of guy. I mean, he's never shown any . . . How can you even suggest such a thing? He's lying down the hall in a coma and you . . . How dare you?"

"A bouquet of flowers was found at the scene. That, coupled with Mr. Littleton being with this man in secret . . . the evidence could lead toward that as a logical conclusion. We've seen things like this before. The wife is usually the last one to find out."

"I know my husband, and that is not something he would do." I stood, unwilling to listen any longer to her crazy insinuations.

As I burst out the door, the other officer stepped forward. I marched toward him. "Please let your partner know I won't be available to answer any other questions from her. Also, I'll be filing a complaint about her insensitivity as soon as I can. I have no idea who the other man is. You'll have to find out from him."

"Ma'am, please calm down. I'm sure she never meant to offend you. We'll identify him another way. Maybe the morgue can get partial fingerprints."

My heart skipped. "Are you saying this other man is dead?"

"Yes, ma'am. He was DOA—dead on arrival—at the scene. We need to notify his next of kin about his passing."

His

DARKNESS. THICK BLACKNESS all around me. Were my eyes open or closed? I couldn't tell. I couldn't move or even feel if my body was there. My mind floated in the never-ending night.

A pinprick of light appeared. It grew bigger as it neared. A flame surrounded by white light. Wind rushed by me as the flame stopped in front of my face. Through the leaps of fire, the outline of a sword appeared. As my vision adjusted, I saw a mighty bronze hand grasping the hilt of the fiery sword.

The blade came to my neck. Heat burned across my Adam's apple. I could not shrink back.

A voice boomed, echoing through the emptiness. "Go," he commanded. "And sin no more."

Chapter Five

Hers

A LITTLE AFTER MIDNIGHT, I walked through the door at home. Dropping my purse onto the entryway table, I kicked off my high heels. Freed from the little points, my toes yearned to stretch and be massaged. They were used to the customary apology after such punishment, but I didn't have the energy.

Upon Sarah's request, her husband had met us in front of the house to pick her up after she drove me home. I still didn't know how I convinced her not to stay overnight with me. I needed to be able to close my door, lie on my bed, and cry into Craig's pillow without any comforting hand caressing my shoulder. If Craig lay in the hospital, alone and hurting, shouldn't I be alone and in pain as well?

Jamie clattered through the door. "I'm starving. Can you make me a sandwich, Mom?"

"Sure." I dragged my feet toward the kitchen. "You want bologna and cheese?"

"Forget about it. I'll make it myself." His voice sounded strained.

I forced myself to turn my sore neck and caught Nicolas twisting his brother's arm behind his back.

"Go up to bed, Mom. We can take care of ourselves." Nicolas sounded so much like his father I had no choice but to obey.

The stairs loomed like Mount Everest, but I managed to take some burden off my wobbly legs by gripping the handrail and pulling with each step. In the master bedroom, the bed summoned me, promising soft warmth. I sat on the edge, fell back crossways on top of the bed, and curled my legs up. Not bothering to slide under the covers, I grabbed the comforter and rolled until it wrapped around me.

Tears leaked from my eyes. When I raised my head some time later, a black smear glared back from the creamy fabric. Maybe I would run a couple of loads through the washer and catch up on the ironing. A few of Craig's dress shirts had loose buttons. I could sew a couple of loops of matching thread to make sure they wouldn't pop off at an inopportune moment.

How could I droop with exhaustion one moment and perk up at the thought of a household chore most women dreaded? I blamed it on my mother. During her cancer, I daily scrubbed the bathrooms, spritzed doorknobs, wiped down the phone and microwave buttons, and washed her sheets. I found the whole process empowering. My actions could enable her body to have strength to attack the disease, to cleanse her body. Never mind that it hadn't worked.

I gathered the comforter, toted it into the dressing area between the his-and-her closets, and stuffed it into the oversized washing machine. After adding the hypoallergenic detergent, colorfast bleach, and fabric softener, I slid down the wall and stared, transfixed, at the window in the front. Round and round went the bedspread, first one way, then the other. Water clicked on and off. Spinning, spinning, black in the center . . . lulling me . . .

At two in the morning, I woke with a start, cold and stiff. My growling stomach reminded me I hadn't eaten since the ham sandwich Sarah brought up to Craig's room from the hospital cafeteria. I transferred the bedspread to the dryer and went into the bedroom.

Silent darkness met me when I opened the French doors. The boys had gone to bed, though I wasn't sure if they were actually asleep. I crept down the hall to the stairs. If they were awake and heard me up, they'd come out and want to talk. I had nothing to say. I didn't even know what to think.

The last stair creaked. I scurried across the entryway and ducked into the nearby office. Why was I hiding from my boys? No one came after me, so I closed the door, crept to Craig's desk, and turned on his desk lamp. A soft glow spread over the shiny surface of his desk. Not a paper on it, no clutter to mar the beauty of the mahogany. Craig filed his mail the day it arrived and paid bills as soon as he received them, removing the opportunity for things to pile up. Just now, though, I wanted to see something with his familiar writing on it.

I pulled open the top desk drawer. His stapler, hole punch, and bins with paper clips and rubber bands were lined up like orderly soldiers on display. The only personal touch apparent was a sticky-backed notepad with a faint design of wind-up chattering teeth in the background.

The next drawer held his cell phone and day planner. Strange. I couldn't envision him going anywhere without his cell. I hit the green button once to see whom he last called. The display was blank. The history had been erased. I toggled over to his phone book. It was empty. My phone number, his office line, his favorite masseuse . . . why had they all been deleted?

Gears whirled in my tired mind. It appeared as if Craig had something to hide. Why else would he destroy all traces of history in his phone? Could the police officer have been right? Was Craig "seeing" someone? The other man who'd been with him?

Plenty of women believed their husbands were incapable of having an affair. Like our neighbor who trusted that her husband was as truthful as she was . . . until another woman showed up proclaiming her pregnancy and pointing to the husband as the father. Or the friend from church whose boss filed charges of embezzlement. Or the men profiled on the news after being arrested in a prostitution sting. Any woman only knew what her husband allowed her to know about himself.

Is it true? Yet it still didn't add up. A man? I couldn't picture it, and I didn't want to try. Unsnapping the planner, I swallowed hard. Would this hold another mystery? Another question to nip at my shaken faith in my husband and our marriage? I flipped back to the first of the year and glanced at the notations. All normal stuff.

In early February, he'd gone to a conference in Las Vegas to learn about some new dental procedure. Had that really been a business trip? He had asked me to come, but I turned him down. The boys needed me to get them to school. Besides, being on the parent committee for the junior high winter ball, I needed to get all those last-minute details in place.

But Craig's trip must have been legitimate because he took the staff from his practice with him: Kirk, the dentist he'd asked to join him as junior partner in his office; the hygienists; even the receptionist, Naomi.

Month after month, page after page, regular activities filled the days and packed the weekends. Craig had been right about being busy, and most of the entries were my choosing for him. Then, the one day he decided to relax, he ended up in the critical care unit in a coma. My poor Craig. He pushed himself so hard at work only to come home to me pushing, pushing for him to spend more time with the boys and our friends. In the early days of our courtship, he told me how much he enjoyed being alone, having time when nothing needed to be accomplished. Did I think he would become a different man? One who loved to be scheduled every minute of every day?

Lord, why is it so hard for me to see how I control him? I thought I was doing so much better since the counseling. Please, God, forgive me and help him to heal soon so I can make it up to him.

I continued flipping pages until I reached June. I read his plans for the week. Everything looked similar to the week before. On Sunday—yesterday, since it was now the wee hours of the morning—the deacons' meeting filled the 12:30 slot. Below that entry, he'd jotted down *Hike the gorge.*

Frowning, I tilted my head. He'd made a spur-of-the-moment decision to skip church, hadn't he? Had he come downstairs to write it just before he left?

Then why didn't he grab the phone? Who went hiking these days without one? Just the other day, Jamie had been ranting about how the government could keep track of everyone at any time by following the GPS locator in their cell phones. Craig had chuckled at our youngest's conspiracy theory and said, "Why would they bother to do that, Jamie?"

An idea flashed across my mind. Nicolas had been asking for a phone for his birthday in two weeks. He would be getting his driver's license, and Craig and I agreed that a cell phone would be a good idea. Maybe Craig had gone ahead and added another line to our calling plan. I picked up the phone and found the menu button that displayed its number. Yep. It wasn't Craig's.

My stomach growled again, and I realized I'd been sidetracked from my main objective of getting a little food into my body. I put the items back in the drawer exactly as Craig arranged them and turned off the light.

Moonlight sneaked through the closed blinds in the kitchen. I pulled the cord and stepped into the puddle of light the moonbeams made on the floor. As far away from the city as we lived—and with our house sitting on a hill—we managed to see some stars. A sprinkling was visible from my spot in the middle of the room.

Lord, what's going on? Why did Craig stop to talk to some guy? He had to know it was dangerous. I don't believe what the police think, so why do I feel like he's betrayed me by being in the accident?

I couldn't sort out any of it. Earlier, my biggest concerns were the cold distance between us and our arguing over his church attendance. I never thought the day would end like this. *Please take care of him. And the boys. And me.*

I searched the pantry for something tempting to my taste buds and seized on my favorite comfort food, chicken noodle soup. After fumbling around in the utensil drawer, I found the can opener, cranked the handle a few times, and peeled off the top of the can. As I dumped the contents into a microwaveable bowl, I noticed the pop-top in the middle of the circle I'd cut away. Craig's voice echoed around me. *"You're too blonde to open a dumb can of soup the right way."*

Pushing his criticism aside, I added water and set the cook time on the microwave. From the counter beside the refrigerator, the answering machine blinked at me. I grabbed a pad of paper and a pen from the message station and hit the play button.

"You have nine messages."

The first message began to play. "Denise, honey," Craig said. "I'm sorry I let you leave upset."

I hit pause and lowered the volume so the boys wouldn't hear it. He called? While I was at church, he called and left a message, apologizing? Maybe he would answer some of my many questions. I punched play and held my breath.

"I just really needed some time by myself. I hope the sermon was good. I'll see you tonight, probably around dinnertime, but don't get worried if I'm a little late. I love you." There was a pause as if he were going to hang up, followed by a noisy fumble. "Oh, and Denise? Can you wash my white shirt? I got ketchup on it when I had breakfast and I don't want it to stain. Yeah, anyway, I changed into a blue shirt. Just in case anything might happen to me. See you later."

"Sunday, 10:18 a.m.," the machine intoned.

Stopping the next message, I closed my eyes and shook my head. He said nothing about taking a friend along or picking up anyone on the way. He even said he loved me. How long had it been since I'd heard those words from him? Did they mean what I wanted them to?

The microwave beeped and brought me back from savoring Craig's declarations, his loving tone of voice. I gripped the bowl with a hot pad, grabbed a spoon, and carried my makeshift meal back to the answering machine. I listened to his message one more time before moving on to the next.

"Denise? This is Gage Browning. We just ended the deacons' meeting and wondered if there was an update on Craig's condition. We've got it out on the prayer chain." He cleared his throat. "Well, bless you all. Bye."

"Sunday, 2:15 p.m."

The third message was a kid named Bulldog asking if Jamie could watch a movie at his house. He didn't leave a last name or a number so I scribbled *Movie with Bulldog?* and dropped the paper into Jamie's slot in the message center. Craig continued to fight his own battle against machines taking over the world by refusing to get caller ID.

Before I finished taking my first spoonful of soup, Gage was back on the speaker, telling me that Sarah had called him and I should ignore his first message.

I breathed a sigh of relief. That girl had been busy as I sat idly by Craig's bed all afternoon. She grilled the doctor and any nurse she could find to listen to her. She brought me food, entertained Jamie when he acted grumpy from the combination of boredom and stress, and managed all the necessary calls.

The next message, a hang-up, I erased. I took another sip of my soup.

Click. I let the time stamp play. "Sunday, 9:55 p.m."

Click. "Sunday, 11:30 p.m."

I shifted in my chair. We didn't usually get a lot of calls like that. Maybe it was friends just checking to see if I was home, but not wanting to bother me by leaving a message.

Click. "Monday, 1:13 a.m."

I must not have heard the bedside phone from the laundry room.

The ninth message started playing. When I didn't hear a click right away, I picked up the pen.

After a few seconds of silence, a voice whispered, "Where are you?"

Click. "Monday, 1:55 a.m."

A man, or a woman? A friend, or a stranger? My spine tingled, sitting alone in a dark house, unsure of whether all the doors were locked or not.

Don't be silly. You're just used to having Craig around. I spooned some more soup into my mouth and relished the contrast of the warm broth and the smooth noodles.

The phone rang and my spoon tumbled into the bowl, splashing droplets of soup onto my face. I wiped my forehead off with a paper towel and picked up the phone. "Hello?"

Silence.

"Who is this?"

Click.

Chapter Six

Hers

THE ALARM BLARED at 6:45. I rolled over and slapped the snooze button. Four hours of sleep altogether. Which, considering the circumstances, wasn't so bad.

The hang-up calls really bothered me. Who had called so late? If the calls were all connected, why did the person leave such a short message and then refuse to talk when I answered the phone? I racked my brain trying to figure out if I recognized the voice. I had listened to the message again and again, but the recording was fuzzy and the words muffled.

The alarm blasted again. This time, I turned it off and trudged to the shower. The warm water made me feel even sleepier, so I lowered the temperature on the digital display. The boys, no doubt, were still asleep.

I pulled on a pair of jeans and a scoop-necked blouse, accented with a wispy pink scarf, and slipped into some brown square-toed heels. I stared at the answering machine as I entered the kitchen. No new messages. At least I wouldn't have any fresh drama to deal with.

While my bagel toasted, I used Craig's planner to look up his junior partner's home phone number. I pressed the digits into the keypad of my cell phone and left it flipped open while I smeared strawberry-flavored cream cheese over both halves of the bagel. I took a bite and chewed as I hit the call button.

"Hello, Craig. What's got you calling me so early?"

I set the bagel down. Despite the prevalence of caller ID, I was still flustered when people answered the phone knowing what number was calling. "Kirk?"

"Yep?"

"It's Denise. Craig's in the hospital in a coma from a car accident."

"What?"

"He's in bad shape. I need you to take over at the office for the time being."

"Oh, Denise . . . I'm so sorry." A shocked silence vibrated over the connection. "What . . . When did this happen? I mean, he just walked out of here on Friday and . . . What do the doctors say?"

"They're going to bring him out of the coma as soon as the swelling in his brain goes down, then we'll know more. For now, he's stable enough that I came home. I would have called you sooner, but . . ." Swallowing suddenly became difficult.

"Don't worry about a thing. I've got it covered. Naomi and I can double-book today and reschedule the rest of the week as we need to."

Naomi. She was more than just a receptionist, she was a family friend. "Kirk, would you mind telling her and the rest of the staff? It's hard for me to put into words."

"Whatever you need, I'm just a phone call away."

"Thanks. Craig will be so relieved to know you're taking care of the office. When he wakes up, I mean."

"It's the least I can do."

"Kirk? I don't have any idea . . . I'm not sure when he'll be back to work."

"Don't worry, Denise. We've got it covered."

I hung up and forced down the rest of my bagel. The boys needed to be woken up, rushed through showers, and fed. Maybe they could bring along a game or a puzzle to help pass the time at the hospital.

○○○

The next day started the same way: my body weary from lack of sleep and wired from stress. Nicolas and Jamie finagled a later hour of leaving for the hospital so they could sleep in. We wouldn't arrive at St. Andrews until around noon.

The coffeepot, which I had programmed the night before, turned on at eight, and the aroma of fresh-roasted beans floated up the stairs into my room. I threw back the covers and slipped into my satin robe. The morning newspaper was not on the welcome mat as it should have been. I fished it out of a rhododendron by the office window and carried it inside the house.

All the carbohydrates and fast food of the past two days weighed me down. I decided to make healthy eating more of a priority. Otherwise Craig might wake up to twice the woman he'd left behind. Breakfast, then, would be a bowl of low-fat granola and an orange. I opened the newspaper and spread the front section across the kitchen table.

Halfway through my crunchy granola, I read the Metro section headline. *Unidentified Accident Victim Named.*

I sucked in a chunk of oats and gagged. Yesterday, I steered clear of the paper and the TV, though the boys said the crash made the news. Only the Lord knew what information the police provided to the media.

"Count your blessings," I told myself. The headline could have said *Homosexual Affair Discovered When Lover Dies.*

> *The body of a 43-year-old man who died in a fiery accident on I-84 was identified as William Ray Rodain, of Portland. On Sunday, Rodain was killed when a Honda Accord driven by Louise Hiller hit an unoccupied Mustang convertible belonging to Craig*

Littleton. The force of the impact carried the unoccupied vehicle into both Rodain and Littleton, who were engaged in a heated exchange in front of the Mustang, according to witnesses. Littleton, who was pulled to safety before the car exploded, remains in critical condition at St. Andrew's Hospital. Hiller, who was wearing a seat belt, escaped injury when her airbag deployed.

The release of the name of the deceased was delayed to allow for notification of family members. Police are asking for anyone with information about the accident to please contact Detective Marshall at the Multnomah County Sheriff's Office.

Cold, bare facts. No emotions. But I learned something I hadn't known before: their "exchange" was heated. Who was this man? The name William Rodain meant nothing to me. How was he connected to my Craig? How I wished Craig were awake to answer some of these questions. I closed the paper and put my bowl in the dishwasher.

The doorbell rang.

In the reflection of the stainless steel double oven, I caught a glimpse of my robe, unshaven legs peeking out the bottom, and a mass of hair sticking up like a rooster's crest from my head. "Oh, no." I groaned. Shuffling to the door, I begged for mercy. *Please let it be Sarah.*

I peered through the beveled glass window. A man in a cheap suit stood on the stoop. I cinched the belt of my robe, smoothed my hands over my hair, and opened the door halfway. "Yes?"

"Denise Littleton?"

At my nod, he launched into his spiel. "Ma'am, I'm sorry to be bothering you—" his gaze inspected my appearance "—so early in the morning, but I have some questions for you."

"Who are you? What is this about?"

"Sorry, ma'am. I'm a detective. Detective Marshall, actually." He flipped open his badge and tilted it my way. "I need to obtain some more information about your husband."

For just a second, I considered calling the local precinct to confirm he was legit. Instead, I sighed and opened the door wider. "If you don't mind waiting in the living room for a few minutes, I'll be right there."

"That'd be fine, ma'am." He stepped over the threshold and wiped his feet, scanning the entryway.

I pointed him in the right direction and rushed up the stairs. My clothes from yesterday were still on the floor where I'd stripped them off in sheer exhaustion the night before. I shrugged off the robe, whipped my nightgown over my head, yanked on the jeans, dropped the blouse over my undershirt, and twirled my hair into a sloppy French twist.

As soon as my bare feet hit the kitchen tile, I offered refreshment. "Coffee?"

"No, thank you." Detective Marshall sat on the middle cushion of the sofa. He faced the snack bar where I busied myself with pouring a cup.

"All right." I edged around the bar and took a seat in the recliner farthest from him. "If you're going to say the same things that woman said at the hospital, then I'd like to get this finished before my sons wake up."

Detective Marshall shook his head. "I've been informed of what Officer Rylant said. That was conjecture. We have to do a lot of that if we can't speak to the principals in the case. With both men incommunicado, anything you can tell us would save us from more conjecturing and give us a clearer picture of what happened late Sunday morning."

"I'm not trying to be difficult. I really don't know about the other man, Will . . .William Rodain." I shrugged and bit my lip.

"So you've read *The Oregonian*?" He pulled out a notepad.

"Today's article, yes. That's how I learned his name." Maybe I could use this impromptu interview for my benefit. "And that's how I found out about their argument."

Detective Marshall uncapped the pen using his teeth and scribbled a note. "What argument?"

Did I know something he didn't? Leaning back into the chair, I leveled my gaze. "If you share all the information you have about my husband, I will tell you everything I know."

He lowered his notes. "I expected no less than full honesty as soon as I found out Mr. Littleton was involved in the leadership of your church. You don't have anything to hide, do you?"

Groaning, I berated myself. Why couldn't I think before I spoke? "I'm sorry, Detective. I didn't mean to sound adversarial. I feel like I've been left in the dark. I'm just asking for a little illumination so I can know what's important for you to know, and what I can keep private. Contrary to what you might have heard, not every church leader is a duplicitous, lying snake."

"You believe your husband was a transparent, honest man. Is that what you're saying?"

I squirmed. I couldn't go so far as to agree with that, but I had to say something in Craig's favor. "He didn't do the things Officer Rylant accused him of."

The detective scratched his chin. "Do you and your husband usually attend church together on Sunday mornings?"

"We do."

"Why wasn't he with you this past week?"

"He told me just before we were supposed to leave that morning that he needed a break from our usual routine. He wanted to go hiking in the gorge."

"Does he have a hiking partner?"

I shook my head. "Like I said, this was not a normal occurrence. He's been under a lot of stress at work."

"What do you know about Mr. Rodain?"

"Just what I read about him in the paper. It's not like Craig called this guy and asked him to meet on the side of a busy highway." I shuffled my feet on the carpet. "He was going hiking, you know?"

"We've obtained your husband's cell phone records." The ominous tone of his delivery warned me I would not like what he said next. "Over the last few months, Mr. Littleton placed many calls to

Mr. Rodain's home phone. Including on the morning of the accident."

When I was seven, playing on the monkey bars, my hand slipped. I hit the ground flat on my back, and the world around me faded into black. Slowly, my vision returned with an increasing circle of scope, but my breath had been knocked out of me and my lungs simply could not draw the air I sought.

The same breathlessness slammed me as I sat in the recliner. Air would not enter my nose. My mouth wouldn't open.

I will suffocate from hearing this.

"Ma'am? You need to breathe."

At his command, my mouth flew open and I inhaled a great amount of sweet, beautiful air. Gasping, I leaned forward and dropped my head between my knees.

Detective Marshall knelt in front of me. "That came as a huge shock to you, didn't it? I'm sorry. From the way you were trying to negotiate information, I thought you knew more than you were saying. Can I get you some water?"

"No." I waved him off. "I'll be fine in a minute." Once the truth sank in, I would want to hear the rest of the detective's news.

When I raised my head, he walked back across the room and resumed his interview. "How has your relationship been with your husband?"

"Um . . . I'm not so sure, now. I've been in counseling for the past year. Craig refused to go. But I never thought he was hiding a secret life from me. I assumed we were just growing apart, the typical marital problem."

"Do you think he *does* have a secret life?"

I snorted. "What other possibility is there? He'd been calling William Rodain, met with him after lying to me. And the bouquet of flowers . . ."

Detective Marshall tapped his pen on his knee. "There might have been some hiking event. Could even be the link between the two men. An outdoor social activity."

"Why wouldn't he tell me about his 'hiking' buddy? It doesn't make sense."

"Simple explanations are the best. That there are parts of your husband's life he did not share with you does not mean he had bad intentions. Maybe he was going to surprise you by entering the Portland marathon."

Upstairs, a shower started. At least one of the boys was awake. "Isn't that conjecture, Detective, which you mentioned wanting to avoid? What can you tell me that's for sure?"

"We'll keep running scenarios until we find one that fits the facts, which are these: your husband and Mr. Rodain had some degree of relationship, and they were arguing at the time of the accident." He stood. "That will do for now. I'll be calling if we have any other questions."

I walked him to the door. "What did Mr. Rodain's family have to say?"

"Pardon?"

"The newspaper mentioned his next of kin. Did they have any answers for you?"

Slipping his notepad into his pocket, Detective Marshall stepped toward the door. "The only person we needed to notify was his daughter. We chose not to interview her."

"Why not? Is she too young?"

"Ma'am, Samantha Rodain is in the same hospital as your husband. She's currently awaiting a bone marrow transplant for leukemia."

Chapter Seven

Hers

CRAIG'S CONDITION hadn't changed. For the third day in a row, I sat next to his bed, reading magazines and books aloud, even some passages from the Bible. Every few hours, Sarah called for an update or to offer to come sit with me, which I declined. For some reason, I wanted it to just be our family.

If my mom or dad were alive, they would have insisted on being with me. I had no siblings, and neither did Craig, though once something he said made me wonder if he had a brother, but he'd shut down as soon as I pursued it. His dad had left their family when Craig was young. His mother died the year before we met. Craig just refused to discuss his childhood with me. It was as if his early life had never really happened, like he'd severed that period from his life.

My family would be different. I refocused on Nicolas and Jamie. The kids and I played card games using the foot of Craig's bed as a table. We bought snacks at the cafeteria. The day passed slowly, as all the others had, and we left for home.

After we swung by for Chinese takeout, I cleared my throat. "Jamie, Nicolas, I really appreciate how you've come to the hospital every day to see your dad, but he wouldn't want you to spend all of your summer vacation stuck in a stuffy hospital room. You want to have the day off tomorrow?"

"Cool! Can I go to Bulldog's house? Or can he come over?" Jamie bounced in his seat.

"The rules of our house are still the same, Jamie. No guests over unless Dad or I are home. If Bulldog . . ." The name stuck in my throat. I almost smiled at the thought of a pimply faced, scrawny preteen calling himself Bulldog. "If one of his parents will be at his house, I'm fine with you going over there. If not, you guys can go skateboarding in the park."

"Sweet! Can I use your cell to call him now?"

I handed Jamie my phone. "What do you say, Nicolas?"

He squinted out the passenger window. "If you don't think Dad would care, it'd be nice to stay home for a day."

The next morning, I left the house alone. My brain reeled as various thoughts—thoughts Detective Marshall had thrown into the mix —spun through it. He'd given me an idea.

Instead of walking straight to the elevator, I headed for the information desk. "I'm wondering what room Samantha Rodain is in, please. R-O-D-A-I-N."

"Seventh floor, ma'am. Check in at the station."

My finger shook as I pressed the elevator button for the seventh floor. What was I going to say to Samantha? To her, I would be a strange woman. I knew nothing about her other than that her father died three days ago and she battled leukemia. Neither of those topics were great conversation starters.

And how could I make myself walk into her room? I had grown accustomed to Craig's room. But Samantha's? And cancer? How would I not picture my mother wasting away?

Lord, I just want some answers. . . .

The nurse at the station directed me to wash my hands thoroughly and don a medical mask and a smock. "Want to keep all the germs out of her room," she said before leading me to Samantha's door. She knocked and leaned her head in. "Samantha, you have a visitor."

I half-expected to see a tiny child. Instead, a teenage girl propped herself up on her elbows as I entered. She looked about the same age as Nicolas. Her hair was so silky and perfectly styled, I knew instantly she wore a wig.

"Hi, Samantha. I'm Denise." I held out my hand.

She reached forward and gave it a faint shake. "Are you from the child protective custody people?"

"No, sorry. I can leave if you're expecting—"

"Stay. I didn't want to talk to them anyway." She offered a small, genuine smile.

"Yes, I don't suppose I'd want to either."

"Wanna pull up a chair? Most of the volunteers get sucked into an epically long game of Monopoly when they come in my room." Samantha reached for the controls on the rail. The head of the bed rose with a hum, lifting her into an upright position. "I'm always the shoe, though, so you'll have to pick something else. And I get to be the banker."

I surveyed the room. "Today's your lucky day, because I'm always the iron." I wheeled the table with the Monopoly box on it to Samantha and swung the tray around to extend over the bed. "Are you ready to lose?"

"Bring it on." She shuffled the chance cards and laid them facedown in their spot. "You must be a new volunteer, or you would know that everyone I play loses."

"Yes." I swallowed. What could I say that wasn't a lie? My omission of who I was and why I was there already constituted an untruth. "I've never been in this wing before."

"Oh, then maybe I should go easy on you and let you win."

Samantha counted out the starting money and handed me my stack of fake bills.

"I hear you've had a tough couple of days," I said gently. "Maybe I should go easy on you."

Her hand stilled over the dice. "They told you about my dad?"

The pronoun *they* could have referred to anyone not in the room with us. I murmured affirmatively. "How are you?"

"I'd rather not talk about it. Let's just play the game." She examined the ceiling and blinked a few times.

"Of course. I'm sorry. I lost my dad when I was young, too. I didn't really have anyone to talk to except my mom." I remembered that day. Waking up to my mother's scream, running into my parents' bedroom, and seeing my mother straddling my father's chest as she shook his face and begged him to breathe. A heart attack had taken him as he slept.

"At least you had your mother." She rolled the dice and moved eight spaces. "I'm buying Vermont Avenue."

My experiences with Nicolas had taught me that when teenagers said they didn't want to talk about something, the opposite was really true. "Where is your mom?" I rolled double ones and picked the top card from Community Chest. *You inherit $100.* I showed the card and she passed me the light goldenrod bill.

"She died two years ago. It's been me and my dad ever since." Her voice caught.

I pretended not to notice, rolled again, and moved seven spaces. "I'd like to buy Connecticut, please."

"Which means I'm a ward of the state, now." She handed me the deed.

"Don't you have any aunts or uncles? Grandparents?"

Samantha rolled the dice, slid her pinkie into the shoe token, and moved it along the board to the next space. "Our neighbor, Mrs. Van Horn. She's been in to see me almost every day since I was admitted. She said I could live with her, but she doesn't have insurance. I have to be in foster care's custody to have my treatments paid for."

Despite the mystery surrounding my husband and her father, my heart went out to her. How could it not? She wasn't responsible for what happened. "How long have you been here?"

"Three months. I only have one more week of chemo and then we'll see what happens."

The thought of the poor girl going through treatment without a parent by her side brought tears to my eyes. How would my mother have done it without my support? How could Samantha anticipate leaving the hospital when she would leave with strangers? She was either very brave, in shock, or a mixture of both. "Do you want to tell me about your dad?"

Samantha glanced toward her window, her face blanching. "He knew he was going to die, I think. I'm not sure how. But he's been talking about how strong I am, how I don't need anyone around, how much he still misses Mom. . . . When the police came to tell me he'd been killed in a car accident, they said he didn't suffer at all. That he died immediately." She reached up and touched her cheek. "He was here the night before. He kissed me and said he loved me. That's my last memory of him."

"So you were close to your father?" I closed my eyes as I asked this. *I'm a horrid person to be deceiving her, picking at her wound for my own selfish reasons.*

"I don't really want to play anymore." Samantha pushed the table away, rolled over, and put her back to me. "I'm going to take a nap."

I couldn't leave the visit on that note. Somehow, I wanted to redeem my time with her. "Can I pray for you?"

She didn't answer.

"Lord," I said, "be with Samantha. Show her she is not alone. Protect her—" *from people like me, who take advantage of her suffering for their own personal gain* "—and put Your healing hand on her body. Forgive me for—" *lying and pretending to be someone I am not* "—bringing up her hurt. Please let her find someone to confide in as she goes through this hard time."

She didn't move. I wondered if she was already asleep. Her color had changed so much, from the slight pink in her cheeks as she first rolled the dice to her pale visage after I asked about her father. As I walked out the door, I glanced back at the bed and saw her shoulders quiver as though she were holding in sobs. How could she grieve such a private hurt with nurses coming in and out all the time?

I stopped at the nurses' station. "I was visiting with Samantha Rodain. She's taking a rest, and I was hoping she'd be left alone for a little bit. If her schedule of care allows it, that is."

"She's not due for any antinausea meds until after lunch. We'll try to give her some peace and quiet." The nurse smiled up at me from her seat behind the counter. "That's sweet of you to think of telling us."

Sweet. That's me. For all the guilt I now carried from my deception, I hadn't obtained any information that helped me understand how William and Craig were connected. I took the elevator to Craig's floor and confessed everything into his unhearing ears.

His doctor came in later and told me skin grafts were ready, and he would be doing reconstructive surgery on Craig's face the next day. I would see my husband's face for the first time since the accident. I'd caught glimpses of his torn skin as the nurses changed his dressings, and I couldn't imagine being able to kiss him or caress his cheek without causing him more pain. A new face for my husband would make that possible. A few hours later, the hospital walls began to waver. I decided to go home and get some rest.

Yawning, I pulled into the driveway and shut off the engine. I got out and walked down to the mailbox in the twilight. The boys would not be expecting me for a while. We never returned home from the hospital before eleven.

A large bush along our fence rustled.

I stopped. Probably a neighbor's dog. Tucking the handful of mail under my arm, I strolled up the sidewalk to the front door. The night air filled my groggy lungs, and the first star twinkled down at me.

I unlocked the front door and dropped the mail on the entryway table. "Boys, I'm home." It would take no time at all for me to whip up some toasted-cheese sandwiches on wheat bread and tomato soup with organic milk. If they hadn't already scrounged up dinner.

Nicolas popped his head around the corner of the kitchen. "Mom . . . you're home?"

"That's what I just said, in case you can't tell by looking at me. Why? Aren't you happy to see me?" I smiled.

"Um . . . sure."

His hesitation jump-started my suspicion. "What's Jamie done?" My shoulders fell and I stepped forward, passing Nicolas and entering the kitchen. Heather McCallister leaned against the counter with her hands covering her face. I frowned. "Heather?"

"Mom, I can explain." Nicolas twisted me around to look at him. His face reddened, though parts remained a splotchy white. "Heather came by after lunch, and we were sitting outside on the front steps. It got really hot, so I didn't think you'd mind if she came in for some ice cream."

I crooked my arm and dramatically examined my watch. "And nine hours later you're both inside with no parents because . . . ?"

"We ended up watching a movie and then we were playing foosball in the bonus room, and time just got away from us."

"Nicolas, what are our rules?"

He held up a hand as if to calm me down. Personally, I was impressed that I hadn't gone ballistic. What was the boy thinking? Having a girl over for hours with no supervision? Was he looking for trouble? Or did he lack any sense of what temptation was?

"I know, normally, we can't have friends in the house while you or Dad aren't here, but it isn't normal around here. And it's not just anyone . . . it's Heather."

I swiveled to look at Heather. Her hands had fallen from her face, but her gaze was fixed on the floor. "Have you noticed that she's female, Nicolas?"

"Mom!" Color flamed across his face, consuming the red splotches. "Do we have to do this in front of her?"

"All right." I spun around. "Heather, could you please call for your mom to come get you?"

"No need, Mrs. Littleton. I drove myself." She picked up a cute little handbag from the counter and scuttled toward the door. "Sorry. I didn't mean to cause any trouble. I hope Dr. Littleton is doing better."

I stalked to the curtains in the office and watched her run down the sidewalk to a small car parked several doors down. Her discreet parking job didn't make things look any better for Nicolas. Another car parked past hers started up and drove the other direction, away from the house.

Turning back to Nicolas, I launched into him. "What in the world were you thinking? You're using your father's accident as an excuse for disobeying me? Why would Heather be parked so far away if you weren't hiding her being here? I don't buy it that she just happened to show up."

If he'd been thinking more logically, he might not have wanted Heather to leave. I had to maintain proper decorum in front of her. In her absence, I could say whatever I wanted. With all that Craig was going through, I didn't need more to worry about, and Nicolas knew it.

"You're the responsible one. What kind of an example are you setting for your brother?"

He dropped his head. "Jamie's been gone all day. He doesn't even know Heather was here."

"So, you were *alone* with Heather all afternoon, all evening?" I shook my head and sniffed. "I expect so much more from you."

"You act like I'm perfect, but I'm not, Mom. So I screwed up." His voice sounded strained. "Heather's easy to talk to. I wanted to be around her and tell her about Dad."

The front door burst open. "Hey, Mom. Bro." Jamie breezed in.

I put my hands on my hips. "And where have you been?"

"At Bulldog's. His parents found out about Dad, and I mentioned you were going to be at the hospital, so they asked me to stay for dinner. His dad barbequed these thick ol' steaks, and I think I ate about five ears of corn. And for dessert, his mom made peach cobbler, and we made our own ice cream by squishing bags with—" Jamie squinted. "Why's he crying?"

Over my shoulder, I saw Nicolas bolt up the stairs. A moment later, a door slammed.

"So you had a good time?" I guided Jamie into the kitchen, hoping to distract him from his brother's drama.

"Yeah." Jamie grabbed a snack-sized bag of chips from the pantry. "Do you think I could go over there tomorrow, or should I go see Dad?"

I'd forgotten to tell either of the boys the good news. "Tomorrow's a big day. They're going to perform plastic surgery on your dad. After they're done, I think he'll look like George Clooney."

"Mom! George Clooney's gross!"

"What?" I pushed his chest. "Wouldn't it be cool if Dad looked like a famous person?"

"Yeah." Jamie munched a chip. "But don't pick some old guy. Maybe ask the doctors for a Tony Hawk."

"I don't even know who that is."

Giggling, probably at my ancientness, he started up the stairs. "Okay, I'll come with you."

I followed him. "Good night, Jamie. I love you."

He turned at the landing and gave me a one-armed hug. "Love you, too."

I rapped on Nicolas's door. "We're leaving at nine o'clock for the hospital." I waited for a response. "I love you, Nicolas. Good night." I kept my ear to the door for a few minutes more.

What else could I do?

Chapter Eight

Hers

A WEEK LATER, scans showed the swelling had gone down in Craig's brain. Dr. Rossing took me into the hall. "We're bringing Mr. Littleton out of the coma now by decreasing his sedation, though he will still be on pain meds. He's really doing far better than we expected. The bones in his legs have both set correctly. His lungs are functioning well and show no aftereffects of the puncture, though his ribs will cause him a lot of pain for a month or so."

"What should we expect from here on out?" I rubbed my lips together, desperate for Chapstick.

"Physically, it will be a long, steady recovery. He'll need to remain hospitalized for about a week longer to regain his strength, get used to eating with the damage to his facial muscles, familiarize himself with using a wheelchair . . . those kinds of things."

"Thank you, Dr. Rossing." I shook his hand. "Craig will be so appreciative once he knows what all you've done for him."

Dr. Rossing dipped his head. "It's my job. I'm glad to do it."

His

DARKNESS FADED INTO a cool, pale light. As the world brightened, a weight settled on my chest. I became aware of each agonizing breath. My rib cage strained and screamed at the act of inhaling and complained with each exhalation.

A dull pain throbbed in the tips of my toes, crawled up my legs, and grew into a ferocious beast. My ears buzzed. Each heartbeat thudded, echoing in my head. The torment drew from my extremities, gathered speed in the center of my being, and gushed up until I feared I could live through it no longer. Like a crowd that had jumped to its feet to celebrate a goal but tired of cheering, pieces of pain fell back into their seats and the noises quieted.

"Craig?"

The whisper pierced my consciousness. Such warmth and love dwelt in that single word that I tried to open my eyes. My eyelids felt as though they were made of lead, but I managed to strain and look toward the speaker through small slits.

"Oh, Craig, honey. You're awake." Even in her excitement, she spoke quietly, seemingly mindful of the pounding in my brain.

I'd brought her joy, and the struggle to widen my eyes became worth it, just to see her smile more clearly. She hovered over the bed, beautiful blonde hair the color of corn silk falling on either side of her face. A hint of mint drifted from her mouth. Soft lips stayed curved into a gentle smile even as tears gathered in her green-flecked eyes.

As I opened my mouth to thank her for being there, a searing explosion ripped across my left cheek. I gasped and squeezed my eyes shut. The pain rose to its feet again—the crowd cheering for another score.

"Oh, baby. I'm so sorry. Let me get the nurse. I'm sure she can give you something for the pain."

Her sweet voice faded as she left. Soon, she returned with someone else. An icy sensation snaked up my arm and the pain subsided. Exhausted, the last thing I knew before escaping into sleep was the soft touch of a dry cloth upon my sweaty brow.

Hers

I WIPED CRAIG'S FOREHEAD with a washcloth, glad the drug took effect so quickly. No longer bandaged, his hair looked greasy, so I wiped that as well. The few moments I'd been able to stare into his familiar blue eyes gave me a calling: to keep his pain at bay and provide him with any comfort I could. Now that he had regained consciousness, my efforts would be worthwhile.

He had tried to speak, I could tell. His grunt as he opened his mouth sounded as sweet as "I love you" to my ears. He was alive. He was awake. In a matter of time, with plenty of loving care, he would be back to himself. *Maybe he'll be even better than he was before.*

Craig had never really needed me during our marriage. After he was released from the hospital, he would. A new closeness could grow between us as he depended on my help. And we'd have all that time to talk. Plus, the boys could spend quality time with their dad until school started back up in September.

I grabbed my purse from the table next to Craig's bed and snaked my way through the hallways until I found the outdoor balcony. I fished my cell phone out and called home.

"Littleton residence. This is Jamie."

"I've got great news." I slung my purse over my shoulder. "Your dad's out of the coma."

"He's awake? Can I come see him?"

"They just gave him something for the pain, so he's asleep, but I'm sure he'll wake up again later. Want me to come pick you up?" I paced across the cement, ignoring the small group of scrub-suited smokers at the picnic table.

"Yeah. I'll take a shower and be ready when you get here."

"Jamie." I laughed aloud. "It's three in the afternoon."

"So your point is?"

"Never mind. Put your brother on the phone."

"Uh . . . I'll have him call you back in just a second, 'kay?"

My sixth sense perked up. "No, I'll just hold on while you get him."

"Well . . . he might be in the shower."

"I can wait." I put a hand on my hip and stared out over the Portland skyline. Something strange was going on. I heard Jamie's huffing and figured he was climbing the stairs.

"I can't find him, Mom."

"Jamie, what's going on? You'd better tell me now since I'll find out eventually, and then you'll be in even more trouble for hiding it."

He sighed. "Nicolas took off this morning. He wouldn't tell me where he was going because he said I wouldn't have to lie to you when you asked."

"Arrr!" I snapped my phone shut and stuffed it back into my purse. Jamie would be ready when I got there. If Nicolas wasn't home, then his natural consequence would be to not see his father today. I refused to waste precious moments waiting around.

In record time, I made it back to the house. As predicted, Jamie was ready to go. Surprisingly, Nicolas also waited by the door with a backpack.

"I brought some snacks and the games." He nodded at me as he climbed into the back of the SUV and let Jamie have the front seat.

"Thanks. That's so thoughtful of you." Acidic sweetness. I backed out of the driveway and headed to the hospital. "Have a good day, Nicolas?"

"Yeah. It was okay."

"What did you do?"

"Heather picked me up and we went straight over to Aunt Sarah's house. You can call her and ask if you don't believe me."

Since Sarah had known my children from birth, they'd taken to calling her "Aunt," and Ethan "Uncle." With no kids of their own, they doted on Heather and her brothers. As the kids grew older, Sarah's house morphed into the favorite hangout. For some unfathomable reason, plentiful junk food, the newest gaming systems, and an outdoor pool appealed to the church kids. Go figure.

Of course Nicolas would rather be there than at the hospital.

"If that's where you say you were, then I believe you." I merged onto I-5. "You're still trustworthy. You made one mistake. I thought about it a lot last night. The enemy will try to use this mistake to start you down a path you don't want to go down. He'll try to deceive you into believing that I don't trust you. That you need to start hiding things and sneaking around."

"Like he did today," Jamie muttered, apparently quietly enough that Nicolas didn't hear.

I kept glancing in the rearview mirror at Nicolas. "Please understand that you don't need to keep making bad choices. I'm not going to give you any consequence for having Heather over. Consider this a small taste of grace."

Nicolas met my gaze. "Thanks, Mom."

"However, if you choose to break our rules again, the full wrath of your father and me will fall on you. Understand?"

Nicolas grinned at my attempt at toughness. "Yes, Mother."

"Oh, I just remembered!" Jamie bounced in the seat. "A reporter called today. I actually got interviewed for the paper!"

Out of one frying pan, dropped back into the hot grease of another. "James Henry Littleton, what are our rules about talking to strangers? Especially over the phone?" My tinny voice rose with each syllable.

"It wasn't a stranger, Mom. It was this lady from *The Oregonian* asking about how Dad got hurt and how he's doing now. She had a bunch of questions about him. At first I thought I recognized her voice, but she says she's never met me. She was real happy to hear he was coming out of the coma."

The reporter must have called in the thirty minutes between my call to home and my arrival at the house. "Can you remember her name?"

"Yeah. It was . . . like . . . maybe . . .Tina?"

"Do not ever speak with anyone else who calls the house and asks about Dad unless they're friends or family." Letting go of the wheel for a split second, I raked my fingers through my hair. "Did an alien invasion come and remove both your brains? I'm having conversations I never thought I'd have to have."

"It was still pretty cool. You think my name will be in the paper?"

"Sure," Nicolas said, "and it will say that you stay home alone and that we have lots of money. Maybe the reporter will give our address to a psycho who wants to make an easy buck or two."

I jumped in before Jamie could throw a comeback, or anything else, at his brother. "Please, boys, do me a favor. Stay out of trouble at least until your dad is fully functional."

They managed to keep their bickering to a minimum on the rest of the trip to the hospital. I may have temporarily forgotten how to get to St. Andrew's the day of the accident, but I'd driven the route so many times since that I could probably still find my way if an alien *did* abduct the contents of my skull.

As we entered Craig's room, he turned his head toward the door. A simple movement, but it proved that he was conscious and aware of his surroundings.

"Craig." I rushed to his side. "I'm so glad you're awake. I brought Nicolas and Jamie with me." I pulled them closer to the bed. "Boys, say hello to your father."

In unison, they said, "Hi, Dad."

"Hello," croaked Craig.

It seemed as though we all burst into tears and started talking at once.

Jamie touched his dad's hand. "I wish I'd gone with you, Dad. Every night, I think about how different it could be—"

"How do you feel?" asked Nicolas.

As he spoke, I blurted, "I've missed you," instead of what I wanted to say: "What happened that day? Where were you going? Who is William Rodain? Who was on the phone? Do you love me?"

Craig blinked a few times.

We hushed up. I knew I wouldn't be able to get any answers from him, not in his condition. I had been unconscious only once, when they extracted my wisdom teeth during my senior year of high school. I remembered breathing in deep breaths of flavored air one minute and waking up the next, the surgery completed. That was my only comparison to Craig's emergence from the coma eleven days after the accident. Did it feel as if he'd been hit by the car moments ago? Was the agony of his injuries still at the forefront of his mind? Where had his mind been? Had he heard all of my whispered words, my prayers for his recovery?

He motioned for me to draw closer. I leaned down and tilted an ear toward him. What was he going to say? What words were worth the effort of speaking so soon after reconstructive surgery?

He licked his lips, and I drew nearer still.

"Who . . . ," he whispered. "Who are you?"

Chapter Nine

His

I DON'T REMEMBER ever making a woman cry like I made that blonde woman cry. She wept in the chair beside my bed for quite a long time. The two boys who came in with her stayed close by. The taller one said something to the shorter one about "Mom feeling overwhelmed."

They were fine-looking boys. The woman had called me their father, but it didn't seem like I was. I couldn't recall, though, if I was a father or not.

As abruptly as her tears started, her sobbing ended. She tucked her blonde hair behind her ears, wiped her face, and came to the edge of the bed. "Craig? What do you mean, who am I?"

My dry throat creaked with protest as I tried to answer. "Water," I said. The taller boy found a cup and filled it with tap water. The woman inserted a bent straw and put it to my lips. I could not round my lips enough to suck. I tried again, this time shutting my mouth in a flat line over the straw and drawing at the water with my tongue. A cold sip fell into my mouth and moistened my throat. I drank my fill before releasing my hold on the straw.

"Does it hurt to talk?" The blonde gazed at me with worried eyes.

I nodded. "What you name?" Not moving my lips took less effort and, though mumbled, my words were distinguishable. Proper grammar be hanged; it was the best I could do under the circumstances.

The boys exchanged a look. She must have noticed because she asked them to go into the hall. They obeyed quickly. Whoever *was* their father should have been proud.

She turned back to me. "Are you saying you don't know my name? Just nod if I'm right."

I nodded slowly. My head pounded if I tried fast movements.

"Oh, Craig." Her voice broke. "I'm your wife, Denise."

"Where?" I meant to ask how we could be married if I didn't know her name, but I couldn't find the right words.

"Where are we?"

Frustrated, I shook my head.

"We're in the hospital. You were in an accident. Do you remember the accident?"

"No." I grimaced from the pain the exhalation caused. "Hurt to breathe."

"Broken ribs punctured your lung." Her voice took on a monotone quality. "During the accident, your legs were broken, and you had some swelling in your brain. They've kept you in a coma while you've been healing."

None of that seemed familiar, but it provided an explanation for my aches and my surroundings. "How long?"

"Almost two weeks. I kept a newspaper article about it if you'd like to read it." She took newsprint clipping from her purse.

Two weeks? If I believed her—and since I didn't think she was telling the truth about being my wife, I *did* have reason to doubt her timeline. "Who I?"

She—Denise—swallowed hard. "Your name is Craig Littleton.

You're a dentist, head of your own practice. Does this sound familiar?"

"Not sure." Years ago, I'd read a book where the protagonist woke up in a hospital, remembering nothing about who he was or how he got there. The staff told him everything he was supposed to know. It all seemed normal until a "nurse" fell in love with him and told him the truth. The staff was fake, as was the hospital. The whole operation was a front to get classified information from him. In reality, he was a top-level, super-secret spy.

Am I a spy? I didn't think so, which begged the question: *How can I recall the plot of a book I've read and not know who I am?*

"Those are our boys that I sent into the hall. Do you remember them?"

I shook my head. Gingerly.

Disappointment clouded her eyes. "Nicolas is the older one. Jamie's younger."

"More . . ."

A glimmer of hope shone through the disappointment. "Nicolas was born soon after you started practicing dentistry. He's our serious, dependable boy. Always trying to figure out what the right thing is and then doing it. Though . . ."

I waited until she remembered she was talking to me.

"Since you've gotten hurt, he seems to be pushing the limits. I'm worried about him." She turned her gaze back to me. "I think he's hitting the age when he really needs a strong father figure."

Part of me responded, wanting to be a good father. But how could I help him if I didn't even know him? "Jay?"

"Jamie." Denise smiled. "He's surprised me with how helpful and obedient he's been. There have been times I've gotten on him about his attitude, but I'm beginning to think it's just his crazy spirit."

"Wild?"

"Yes, he's wild. You've always understood that better than I. He's never been one to show his emotions as much as Nicolas, but he's beaten himself up about not being with you that day. Deep down, he doesn't think you would have gotten hurt if he'd been along for the ride."

They cared for me, that much was obvious. Did I care for them? "Back in."

She pursed her lips. "You want them to come back in?"

At my nod, she stood and went to the door.

The boys reentered the room.

"Your dad's having trouble thinking clearly. If he seems confused, it's probably from his medications."

"Nic . . . Jay . . ." I forced out the words and watched their expressions carefully. The light in their eyes coming from my apparent recognition did not seem to be manufactured. And Denise could have been right. Once I was off the IV and the medications, maybe my memories would come rushing back. If that was the case, I needed to behave as if I knew what was going on. I didn't want to hurt my wife and children with my words while I floundered in this altered state of reality. Otherwise, once I came to my senses, there would be a lot of damage to repair. After my "family" left, I would ring for a doctor and see what he had to say. Until then, I would play along as much as possible.

"How's school?" Words came more easily.

"We're on summer break, Dad," Jamie said.

"No summer school?"

They cracked smiles and seemed to relax.

"Nicolas is doing a lot of studying, though." Jamie smirked. "Studying Heather McCallister every chance he can get."

Nicolas narrowed his gaze. "Better than majoring in slacking off and sleeping."

"You know—" Denise broke in "—your dad's pretty tired, I bet. Let's give him a chance to rest for a while."

They gathered their things.

"Need to . . ." They didn't seem to hear me over their ruckus, so I waited until the room quieted. "Talk to Jay alone?"

Denise hesitated, then put her hand on Nicolas's back and guided him to the door. Jamie scanned the room, seemingly unsure of being alone with me.

"Son?"

At that word, he came close.

"Sit."

He jumped up onto the edge of the bed.

I gritted my teeth against the wave of pain. "Mom say you help a lot."

Blushing, he said, "Not too much."

"Keep it up. She need that."

"Okay."

"Jamie, don't feel bad you not with me. This all God's plan." I blinked. *God's plan?* Somehow, though, I believed it. "Send Nick?"

"Sure." He slid off the bed. "But don't call him that or you'll make him mad." He left and his brother appeared.

Nicolas sat on the bed without being told to. "Dad?"

"You need be good for Mom."

Hanging his head, he stared down at his hands.

"Hard on her. You be help." I thought I should say the same thing I told Jamie. "God's plan."

"If you hadn't skipped out on church, none of us would be going through this. And now you want to talk about how it's all part of God's great plan?" He stood and straightened his shoulders. "What were you doing, Dad?"

Squinting my eyes, I peered up at him. "I not go church?"

"No, and there's all kind of ugly rumors going around. They're sick, some of the things my friends have heard. So what were you really doing?"

"I don't know." I didn't have to tell him I didn't remember anything about my whole life. "What I say I doing?"

"Going hiking."

"Then I hiking." The intensity of the conversation made me forget about the torture of enunciating. I closed my eyes to keep from crying out.

Nicolas snorted. "That's not the way it looks to anyone else. And now you have this great excuse of not remembering. How convenient."

He threw his hands in the air and walked out of the room.

Powerless to stop him, I lay in bed and watched him leave. Why had he acted so differently than Denise described him? Or was this the subtle rebellion she alluded to? Did he really think I was pretending to not know who I was?

Right. It's so much fun, maybe I could write a story about it. Here's the first paragraph: "They say my name is Craig. Denise—she's my wife—cries over me and says how glad she is that I'm awake. But it seems that she can tell just by the look in my eyes that I don't know her."

Perfect.

But what kinds of rumors were going around about me? And why did they affect Nicolas so much? The explanation hit me. For the rumors to matter, he had to believe they held at least a kernel of truth.

Hers

NICOLAS CHARGED FROM the room. "I'll meet you at the car." He raced down the hall, tennis shoes squeaking. A few of the staff in the hallway turned to watch his hurried exit.

Craig could barely even speak, and he couldn't think very well. What could he have said or done that upset Nicolas? I frowned. "Jamie, do you want to go see what's up with your brother? I'm going to check on your dad and make sure he's all right."

He nodded and drifted in the direction Nicolas had gone.

Craig's eyes were closed when I entered the room. "Honey?" I could tell by the erratic lift of his chest that he wasn't sleeping. "What happened with Nicolas?"

"Don't know." He opened his eyes and stared at me. "Don't know anything."

My heart broke for him. I'd been feeling caught up in a whirlpool for quite some time. I was almost getting used to it. But it was Craig's first day of uncertainty. I did not envy him one bit.

"It'll all come back to you soon. I'll ask what drugs they have you on, see which ones could be doing this to you." I took his hand and turned it over. They had removed the bandages to allow the rest of the abrasions to heal in open air.

He weakly grasped at my hand.

"It's just a weird side effect. You'll be fine soon." I glanced at the casts on his legs, tracing his hurt body with my gaze until I reached his face. A bandage twisted around his head, hanging down over his eyebrows. Stitches ran in a semicircle on his good cheek. I laid my other hand on his chest and felt the bumpiness of a wrap, probably to keep his ribs in place as they mended.

"Denise, I don't remember you." Garbled and scratchy, his words squeezed out of his stiff jaw. "I don't remember those boys. How can be side effect?"

"I don't know, Craig." I bit my lip. He didn't say a word about it. "You don't remember everything right now, but that can be good. You've got this whole great life waiting to be discovered. You can make it what you want it to be."

"What would you . . . change?"

I rubbed my thumb along the ridge of his hand. "I think we'd talk more. That's what I'm praying for. The accident helped me see how much I take you for granted, and I don't want to do that anymore."

"You think God's plan?"

"Of course. Of course, He always has a plan."

"Nicolas got mad." Confusion reigned in his eyes. "What people saying about me?"

I shifted my weight on the bed. "He got riled up when you talked about God?"

"He think I lying about hiking."

"Oh." It was all I could think to say, not having any answers to give to him.

"Did I?"

"Did you what?"

Craig squeezed my hand. "Did I lie?"

"Oh, honey. There are a lot of unknowns right now. I'm not sure what Nicolas has heard or what he thinks happened." I pulled the sheet up to fully cover Craig's shoulder.

"Am I a liar?"

I stared into the depths of his eyes. "We have a fresh start, Craig. We don't have to be defined by how we were before this. The thought of losing you has made me realize just how much I need you. If you lied before, you can't change that. But you can decide to tell the truth from this point on."

He nodded, his gaze searching my face.

"I'd better go see to the boys. I'll come back tonight." I couldn't break eye contact. Finally, I whispered, "I love you."

"I give you truth, Denise. I don't know you. Can't say love you . . ." He blinked. "But I want . . . to remember how to."

Chapter Ten

Hers

"HE DOESN'T REMEMBER ME." I stood in front of Dr. Rossing, my heart beating like . . . like the heart of a woman whose husband of nineteen years just said he couldn't remember her or their family. "What is going on?"

"Calm down, Mrs. Littleton." He put his hands on my shoulders. "I know it's come as quite a shock to you, but this type of problem is fairly common after acquiring head injuries in motor vehicle accidents."

I shook his hands away. "Craig's never been the common type of guy."

"I understand. Though none of the MRIs or other tests we've run has shown any brain damage, this appears to be stemming from the swelling. As Mr. Littleton has returned to a conscious state, we've begun to suspect a diagnosis of traumatic brain injury."

"What does that even mean? It sure sounds like brain damage to me." My hands trembled from adrenaline. It was one thing to put on a face of calm for the boys and for Craig, but now that the boys were waiting at the car and I was alone, I allowed myself to give in to the building panic. But I wouldn't let it overtake me. I clamped my lips into a straight line and clasped my hands behind me.

"Before the subarchnoid intraventricular hemorrhage reabsorbed, it placed quite a bit of pressure on the brain. Because his memory is affected, I'd guess that his hippocampus sustained some damage, yes. But all other areas of his brain are functioning correctly. Frankly, after the trauma he endured, I find that fact amazing."

"When will he remember us?" That was really all it boiled down to. All the other questions turned to mush in comparison.

"Let's go into my office." He led me into the small, private space and settled into his chair.

"When, Doctor? Is this how he'll be for the rest of our lives?"

He leaned forward, put his elbows on the desk, and rubbed his face. "Injuries are so individual, I hesitate to speculate."

"Please, do. Please speculate. Any idea of what I might be facing will help." I wove my fingers together. As I willed my heart rate back to normal, the shaking ceased.

"There's an exciting study related to memory." He met my gaze. "If you'll pardon the fact that it was done with rats, I believe you'll be interested in the end result."

I gave a small smile. "Go ahead, the whole thing smells of a rat anyway." Humor was the best medicine, right? The fact that a rodent could help predict what might happen with my highly educated husband wasn't so far-fetched.

Dr. Rossing chuckled. "The study focused on three groups of rats, all with hippocampus damage. The group who was raised in, and spent considerable time in, the test environment pre-injury continued to recall the most direct paths to the rewards in the maze after their 'accidents.' In humans, this translates to meaning that a person with a damaged hippocampus could function in—even remember—familiar places."

"And for Craig?"

"As soon as he is physically able, we will release him. The sooner you get him home, into a familiar environment, the more quickly his memory will come back to him, though it could begin returning even before his release. This does not mean he will be able to function in the same manner as before. Being expected to return to family roles, even doing household chores, can be quite taxing after a TBI, or traumatic brain injury as it's called."

"Will he be able to work again? He's a dentist."

Dr. Rossing rolled his chair back from the desk and stood. "Dentistry is a very fine motor skill. Mr. Littleton might need quite a lot of recuperation before rejoining his practice. Maybe even some occupational therapy."

I stood also. "What time frame are we looking at? How long will I need his partner to cover for him?"

"It's hard to say, Mrs. Littleton. The first few months should give you some idea of how long it will take for your husband to jump back into the normal world." He buttoned the top of his lab coat. "Now, if you'll excuse me, I'm late for my rounds."

His

ABOUT AN HOUR AFTER Denise left, Dr. Rossing strode into the room. Strange. I could remember his name after one introduction. And every event since regaining consciousness was clearly etched in my memory. I'd gone back to review them often, the few memories I could access.

No blank space loomed in the recesses of my mind. It was more like a fresh document had been opened and my new life was being written. On some disk drive, the remainder of the memories, the first section of my life, was fully intact, but I lacked the program to open the file.

The small amount of information I had gathered about my past life was a mixed bag. On one hand, I had a gorgeous wife and beautiful kids. On the other hand, Denise seemed to be acting as though our marriage had not been in the best place, and at least one son did not respect my decisions preceding the accident. How could I not remember them or that day?

The doc might have some answers.

"How are you doing today, Dr. Littleton?" He scanned my chart as he stood by the bed.

"Talking is getting easier."

"I hear that. Some of the roughness is caused by irritation from the tube you had down your throat, but they'll work on improving the clarity of your speech in rehab. Anything else?"

"My neck hurts and my vision's fuzzy."

"Any nausea? Ringing in the ears?"

"No." The working vocabulary this new life supplied astounded me. How could I understand those words? Know how to spell them? Define them? And not be able to define myself?

"Are the lights too bright?"

"It could be darker."

He examined my eyes and then dimmed the light. "I spoke with your wife, and she mentioned you were having a hard time remembering."

"Might be an understatement."

He seemed to be able to decipher my mumbling as well as Denise and the kids had. "I appreciate your calmness, Dr. Littleton. I'm sure it's very scary to wake up and not know the loved ones gathered around your bed, but your memory will return. The bad news is I can't anticipate when that might happen." He drew back, clicked his pen open, and made a note. "Yet, I do anticipate it in the future. A week, a month, maybe longer, and all those images of the past will start flooding back to you."

"How can I talk? Think?"

"Your thought process seems clear to you? Word choice?"

"Mostly clear, what there is of it."

"Another thing to be thankful for, then. It appears that the only thing affected is your past. After a head injury, we're always watching for memory loss. It's usually the first symptom to show up and the last to leave. Do you want to know the word for what you've got?"

"Sure. Slap a label on me."

"Post-traumatic amnesia, specifically retrograde. Short-term memory tends to be spotty, so I won't expect you to remember the phrase."

His joke reminded me of one of my concerns. "That's another weird thing. I remember everything from the moment I woke up."

"Ah." He narrowed his eyes and scrutinized me. "You might be repressing the past for some reason."

An unconscious repression? "Could I do that?"

"Are you aware of any mental illness in your history?"

"I'm not aware of anything in my history."

Dr. Rossing scrawled something on a paper. "I'm going to set up an evaluation with the resident psychiatrist."

"You think I'm crazy? That I'm doing this to myself?"

"The brain is a marvelous, complicated thing. There might be an injury we've yet to find." He patted my shoulder. "In the meantime, stay on top of the pain. If you allow your body to go without medication, that's *not* something you'll want to remember."

Hers

"LET'S CELEBRATE." We needed a short vacation from the drama, so I veered off course from our usual route home.

The boys cheered as we pulled into the parking lot of Krispy Kreme.

Warm, sweet smells crept into my nose and crawled down into the empty pit of my stomach as soon as Nicolas opened the door for me. Still, I exercised self-control and followed the path of one flat, uncooked doughnut on the warming tray. Up and down it went, growing, rising so slowly I couldn't ever see a change, yet at the end of the tray, when it dropped into the hot oil, it had doubled in size.

Bobbing along, it made its way to the flipper and revealed its golden brown underside for the first time. It jostled onto the slatted conveyor belt and glided under the glistening white sheet of icing, appearing on the other side like a hot, moist, air-filled cloud. As the employee plucked doughnut after doughnut off the cooling circuit with a single chopstick, I positioned myself in line to receive the free sample I had watched throughout its journey.

I grabbed the waxed paper square that held the bundle of cloud fluff. Biting into the yeasty treat, I closed my eyes and sighed. I opened them to see the boys laughing at my display of pure desire. "I have few pleasures lately. Let me enjoy my doughnut." So much for my resolution to eat healthier.

I let the boys pick the varieties to fill two boxes. One of the boxes would either end up at the nurses' station next to Craig's room or . . . I thought of a teenage girl who probably hadn't savored a Krispy Kreme in months. She wouldn't have to know who brought them.

When we drove up our street, Jamie noticed a car blocking our driveway. "Why are the police here, Mom?"

"What makes you think it's the police?"

"It's an unmarked car. I can tell."

I shrugged. "Something connected to your father, I'm sure. Maybe they heard he's conscious and want more information. Whatever it is, it's not a conversation you boys have to be involved in."

I signaled a turn into my driveway and the cruiser pulled forward, parking in front of the mailbox. "Go ahead into the house and I'll try to be quick."

Taking my sweet time, I gathered my purse and cradled the papers I received from a nurse about Craig's diagnosis, balancing the boxes of doughnuts atop the pile. I bumped the car door shut with my hip and turned to face the detective I'd spoken with before.

He flashed his badge once again. "Detective Marshall."

"Of course, Detective. What can I do for you?"

"Need any help with your packages?" He reached out toward the boxes.

I turned to the side. "Yeah, right. Like I'll let a cop carry my doughnuts."

Feigning shock, his mouth gaped open. "I see you're feeling quite spunky compared to our last visit."

"I might wear out at any time. We've had a long, emotional day, what with Craig's waking up. Can we get right to the point? Why are you here?"

"Your husband's awake now, is he? Congratulations."

"Thank you." I started down the sidewalk toward the house.

Tailing me, the detective coughed. "We've had a breakthrough in the case."

An answer to prayer. Finally, the police were getting to the bottom of this mess. "Then come right in. You know where the living room is." I slid the boxes onto the kitchen counter, washed my hands, and took a dessert plate out of the cabinet.

When I approached the couch with a chocolate-glazed, cream-filled doughnut on the plate, the detective sat up straighter. "Changed your mind about me, ma'am?"

I handed him the plate. "You get one now. If you've got good news, you'll earn another one before you leave."

"Do you always drive hard bargains?" He polished off the doughnut in a few bites. "Mighty tasty, thanks."

"Your news? What's the breakthrough?" *Please, Lord, let it illuminate the darkness surrounding that day.*

"We've found the link between your husband and—"

The phone rang.

"Don't worry about it. I'll let the machine get it."

He nodded. "As I was saying, the investigation found—"

"Mom," Jamie yelled from upstairs. "Kirk's on the phone. He says it's an emergency."

"Just one moment. It's Craig's partner from the office." I excused myself from Detective Marshall and picked up the extension in the kitchen. "Kirk? What's the matter?"

"Oh, Denise, boy, am I glad you're home. I've tried your cell all day long."

I snagged it from my purse and flipped it open. *12 Missed Calls.* I'd put it on vibrate when I first arrived at the hospital and I never turned the ringer back on. "Sorry, Kirk. Why were you trying to reach me?"

"Diane's out with the flu and—"

"I'm sure that leaves you a little shorthanded, but can't you work it out?"

"Naomi quit."

I stood there, stunned. "What? She's been with Craig since he started the practice. She wouldn't just quit."

"When I got to the office today it was still locked up. Her letter of resignation was on my desk. Actually, Craig's desk, which I'm using at the moment. The patients started arriving a few minutes later, and I basically ran the whole office single-handedly. I have no idea how to do the billing, so I had people leave all their contact information. I even had them making their own copies of their insurance cards 'cause I was so busy."

"Didn't Jennie help out?"

"Nope, she said she's a hygienist and that's the only job she's going to do."

"Oh, Kirk, what are we going to do?" I slumped against the counter. Naomi was the oil that kept the office running. We had never worked a day without her. If Craig was there, rain, shine, or black ice, she was by his side. "Did Naomi give any reason for quitting?"

"Not a hint. And she's not answering her phone either."

"I don't even have a clue. . . ."

"When I still couldn't get hold of you by three, I took the liberty of calling a temp agency my friend recommended. They'll have someone here tomorrow, though I'm not sure how smoothly it will go."

"Sounds like anything will be better than today," I said. "I'm sorry you had to go through all of that. I've been at the hospital all day."

"I figured, but I didn't want to bother you there in case Craig wasn't doing too well or—"

"No, no. He woke up today, so hopefully . . ." What could I say? The doctor's negative outlook on Craig's returning to work didn't have to be true. God could do the impossible. He brought Lazarus out from the grave, and I bet ol' Laz was back to work the day the feasting and parties ended. "Hopefully, it won't be too much longer until Craig's back to work."

"Oh." Relief permeated Kirk's tone. "Great news, Denise. I'm so happy for you."

A presence hovered behind me, and I turned to find the detective a few paces away. "Oh, I've got to go. Hiring a temp sounds like a good plan to me. I'll call you tomorrow to see how it all worked out, okay?"

"Sure."

I hung up.

"An emergency having to do with Mr. Littleton?" Detective Marshall folded his arms.

"Well, his office actually. Our longtime secretary just up and quit with no warning today."

"When her boss is hospitalized after a life-threatening accident?"

I bit my lip. "Doesn't make too much sense, does it? She's always been so loyal."

"We'll need to interview her soon."

"Why?"

"We've been going through Mr. Rodain's papers, personal effects, and so on. Turns out that your husband was his dentist."

Chapter Eleven

His

"DR. LITTLETON?" Someone gently shook me awake. "I need to check your blood pressure."

I lifted an arm, ribs protesting the simple move.

The nurse slipped the cuff over the patches of bandages on my forearm and settled on an unabraded spot of skin on my upper arm.

Glancing at the clock in the dim early morning light, I counted my hours of sleep. Only three so far. I'd try to fall back asleep after the nurse left, but not being able to lie in any position except flat on my back was wearing thin. I usually slept sprawled out on my stomach, limbs stretching in every direction.

What? How do I know that? The only way I'd slept since losing my memory was on my back, yet I could clearly picture a skewed view of the white sheets on the bed as I opened one eye, face smashed against the mattress.

A memory. Albeit a small one. I couldn't picture the bedroom beyond that blurry viewpoint of a single eye, but it gave me hope that my world would slowly expand, that I might rediscover who I was.

Was Denise beside me in that bed? I couldn't tell.

Sticking a thermometer in my ear, the nurse pushed a button and took my temperature. "You're running a slight fever. I'll have the doctor check your dosage of antibiotics. We need to be sure none of your abrasions or your stitches on your face are getting infected." She peeled back the dressing on my reconstructed cheek. "Looks all right to me. I'll leave them in place until the morning, but I'll make a note that all your wounds be given a thorough cleaning before they're rebandaged."

"Thanks," I mumbled, turning my head away from her. My face throbbed. "Could I have a little more pain control?"

"Of course." She adjusted my IV and left.

In a short time, the throbbing eased and I was able to concentrate more on the memory I had of sleeping in a soft, white-sheeted bed. With the intense, gentle movements of a paleontologist, I tried to unearth more of the memory. My efforts proved futile.

An hour later, I pressed the call button.

The same nurse appeared in the door. "Can I get you something?"

"A sleeping pill, please?"

"Be right back." She returned with a cold cup of water and the pill.

She transferred my old straw into the new glass as I slid the pill into my mouth. I drew in some water and swallowed. I gazed at the ceiling until my whole body began to relax and my eyes fell closed.

"Craig?" The bed depressed at my side as someone's weight settled next to me. Fingernails raked through my hair and a kiss pressed my lips. "I couldn't come before now. I'm sorry."

"It's okay," I whispered. All I wanted was for the pleasant stroking of my hair to continue. The root of every strand registered pleasure as the fingers massaged my scalp. Perfume drifted over me. The scent brought to mind a bouquet of bird-of-paradise, a wild, exotic blend of brilliant colors and sharp edges. I moaned and leaned my head into the touch.

"I've been so worried." Her honeyed voice melted into my mind. Such care and yearning filled her words. "I had to come."

"Glad you did." I tried to open my eyes to look into the face of this goddess who comforted me, but my lids were too heavy.

"What are we going to do?"

I didn't know what she meant, but I knew what I did not want her to do. "Don't leave."

"You want me to stay? I'm already risking so much to be here. I've been so scared." Her voice sounded tight, and I thought she might be crying.

I again tried unsuccessfully to open my eyes.

"Shhh. . . ." I tried to reassure her by feeling for her hand and patting it. Her fingers closed around my palm and the long nails I had earlier enjoyed in my hair rested on my skin. "Be okay."

"Why didn't you call me? At least just to let me know? You could have even had Denise tell me what happened." She gave my hand a squeeze. "As far as I know, she still doesn't suspect a thing. Like you always say, she's just a stupid blonde."

I drew my hand back. "Don't talk about her that way," I muttered, managing to open both eyes to a slit. Denise had been nothing but kind to me from the moment I awoke. I didn't appreciate some other woman putting her down.

"Why not? I'm just repeating what you've said a billion times before."

Through the haze of my mind, I realized I didn't know who was sitting next to me, and I didn't know why she was stroking my head. I didn't want her to stay after all. "Go away."

"What?"

"Leave." I turned my face the other direction and the stitches in my cheek pulled taut.

"You're throwing me out?"

I kept quiet.

"I don't know who you think you are, but no one messes with me like this. I told you I was done waiting around and I meant it."

The weight lifted from my bed. As my hips rose with the motion of the mattress, my ribs complained. I groaned.

"Oh, that's right. You're in a lot of pain, aren't you?" She stepped closer and the bed bounced. Splinters of torment pricked my chest. "Aaahh!" The shaking continued. I forced my eyes to open farther and caught a glimpse of a dark face hovering over me, kinky curls bouncing as she pushed her hands up and down on the mattress. "Stop! Please, stop!"

She turned and left the room.

From my half-conscious state, I quickly fell back into more congenial dreams.

Hers

I STOPPED BY CRAIG'S practice on my way to the hospital. His office was centered in the small business park on the short block. Young trees stood alongside the walkway, and flower beds lined the brick exterior. Inside, the front desk looked like a hurricane had touched down in that exact spot.

A strange man sat behind it, shuffling through a stack of papers. He glanced up. "Do you have an appointment?"

"No, I'm the owner's wife, stopping by to see how things are going."

"Good." He relaxed his shoulders. "Maybe you can help me figure out what I'm actually supposed to enter into the computer from the forms."

I went around through the door into the office. Five minutes later, he was well on his way to getting us caught up from the day before. Mentally, I made a note to have Kirk see how long we could keep him. Maybe we could hire him on as permanent staff. Just because we were used to having a female secretary didn't mean it had to be that way. In fact, I liked the idea of a change. Things might end up being very different by the time Craig got back to work.

Through the open door of an examination room, I saw Jennie seated and leaning over a patient. "Jennie, when you're finished with that cleaning, I'd like a word with you."

She glanced my way. "In a minute, Denise. I'm almost done anyway."

The patient, an older woman with a blue bib draped over her fluorescent lime blouse, craned her neck to look at me. "I was so sorry to hear about your husband."

I laid a hand on the doorjamb. "He's taken a turn for the better, I'm glad to report. Thank you for still coming to this office."

"Well, why wouldn't I? They always take such good care of me here." She lay back down and opened her mouth at Jennie's request.

I found Kirk in Craig's office behind his desk. "Denise, it's so good to see you." He stood and drew me into a loose embrace. "We're doing the best we can."

"That temp is a very quick learner. I think we should try to keep him around as long as possible."

"You're the boss."

I smiled. "I guess, in a way. You better be on your best behavior, then."

Jennie peeked around the door. "Denise, I'm done now."

"Kirk, would you mind giving us a few minutes?"

"Not at all." He moved his lanky body toward the door. As he passed me, he whispered, "Good luck."

I studied Jennie. She had returned from a Caribbean vacation the week before the accident. "I like your hair."

"Thanks." She reached up to touch it. "I just took the braids out."

"Oh." The silence lengthened awkwardly. I wasn't used to dealing with the employees in an authoritarian role. *Lord, help me.* "Yesterday was pretty hectic, huh?"

"Not really. I got all my work done just fine."

"Kirk mentioned that you didn't help out much up front."

Jennie put her hands on her hips. "Look, I didn't study to be a hygienist only to do secretary work. I did exactly what I was hired to do."

Perching on the edge of the desk, I fought the urge to glare at her. "There are times, Jennie, when we must all go above and beyond our job descriptions. I'd like to think that you have enough loyalty to Craig to pitch in a little extra to keep this business running smoothly until he gets out of the hospital and back to work."

"Did you want me to find a different place to work? 'Cause there are plenty of places I can go that will only expect me to do my job."

We couldn't afford to lose another employee, so I forced a smile. "No need to go jumping ship. I understand your position. If we can keep that temp around, we shouldn't need to ask for any extra help from you."

"Great. Can I go on to my next patient now?"

"Be my guest."

Jennie had never been my favorite person in the world, but her name now fell considerably lower on the list. The only reason I could think that Craig had chosen to hire her in the first place was her perky cuteness. Maybe I should place an ad for a new hygienist. By the time Craig got back to work, things might look extremely different.

Kirk strode back in. "I didn't hear any swearing or breaking glass, so it must have gone well."

I pretended to wipe sweat from my brow. "I keep trying to act in a godly way with her but it's hard work, though, since she doesn't speak my language."

"English?"

"No, human. She's clueless, absolutely no compassion. She was such good friends with Naomi that she must be grumpy about her quitting."

"Well . . ." Kirk opened a filing cabinet and plucked out two candy bars. "She's pretty young. Maybe she'll do better as she ages." He threw a miniature Milky Way toward me.

"Are dentists supposed to have candy stashes?" I raised an eyebrow. "Never mind, I won't tell on you. I've got to check on a file before I leave, but I'm heading to the hospital after that."

"Tell Craig hello." Kirk tossed me another candy bar. "And give this to him."

"He's only eating really soft foods or liquids, as chewing hurts his cheeks too much, but I'll give it to him as incentive. Maybe he can suck on a piece." I tucked it into my purse.

During the time I'd been in the back, the temp had almost finished the stack of papers. "Good job," I told him.

He shrugged off my congratulations. "It's pretty easy once you know what you're doing."

I walked along the open shelves of alphabetized files until I came to *R*. Running my finger along the names, I scanned for *Rodain*. "Kirk?" I hollered.

He jogged up to the front. "Yep? Need more candy?"

"Why isn't William Rodain's file here?"

"I didn't tell you? The police confiscated it about an hour ago. They were waiting outside when we opened."

I hung my head. I was too late. How was I ever going to find any answers?

"But . . ." He motioned for me to follow him. "I made copies first."

I hurried to his office after him, hugged him hard, and started flipping through the pages. "Do you remember him?"

"Nope. He was fairly new. I double-checked his file. I've never seen him as a patient. Craig did his care on days I was out of the office. Rodain's initial complaint was grinding his teeth in his sleep."

I reached the end of the documents. "Everything seems pretty normal in here."

Kirk nodded. "That's what I thought, too. Nothing remarkable at all."

"He never mentioned William Rodain to you?"

"No. You might want to ask Jennie."

I raised my eyebrows. "Suppose I have to." My skin crawled as I went back to find Jennie. Why did I find her so revolting? I couldn't put my finger on it, but something about her bothered me. She came out of the room I'd first seen her in. "Jennie?"

"Can I help you with something else, Denise?" Sarcasm coated her words.

I wanted to take her tanned little face between my hands and pop it open like a zit. "One more thing. Did Craig ever talk about seeing any of his patients socially?"

"Like who? Are you afraid he was sneaking around with some girl behind your back? I heard on the news that no one knows why he—"

"No. I trust Craig completely." I set my jaw. "I'm asking about a man named William Rodain."

She stopped short. "No. I don't think he ever mentioned him. Craig really tries to keep business separate from pleasure."

"Fine. Thank you." I left the building. Her snotty statement played over and over through my mind as I drove to the hospital. At first, when the detective told me they discovered the link between Craig and William, I had been overjoyed. Craig was William's dentist. William was just one of his patients. But as I lay in bed last night, my imagination tore hole after hole in the simple explanation.

Jennie's declaration rang true. Craig never mixed work with recreation that I knew of. He whined about going to charity events and parties that were vaguely connected to work because he felt he was going as Dr. Littleton, not as Craig. He wheedled his way out of so many evenings and forgot to tell me. Dressed to the nines and ready to go, I would find Craig in front of the computer in his sweats. His explanation always carried the general gist, "Oh, Denise. Didn't I tell you? I got Kirk to go instead." I would climb back up the stairs, look in the mirror, and stash all my finery away until the next scheduled event that he'd tell me was coming up. Every now and then, we actually went to a party and he'd act so unsociable, I'd wish we had stayed home.

Yes, hiking wasn't quite on par with a formal evening out, but it still didn't make sense for Craig to lie to his family to spend a day on a trail with a patient. There had to be an explanation, but I didn't think a professional relationship was the only connection between my husband and William Rodain.

Was it pleasure? Was it business? Maybe William was a wealthy man, someone with whom Craig wanted to remain in good graces. Maybe the only reason that Craig lied about where he was going was because he didn't want to get a huge lecture, or start an enormous fight over his choosing to woo some big client rather than go to church.

It didn't excuse his actions, but it made a little more sense than a strictly dentist-patient relationship. Pulling into a space in the parking garage, I wondered if I might be able to get more information from Samantha.

Once inside, I passed the nurses' station without stopping, washed my hands, and grabbed a mask. My stomach seized at the thought of how often I had done the same to visit my mother. During our last visit, Samantha talked of only needing one more week of chemotherapy. If she had been released, I would need to track down that neighbor lady Samantha mentioned.

Samantha sat in her bed, drawing on a sketch pad.

"Hey," I said from the door. "Played any good Monopoly lately?"

She glanced up. "Oh, hi." She motioned for me to enter and closed her pad before I saw what she'd been working on. "I was hoping you'd come back sometime."

"After our great visit last time, right?" I dropped my purse onto the chair. Oh, I'd forgotten the doughnuts.

"Everything was so fresh with my dad. I wasn't ready to talk about it yet." She flashed me a smile.

"Well, we don't have to talk about anything you don't want to, okay?" A vase of flowers with a *Congratulations* balloon bobbing above it stood on the table where we played Monopoly. Had she gone into remission? "Why are you still here? I thought you might be at your neighbor's by now."

Samantha tossed her head. "They scheduled my transplant. I've got to stay in here to keep healthy."

"So it won't be too long, huh?"

"They're busy setting it all up." Giggling, she stretched both arms over her head. "I'm getting healthy marrow."

Her joy, in the midst of her tragedy, touched my heart. "I've prayed for you every night. I'm so glad God is working it all out."

"Enough about me." She beamed. "Why'd you stay away so long? I kept asking the nurses when you'd be back to volunteer, and they didn't even remember who you were."

I shifted my feet. "Like I said, that was my first time."

"When are you coming next?"

"Well, I can see you as often as you'd like."

"I don't want to put you out."

"Oh, no problem." I cleared my throat, crossed my arms. "Actually, my husband is a patient."

She nodded in a knowing way. "What kind of cancer does he have?"

"Oh, no, he was in a car accident, then a coma, and now he has amnesia." I raised my eyebrows and nodded at her look of incredulity.

"So, he, like, doesn't remember anything?"

"Not much. Do you want me to stop by tomorrow?"

"That would be great, if you're not too busy with your husband."

Spending time with Samantha was important, too. "Maybe you can tell me a little more about your dad."

Chapter Twelve

His

WHEN DENISE WALKED in a little before noon, I still hadn't made a decision. Should I tell her an unidentified woman came on to me while I was in a drug-induced slumber? But what good would it do? I didn't know anything about the woman or why she visited me. Maybe I had dreamed the whole episode.

What kind of guy was I? I didn't know that either. Maybe I had a hidden life. Nicolas's outburst could be explained by that, if he gave heed to rumors. Obviously, the woman wasn't connected to the accident since she hadn't known about it. I knew that another man, one named William Rodain, had been killed while I lived. No one else had been injured, the doctor told me, because the driver of the car that hit mine was saved by her air bag.

"Hi, Craig." Denise pushed my hair back from my brow and kissed my forehead. "How's today been?"

My mind whirling, I tried to form a coherent sentence. "Not too bad." What if the woman driving the car that hit me was the same woman who came to my room in the early hours of the morning? A stalker. A deranged woman who'd been spurned by me, a faithfully married man. "Denise? Did I ever say anything about someone following me in the weeks leading up to the accident?"

"Why? Do you remember being followed?"

"I'm trying to figure out what happened to me. Do you know who was driving the car that hit mine?"

Denise opened her purse. "I still have the newspaper article I showed you right after you woke up. It says the woman's name."

I took the clipping and found the name. Louise Hiller. Nothing. No bells ringing, no sudden realizations. "Does Louise Hiller mean anything to you? Did I know her?"

"Not that I know of. Why?"

I promised to tell her the truth . . . and now I was holding back because I was afraid. Afraid of how Denise might react knowing another woman had been at my bedside. Afraid of being left to figure out my past alone.

Afraid of who I really was.

I had to face it sometime. "Someone came to see me this morning."

Denise pulled a chair up to the bed. "Who? The physical therapist they've been talking about?"

"A woman. And she knew me."

Confusion swirling in her gaze, Denise sought me out. "Who was she?"

"I don't know. She didn't introduce herself."

"How do you know she knew you?"

"She called me by name . . . and she kissed me." I braced for the fallout. Though I felt guilty for enjoying the mystery woman's touch, I had done nothing to lead her on.

Denise's jaw dropped. "She kissed you?"

"On the lips."

"What did she look like? What did she say? What did you do?"

"I don't remember a lot, but—"

"Are you always going to say that?" She stood, arms tight against her sides. "You're like a broken record. 'I don't know.' 'I don't remember.' When a woman kisses you, you have to remember!"

"Calm down, Denise. I'm sorry. I'll tell you everything I know. She came in after I'd taken a sleeping pill. She woke me up, but I was still in a dazed stupor. That's how I woke up. To her kissing me."

"And *then* Prince Charming remembered he was married to me?" Clipped words aside, I figured she was calming down and wouldn't be running out on me. She sank back into her chair.

"She said she was scared to come, and she said you were stupid, so I told her to leave."

"Did she?"

"After shaking my bed until my ribs felt like a jumble of pick-up sticks."

"Oh, Craig." Denise shook her head slowly. "You'd better get your memory back soon because I don't know how long I can handle this."

I reached out my hand as far as the IV tubing would allow. "I'm sorry. It happened to me. It wasn't something I chose. I told her to leave as soon as she said one bad word against you." That had to mean something. Even in a half-delirious state, I defended Denise's honor.

"What would she have against me? She's kissing *my* husband and insulting *me*?"

Pressing my head into the pillow, I closed my eyes. "She got angry when I told her not to call you a stupid blonde. She said I'd said it so many times before."

Her voice trembled. "Who was she, Craig?"

I opened my eyes and saw a tear fall from the tip of her cute nose. "You are not stupid. I think you're intelligent and lovely and kind. And if she came back in right now, while I'm in my right mind, I would tell her so and grill her for any details I could give you."

She finally took my hand and laced her fingers through my own. "Could it have been the Louise that's mentioned in the article?"

Denise snorted. Even her snort was adorable. "I caught the tail end of the interview with her on the news a few days after your accident. She's got to be in her seventies, if she's a day."

"No." I squinted. "The woman who kissed me was definitely not a gray-haired old lady."

"Can you describe her?"

The silhouette of the woman came to mind first, followed by the few features I thought I recalled. "I'm pretty sure she had short, really curly hair. And dark skin."

She ripped her hand from mine.

Hers

DARK SKIN? Curly hair? Jennie fit that example. No wonder she snipped at me and chose to be so unhelpful at work. She'd been having an affair with my husband! Okay, maybe calling it an affair was too strong of a word for the kiss I knew about. But what *didn't* I know about?

"It was Jennie," I muttered. "That conniving, sneaky, snotty little—"

"I don't think that's her name."

I raised an eyebrow.

"Somehow, it doesn't seem to fit her."

"Aw, what do you know anyway?" Like I was going to listen to the man with amnesia when I finally figured out a portion of the riddle. "She's your hygienist. She's cute and young and you probably went over to her apartment after work any day you had the urge. Even at lunchtime, if you wanted."

Craig frowned. "Denise, that doesn't seem fair. I have no idea what I did or didn't do, but even the thought of cheating on you is repulsive. Really, it's making me feel nauseated."

"You know what?" I stood and walked backward toward the door. "You just stay in your cozy little bed and let your body heal from the accident that happened when you lied about where you were and what you were doing while I go figure out what kind of disgusting affair you were having with your assistant, 'kay?" I whipped around and stormed out of the room.

Of all the nerve. For Craig to be upset over his choices, making me feel as if I were the one being unfair.

Enough of being the wife in the background, the "stupid blonde." I wove my way through traffic, swerving past the slower cars, and jerked back into the parking lot of Craig's office. Bursting in the back without a word to the temp, I searched for Jennie. Instead, I came face-to-face with a strikingly beautiful African American woman. "Naomi?" I froze in place. "What are you doing here? I thought you quit. Kirk said he couldn't get ahold of you."

"I've been out of town. Just stopped by to pick up my last check." She stepped to the side of the hallway as though she wanted me to pass her by and let her on her way.

Instead, I moved in front of her. "What happened? You've been with Craig since he started this business. We need you here right now the most."

"An emergency came up, so I couldn't work the last two weeks I was scheduled to." She focused her gaze on the picture that hung opposite us, a photo of Craig fishing the Deschutes River.

"You only had two weeks left?"

"Craig didn't tell you? I gave my notice the day before he was in the accident."

Surprise. Yet another thing Craig had *not* told me. "He failed to mention the fact that you were quitting. But why did you give notice?"

"I'm moving." She rubbed a hand over her hair, which was pulled back tightly into a ponytail at the nape of her neck. A black tuft of hair curled out at each temple.

I thought Naomi loved Portland. She'd been to barbeques at our house, and frequently mentioned how our kind of neighborhood was where she wanted to live. Once, she had even told me she would love to live in my house. "Where are you going?"

"To Mexico. We found a place in a little town by the beach."

"We?"

"I mean the real estate agent helped me find it. I'm going to be living there alone."

"Oh." Had my entire universe slipped off its rocker? No one made any sense anymore. Jennie was most likely having an affair with my amnesic husband. My good son was breaking house rules. My wild child was showing a softer side. And now—with only two weeks warning—sweet, dependable Naomi planned to jet off to Mexico and live by the beach.

I shook the random thoughts out of my head and refocused on my current problem: getting down to the bottom of Craig's pre-accident secrets. "Do you remember a patient who came in here named William Rodain?"

Naomi scrutinized her watch. "Wasn't that the man who died in the accident?"

"Yes, but he was also Craig's patient. You must remember him. You're always so good with names. That's one of the reasons all Craig's patients love you."

"He came in a few times. There was nothing distinctive about him." She explored me with her gaze for the first time. "How's Craig doing?"

"He's awake and talking now."

"So I heard."

"But he's still in a lot of pain."

"I'm sure he'll get over it." She stifled a yawn. "Well, I've got to get going. Need to finish packing."

The lack of sympathy in her voice surprised me. Was she feeling that uncomfortable about quitting when we needed her so? *Never mind, you have enough problems of your own.* "Have you seen Jennie?"

"She left for lunch right before you got here." Naomi gave me a small wave and darted out the door.

I checked my watch. *12:30.* Craig had set up the office with later lunches so they could squeeze one or two clients in during the noon hour. Jennie wouldn't be back until 1:30. With an hour to kill, I closed myself in Craig's office and pulled out the bag of miniature candy bars.

Lord? I unwrapped a dark chocolate and popped it in my mouth. *Help me to confront Jennie with the right attitude. I know whatever is going on between her and Craig is not pleasing in Your sight. I want to let her have it without ruining the witness I've tried to build with her. I've already got the anger part of "righteous anger" taken care of, but I need You to keep me from calling her names or saying things I will regret. I know You love her, too.* I opened another candy. *Please . . . give me guidance. Lead me to the answers I so desperately need to find.*

I tried to pray for Jennie, but my mind kept wandering back to my unexpected encounter with Naomi. Was she really leaving us for Mexico? Of course, she loved to swim, so the beach made sense. She always brought her suit along to our barbeques. She played diving games with the boys for hours. I pictured her stepping out of the pool and toweling off her hair. Any color of suit contrasted beautifully with her dusky skin.

Curly hair? Dark skin?

Jennie hadn't visited Craig this morning. Naomi had.

Chapter Thirteen

His

"DR. LITTLETON, how would you like to get out of bed today?"

I rolled my head toward the door as a stocky nurse pushed a wheelchair into my room. "That sounds like it will hurt."

"Probably will." She set the brake. "But it'll be worth it to see a different view, won't it?"

I'd only been awake a little more than twenty-four hours, but it seemed as if I spent all my life in a small, antiseptic, white-walled room. "I'll give it a try."

The nurse raised the head of the bed as high as it could go, putting me into a sitting position. "We're going to swing your legs over this side of the bed as you pivot."

Lifting with my thigh muscles, I tried to help move my legs, but with the weight of the casts and my lack of activity, I didn't think I helped much at all. As she lowered my legs to dangle off the side of the bed, my calves throbbed. My ribs ached beneath their tight wrap. Swirls of gray flirted with my vision. "I'm feeling light-headed."

She put one hand on each shoulder. "Drop your head and close your eyes. We'll stay in this position until you get used to it."

A few moments later, I could open my eyes without feeling faint. "I'm okay now."

She let go of my shoulders, maneuvered the wheelchair closer, and lined it with a clean blanket. "Throw your right arm over my shoulder. I'm going to keep your weight off your feet and swing you into the chair."

I analyzed my body. I figured I was about six feet tall. She was just over five feet. Though I'd surely lost weight while in the hospital, I still outweighed her by at least forty pounds. "Don't you need someone else on the other side?"

"I'm stronger than I look. Plus, I've got the proper training." She nudged her shoulder into my underarm and wrapped my arm around her back. "On three. One . . . two . . ."

Three found me seated in the wheelchair. My feet hadn't supported any of my weight, and my ribs hadn't twisted too badly.

She hooked the IV bag onto the pole coming up from the back of the wheelchair, positioned what I affectionately referred to as my "bladder bag" next to me, lifted my feet onto the footrests, tucked the edges of the blanket around my body, and released the brake. "Where do you want to go?"

"Anywhere I can see a tree."

She chuckled. "Been awhile, huh?"

"It's still summer, right?"

"You don't miss a thing, Dr. Littleton." Laughing, she rolled me down hallways until she reached an outdoor balcony. Hitting the handicapped button, she waited for the doors to open.

Warm, pollinated air whispered over me. The hospital's circulation filters removed all the germs and odors from the indoor air, but they also stripped it of its personality.

She parked me next to a picnic table. "I'll check on you in a few minutes."

I nodded and closed my eyes, letting the sun beat down on my face, its bright shape penetrating my eyelids. Judging by the sun's height in the sky, high noon had already passed. In the distance, a songbird trilled a glorious tune. I searched for it. Large aggregate concrete tubs held mature trees. A breeze rustled their leaves. Natural sounds filled my ears. The only background noise I'd heard since waking up was the beep and hum of medical equipment. I rested in the softness of the Lord's creation, relieved to be free from the harsh, man-made soundtrack of the hospital.

The doors opened and a pair of doctors strolled through, unlit cigarettes already set in their mouths. Even the smell of their smoke woke my senses, reminded me there were so many odors I would experience anew.

After Denise had stormed out, a male nurse cleaned my wounds and redressed them. My skin was healing so quickly he used far fewer bandages this time than before. I twisted my arm to look at the abraded area. All the hair had been scraped off. A thin, shiny scab covered half of my forearm, dipping in at the meatiest part instead of rounding out as it should. I would always carry the scars.

I ran my fingers gently over my cheek. The man had given me a mirror to see my face for the first time. They had shaved one section of my head in preparation for inserting a shunt. A fine, dark stubble covered that part of my scalp. Deep purple lines traced the irregular patchwork of stitches on my cheeks. My nose and eyes looked familiar, but the majority of my face had been altered. Whether by the accident itself or the subsequent surgery to repair the lacerations, I did not know.

I felt broken, looking in that mirror for the first time, wondering what Denise saw when she looked at me. Even wondering what that other woman thought. But sunshine warmed my body and made me feel as though the Lord were knitting me back together. Somehow, I had faith He would knit my memories back together, too. If I could convince the nurse to leave me in the wheelchair for a while when we got back to the room, I would request a Bible, sit by the window, and delve into Psalms.

The doors opened again and Denise stepped onto the balcony. During the seconds it took her to spot me, I studied her. A gauzy skirt of brown shades swirled below her knees while a matching scarf hung atop a white blouse. Pointy-toed, high-heeled sandals accentuated her toned calf muscles. She brushed her hair back, and highlights sparkled in the sun.

And then she turned her eyes on me. Mascara smudged under her lids. *Lord, what have I done to her? How could I cheat on a woman who obviously loves me so much?*

Striding toward me, she managed a smile. "Good to see you outside enjoying the fresh air, though it gave me a fright when you weren't in your room."

"Thought I died, did you?"

Shaking her head, she sat next to me at the picnic table. "I thought you needed emergency surgery."

"I hate to make you worry." I stared at the view. "It seems I've done enough of that for a lifetime already."

We sat side by side, listening to the birds, and somehow the mood changed. The melancholy gave way to sweetness. Just being together was enough.

She placed a graceful hand on my chin and turned my face toward hers. "You're different now, Craig. You're softer, and you listen more, and . . . it's like you feel more deeply. We're more connected than we have been in years." Her gaze held fast.

"I'm sorry for that, too." Like a magnet, I was drawn closer to her.

"What?" she whispered, leaning toward me.

"That you feel more loved by a man who's just getting to know you than you did by the man who lived with you for years." I stretched farther, closing the distance between us, pressing my lips against hers. Only after her eyes fluttered closed did I shut my own.

She pulled back, as if a whip had cracked across the dreamy atmosphere. "You were having an affair with Naomi."

"Naomi? Who is she?" My heart beat even more erratically than the kiss could account for.

"Your receptionist." She opened her purse. "We've been friends with her for years and years. She helped us start the practice. I trusted her around the kids, with you. . . ." Denise wiped her nose with a tissue. "How could I not have seen it? It must have been going on all along. She wanted my house, she said once, but what she really wanted was my life. My husband, my kids." Her hand shook as she wiped her nose again.

"I don't remember her."

"Why didn't you tell me the mystery woman was African American? It would have narrowed my search."

"Didn't I? I said 'dark skin,' but I guess I couldn't think of the right term. How do you know it was her?"

"I went to your office to confront Jennie and ran into Naomi instead. I didn't figure it out until she was already gone, but then it all clicked into place. Her quitting, her indifference to your pain, not looking me in the eye, acting strangely."

"You're sure?"

"Completely. I'd stake my life on it."

"And yet you came back to the hospital to see me?"

"Craig . . ." She wrung the tissue. "First I sat in the car and had a good, long cry. But I love you. I promised to stay by you in sickness and health, for better or worse. You just came out of a coma, for crying out loud. I'm not going to leave you when you're at your sickest, when we're at our worst."

"I disagree."

She whipped her head toward me. The look in her eyes said I'd better explain what I meant. Quickly.

"I don't know much, but I don't think we're at our worst. Before the accident sounds pretty terrible. I was cheating on you. . . ." I had to swallow a huge lump in my throat to continue. How strange it was to be confessing to something I did not remember doing. "I was lying and running around. Abusing your trust and depriving the boys of the right kind of father. No matter what else I find out about the old me, that is not who I want to be."

"Oh, Craig." She leaned in for another kiss. "I don't know why . . . maybe I shouldn't, but I believe you."

"Can you bring the boys by this evening?"

"Maybe I could bring some food too, and we could have our first family dinner. Are you up to it?"

I nodded. "If you brought me a bean burrito from Taco Bell, I could probably chew the soft tortilla."

She tipped her head. "You hate Taco Bell."

"I do?" I smiled. "It sounds delicious to me right now. What do the boys think of it?"

"They love anything that's not good for them."

"Tell me more about the boys. What are their favorite things to do? What do I usually do when we spend time together? Is there anything I should know before we hang out?"

"Well . . ." A faraway look stole into her eyes. "You have a special hug you do with Jamie where you squeeze the back of his neck."

"Why squeeze?"

"When he was a little boy, he'd try to bite you."

"He'd bite me?"

"Yeah, you let him watch some vampire show I didn't think he was old enough to handle, and he started biting us on our necks whenever we'd hug him. To protect yourself, you always held on to his neck just tightly enough so you could pull him away. Sometimes I noticed you walk by him and squeeze his neck."

"I can handle that. What about Nicolas?"

"That's easy. You pull on his ear. He loves it."

"As old as he is?"

"He's young at heart." Denise tucked the blanket more tightly across my lap. "Are you warm enough out here?"

All I wore beneath the sheet was a thin hospital gown. Despite the sunshine, a chill had crept over my weakened body. "Going inside would be fine."

Denise released the brake. "You look tired, Craig. You should take a rest so you'll have energy for the boys."

"Thank you. I really appreciate the way you've been taking care of me."

"You're welcome." The wheelchair stopped. With a choked voice she said, "It's all I ever tried to do, but often you misinterpreted my motives. I'm glad you understand me now."

She wheeled me back to my room and rang for the nurse to help me into bed. After getting an extra blanket from the top of the closet, Denise spread it over me.

Truly, even though I'd done nothing but sit, I was exhausted. "Thanks." My eyes drifted closed.

"I'll be back in a few hours with the boys and a Taco Bell dinner."

She kissed my lips again. Boy, this kissing business sure was agreeable. I hoped to continue it for the rest of our lives.

"I'm going to bring in extra for Samantha."

"Samantha?" I opened my eyes. "Is she someone I know?"

"I don't know how you would. Unless she came into the office with her father."

"Who's her father?"

"William Rodain."

I couldn't keep up with the conversation. "Why would you be taking dinner to his daughter?"

Denise perched on the bed. "I haven't told you everything, Craig, not because I'm trying to keep things from you, but because I don't want to add to your stress. I want you to focus on getting better and coming home."

"What haven't you told me?"

"William was a patient of yours."

"I gathered that from your earlier comment. What about Samantha?"

"She's a patient in this hospital . . . in the cancer ward. She's got leukemia, but they've scheduled a bone marrow transplant, so things are looking up. When her father died, she became an orphan. Her mom's been gone for a few years. I started visiting her to find out about her dad, but now I feel sorry for her. She doesn't have any family at all."

I couldn't find a comfortable way to sit, so I propped myself on both elbows. "Do we have money to spare?"

"You've always taken care of the finances, but I'm sure we're doing fine."

My cheek itched and I lay down to rub a knuckle along the stitches. "We need to take care of that girl."

"What do you mean?"

"If I hadn't been arguing with her father—and no one seems to know why I was—then he wouldn't have been in front of the car, and he wouldn't have died."

"How can we help her, Craig?"

I'd already come to expect her helpfulness. No matter what I suggested, Denise backed me up and did her best to make my suggestion a reality. "Check with the hospital. See if we can pay for her care."

Chapter Fourteen

Hers

PAY HER BILL? The Craig I knew would never have suggested we use our own money to pay for a stranger's medical care. Not without a lawsuit requiring him to do so. Yet it sounded like the perfect way to help Samantha out. She wouldn't have to make a choice about where to live after the bone marrow transplant was done based solely on keeping health insurance.

Trying not to sound too shocked, I moved toward the door. "I'll check up on that right now."

A scrubs-wearing woman stood at the nurses' station looking over a file.

"Excuse me?"

She snapped the file closed. "Yes?"

"Who would I talk to about billing information?"

"Your insurance company would be the best place to start. They can tell you exactly what your coverage is."

"If I wanted to talk to someone here at the hospital?"

"Just call the information desk in the lobby and ask for the billing department." She put the file underneath her arm and walked into the room across the hall from Craig's.

"Of course," I muttered. "Even a dumb blonde should be able to think of asking the information desk for information." Craig would have said the same thing if he'd—no, he didn't seem to think of me in the same demeaning manner. He sounded heartfelt when he complimented me. He even called me "intelligent."

A phone sat on the counter. I really didn't want to have Craig listening to every word I said no matter how kind he'd been lately. I pushed the extension for the lobby, which was marked on a card taped to the phone.

"Hello. How may I help you?"

"Yes, can you connect me with the billing department?"

"One moment, please."

A *click* later, ringing filled the earpiece again.

"Billing."

"Hello." I glanced up and down the hall to see if a nurse was on her way to ream me out for using their phone. "I'd like to find out what the balance is on a patient's account."

"What's the patient's name?"

"Samantha Rodain."

"How do you spell the last name, please?"

"R-O-D-A-I-N."

"And who am I speaking with?"

"My name is Denise Littleton."

"I'm sorry. You're not on her list. Until she has given approval for you to access her account, I am unable to give you any information."

"I'd just like to find out how much she owes for her treatment."

"Again, I'm sorry, but that information is not available to you. Is there anything else I can help you with?"

"Please . . ." I drew a deep breath. "Please just listen to my story for a minute. I know that Samantha has leukemia, and she told me they're getting ready to do a transplant. The whole process has got to be extremely expensive, not to mention the months she's spent in the hospital for chemotherapy and other treatments. I also know that her father died, leaving her an orphan. My husband was with her father when he died, which makes us feel responsible for her. I'm not asking for information about her health, her past history, or even her address. All I'd like to know is how much we can give you to pay off her bills."

"Ma'am . . ."

"Please." I waited, my chest heaving after such a long speech.

"Mrs. Littleton, I really can't tell you. But . . ."

"Yes?"

"It's not necessary. What you want to do is a very kind, charitable action, but it's not necessary. Do you understand?"

A light dawned. "Oh."

"But I didn't tell you anything."

"Yes, thank you. I understand completely. You can't tell me anything, of course. Forget I even asked."

"Yes, ma'am. I've forgotten already."

I hung up the phone and rested my elbows on the counter. Who paid Samantha's bills? Her hospital stay must have run up thousands of dollars no matter how great her dad's insurance was.

I peeked in on Craig. Sleeping already. I mulled the problem over on the drive home. A stack of mail threatened to topple as I set my purse down next to it on the entryway table. The boys had been faithfully putting the mail there, and I'd been faithfully ignoring it. I flipped through, tossing junk mail in the trash can and separating bills from personal correspondence. Our auto insurance was due. The bill must have been mailed before the company totaled out Craig's car, as it was still listed on the statement. At least it was well insured.

Insurance. William Rodain must have had life insurance. If the executor of his will had received the payout, Samantha's bills would be a natural expenditure. As his sole heir, all the benefits probably went straight to her.

Or maybe the hospital wrote off her expenses when they became aware of her situation.

I took the business mail into Craig's office and opened the next envelope. My steps left prints in the vacuumed carpet. Hmm . . . our bank statement. The checking account's balance looked normal, but savings had dropped considerably. On the first of the month, a huge withdrawal—over $30,000—stopped me cold. Strange. Craig hadn't made any large purchase that I knew about. Did he move a big chunk of savings into our mutual fund?

I looked up the number for our financial guy and dialed. "Hey, Nathan. This is Denise Littleton. What's the current net worth of our portfolio?"

"Hello, Denise. So sorry to hear about Craig. How is he?"

Apparently, news traveled quickly. "He's doing well. Should be coming home soon."

"And you're taking care of all the little details, huh? Good for you. Every man needs a woman who'll take the lead when he's unable. I'm bringing your portfolio up on the computer right now."

Yep, playing at banking. *A sad state of affairs when patronizing words feel like a compliment.* I waited, spinning slowly in the office chair. I could hear Nathan breathing but, otherwise, he remained quiet. "Nathan?"

"Um . . ."

"What?" I stuck my heels into the carpet to stop my lazy revolutions. "What's the matter?"

"Denise, there's hardly any money left."

"What do you mean?" The office spun around me.

"Craig called three weeks ago. He spoke to my assistant. According to her notes, he moved about ninety-five percent of your money into a trust fund he was setting up."

"A trust fund? For the boys?"

"Don't know. I assume so. There's nothing else in the note."

Where was our money? What did Craig do? Did we even have enough to support our family? To pay the house payment?

"Denise, I'm sorry. I'll talk to my assistant and call you back if I find out anything more."

"Thanks, Nathan." I hung up, imagining the conversation I could have at the hospital.

"Craig, almost all of our savings are gone. You made two huge withdrawals and said you were putting the money into a trust fund. Where's the money, Craig?"

"I don't know."

And he'd stare back at me with those soft, warm eyes that seemed to hold no secrets from me. He'd take my hand and apologize again for something he didn't even remember doing.

What was the point? He'd only feel worse, like he'd let his family down again. I wanted him to get better and come home as soon as possible so his memory would return. I could keep this bad news to myself until he recalled his life before the accident.

At every turn, secrets reared, growling and snarling. What else remained undiscovered?

What if, when the amnesia burned off like fog under a strong sun, he reverted back to his old personality? Would he tell me what he had done with our money? Would he confess the details of his affair?

Denise! I clamped a hand over each side of my head. *Are you actually hoping he never regains his memory? Dear Lord, What kind of a woman am I?*

But if Craig never remembered the affair . . . To me, if he didn't have memories of being with another woman, it would be as though he never had been. *But he has. He slept with someone other than you, his wife.*

For the first time, I let myself think about his strong, nimble hands moving across Naomi's sleek, supple body. Bile rose in my throat. I held my head over the office trash can until I was sure my stomach could hold its contents.

From that bent-over position, I had a great view of the floor. Another set of footprints laid a different path in the carpet than I had walked. I'd have to remind the kids to stay out of their father's office. Rules were rules.

I reached for the phone once more. "Hello? This is Denise Littleton. I need to make an appointment for a complete STD screening."

His

AN OLDER, AFRICAN AMERICAN man strode into my room, wearing a dark blue suit with a pin-striped shirt. Even limping slightly, he walked with confidence. "Craig. Good to see you." He stuck a big paw of a hand out.

I shook it as best I could. "I'm afraid you have the advantage of knowing me."

He chuckled. "Just hoping for the best. Though, if you don't remember your own pretty wife, you'd better not remember me." He stuck his hand out again. "Pastor Miles."

"Pleased to meet you," I said, causing him to break into a full belly laugh. Using the remote, I shut the TV off in the middle of a toothpaste commercial.

Pulling up a chair with one hand, he used the other to wipe laughter from his eyes. "You're doing better than you look, I expect."

"Having seen myself in the mirror only recently, probably so."

"I came by a few times while you were still in the coma. Brought that plant over there." He pointed to one of the pots crowding the windowsill.

"Oh. I don't remember. Should I also know why you're limping?"

"About a week after your accident, I popped in at youth group, wanting to show them that the senior pastor's not some has-been old guy. They were in the middle of a skateboarding relay." He slapped at his left hip. "Took a nasty spill and ended up not able to get around myself for a while."

"Guess you showed them."

He grinned, placing his elbows on the armrests and studying the room. "Nice place you got here."

"Home, sweet home . . . for the time being."

"How long do they think you'll be in?"

"If I can start getting around on my own, I'll be getting out soon. At the very least, I'd like to be able to make it to the bathroom so Denise doesn't have to deal with any of that."

"Where is your lovely wife? I was hoping to visit with her and you at the same time."

"She's bringing the boys back here for dinner. Our first one as a family since the accident." My mouth watered at the mere thought of cheesy beans.

"Sarah's been keeping us updated, so I haven't talked to Denise lately."

"Sarah?"

"Excuse me." Pastor Miles dipped his head in a quick apology. "Sarah is Denise's closest friend. She's been making sure the boys are checked on during the day, and she's got a whole platoon of people ready to do whatever they can to help. One group is mowing your lawn and doing the other yard work today. I think tomorrow, a group of women is planning on cleaning the whole house, top to bottom."

"Thank you." Tears welled up. I didn't feel like I knew the man who sat beside my bed, but his love, and the love of others from the church, was undeniable. Palpable. "Until I can take care of my family, I'm glad there are people who will."

Pastor Miles leaned forward. "You rest assured, Craig Littleton, we will support you any way we can."

"Will you pray with me?"

"It'd be my pleasure. My wife and I have not missed a day since the accident of praying that your health would be restored."

"Would you pray for my mind? Do you know how many commercials for toothbrushes, mouthwash, even gum, are on during the day that mention they're recommended by dentists?"

One corner of his mouth turned up. "Not really."

"Quite a few. And every time I see one, I try to guess if I would recommend that brand. Is that the free sample we give out after every cleaning? When I think about being a dentist, I don't even remember what the hook thingy they scrape your teeth with is called. I can't remember a thing about my office, or my coworkers, or my job. Unless it all comes flooding back to me, I have no idea how I'm going to support my family." I shook my head. "I'm afraid I'm going to lose everything if I don't remember."

He closed his eyes and held his hand out over my body. "Lord Jesus, please heal this man. Restore him to his right mind, Father. Give him peace and strength to deal with what lies ahead." He paused.

"And . . ." I waited until he opened his eyes and looked at me. "And, I'm afraid to remember."

"Why are you afraid?"

"Because I don't think I've been a very good husband or father. The few things Denise and I have figured out . . . I'm afraid of what is still lurking in the shadows. And if I remember the past, and need to tell Denise things that will hurt her even more deeply, then I might lose it all anyway."

His eyes narrowed. "What have you been figuring out?"

"There are truths about me that I hate." Unable to meet his gaze, I turned aside. "I had an affair. I was unfaithful to Denise, and really, to my boys, too. With a woman I worked with."

"You remembered this?"

"No. The woman came to see me here, and Denise was able to piece together the whole story."

"Aw, Craig. I'm sorry." He sighed.

"Not as sorry as I am. How could I have risked losing my family like that? Was I a complete idiot before this?"

"Are you really repentant? Do you truly want to turn away from the sins of your past?"

"When I was unconscious, I had a dream." I swallowed. What would he think of my claim? "A vision, really."

"Of what?"

"An angel. He told me to go and sin no more. I want to obey that."

"I see." Pastor Miles rubbed his hand under his chin. "I'm going to tell you this because I believe you do want to turn away from sin. Craig, you had a spirit of arrogance. You chafed against accountability. You thought yourself incapable of falling. The elders met the night before your accident to discuss removing you as deacon."

"A wise move, apparently." My chest tightened. Now I could add the whole church to the list of people I'd let down.

"Take his fear," he prayed, his hands hovering over me again. "Remove all doubt and self-loathing from this man. Create in him a new heart, a soft heart, a heart open to Your leading and fully devoted to Your kingdom, to his wife, and to his family. Make a clear path for him to follow, Lord. And as he has confessed his sins, now throw them to the bottom of the ocean to be held against him no longer."

Chapter Fifteen

Hers

"DID YOU HAVE FUN last Friday night?" Sarah steered her car into the parking spot farthest from the mall doors. "I mean, as much as you can in the hospital with a husband who doesn't remember you."

"On an amnesic, hospital fun-o-meter, I'd give it a ten." I hopped out of the car, pushed the strap of my purse over my shoulder, and shut the door. "Craig ended up judging a belching contest between the boys. I laughed so hard, I thought my sides were going to split open. A nurse even came in and told us to keep it down."

Swinging our arms at a brisk pace, we powered toward the mall entrance.

"Craig got a kick out it?"

"Sometimes he seemed like his old self. We were a normal family having a typical dinner, and it felt so good." We moved to the side as a car crept past. "Pastor Miles had stopped by right before I got there."

Sarah nodded. "He mentioned wanting to the last time I talked with him, but the fall he took really slowed him down."

"Craig told me."

"People are calling every day, wondering how they can help. Asking if they should come visit Craig."

"What have you told them?"

"That you'll need more help when he comes home and visitors might overwhelm him for a while. I've got meals lined up for a month, if you want them."

"Thanks. I'm sure I won't need that many. I like the idea of cooking for him myself."

We crossed the remainder of the parking lot in silence. Sarah never talked just for talking's sake. Another reason she and I got along so well.

She bumped me with her hip. "Thanks for coming with me."

"You were right. I needed a break. What could be better than a pair of new high heels?" I held the door open as Sarah breezed into the mall. "We're starting with shoes, right?"

"Then moving on to dresses and accessories, girlfriend." She snapped her finger over her shoulder and swayed her head.

I waited until we were looking at earrings to tell her about the money.

"Are you saying you're broke? And I dragged you out shopping?" She slapped her forehead.

"No." I put my hand on her shoulder. "It's not that bad. We've still got a little put away. And I'm sure I'll find where the trust funds are that he set up for the boys. At least they'll still be able to go to college. Plus, some money is still coming in from the office."

"What did Craig say about the missing money?"

"Nothing. I didn't tell him."

"Girl." Sarah whirled to face me. "Why not?"

"He's got enough on his plate without me asking questions he doesn't have answers for. He'll just feel guilty."

"But maybe he'll remember. Maybe the money is connected to

why he was with that guy in the car, why he lied to you. Maybe the money is the key to breaking open this whole thing."

I hadn't thought of that. "Sarah, there's way too much for us to deal with as it is. The questions can wait."

"I don't get it. The Denise I know doesn't back away from challenges. What's the harm in asking?"

"I told you. I don't want to worry Craig."

"Oh, right, you should protect him the same way he's always protected you from that in the past." Holding a pair of earrings next to her ear, she peeked in a skinny mirror at the corner of a carousel of merchandise. "After all, he didn't have anything to do with your current predicament."

"Don't you think I've felt that way, too? Like he made his bed, so let him lie in the filthy, stinky thing with whoever else is in there." Tears sprang up. "But then I think about being without him, and I ask myself what I would want him to do if the roles were reversed, and I pray for the strength to treat him as the man I love. I weigh everything on the scale of whether it will make our lives together better or not. If it doesn't, I throw it on the thought trash heap."

Sarah stared at me. "Go back to that first thing you said."

"What? That I don't want to be without him?" I bit my lip to keep the tears at bay.

"No." Tipping her head, she scrutinized me even more intently. "About whoever else is in the bed with him."

"I didn't say that." Heat flamed on my blushing cheeks.

"Yes, you most definitely did." She stepped closer to me. "What did you mean by it?"

"Nothing."

"Was there someone else in his bed?"

"I don't want to talk about it. It's too humiliating." I fiddled with a pair of pearl studs.

"Who was it? When?" Sarah gasped. "Was it that single girl who plays on the worship team every now and then? She's made eyes at Ethan a couple of times when she thought I wasn't looking."

"No." I moved to the next display. "Can we not talk about it, please?"

"My poor Denise." She came up beside me and encircled me with her arms. "Honey, I'm so sorry."

The tears fell, dripping off my face onto her shoulder. As I sobbed, she held me and patted my back. Even though I knew we made an odd sight—me towering over my friend, crying my eyes out, hugging in the middle of the mall—I let her comfort me.

"That jerk! I'll rip his head off with my bare hands. I'll throw his body to those wild dogs my neighbor has."

"Sarah."

"Don't you dare defend him, Denise. After all these years that you've talked about how often he turns you down when you approach him. I've always had a suspicion there was someone else."

"Why didn't you say anything?"

"You had to know." She pulled back. "Didn't you?"

"Once, I asked him if he was seeing someone on the side. I didn't even call it an affair, but I wondered aloud if he was enjoying another woman's company more than he enjoyed mine. He swore—he swore up and down he would never cheat on me. Craig acted so offended I entertained the thought that I ended up apologizing for not trusting him."

"And you believed him?"

"It's either believe him or think he's lying and turn into a wife who follows him around, checking up on him, going through his phone and his wallet. Or I could have hired one of those girls who pretends to flirt with the husband to test his response."

"I would have put money in on that."

"No, you wouldn't have. You're not sneaky either."

She rolled her eyes. "Okay, not really. But I would have gotten in his face about it."

"You're letting anger speak for you." I offered a little smile. "I know about that."

We left the store and moseyed over to Orange Julius.

Sarah pored over the menu, but I knew her mind was elsewhere. "Aren't you angry with Craig?"

I waited until we bought our drinks and sat at the café tables in the middle of the walkway. "Not as angry as I have been at Naomi."

Sarah, sucking on her triple berry smoothie, choked and coughed. Coughed again. Gagged and choked and coughed until every single shopper stared at us. "You . . ." cough ". . . have got . . ." cough ". . . to be . . ." cough ". . . kidding."

Standing, I thwonked her back a few times until she stopped choking.

"Thanks, but you *are* kidding, right?"

I sat back down. "I thought you might have figured that out already since you had so many 'suspicions' for so long."

She wiped her mouth with a napkin. "Naomi? Never saw that one coming."

I handed her another napkin and pointed to my right cheek.

She rubbed at the mirror image of the spot on her face. "I assumed it would be a white girl like you. Never really thought of Craig going for anybody so different."

I shot her a reproving look. "Do you like it when people make a big deal over you being Asian? We're all the same underneath."

"Underneath what? The covers?"

I gasped. "Do you have a censor? Are there any comments you choose not to make?"

"Rarely." She grinned at me, then turned somber. "Seriously, I can't believe, with a woman like you at home, that Craig would be sniffing around elsewhere."

"One thing I've figured out from counseling, even before I knew he'd been unfaithful, is that it's not about me. Craig has issues he needs to deal with. I'm not responsible for the decisions he makes." I gathered up the trash. "Let's burn the smoothie calories off as we take them in."

We ambled past a suitcase store, a children's boutique, and a bookstore. A row of massage chairs lined the front of an office supply store.

"Close your eyes and pretend we're at a spa." Sarah pushed me into the nearest chair and switched on the vibration and heat.

"Mmm." I took a sip of strawberry smoothie. The coolness on my tongue contrasted the warmth spreading over my back. Pulsations of energy soothed my tight muscles.

"And yet you've been at the hospital for hours almost every day." Sarah's comment seemed to come out of nowhere, but I knew she was really asking why I was still by Craig's side after finding out what I now knew.

"He's my husband." I nestled back into the depths of the chair.

"You're staying with him?"

"Strange as this may sound, I like being with him."

"Uh-huh." Reclining in a huge chair, Sarah kicked her legs up onto the footrest.

"He's different since he woke up."

She flipped a dismissive hand in the air. "Dalmatian, that's what he is."

"Come again?"

"Oh, he's a cute little white puppy, fresh and adorable. He needs you. But when his memory comes back, his spots will start showing and you'll have a temperamental, demanding, fully spotted dog. A man can't change his spots."

"I think he has. When he looks at me, he looks at me the way he did when we first met, not like I'm some wife who's so ordinary and predictable she might as well be a reading lamp."

"Know who you sound like? You remind me of Heather when she talks about Nicolas. You're twitterpated."

I rolled my neck back and forth. "He is really cute."

"Nicolas?"

I giggled. "I was referring to Craig."

Sarah propped herself up on an elbow. "Have you kissed him?"

Looking to the side, I wiggled my eyebrows.

Her jaw dropped and she rolled onto her back. "Closed or open mouth?"

"Sarah!"

"What? He's your husband. It's okay to admit it."

"We've been strictly G-rated. It's like we're this Disney couple and the spell cast over my prince has finally been broken. Our lips barely come together and fireworks go off." Talking about Craig and our budding romance made me miss him. "Come by the hospital right now and see for yourself."

"I don't want to watch your make-out session." Sarah stood. "But, sure, I'll look into his eyes and tell you what I see."

"I have someone else for you to meet too."

Despite all her begging during the drive over, I wouldn't tell Sarah who the other person was. I really didn't have any reason for the secrecy other than to drive her nuts.

"Male or female?"

I pressed the button in the hospital elevator.

"Young or old?"

I handed Sarah a mask.

"Someone you've mentioned before or a complete stranger?"

I led her to the scrub sink.

When we walked into the room, the first thing I noticed was Samantha's baldness. I'm sure it was the first thing Sarah noticed too. Samantha also wore a mask.

"Denise!"

"Hi, Samantha. I'd like you to meet my best friend, Sarah."

Sarah stared straight at Samantha and acted as though there was nothing out of the ordinary in this introduction. "So nice to meet you."

Samantha ran her hands over her smooth head. "I'm going *au naturale* today to celebrate."

"What are you celebrating?" Sarah's voice sounded interested. Truly, I think she already was. My friend had a unique ability to connect and care about a person in a very short amount of time. Her ministry of being with AIDS patients during the last stages of their disease meshed well with her gift to touch a heart deeply and quickly.

"Tomorrow, I'm getting a transplant." Samantha shadowboxed in her bed. "Going to kick that leukemia once and for all."

"Good for you."

"Wow." I walked to the head of the bed. "That happened quickly."

Samantha stared up at me, a twinkle in her eye. "I don't really have a lot of time to waste, Denise."

I patted her shoulder. "When will you be ready for more Monopoly?"

"I've got one more round of chemo after the transplant itself. Really takes a lot out of me. I'm not much fun during the treatment, but after that, I'll be back to myself."

"I'll still come see you, if you'd like. I could read to you, or rub your feet, or paint your nails."

"Oh . . ." Sarah moaned. "Her foot rubs are to die for."

The word *die* dropped like a grenade in the room. It hit the ground and rolled pinless on the floor. I held my breath and waited for the explosion.

"I'm sorry." Sarah cringed. "Denise was just reminding me that I needed to censor the words that come out of my mouth."

"I'm not afraid of dying." Samantha gazed up at the ceiling. "In some ways, I'd rather die than keep fighting. It'd be easier. No more pain, no more needles. I'd see my mom and dad again." She choked up. "I miss them."

I looked around for a tissue box. I handed a tissue to Samantha and pulled two more out for Sarah and myself. "You shouldn't have to go through this alone."

"Jesus is with me . . . all the time." Samantha wove the tissue through her fingers. "When Dad would have to leave . . . when he couldn't be with me . . . he'd pray and ask Jesus to hold my hand."

How could a teenager possess such great faith? I had my health, my husband was recovering his, we had a home and family and friends . . . and still I questioned whether the Lord was with me or not. Still, I felt alone. Still, I felt the need to misrepresent myself to Samantha, to lie, to manipulate the situation so I could feel in control of my fate.

Lord, give me faith like a child. Let me reach out and trust You to hold my hand.

I twisted my hands together. "Samantha, I have something to tell you after the transplant. The next time I see you. Don't let me forget."

She nodded, and didn't seem curious at all. Maybe because she had more important things to think about.

I didn't really think I would forget that I needed to confess who I was, to reveal that my husband was with her dad the day he died. However, I did want her to hold me to it so I couldn't talk myself out of it later.

"Will you pray with me again?"

I blinked back unbidden tears. Could God still use a liar like me? "I would love to."

Sarah and I held hands and placed our other hands on Samantha's shoulders.

"Father God." I squeezed Sarah's hand. "We know You are Samantha's Father. We know You are holding her hand and will be with her tomorrow as You have been with her always. Help this new marrow to bring new life to Samantha. Give the doctors wisdom as they continue to treat her. And we praise You for what You are doing."

After a pause, Samantha said, "Amen."

Sarah echoed it and we said our good-byes.

Once we were in the hall, Sarah nudged me. "Is she really an orphan with cancer? How did you get connected with her?"

"Her last name is Rodain. William was her father."

Sarah stared at me in apparent disbelief. "And how did you become her favorite visitor?"

"She doesn't know who I am." The elevator pinged and we walked on. "Don't worry, I'm going to tell her. But she's all alone. When I told Craig about her, he told me to take care of her. He even wants to pay her hospital bills."

"No way." Sarah leaned against the side of the elevator. "Do the boys know about her?"

"Why would they? Needless to say, they don't know about Craig's affair, either."

"I wouldn't be so sure."

The door opened and we exited onto Craig's floor. Sending a quizzical look at Sarah, I started down the hallway.

"From little comments Nicolas has made to Ethan and me, I'm pretty sure he thinks his dad was up to no good."

I sighed. "What should I do?"

"Talk to him, Denise. You're getting all wrapped up in Craig—which is completely understandable—but your boys are feeling lost."

"They've mentioned that to you?" Jealousy panged across my middle. If anyone had asked me a month ago, I would have said the boys and I had a great, open relationship. I tried to be their best friend without sacrificing my maternal authority.

"No, not really."

"Then how do you know?" Maybe Sarah was projecting her own ideas of what the boys were feeling.

"I look into their eyes as they speak and I see what they're not saying."

I understood. Sometimes the most legitimate feelings hid behind words instead of strutting out and demanding attention.

Chapter Sixteen

His

DENISE WALKED IN with a lady I couldn't remember ever seeing before. *Lord God, please don't let this be another woman Denise unearthed that I had an affair with.* As soon as I saw them both smiling at me, the paranoia eased.

"Hi, honey." Denise kissed me, raised an eyebrow at the woman, and they both laughed. I didn't mind one bit being left out of the joke. There had been few joyous sounds in my memory, and I wanted to savor this, even if I wasn't involved.

"I missed you." I squeezed her hand.

"Sarah took me to the mall."

Turning my head to face the woman, I grimaced from the twisting movement. "You must be Sarah."

"Pleased to make your acquaintance, new and improved Craig."

"Oh, I'm the new model, huh? The less a man knows, the more valuable he is?"

Her eyes sparkled and she smiled. "You didn't grill Denise about her expenditures at the mall. So, in that aspect, yes. It's a benefit that you can't remember your previous life."

"By your familiarity, I'm guessing you must rib me quite often."

"See?" She flung an arm toward Denise. "I think he's smarter than the old Craig, too."

I caught a sarcastic barb in the backhanded compliment. "I'm also more intuitive." Squinting, I rubbed my palms together. "I'd go so far as to say that you and I didn't really get along very well in the past."

The teasing expression disappeared from Sarah's mien. She gaped at me. "How do you know that? I've been perfectly civil for the last two minutes."

"A magician never reveals his secrets." I expected some type of positive reaction from the women, a giggle or the next comment in our quick repartee. Instead, an awkward silence fell.

"Um . . ." Sarah gestured toward the door with her thumb. "I'm going to get some coffee. You guys want some?"

We mumbled no, and Sarah left.

"Was it something I said?"

"Really, Craig, how did you know that you and Sarah don't get along?"

"She looked surprised when I started playing along with her, so I must not have paid much notice to her. Obviously, she didn't think I was the greatest man before the accident, calling me an upgrade. She and I must have rubbed each other the wrong way. I thought we could joke around about it in the same passive-aggressive way she had just told me my amnesia was a blessing."

Denise let out a huge sigh. "For a moment, I thought you had remembered her . . . the past."

"Do we have a particularly bad history?"

"You're up to hearing it?"

"Hopefully I've already heard the worst about myself."

Shoulders slumping, Denise seemed to turn inside herself. "Back when we met Sarah and Ethan—that's her husband—I was pregnant with Jamie. I first saw Sarah at a library story time for Nicolas. She doesn't have any children of her own yet, but she'd taken her niece to hear the guest children's author read. We hit it off right away. She started coming over almost every day to hang out with me. You were pulling long hours getting the office up and running. I don't think you even knew about her for months. Not that I didn't tell you about her, but you didn't hear me, I guess. One day . . ."

"What? I want to know what happened."

Denise crossed her arms over her chest and leaned forward, head down. "The morning sickness lasted all day. I felt horrible and I didn't want to disturb you, so I called Sarah to come over. She played with Nicolas, put him down for his nap, and made me a lunch I could actually eat. She drew a hot, deep bath and convinced me to soak in it. Then you came home." Denise stared at the floor.

"What? What did I do?"

"You'd been drinking." Her voice dropped to a whisper. "I hadn't thought of what it would look like to you. Instead of all the things Sarah had done for me, all you saw was the messy house, the absent dinner, the lazy wife." A tear trailed down her cheek.

Pain stabbed my chest. I touched along the taping over my ribs, but couldn't find the spot that hurt. The source seemed to be deeper within. "I'm a miserable excuse for a man." My voice cracked like an adolescent's.

Denise shook her head. "Our life changed. Her husband, Ethan, came by a few days later and convinced you to go golfing. The next Sunday you took us to their church. You and Sarah have never acknowledged that incident with each other since."

"But she can't help thinking of me the way I was the night we met."

Straightening, Denise glanced at the door. "Deep down, I think she wonders if you ever really changed."

"What do you think?"

Denise's soft eyes turned to me. "I don't know what I thought then . . . it doesn't matter anyway. What matters is the man you are today."

Carrying a single cup of coffee, Sarah sashayed back into the room.

Hers

SARAH'S SUDDEN CHANGE of demeanor didn't faze me one bit. Pretending to be okay came easier than facing the problem. And, truthfully, with Craig recovering from a major accident, now was not the best time to mend an ancient rift.

"So nice to see you doing better with my own eyes." Sarah nodded at Craig. "Denise, are you ready to go? Ethan's expecting me home within the hour."

"Uh, sure." What? Had I expected us all to sit around and have a cozy chat? "Can you give me a moment to say good-bye?"

"Of course. I'll meet you in the hall." Black hair flared around her as she spun and walked out the door.

"She's my ride, so I guess I've got to go."

Craig's eyes pleaded with me. "I've barely seen you at all."

How I enjoyed the new Craig. When I walked into his hospital room, he seemed excited to see me. When I had to leave, it seemed like he would miss me. During the interim, he listened to and looked at me. He saw me as I was, not as I used to be.

An idea bloomed. "Do you think you're up to talking on the phone?"

His eyes brightened. "If you stretched the cord over to the table here, I could manage."

"I'll call you." Blushing, I smiled.

"I'll be here. Waiting." He lifted his chin and his gaze settled on my lips.

Even though his lips felt different, stretched somehow from the wounds and subsequent surgery, they also seemed familiar. "Bye," I whispered, between the sweet kisses.

"Bye."

OOO

Sarah sat on a bench in the hallway. I started toward her, but Dr. Rossing caught me a few steps later.

"Why, Mrs. Littleton, I haven't seen you in a while. What do you think of your husband's recovery so far?"

I signaled to Sarah that I would join her in a minute. "It's quite amazing for only coming out of the coma, what? A week ago? His memory seems to be razor sharp since then. I mean, he's funny, and quick, and kind."

"Just like before, huh? I would think the return of his long-term memory is just around the corner."

I laughed. "Actually, he seems like a different man. He looks the same, but he talks and acts differently."

"You know, Mrs. Littleton, I've had patients whose personalities changed after head trauma. Their families, at times, did not want to accept that the different-mannered relative really belonged with them. Someone who's always been quiet and easygoing can become angry and combative. And vice versa. I'm glad Craig's changes appeal to you, but keep in mind they are most likely temporary."

"So it's normal for people to act unlike themselves?"

"It can show up as a side effect, yes."

"But you're sure that's my husband in there." I smiled at my joke.

"You have the advantage of hard physical evidence that proves he's your husband."

"I do?" It had never occurred to me to doubt it was Craig lying in that hospital bed, but my curiosity loved to be appeased once awakened.

"Yes, because of the investigation the police confirmed your husband's identity. They double-checked his medical records and everything matches up."

"Ah, indisputable evidence."

Shifting his weight to the other foot, Dr. Rossing grinned. "Are you ready for Craig to leave the hospital?"

My heart missed a beat. "He can come home?"

"He'll need some rehabilitation after his casts are off, but he's able to get around with the help of a wheelchair."

I trusted Dr. Rossing knew what he was talking about. "His lungs are fine? What about his ribs?"

"The ribs are going to cause a lot of pain for months to come. They'll heal slowly, on their own timetable. His lungs are functioning extremely well. There's nothing to worry about with his health. As I said before, I believe a familiar environment will speed his memory recovery." He cleared his throat. "Seeing the psychiatrist I've recommended to Craig will help with that, also."

"So when are you releasing him?"

"How's tomorrow?"

I whooped. "That'd be great."

Sarah joined me. "What's going on?"

I grabbed her hands and spun her in a circle. "Craig's coming home."

She squeezed my hands. "How wonderful for you."

"I've got to tell him." I ran back into Craig's room. "Baby, you're coming home tomorrow!"

Joy washed over his face. "I am?"

Dr. Rossing had followed me. "You are. If you feel ready."

"Yes, sir, I'd like that very much." He squinted, sniffed, as though holding back tears. "Home." Desire filled the word to the brim and spilled over.

"Tomorrow it is," Dr. Rossing said. "Mrs. Littleton, I'll have the nurses instruct you tomorrow on further care for his wounds. How to minimize the scarring and such. Plus, we'll set you up with a rehab schedule."

"Thank you." I hugged the doctor. He remained stiff under my groping arms. "Oh, I've got to clean the house. Except the church already did. And we're going to need groceries. Craig, I'll call you. Sarah's got to go and I've got so much to do." I scattered kisses all over Craig's face and rushed out the door.

His

HER ELBOW HIT MY CHEST in the flurry of love. Some of my tears had to be from pain, but most evidenced my new hope. I would be with Denise all day until I went back to work. I could eat at my own table, sleep in my own bed, and be with my own family.

I checked the clock and marked the time since she left minutes ago. I wasn't sure how long the drive to our house was, but it had to be longer than a few minutes, or Denise would have gone back and forth for meals during the week. I budgeted a half hour. After she did other things . . . Maybe by the time meals were served and the trays were picked up, she would call. I imagined picking up the receiver and hearing her dulcet tones.

I glanced at the clock again.

Hers

I BOUNDED UP the steps, quickly noting the mowed lawn and weeded flower beds—the church strikes again—and tried the door. Locked. In my excitement, it was difficult to find my keys. As I fingered them in the bottom of my purse, the door flew open.

"Mom!" Nicolas hugged me. "I'm so glad you're back."

"You are?" Wondering what caused his sudden change of attitude, I returned his embrace.

"Jamie told me you were at the mall." He beamed at me.

"Yes." I left one arm around him as we strolled into the house. "Afterward, I saw Dad."

"Do I get it now or do I have to wait until after dinner?"

"Get what?" I tilted my head and grinned at my funny boy. When the experts said hormones caused strange behavior and mood swings, they meant it.

"Yeah, right. I wondered if you would forget, since you haven't been home at all lately, but as soon as Jamie told me where you were—" He wrapped his arms around me. "I love you, Mom."

"Love you, too," I murmured into his hair. What was he talking about? Okay, he thought I'd forgotten something, he was happy to hear I'd been shopping at the mall . . . I searched the outer reaches of my mind. What was today? Craig had been in the hospital nineteen days. *It's Wednesday, I think. Or Thursday.* "I'll talk to you in a minute. Let me run upstairs first."

"You don't have to wrap it," he yelled up the stairs at me.

Luckily, I had reached the landing so he couldn't see me. I doubled over with shock. I'd forgotten Nicolas's birthday! And not just any birthday, but his sixteenth! *Oh, Lord, what am I going to do?*

I staggered to my room and closed the doors in case he tried to peek at the present he believed I bought for him. A party? I could make last-minute reservations at his favorite restaurant. But friends? He would expect me to include some of his friends. He always invited a few of his pals to his parties. And I needed a gift.

The phone. If I could sneak into Craig's office, I could wrap up the cell phone I'd found in the drawer. I didn't know if it was activated, but Nicolas would understand his dad was planning on doing it before the accident. I slipped down the stairs, snagged the phone, and rushed back to my room. From under the bed, I pulled out the wrapping paper tote and found a not-too-cutesy, tiny gift bag. Stuffing crumpled tissue paper into the bag, I thought of which friends Nicolas would want at his celebration.

I dialed a number from my bedside phone and waited.

"Hello?"

"Hi, Heather. It's Mrs. Littleton. Are you busy tonight?"

"Not really. What's up?"

"It's Nicolas's birthday."

"Yeah. I already gave him his present this afternoon."

Of course. A teenage girl remembered my son's birthday, while I forgot. "Then it will be an even bigger surprise to him. Could you meet us at the Copper Monkey in forty-five minutes?"

"I'll ask my mom." An agonizing moment later, Heather came back on the line. "Sure. I'll be there."

"Thanks. I really appreciate it. With all that's going on with Nicolas's dad, the dinner's kind of eleventh-hour."

"You've had a lot to deal with, Mrs. Littleton. Nicolas understands."

❍❍❍

Craig must have set up the phone fully, since Nicolas called all his friends from the restaurant. They met us for a game of laser tag after dinner. Once they were worn out, I treated the whole gang to made-to-order ice cream, their choices of topping blended into their favorite flavors, at the Cold Stone Creamery. We didn't get back until almost midnight. As far as I could tell, Nicolas never figured out I'd forgotten his big day.

Jamie went up to bed, and Nicolas and I lounged on the couches in the bonus room.

Nicolas flipped his phone open, snapped it closed. "When can you take me to the DMV?"

"Oh." I rubbed my forehead. Craig had promised we would be first in line when the DMV opened on Nicolas's sixteenth. "Maybe tomorrow? They're open on Fridays, right?"

"I think so." He pushed a few more buttons, trying out the features. "Thanks, Mom. I know you're busy."

"You'll run to the store for me, won't you, whenever I need anything?"

"Yeah, I'll be your gofer."

"Good. Let's get to bed, my boy, so we can get up bright and early. You can practice driving before your test."

My pajamas never felt so good. I washed off my makeup and climbed into bed. What a long day. First shopping with Sarah, then visiting Samantha, hearing that Craig would be coming home, throwing a party . . .

Tomorrow!

I hadn't even told the boys Craig was coming home. *Calm down. If you do the DMV early enough with Nicolas, it shouldn't interfere with Craig's release.* And I could make his homecoming a surprise for the boys.

How different would our house be with Craig around? Jamie and Nicolas wouldn't feel left out anymore. I could relax—finally—and get things done around the house. Maybe I could help Craig out to the patio and work in the garden. Black plastic six-packs of petunias and lantana sat in the side yard, waiting to be planted. If anyone had thought to water them, the plants might still be alive.

I pictured Craig, stretched out on the chaise lounge.

Craig. I might lose my head if it wasn't attached. I found the scrap of paper where I'd scribbled his extension and dialed.

Six rings later, he picked up with a groggy hello.

"Hi. I'm sorry it's so late. I figured it was better to call and wake you than not to call at all."

"I was worried about you."

Over the phone, I heard anew the raspiness in his voice. The tube they'd put down his throat when he was on the respirator must have caused permanent damage. Or maybe he needed more healing time to sound like himself. "Tonight was Nicolas's sixteenth birthday."

"Oh, I forgot you told me that."

"I didn't even tell you because I forgot myself."

He sucked in a deep breath. "Uh-oh."

"That's one word to describe what went through my mind. I feel like the worst mother ever."

"What did you do?"

"We went out to eat and got some of his friends to meet us."

"He had fun?"

"No doubt." Talking to Craig made it seem like a bump in the road, not a major stumbling block.

"I have something to ask you."

"Okay. What?" I clenched the phone, wary of what might come next.

"It's very important. I've been thinking about it all day and I need to know the truth."

"Yes?"

"What did you buy at the mall?"

I chuckled. "Not a thing, I'm proud to say."

"After Sarah's comment, I knew I would be remiss if I didn't bring it up."

"Your money is safe for now." Slight exaggeration.

"Good."

I sank back onto the pillows piled at the head of our bed. "Nicolas loved his cell phone. You picked that out for him, by the way, before everything happened."

"I think that's one of the first positive things I've heard I did in my old life."

I wasn't quite sure what to say. Truly, there were not a lot of compliments I could give about Craig's pre-accident behavior. "I visited Samantha Rodain right before we saw you and she had good news."

"She did?"

The back and forth. Being in my own bed, conversing with a masculine voice. Shivers of delight trickled over my tummy. I was having an intimate connection with my husband. "She's getting her bone marrow transplant tomorrow."

"What does that really do for her? Is the leukemia gone?"

"I'm not sure exactly what happens. Marrow makes blood cells, so I guess she'll have healthy blood."

"How did she seem?"

"Ready to have it done. She's around the same age as Nicolas, and she trusts the Lord more than I do."

"So she's about sixteen?"

"Yep. Which reminds me, I've got to take Nicolas to the DMV tomorrow for his driver's test so I won't be in as early as I'd planned to see you."

"What time's his appointment?"

"He doesn't have one. We'll just walk in and grab a number."

Craig cleared his throat. "Won't work. You have to make an appointment."

I hadn't taken a driving test in years, but I should have been able to do something as simple as follow through on my promise to Nicolas. "Now how would you know?"

"I dunno. It's a guy thing, I guess. It's in my head and I know I'm right."

"Fine." I would rather not pursue the subject than have him remember the snide comments he used to make about my abilities to check the oil in my car, start the mower, or drive a stick shift. His memory of my relationship to motors might return.

"Did she talk about God with you?"

"Who?" I blinked. "I thought we were talking about Nicolas."

"But you said Samantha trusts God, and I wondered how you knew that."

I rubbed my forehead. "Yes, she said so."

"Did she look very sick?"

The thrill of speaking with Craig waned and irritation waxed. The whole conversation didn't need to focus on a stranger. "She had a mask on, but she sounded strong."

"Is there anything we can do for her?"

"You already had me—"

"Did she seem scared to be alone?"

Pushing my head into the pillow, I stared at the ceiling. "I don't understand you at all. Why are you so focused on Samantha Rodain? I want to talk about our family, not somebody else's. We should be talking about our children, our dreams, our future."

"I'm sorry." He sounded genuine. "I just feel a huge amount of responsibility for her."

"And you should for your sons, too." I clipped my words. "'Cause you caring more about Samantha than about them is really getting old." I hung up the phone. It wasn't enough of an action to ease my frustration, so I threw Craig's pillow across the room.

Chapter Seventeen

Hers

I DABBED CRAIG'S favorite perfume on each wrist and behind my ears and ran the brush through my hair one more time. When Craig studied pictures or videos of him coming home, I wanted him to see me as an attractive, happy woman. Not the crabby lady who hung up on him the night before.

Why? Why did I do that?

A glance at the calendar reminded me I could blame my hormones. Dumb excuse. I had practiced my apology all morning. Soon I could deliver it.

"Mom!"

I took the stairs at double speed. "What, Jamie?"

"It's time to go. You told me to be ready by nine and I am. So let's go." He stood in the entryway wearing slacks and a striped shirt, his hair neatly combed. He seemed to notice my perusal of his person. He blushed. "Dad likes it when I look 'professional.' "

"He does." I kissed the top of his head, picked up the keys, and turned toward the kitchen. "Nicolas, are you ready?"

He ambled in, still in sweats and hair askew, munching an apple. "I decided I'd wait here at home."

"Is this because of your driver's test?" I stepped toward him. "Your dad was right. I called and set up an appointment for next Thursday."

He leaned against the wall, one foot kicked behind the other.

"I'm sorry. I know I promised we'd do it today but, like we talked about earlier this morning, waiting a couple of days isn't so bad, is it?"

"No, Mom." He shrugged and stared at the floor. "I'm fine. Go get Dad."

I glanced at Jamie and then back at Nicolas. Had their personalities been transplanted into each other's bodies? Jamie now seemed eager to please, dressed well, and obeyed. Nicolas acted as if he couldn't care less what I wanted him to do. Actually, he didn't seem to care much about anything unless it concerned him. The sixteenth year boded badly so far.

"All right." I pointed to the camera bag and jiggled my keys. "You can videotape us all coming through the door. Jamie, we're off." Ushering him into the garage, I smiled over my shoulder at Nicolas. "We'll be back soon and we'll come in the front. Fewer steps for him to maneuver than the garage."

Jerking open the passenger-side door, Jamie smirked. "I didn't have to say 'shotgun' and I still get the front seat."

I climbed into the car. "Enjoy it while you can. Once your brother gets his license, he'll want to drive everywhere and . . ." I tilted his chin and made him look into my eyes. "A gentleman would never ask his mother to crawl into the back."

"Why not? Do your imaginary brakes only work in the front?"

Grinning, I put on an innocent tone. "Whatever are you talking about?" I pulled out of the garage and backed into the street.

"What you do when Nicolas drives. Does that only work up here?" He raised his right foot and dropped it to the floor.

I played along, tapping the brakes at the same time his foot hit the floor. For just a moment, a look of sheer amazement passed over his face. I was still giggling when I parked at the hospital.

When we walked into Craig's room, the bed lay empty. I had grown accustomed to seeing him lying down. Aside from the day I met him on the patio, he always had been supine under his sheets. This morning, he sat in a wheelchair in the corner of the room.

"Jamie, come here and give your ol' dad a hug, huh?" As Craig wrapped his arms around Jamie, he winked at me and squeezed the back of his son's neck.

I knew the effort each movement took and I hoped Craig wouldn't push himself too hard.

"You're really coming home?" Hope pervaded Jamie's question.

"I sure am."

A nurse bustled into the room, followed by Dr. Rossing, as if on cue. She smiled at us and took Craig's arm. "One last check of your blood pressure and pulse for our records, Dr. Littleton, and you'll be good to go."

Dr. Rossing pulled me aside. "I've printed off everything you need to help Craig in his recovery." He held out a stack of papers. "There's more information on the long-term effects of traumatic brain injuries and retrograde amnesia. During these first few weeks, it's important not to pressure him to remember. Explain your routines, explain your schedules, explain everything. Make sure he rests, gets enough sleep, eats well, doesn't smoke or drink alcohol, and does the home exercises the rehabilitation program recommended. He also needs to see the psychiatrist as soon as possible."

"Do you really think he'll be okay at home?"

"We wouldn't release him if we didn't feel he was ready to go." Dr. Rossing patted my shoulder. "Don't worry, Mrs. Littleton. He's got a long road ahead of him, but it's in the direction of complete recovery."

"Thank you." I shook his hand. "I appreciate everything you've done for him."

"Here's my card." Before handing the small rectangle to me, he scribbled something on the back. "Try my cell if anything abnormal occurs, though I don't believe it will." He wished Craig good luck and left the room.

The nurse waited behind the wheelchair. "Ready?"

"Don't I need to sign him out or something?"

"Nope." She grabbed hold of the rubber grips on the wheelchair handles. "We got all the paperwork out of the way earlier this morning. Dr. Littleton rang for us as soon as he woke and jump-started the whole process."

I pictured him pulling on the bedside cord, his first waking thoughts about coming home to his family. As I walked toward him, he glowed. He must have convinced them to help him shave, too, because the scruff had disappeared and his cheeks were smooth between puckered lines where stitches had been. Bending to kiss him, I rubbed my thumb on one velvet patch of softness midst the scars. He had suffered through so much.

"Gross." Jamie pulled me back. "You'll have plenty of time for that when we're home. Behind closed doors."

I exchanged an amused look with the nurse as Craig chuckled.

Jamie and I stowed Craig's possessions, a mishmash of flowers, cards, balloons, and books, onto the cart the nurse provided. Gathering the plants from the windowsill, I pricked my hand on a cactus. "Who was this from?" I held it up for Craig to identify.

"No clue. Is there a card?"

I pulled the white rectangle from the forked plastic and opened the tiny card. A lipsticked kiss print.

Naomi must have brought it on her early morning visit. I flashed him the card and dumped the cactus in the trash.

"Mom, that was cool. Don't throw it away." Jamie reached for the garbage can.

"Jamie."

His hand stilled at my tone.

"We are not taking that cactus home, understand?" I bristled as much as the desert plant. And with good reason.

Jamie led the way out of the room and toward the elevator. Sunshine greeted us when we exited the hospital. Craig raised his head to the warmth. In the flower beds, bees buzzed over the color-drenched blossoms.

I angled the cart to keep it from rolling. "If I'd known we would be out so quickly, I would have parked in the loading zone. Be right back." I sprinted over the crosswalk, into the parking garage, and up the stairs. By the time I reached the car, my blouse was sticking to my sweaty chest and my throat tasted of metal from my sudden exertion. I flipped the air-conditioning onto high and twisted my way down the structure toward the exit. They were probably wondering what was taking me so long.

I pulled up to the sidewalk in front of the trio. Jamie squatted next to his dad, holding hands. The nurse batted an errant get-well balloon away from her face. Putting the car in park, I set the emergency brake. The nurse wheeled Craig to the passenger door.

I popped out and hurried to the other side of the car. "Now how do we get him in?"

Craig grinned at me. "I'm not a baby. You don't have to talk about me like I'm not here. I can open my own door."

"I'm sorry." I bowed and grandly gestured toward the car.

"I forgive you."

When his efforts to pull the handle open failed, I glanced at the nurse. She shook her head once and put a finger to her lips.

"So." Craig turned to see the nurse. "How do we get me in?"

Jamie cracked up, and I smothered a laugh by tightening my chest and holding it still.

The nurse pulled the door open and pushed the wheelchair into the angle of the door and the car. "Put one hand on the seat and one on the door and pull yourself up. Denise and I will brace you. Your son can move the wheelchair out of the way as soon as you're out of it."

Craig did as he was told, though it wasn't until the third try he actually made it to his feet. He teetered and started to fall back. Jamie whipped the chair out of the way, and the nurse and I lunged forward, grabbing onto Craig.

He moaned. "Do you play pro ball or what? My ribs can't take a tackle very well."

"You shouldn't have hit the bottle so hard today." I rubbed my hand along his bicep. His muscles didn't feel quite as large as they had before, and I remembered his arms as being hairier. The coma and bandages changed his body just as much as the amnesia changed his mind. "You're tipsy, and it's not even noon yet."

"Har-har." But the corners of his mouth turned up.

I tried to imagine what it would feel like to be in the body of a strong runner and wake in a weak one. So weak it couldn't even get into a car by itself. I was proud of Craig for making the best of it, for not giving up, for trying until he succeeded.

With our help, he turned around and sat on the edge of the seat. We lifted his feet onto the floor mat, and he spun until he faced the windshield.

As Jamie put the bags into the trunk, the nurse showed me how to fold the wheelchair. I stowed it in the back, fit the mementos from Craig's hospital stay around it, thanked the nurse, and climbed into the driver's seat.

"All set?" I wrapped my fingers around the steering wheel.

Craig nodded and stared out the window.

The import of driving suddenly occurred to me. The last time my husband drove anywhere, he ended up in the hospital. Was he afraid to be back in a vehicle? Did he remember any of it? Maybe not in his mind, but his body. The physical acts of moving, turning, braking. Would they bring back the feelings of the accident?

Keep us safe as we drive home, Lord. Please let Craig's coming home be a good thing.

His

MY INSIDES WERE FULL of butter, I think, from how long my stomach had been churning. The barrage of colors and sounds, the number of people coming into or out of the hospital—I grew dizzy with the newness.

Denise didn't seem to notice how overwhelmed I was. When she took off for a six-story building across a narrow street, I somehow knew it was a parking garage. How could I find the right words for that and yet not know the color or make of the car Denise would be pulling up in?

Jamie reached for my hand.

I held on to him, tethering myself to the present. "Where's your brother?" I'd been surprised not to see Nicolas after Jamie entered the room, but I tried to keep his absence from hurting.

"He's at home. He's grumpy because he couldn't get his license today so he's taking it out on Mom."

A perceptive boy, my son. But while Jamie thought Nicolas only had it out for Denise, I added myself to the equation.

A champagne Denali stopped at the curb and Denise jumped out. *I guess that's our car.* But I still had no idea what our house looked like, what kind of mower we used, or what style of slippers I wore.

As we merged onto the freeway, Denise ran her fingers along the steering wheel. "I'm sorry about last night. I shouldn't have hung up on you."

I gripped the armrest as we avoided a vehicle changing lanes without using a blinker. "If I knew our number, I would have called you back."

Flipping on the turn signal, she slid into a space in the next lane barely bigger than the Denali itself. "In our marriage vows, we promised never to go to bed angry."

"I didn't mean to make you mad." I adjusted the seat belt away from my neck. Breathing became less of a chore. "I can't explain why

I feel so strongly about taking care of Samantha. Nicolas is my son. I understand that. I want to hear everything you want to tell me about him. And Jamie. I'll be loving them for the rest of my life, but Samantha . . . she has no one."

Denise sighed. "I get that. I'll try not to overreact."

"Who's Samantha?" Jamie piped up.

"Never mind," Denise said. "You don't know her."

Now aware of Jamie in the back, listening to every word, I said, "Denise, you reacted emotionally. Think of all the stress you've been under. And not just you, but the kids, too. Pressure creates fissures. But we can patch cracks."

Denise's eyes glistened, and she didn't speak again until we got home.

Somehow I managed to slide out of the car seat and into the waiting wheelchair without causing myself excruciating pain.

Denise set the chair's brakes. "As soon as we get you up these little steps in the sidewalk, we'll be home free. You'll be able to spin all around the lower level and reacquaint yourself with the house."

Jamie helped her carry the bags through the front door while I waited on the driveway. Quiet settled like Mount St. Helens' ashes on the neighborhood. None of the kids on our block were out playing hopscotch, riding skateboards, or playing basketball. Naptime?

Judging by the size and appearance of the houses, many of the families had probably enrolled their older kids in expensive summer programs destined to make students' SAT scores jump or to train athletes to be the next Wilt Chamberlain.

Fine by me. I didn't need a cute little squirt riding up on his Big Wheel and asking me why I had taken a purple Magic Marker to my face and played dot-to-dot with my freckles.

Denise came down the walkway. Though she smiled at me, her gait seemed stiffer and her shoulders higher. "Think we can make it up these steps?"

"Don't tip me out." I clutched the arms of the wheelchair as she spun me around and wheeled me backward to the first step. She pulled as Jamie pushed, and we made it to the doorway.

As we rolled over the threshold, I expected to hear Nicolas greet me, but no one stood in the foyer. "Where's Nicolas?" I asked Denise. "Jamie said Nicolas would be waiting here to welcome me home."

Her smile faltered and she shot a look at Jamie. "You'll see him very soon."

Fatigue swept over me, and my knees shook even though they hadn't done any work. I must have been tightening the unused muscles more than I realized.

Denise and Jamie gathered around me.

"Are you okay, Dad?"

I nodded, but caught a look at myself in the full-length mirror hanging beside the entry table. My face had turned white except for the scarlet gashes across my cheeks. I ignored the ugly hue of my reflection's wounds. Yep, I would have sent any neighborhood kid screaming for their mommy.

"Do you want to rest?" Denise bent down, a concerned look on her face.

"I hadn't realized how tired I was. Getting in and out of the car wiped me out."

"I made up the hide-a-bed for you."

"Oh." My disappointment must have been evident in the timbre of my voice.

She dropped to a knee in front of me. "Why? What's the matter?" A prism hung in some nearby window, floating a rainbow on Denise's neck, melting into her hair.

"I guess I've been looking forward to sleeping in my own bed, that's all." I thought of all the ways it could be worse. Of the hospital calling and asking me to come back in for more surgery. Of them inserting another IV or catheter. Or even of spending another night in that plain, cold atmosphere.

Denise gestured toward the stairs. "I don't see how you could manage it, honey. Our bedroom is the hardest room in the house to reach."

"Yeah, Dad." Jamie nodded. "Those are honkin' big stairs compared to the little steps outside."

"No, no. Of course, you're right. A bed on the first floor is only common sense." The wheelchair squeaked as I turned it around. "Can you show me the restroom first?"

Denise maneuvered me into the half bath next to the hall closet and closed herself out of the room.

I had just gotten into the wheelchair. How could I expend more energy to get onto the toilet? Lifting the lid, I planned how I could leverage my body to arrive on my desired destination. I hoisted my body up gripping one arm of the wheelchair and pushing against the half wall built to separate the toilet from the pedestal sink. Landing on the toilet, fully clothed, I caught the wheelchair in mid-fall.

"Are you okay?" Denise's voice came through the door.

"Yep. Just great." I righted the chair, wriggled my pants down, and did what I needed to do. Getting back in the chair was easier.

I rapped on the door with a freshly washed hand and rolled back for Denise to open it. Letting her push me to the bed, I scanned my home. Pillows covered the top half of a hide-a-bed. A couple of blankets lay across the bottom. Off to the side, a table held a remote, a box of tissues, a few magazines, and a picture frame. As I wheeled closer, I recognized Denise with her arms around a man who looked kind of like the man who stared back at me in the mirror.

Denise followed my gaze. "Do you remember that day?"

Did I? Fallen leaves littered the background of the photo. We were outside, in a grassy area. Behind us, part of a statue could be seen. "Not really."

Denise waited until I hoisted myself onto the bed before asking her next question. "Do you remember the house?"

We had passed through a gorgeous kitchen: granite countertops with custom backsplashes and matching, top-of-the-line, stainless steel appliances. I lay in the living room, facing a flat-screen TV almost as large as my bed. Outside massive French doors, the lawn wandered between raised flower beds. Profuse colors spilled over the cedar boxes, filling the view with life.

I closed my eyes. "Nothing seems familiar yet."

"Don't worry." Denise sat on the edge of the bed and stroked my forehead. "The doctor didn't say it would happen right away, but being here should help you remember."

"Yeah." Sleep darted around my consciousness.

"Promise me something."

"What?"

"If you remember anything, or think something feels familiar, even just a feeling of déjà vu, tell me."

"I promise." My eyes opened for a moment, then closed again with heavy lids.

When I awoke, a blanket had been tucked around my body. With the blinds drawn, a warm darkness surrounded me. Did it smell like home to me? Did it look like home? Most importantly, did it feel, deep down in my gut, like home? I couldn't tell. Yet.

As I searched for a clock, my body ached. I took inventory. Ribs burning, cheeks pounding, legs itching: I prayed for relief. If only I had taken my pain pill before napping, I wouldn't be paying such a high price upon waking.

Hers

IT SEEMED LIKE SERENDIPITY that our bedroom was on the second floor. Yes, Craig was my husband. He had a right to sleep in his own bed. But did he know I was his wife? Did he remember me in his heart, if not his mind? The dichotomy of our marriage confused me.

I wanted to wrap my arms around him, kiss him, and whisper, "I love you." What would he do in response? I was hesitant to hug him for fear of hurting his ribs. Kisses seemed forward. I initiated them so often because I was the more mobile one, but he must enjoy them. He could ask me to stop if they made him uncomfortable.

Did I feel ready to wake up with his scarred face on the pillow beside me? Yet the choice had been made for me. The limits of our physical relationship were drawn by Craig's injuries—a small silver lining in the storm cloud that dumped a flood of grief on our lives.

Hearing a noise from the living room, I pup-tented my book on the arm of the recliner in Craig's office and went to check on him. He sat up in bed when I approached.

"Can you bring me pills and a glass of water?" The wildness of a hurt animal lurked in his eyes.

I rushed to the counter in the kitchen and dumped the recommended dosage into my palm. After filling a glass of water, I offered the medication to Craig. "Is it bad?" I'd never seen him in so much pain.

"Like a semitruck ran over me." He groaned.

"Don't exaggerate. It was just a Mustang convertible." I watched the line of his mouth. *Yes!* I had coaxed a small smile out of him.

The front door opened, and Craig tried to peer around me. "Is that Nicolas?"

I raised my eyebrows. "I'll go see." Forcing myself to walk slowly so as not to arouse Craig's suspicions, I made for the door.

Nicolas stood with his back against the open door, waving toward the street. I got there in time to see Heather's car disappearing down our road.

"Nicolas Arthur Littleton," I hissed. "Where have you been?"

"Out." He glared at me.

"Where is this attitude coming from, young man?" I pushed him off the door and shut it before the neighbors could tell what was happening. "You were supposed to be here, video camera in hand, when your father came home."

"He's home?" Nicolas ran a hand through his hair.

"Yes, he's in the other room and—" I glared at my son and shook my head. "Don't try to change the subject. You're in big trouble. I want to hear some kind of explanation for your absence on such an important day." My voice had risen despite my resolve to keep quiet. "Go to your room. I'll be there in five minutes."

He slunk toward the stairs, taking a wide berth around me when he passed.

"And you better be ready to tell me what in the world you were thinking when you chose to go off with a friend instead of being here to greet your father."

He mumbled something that sounded like "girlfriend."

I rolled my eyes. "Go!" I jabbed a finger toward his room. Smoothing my shirt and blowing my hair off my face, I glided back to the hide-a-bed.

"Was it Nicolas?"

"It was." I stopped about ten feet from Craig. The dim light might disguise my red cheeks and delay his questions. "I need to go chat with him for a few minutes before you see him." I pointed to the bell I'd placed on the table while Craig slept. "Ring if you need me."

"Okay."

Chat? I stomped up the stairs. *I'd like to spank him and put him to bed without dessert. If he's going to act like a disobedient little boy, I should treat him like a disobedient little boy.* No need to make a fist with my hands to knock on the closed door, as my hands were both in that position already.

A dull grunt answered the knock. I took it to mean permission to enter. Nicolas lay sprawled across his bed, the telltale white cords of his earbuds hanging from his head. I yanked on the cords.

He lurched upright. "Hey!"

"Give it to me." Palm up, I stuck my hand out and waited until my sullen teenager put the player in my hand. "Now talk."

"What is there to talk about? Just ground me and let's be done with it."

"What is there to talk about?" Incredulous, I stared at him. "For starters, you left the house without permission."

"I needed to see my girlfriend. There's nothing different about it than when you said you had to unwind and talk to Sarah yesterday."

Breathe deeply. Count to ten slowly. Pulling Nicolas's desk chair over, I sat. "You know that is not true. Two adult women getting together is far different from a boy sneaking out of the house to see a girl." Resting my elbows on my knees, I rounded my back as tension settled around my spine. "And you're not allowed to have a girlfriend."

"You and Dad both said I could." He swung his legs over the side of the bed. "The rule was no dating until I turned sixteen. Which was yesterday, in case you don't remember."

I hit my knuckles against my head. He had me there. When we made that rule, I don't think we remembered how young sixteen was. In my mind's eye, I pictured Nicolas as a towheaded toddler. Sixteen had seemed ages away, a safe number to set for the milestone of becoming involved with the opposite sex. "You're right." I looked up. "I forgot about that. But if you think that what you did today will allow you that privilege for the next couple of weeks, you're dead wrong."

"I'm grounded from dating for *weeks*?" He jutted his head forward.

"No seeing Heather except at church. No calling her. No e-mailing, no texting, and no whatever else you kids do now. No contact." His cell phone lay on the nightstand. I pocketed it.

"Mom! It's not fair!"

"Your father has been asking about you. I'll give you time to calm down, and then you will come and have a civilized conversation with him."

"You don't know anything about Dad!"

I ignored his outburst. "Maybe you'll even find your manners and apologize for not being here." Slowly counting to ten, I calmly walked away.

Downstairs, I pulled chicken tenderloins from the freezer. Carrying the bag with me, I stuck my head into the living room. "Sweetie, I'm going to get dinner started. Nicolas will come see you in a few minutes."

He nodded, the animal-like look gone from his eyes. "Where's Jamie?"

"He went to a friend's house. Since you were sleeping, I thought it would be okay for an hour or so." I checked my watch. "He should be home in a few minutes."

"I figured he was gone." Craig stretched his arms. "Seemed too quiet around here."

"Dinner will be ready in about thirty minutes." I poured olive oil into a frying pan and puzzled the chicken pieces to fit as many as possible. After adding teriyaki sauce, I doctored it with ginger powder, drained pineapple, and diced green pepper.

A cup of rice, twice as much water, some butter, and salt went into a saucepan. I set the timer. Nicolas stalked past me as I stirred the chicken, but when I heard his voice as he spoke to his father, he did not sound angry.

He sounded hurt.

Chapter Eighteen

Hers

"NICOLAS, GET SOME CLEAN silverware out of the dishwasher, please." I poured pancake batter into the electric skillet as Jamie wheeled Craig to the little table we tucked in the nook.

"What day is it?" Craig asked.

"It's Sunday." I tipped the bowl back and twirled it to catch the large drip hanging on its rim, moved to the next spot on the hot surface, and poured.

"Are we going to church?"

I glanced up to find a serious expression on his face. "Really? You want to go to church?"

"Yes. Is that a surprise?"

"It's so hard for you to get out." Glancing down, I gasped. I had poured the entire contents of the bowl into the skillet. "You've only been home two days."

Jamie sat at the table. "I'll go if Dad wants to."

"Me, too." Nicolas set a stack of four plates on the table. "If I'm not grounded from it."

Bubbles formed all over the rectangular pan of batter. I grabbed the spatula and sliced the surface into eight equal pieces. Flipping the sections, I thought about going to church as a whole family. Was Craig really up to it? Or was he exhibiting the first real signs of cabin fever? He'd been virtually held hostage inside his hospital room or home for a total of three weeks, even if he'd been unconscious for some of it.

I transferred the pancakes onto the platter and carried it to the table.

"Squares, Mom?" Jamie screwed up his eyebrows as he speared one and dropped it on his plate.

"Circles are too normal. We're not a normal family anymore," Nicolas said.

"Nicolas!" I shot him a look that said "be quiet, or you'll have square pancakes coming out your nose."

"I'm going by *Nick* now." He slathered his pancakes in butter.

I swallowed. He had to grow up sometime, but why couldn't it have been when his dad was a full participant in the family? "Okay, let's go to church. We can make it to the second service without rushing."

When we finished eating, I ran upstairs and grabbed a pair of Craig's slacks, a dress shirt, and a patterned tie. I sent them back down with Jamie. "Cut along the seams until they fit over the casts," I yelled over the banister.

It seemed odd that, though we'd been married for so long, Craig seemed wary about my aiding him with his personal matters. The nurses had seen more of his body than I had since the accident.

Not that I wanted to.

Well, I did . . . but a strange electricity zapped through me when I touched him. His kisses, always when the boys were occupied elsewhere in the house, hinted at a deep passion. What would happen to that new romance if he allowed me to become, in essence, his home health aide?

I showered, dressed, and did my hair. We all helped Craig get into the passenger side of the car. Buckling, I glanced around. Rare was the time when Craig and I went somewhere that he didn't drive. Nicolas smiled at me when I looked his way. Since his affection had become even more rare, I treasured it to a greater extent.

Once in the lobby of the church, I stared at the spot between the two ficus trees where I first took the call about Craig's accident. Though our church was large and diverse, not too many people used wheelchairs—which made us stick out like a tall blade of grass in a newly mown lawn. Had it really been only a few weeks? My life had changed so completely, it didn't seem possible.

His

DENISE WHEELED ME UP to a man at church. As soon as I saw his face, a name popped into my head. My first time to recognize someone amid a crowd. I stuck out my hand. "Pastor Miles. Good to see you."

"Well, Craig." He clamped his paw over my hand and squeezed a little of Christ's love right through my pores. "It is so good to have you here again."

"Oh, I don't have a problem with hearing, sir. It's my memory that has issues."

"Pardon me?"

It took a moment for my play on words to translate to him, but once it did, a car driving by outside could have heard his guffaw.

"You can *hear* . . . and you're *here*!" Once his laughter wound down, he said, "I've got to kick off the service now. Would you mind coming up front?" He placed a hand on my shoulder. "Many people have been praying, and they want to hear how you're doing right from the horse's mouth."

I had no time to answer before the wheelchair moved toward the ramp leading up to the stage. If Denise were that anxious to let everyone in on the grand update that I was home and still clueless, I would be more than happy to let her do the talking. As we neared the front, the crowd's stares prickled my skin. Flushing, I took comfort knowing Denise was with me. By the time the wheelchair stopped, I was center stage, facing the congregation. Music swelled and died.

The auditorium was huge. Seats fanned out in six sections, and a balcony held even more people above. My gaze settled on a little girl in a middle section. She sat on a man's lap, one arm thrown back around his neck. He had to scrunch his shoulders down just so she could reach. With pigtails sprouting from the sides of her head and a round full face, she resembled a bunny rabbit. I smiled at her, and she gave a wave with her free hand. I blocked out the thought of every eye in the whole place being on me, and focused on her.

"Welcome." Pastor Miles beamed. "We're so glad you chose to meet with us this morning. I've got a special treat for you all today. Craig Littleton is going to give us an update of his recovery. If you are unaware, three weeks ago today, Craig was injured while stopped on the side of the highway."

Did he say I was going to give the update? I turned to look at Denise, but saw a friendly, mustached face glancing down at me. *Mustache?* Who was this man? Where was my wife? Frantically, I scanned the faces along the path we traveled to the stage. Denise stood exactly where we first met the pastor at the far edge of the room, a look of calm expectancy upon her face. This man must have pushed me as we followed Pastor Miles.

"In fact," said the pastor, "we feared for his life."

With everyone watching me, I couldn't glare at Denise. How could she have let me be brought up like a circus freak in front of all these people? She knew I couldn't speak clearly. My lips couldn't form words the way I wanted to without straining my injured cheeks. And she knew I had no idea who anyone in the room was, save her, Nicolas, Jamie, and the traitorous pastor who was about to hand me a microphone.

"But first . . ." Pastor Miles held up a hand. "I'd like for Craig to see how much we've missed him. Won't you stand if you have prayed for this family, cleaned their house, watched out for his boys or Denise in any way?"

Within a few moments, nearly all of the audience rose. Despite my panic, my fear of speaking to them in slurred words with a deformed face, I knew they loved me. They really cared about how I was doing. Tears welled up, and I swiped at my eyes with the back of my hand.

At the pastor's signal, they settled back down in their seats. When the room calmed, Pastor Miles knelt on one knee and held the microphone a short distance from my misshapen face.

"Thank you. I don't know what to say." Taking the microphone, I slowed my speech and put more of my breath into each syllable. If I were unintelligible, hopefully the pastor could translate for me. "Of course, I don't know a lot of things anymore."

A few titters bounced around the crowd.

"I'm weak and I'm tired and I don't really know who I am." I cleared my throat. "Which is just the way we should be when we come to Jesus."

"Amen!" An older Hispanic woman in the very first pew stood and shouted her praise.

"If you want to continue to pray for us, we ask that you pray for our family to stay strong, for our hearts to stay soft, and my mind to be renewed. Thank you again."

Pastor Miles stood and led the church in just such a prayer. As the worship team began the opening song, the mustached man wheeled me back down the ramp to Denise.

Her eyes sparkled. "Craig, I'm so proud of you."

After that, I didn't feel as compelled to tell her how scared I'd been to see her by the wall instead of by my side.

Hers

WOW, HOW THE SPEAKER system amplified the gravelly tone of Craig's voice. Frankly, I was surprised Craig didn't protest when the pastor suggested he give an update on his condition. Craig had never liked being the center of that kind of attention. My husband's new personality kept surprising me. His quick wit seemed more natural now, with so many other aspects of his personality stripped away.

My counselor had warned me about hiding my true feelings from Craig, so when he reached me after his spontaneous speech, I let him know how proud I was of him. Despite what happened in our past, I *was* proud to be his wife.

During the service, Nicolas turned his head Heather McCallister's way more than he faced forward. I still hadn't talked to Craig about Nicolas's new rebellion, his labeling of Heather as his "girlfriend," or his grounding. Yesterday, Craig urged the boys to get outside the house and do something fun instead of hang around with him all day. To Nicolas's credit, he mumbled something about wanting to stay at home and didn't mention a word about the grounding. Instead, they hooked up an old game system to the flat screen and taught Craig how to play a racing game. Hour after hour, father and sons duked it out, striving to win first place, each round punctuated by yells, groans of defeat, and taunts of victory.

Without verbalizing it, and despite how Craig had hurt us in the past, I believe we all wanted to protect him from the hard parts of our life.

At least for as long as we could.

Chapter Nineteen

Hers

"I'M GOING INTO TOWN for a few hours. Anything you want me to pick up?" I wrapped a lavender scarf around my neck and pinned the ends together with an amethyst brooch.

Craig scratched his chin. "You know what sounds really good? A bag of sunflower seeds. Oh, and a Twinkie."

"The yellow, cream-filled thing that can survive a nuclear holocaust?"

"That's the one."

Where had my health food–crazed husband gone? "Okay, I'll pick you up a box. If you think of anything else, give me a call on my cell. I'll be back in time to make lunch and to get you to your rehabilitation appointment. And the boys will be here the whole time I'm gone. Right, Nicolas?"

He nodded from the easy chair. Each of the three males held their game controllers ready, apparently just waiting for me to stop talking to continue their play.

"I won't keep you any longer." My heels clicked as I walked through the kitchen.

My hands shook as I put the key in the ignition, the turmoil in my stomach reminiscent of the day I'd left Craig at home and driven to church. I never thought I'd ever have to do what I was about to do. This would be a Wednesday I'd remember for the rest of my life.

Twenty minutes later, I pulled into the parking lot of the medical plaza. My gynecologist's office faced the back of the building on the second floor. Drawing a deep breath, I opened my door. "Lord, please let there be nothing wrong with me." I scooted between two cars and made my way across the parking lot. "If I do have something, I trust You to use it to Your glory. Maybe it will help one person stay faithful to his spouse."

Or maybe not. I could warn and testify and preach it all I wanted, but a person would do whatever he wanted. The curse of free will.

Don't think like that, Denise.

I also had the free will to forgive Craig or not. What if I *was* HIV-positive? Or what if I had some kind of STD? Would I be able to stay with him?

Where would the path ahead of me lead? Before today, I'd walled off any ponderings concerning the future consequences of Craig's infidelity. So far, my main focus had been getting Craig home and helping him remember his life. As I cracked the mental door open and glimpsed the future, I found the worries, the insecurities, the nightmares I had shoved to the dark sides of my mind.

The receptionist slid her glass window open and smiled at me.

I tried to smile back. "Denise Littleton to see Dr. Brewster."

"Have a seat. It'll just be a minute."

I'd only flipped a few pages of a fitness magazine before the nurse called my name and ushered me into an examination room.

"It says you're here for a full STD panel?"

Glancing around the room, I nodded. "My husband . . . he might have exposed me to . . . I'm not sure what."

"Did he use protection?"

"I don't know."

"Are you comfortable asking him?"

"He wouldn't know." By the look on her face, I knew I needed to explain. "He's suffering from amnesia."

The nurse lifted an eyebrow. "How convenient."

"I've agreed with that at times." Did I want her to think as badly of Craig as I had at my lowest moments? "We're working through our issues, though. He's like a different man without his memory."

"Women might start hitting their husbands over the head if they hear it's an improvement." She winked at me with compassion in her eyes. "The doctor will be in shortly."

I was left with nothing but my thoughts and diagrams of the female anatomy.

A rap at the door preceded Dr. Brewster's entrance. "Denise, how are you?" He'd been my doctor through both boys, delivering them himself.

"Hanging in there. I'll be better after I get these results."

"Yes, I'm sure you will. I'll have Lila come back in for the actual procedures, but I wanted to talk with you first." Squatting, he pulled a wheeled stool underneath himself in a fluid, practiced motion. "Your health is one aspect, but your emotions, your thoughts, and your spirit are also affected by unfaithfulness. How are you dealing with those areas?"

I twirled my wedding ring, thinking of when Craig placed it on my finger and promised to *forsake all others.* "I talk to my friend. My pastor's offered a referral to a good counselor once Craig's more able to participate. And I pray when I don't know what else to do."

"So you have a support system in place?"

"I think there are a lot of people willing to help me."

"Then I'll call Lila back in and we'll get this over with."

His

DENISE CAME BACK from town with smudged makeup and no Twinkies. I didn't ask where she'd been. All through lunch, the boys kept up their chatter. Denise ate sparingly and silently. I watched her.

As she cleared the dishes, I watched her.

As she helped me down the steps to the Denali, I watched her.

She never met my gaze. Somehow, I knew I had failed her anew. But how? I hadn't even left the house while she'd been gone.

As she backed out of the driveway, her left arm followed the rotation of the steering wheel and stopped near its zenith. In the crook of her elbow, a Band-Aid secured a wad of cotton. She'd had her blood drawn. It took me a moment to pencil in the lines between the dots. Blood draws happened at doctor's offices. Denise had not told me where she was going. Silent blame cooled our usually animated conversation.

I clenched my teeth and gazed down at my hands. My wedding band had been in my personal belongings that the hospital returned to me upon my release. I put it back on my ring finger the first night I'd been home, waking on the hide-a-bed and feeling alone in the world. Its cool, heavy feel connected me to my wife, even if we lay in separate beds on different floors of the house.

I risked more than my marriage by having an affair—I gambled with Denise's life.

"I'm sorry." At her quizzical look, I tapped on the inside of my arm. "For putting you through the testing."

She acknowledged me with a nod and turned back to the road. "I figured we were safe from the worst since they did all your blood work at the hospital, but my doctor said it can take six months to show up on a blood test."

"When will you find out about everything else?"

"In two weeks."

She didn't speak again until we arrived at the hospital. She parked in a wider spot near the front of the building. "I'll be okay, whatever the results are."

What could I say? Her declaration seemed overly simplistic, ignoring the reality of most STDs. Did I want to provide her a reality check and invite more blame? If a test result came back positive, I wouldn't ignore my responsibility in the matter, but I wasn't looking for extra trouble right now. Better to let her deal with things her own way. Maybe this attitude was typical for her. How was I to know?

Denise opened my door, wheelchair waiting behind her. I looped my arms around her neck, slid out of the seat, and she swung me into the chair. Her hair smelled like coconut. I resisted the urge to nuzzle her and released my arms.

Signing in at the desk, I reminded myself to be grateful for the chance to have rehab instead of decomposing in a coffin. Horrid thought. But I didn't relish grunting and moaning in front of Denise as I suffered through my first official session of therapy. I wheeled over to the waiting area, straining my muscles with each shove on the tires.

Denise sank down in a turquoise padded chair.

"Would you mind if I did this by myself?"

"You'd rather I not come back with you?"

A loaded question. "I'd feel like a little boy with his mommy along for support."

"I understand." She stood and clutched her purse to her side. "There are some things better done alone." A subtle threat resonated in her voice.

"You don't have to leave. If you want, just wait here."

"No, I have somewhere to go."

"Please, Denise." I reached for her hand, but she stayed beyond my reach. "I'm sorry. I want to be with you all the time, but I also need to learn how to function on my own. How am I ever going to return to the dental office if I can't see a therapist by myself?"

"You're right. I'll be back in an hour." She left without touching me.

Hers

MY TOES SMASHED through the front of my high-heeled sandals as I strode out of the therapy wing. Slowing down, I slid my feet back in the shoes, relieving the pressure. *He wants me to leave. I can gladly oblige.* I passed a framed picture and glimpsed my pouting reflection. Didn't I have enough reason to pout? I'd just been probed and poked to see if I carried the marks of another woman, yet I stood by my husband. But did he even want me to stand by him? No!

I stomped my way to the elevator. When the doors slid shut, I ran my fingers through my hair and dug my nails into my scalp.

Shake it off. Samantha doesn't need to see you like this.

In a month or two, when Craig reaped the benefits of his rehab, I would be grateful he had done it on his own.

Heading toward Samantha's room, I smoothed my hair. A sudden thought stopped me. What if Samantha wasn't there? She might have been released already, and I didn't want to barge in on some other cancer patient. Yes, she might be gone. Or . . . transplants carried risks. Chemo was toxic. Maybe she didn't make it through the surgery. Maybe she did and couldn't recover her strength after the stress it placed on her body.

I backtracked a few steps. "Excuse me."

The nurse on duty behind the desk glanced up.

"Is Samantha Rodain still just across the hall?"

"No, I'm sorry." She studied some paperwork.

What did she mean? And how could I word a delicate question like—

"She's in the playroom at the end of the hall with the children."

"Oh." I turned and started the way she had pointed. "Thank you."

The door to the playroom rested ajar. I peeked in. A masked Samantha sat on a huge purple cushion on the floor reading a book with two bald children pulled up to her side. The little one nearest the door held her arm straight up and rubbed Samantha's fuzzy head. I hung back and listened to the story about some bunnies who found a bungalow and made it their home.

"What's your home look like?" a childish voice asked.

"A little like this bungalow. Cozy and small. This time of year, my dad's climbing roses practically cover the front of the house."

"Can you climb up the roses to get to your room?"

"We only have one level, so I don't have to climb."

A different voice piped up. "I'm going to miss you. I want to go home, too."

"I'll miss you, too. But soon you're going to be all done with your medicine and you'll get to go back to your house. Keep being brave."

"I'm brave, too!" the first voice said.

"Yes, you are. Now why don't you get a puzzle and take it to the play table. I have a visitor."

The children craned their necks and discovered me at the door. Little girls sporting pixyish, feminine faces graced with studded earrings. About the same size and similarly featured, the girls appeared to be twins. Were the odds greater of having cancer if a twin did?

They jumped off the sides of Samantha's pillow and came to me, pulling my hands and begging me to help them pick out a puzzle. After settling on a Care Bear jigsaw, they dumped the pieces on the table and got to work.

"Denise." Samantha drew me back over to the cushion and pulled a chair beside her for me to sit on. "I'm so glad you came."

I pulled another cushion toward us and surprised myself by settling down on it instead of using the chair. Kicking off my shoes, I leaned back onto my elbows. "You look fantastic."

Samantha's face glowed even more at my declaration. "So does my white blood cell count."

"Really?"

She nodded and, even though I couldn't see her mouth, I knew she was smiling. "I'm going home tomorrow."

I tried to recall our last conversation. "They found a home for you in foster care?"

"In a roundabout way." She leaned forward. "Mrs. Van Horn, the neighbor I told you about? She took a fast track of foster care classes to be certified. I get to go to her house, stay insured, and she gets paid to take me in." Samantha played a drum solo on the floor. "It couldn't have worked out better."

"I'm so glad you have a place. I would have offered you our home, but you hardly know me."

"You are such a total sweetheart. Your house is probably awesome and all, but this way I'm right next door to my own home. The weeds must be taking over the flower beds, and I bet the roses need trimmed back. Dad usually does that in the spring, but this year, with me in the hospital . . ."

"The yard wasn't his top priority. You were."

"Yeah." She stared at her lap.

"Is your house being sold? My boys and I can come over and fix it up, however you like, if it's going on the market."

"You have boys?"

"I've never mentioned them, huh?"

She shook her head. "How old are they?"

"Twelve and fifteen—I mean sixteen. Nicolas's birthday was just last week. Should I ask them to help with your dad's house?"

"I own the house. Dad left it to me."

Remembering Craig's insistence that we help Samantha financially, I said, "If it's not too rude to ask, how are you planning to pay the mortgage?"

"I wondered the same thing. Dad always had to scrape at the beginning of the month to make the payments, but the lawyer told me I own the deed free and clear. Or my trust does. I can't touch the money until I'm eighteen."

"So it's all worked out?"

"You shouldn't sound so shocked, Denise. You said you would pray for me. God's in the business of taking care of widows and orphans, right?"

How close I had come to being widowed. Would that have been

easier than facing Craig's past? A wave of hysteria swept over me, passing so quickly I was able to act normally.

"Oh." Samantha's fingers found the charm hanging from her silver necklace and ran it back and forth on a short track before her neck. "You said you had something to tell me?"

Clunk. My stomach hit the floor. I'd said that on the spur of the moment, knowing I would lose my nerve unless I committed myself. But it had been a vague comment, a mere hint of some news. She didn't expect me to confess to hiding who I was. I could tell her anything. "I'd . . . I'd like you to come visit. Maybe Mrs. Van Horn would like a break every now and then."

"Like I'm going to be incredibly hard to take care of." She wiggled her penciled-in eyebrows.

"You *are* a teenage girl, you know." I dangled the largest carrot I knew of in front of her. "We could play Monopoly for hours."

Her eyes lit up. "One time, Dad and I played a game that lasted five days."

"Who won?"

Samantha placed her hand lightly on her chest. "I'm offended that you would even ask."

A smile took over my lips. "I'd come and meet Mrs. Van Horn first, have her over to check out our house." I rummaged in my purse and scribbled my phone number on the back of a receipt. "Call me. We'll set something up."

"Thanks for coming by. I was hoping to see you." She leaned forward and wrapped her bony arms around me.

Hugging her firmly, I whispered in her ear, "You call me if I can help you in any way, okay?"

"Okay." She loosened her grip.

Checking my watch, I stood. "My husband's at his first rehab appointment. I'd better get going to be there when he finishes up."

"Tell him I can't wait to meet him." Samantha's eyes flashed another smile. "And say 'hi' to your boys, too."

"I will."

Before I left the room, she was back over with the little girls, helping them frame in the edges of the puzzle.

Chapter Twenty

His

STOMACH GROWLING, I woke at three in the morning. The only food on the table beside me was half of a peeled banana. My tender cheeks made eating solid food so painful, I figured I had eaten more bananas than a silverback gorilla. I gagged as I imagined eating the remainder of the fruit, its blandness squishing between my teeth.

My bladder complained anyway, so I pulled the wheelchair to the side of the hide-a-bed and hefted myself into the sling-backed seat. After using the bathroom, I wheeled into the kitchen and opened the refrigerator. Propping the door open with my footrest, I scanned the contents. My taste buds begged for salt. I pulled a container of bologna out of the middle drawer. Chewing on a rolled-up slice, I glanced over my other options. I stuffed the bologna package back into place and grabbed a cup of boysenberry yogurt. Wheeling back, I let the door close on its own. On my second try, I found the silverware drawer. Spoon and yogurt in my lap, I pushed myself into the room Denise had pointed out as my office.

A streetlight shone through the louvered shades, illuminating a path to the massive desk in the middle of the room. I pulled the office chair back and brought my wheelchair close enough to set my snack on the desktop.

The contents of the top drawer painted me as a more organized person than I imagined myself to be. Only a day planner occupied the next drawer. Opening the cover, I flipped to the day of the accident. Two entries: *Deacons' meeting* and *Hike the gorge.*

Was that the meeting when the rest of the deacons and the pastor were planning to confront me and remove me from office? How ironic that I would miss that meeting to go hiking and get in the accident I had begun to think of as a blessing. My standing in the church, my relationship with my wife, my reputation with my children . . . all of them had been slipping away. Confused as I currently was, I knew I would have to fight to regain each and every valuable bond.

Strange. No scribbled entries in the next few weeks. Actually, I hadn't written any notes for the rest of the year. "Hike the gorge," I whispered. "Was that the last thing I planned to do in my life?"

Oh, Lord God, no.

My life had been falling apart. Major loss seemed inevitable. I must have given in to the despair. Let depression take control of my choices.

And decided to end it all.

The accident *had* been a true godsend. A protection for myself and my family. The grief Denise would have felt, hearing about my death . . . I couldn't imagine it. The stares of folks wondering what had been so bad in my life that I had been driven to terminate it. A public unveiling of my affair. All my mistakes laid out posthumously for strangers to gawk at.

I dropped my head onto the cool surface of the desk. *Thank You, thank You, Father, for stopping me. What would I have caused without*

Your intervention? Who else would I have hurt? How deeply? If I never remember, if my messed-up mind never returns, I'm fine with that. Continue to protect me from myself.

Eventually, I grew tired of contemplating my failed, self-inflicted death. I peeled back the yogurt top and licked the foil. As boysenberry flavor diffused across my tongue, a memory slammed into my mind.

"You're kidding me. Boysenberry isn't a real berry?"

The server shrugs. "It is now, but it didn't exist before Mr. Knott mixed together the best of raspberries, blackberries, and loganberries."

"However he came up with it, this concoction is delicious." I pour a generous amount of boysenberry syrup over the stack of pancakes waiting before me. I feel a tug on my sleeve, but I don't turn to see who instigates it.

"Can we ride more roller coasters after lunch?"

Nodding . . .

The memory went black.

A pinprick of my past broken through the darkness! Knott's Berry Farm. We had gone there on vacation. Plunking the cup of yogurt down, I stared at the label. A processed dairy food had birthed my first recollection of my past life. Amazing.

Pictures. Our family surely took pictures on vacations. All I'd seen were the family pictures on the walls between the front door and the living room and the huge portrait, visible from the bottom of the stairs, of us all. Where did Denise keep the photo albums? Books filled the shelves in my office, but none of the spines looked wide enough to be an album. I rolled into the living room and searched the built-in bookcases there. No luck.

We probably had a hope chest at the end of our bed, or Denise stored all the pictures in a box in the attic. I would have to wait until morning to ask her to find pictures of that vacation. The only place left to look downstairs was the coat closet. The door swung open with a creak. On the highest shelf, a mishmash of floral and solid print albums taunted me.

Wait. Let Denise get them down for you in the morning. But they were there, within my arm's normal reach if I hadn't been in a wheelchair. My therapist had made me practice standing, but she rigged the exercise to keep most of the weight off my feet. Still, my legs felt like broken necks of glass bottles fitted back together with shards jutting out. *You only need to wait a few more hours.*

I gripped the armrests of the wheelchair and set my feet on the floor. If I could wedge my hip against one side of the doorframe and press with a hand on the other side, I might be able to reach up with my free hand and grab a book.

I used too much force and my shoulder crashed into the frame. I staggered. Empty hangers rained down around me as my face snapped forward into coats. Blindly tossing an arm overhead, I felt for the spine of an album and slid out the first one I touched. I fell back into the chair with my hard-earned treasure, huffing, ribs screaming. The rest of the house slept through my commotion.

Without opening the book, I took it back to the hide-a-bed and crawled under the covers. Had I struck gold and grabbed the one I wanted? Drawing a deep breath, I turned to the first page.

A shot of me on hands and knees. Atop my back, Nicolas dressed as a cowboy, complete with spurs. The narrowness of his face and the intelligent look in his eye made me sure it was Nicolas and not Jamie. Not to say Jamie wasn't intelligent, but his eyes always hinted at mischievous fun. Nicolas looked serious even when he was having a good time.

In the picture below it, I blew on a toddler's belly, but his face was turned away from the camera. On the next page of the album, he had squirmed away from me and displayed a gleeful smile.

Most of the photographs included me with the boys. Every now and again, a picture of a much younger Denise appeared. Near the end of the album, she posed next to a massive waterfall, the beauty in the background offset by her crossed eyes and fingers pulling her mouth wider than a human orifice should stretch. Snickering, I pictured the staid, graceful woman I was coming to know reenacting the moment. Impossible.

Only after I turned the last page did I realize the absence of any amusement park pictures. Also, despite my ability to view the snapshots with fondness, I felt no more connected to those times or places than before I saw myself in them. Randomly, I wedged my index finger between two glossy pages and pried the book open.

My likeness stared back. Was that really me? A rounder face, though I knew I'd lost weight from being hospitalized. Thicker hair, which passing years could explain. And my eyes seemed sadder. Why? When I'd almost lost my life under mysterious circumstances and couldn't recall a moment from my past except an insignificant conversation with a waiter, why would my eyes be more cheerful now?

Hers

I PUT A COFFEE CAKE into the oven and watched Craig sleep as the aroma filled the house. He used to wake up before me, pull on some running shorts, get in a couple of miles, and be showering when I staggered out of bed. Since the accident, he'd been staying up late talking with me or the boys and sleeping in to make up for it the next morning. Once he recovered, would he go back to his solitary fitness routine, or would he place value on relationships as he had lately, investing his time and heart into getting to know us again?

Years of counseling, session after session of asking how I could get Craig to really see me . . . and all he needed was amnesia. Even Nicolas seemed to be thawing. The only complaints he voiced about his restriction centered on his severely limited contact with Heather.

Craig's thigh, sprinkled with curly long hair—more of them gray then I remembered—peeked out of the covers. The sheet tangled around one cast. I tugged it loose and covered him back up. As I drew away, my knuckles rapped against something under the sheets. Curious, I reached under the sheet and pulled out an old album. Kicking back in a recliner, I flipped through the pictures for a time, revisiting those early years.

Craig woke with a stretch. "Morning." The damage to his vocal cords combined with the relatively early hour made the word come out like a growl.

"Good morning, hon."

Craig sat up in bed, raised a bent arm, and pushed against the elbow with the opposite hand. "Where are the pictures from Knott's Berry Farm?"

"You dreamed about a farm?"

He covered a yawn with the side of his arm. "I didn't dream." Dropping his hands to the bed, he gazed at me with powerful eyes. "I finally remembered."

"Remembered what?"

"Our vacation to California, and one of the boys asking me to ride the roller coaster again."

"On a farm?" My eyes grew wide as I kept my laughter in.

Craig drew back. "Are you making fun of me?"

"No." I giggled. "I'm just trying to figure out what happened in your dream."

A muscle bulged along Craig's jawline. "I'm telling you that a memory came back. We went to Knott's Berry Farm. Which, by the way, is an amusement park, not a farm."

"Craig, we've never been to an amusement park in California before. Every time I brought up a family trip to Disneyland, you said you couldn't take the time off work or that we should buy more stock or . . ." I threw my hands up. "You always had an excuse not to go."

He shook his head, keeping his gaze steady. "It happened. It was real."

"Okay." I leaned forward. "Tell me the whole thing. Maybe it's a combination of our trip to the smaller park up in Washington and something else."

"Promise to take me seriously?"

"Yes." Lacing my fingers, I sat back.

"I talked to a waiter. He told me about how boysenberries are a hybrid and then one of the kids asked to go on more rides."

I waited for more.

"So? What do you think? Did I make up the one thing I'm remembering about our past?"

"Do you remember what rides we went on?"

"I only saw that piece of it, being in the restaurant."

"Why do you think the restaurant was at Knott's Berry Farm?"

He looked at me like I was an idiot. "The waiter and I discussed the syrup and how Mr. Knott created the boysenberry."

I bit my lip.

"What?" Irritation edged his voice.

"Craig, they have boysenberry syrup at every pancake house in the country."

He groaned. "Why? Why would I have a conversation about syrup with a waiter about Mr. Knott if it wasn't at *his* restaurant?"

I held up my index finger. "Give me a sec." I went to the kitchen, opened the refrigerator, scanned the door bins, and snagged a bottle. Walking back to the living room, I skimmed the label. "Here." I held the bottle out toward Craig. "Read this."

His eyebrows drew closer as he stared at the bottle. "So, this little explanation of the boysenberry is on every Knott's Berry label?"

I shrugged. "I can't speak for the rest of them, but it's on that one for sure."

"You think I made it all up?"

"We had pancakes on Sunday. Maybe you read the label, saw the pictures last night, and the two images merged into a lifelike dream."

Craig huffed and laid back. "One problem with your explanation, Inspector Gadget. I had the memory before I found the photo album."

Chapter Twenty-One

Hers

CRAIG DIDN'T REALLY SPEAK with me again until after we finished lunch, and what did he start with?

"Take me to the office. Let's see if that jogs a real memory out of this clogged brain."

"Honey." I tucked a strand of hair behind each ear. "I didn't say a thing about your brain. All I'm doing is keeping you from placing undue faith in a flawed memory."

"Terrific. Thank you so much for thinking of me." He wheeled toward the front door. "I'm sure we'll find some solid, true memories at the office."

By the time we were loaded in the car and I gave the boys instructions on what to do—or really what *not* do—while we were gone, compassion took over the better part of my rancor. "A solid memory, you said?" I came to a gentle stop at the sign before leaving our road.

"Yep. Solid as a drill bit." Apparently, Craig found a better place as well.

"Solid as a filling."

"Or a plaster mold of teeth."

"Solid as an X-ray."

Craig laughed. "That makes no sense whatsoever."

"I ran out of dentistry-related items that were hard."

"You know less than I do."

I swatted his thigh and kept driving, grateful he could distract me from thinking about our arrival at the office. Who knew about the affair? Did Kirk? Obviously Jennie had a clue. She had been spiteful to me to get revenge for Craig's "breaking up with" Naomi when she visited him in the hospital. Oh, there were way too many players involved. "If Kirk says anything to you, anything that seems connected to your secrets, you'll tell me, right?" I glanced at Craig, then returned my attention to the road.

"Sure." Craig nodded solemnly. "Who's Kirk?"

I giggled. "He's your partner. Be extremely gracious to him. He's saving our rear ends from bankruptcy by running the practice until you—" I glanced at him again.

"Getting worried I won't make it back there, aren't you?" Craig let out a low, loose whistle. "Makes two of us."

"It will all come back to you in a rush of . . . minty mouthwash."

He tapped his fingers on the dash. "A rush of water from the little squirter they rinse your mouth out with."

"Is that the technical term?"

"Pretty sure."

We pulled into the spot reserved for Craig. I took the key from the ignition. "Ready?"

"If you are, milady."

"Yes, gallant sir. Let me bring your chariot around to thee."

Inside, the wonderful temp—what was his name?—manned the desk again. I hadn't talked with Kirk lately. Did he go ahead with my advice and hire the guy?

"Mrs. Littleton. Nice to see you again."

"Oh, thank you . . ." His name still darted outside my consciousness.

"Charles."

"Yes, of course, Charles. This is Dr. Littleton." I rolled Craig forward and cringed. It felt as if I were pushing a carriage closer to show off my new baby. "Craig, Charles has taken over for Naomi at the desk."

Charles showed no outward sign that he knew more about Naomi than he should. "Wonderful to meet you, sir. I've really enjoyed working here."

"Keep up the good work." Craig nodded with an air of authority. "Denise, can you show me to my office, please?"

A film of dust covered Craig's desk, and the plant in the corner had died. Other than those dismal signs, it looked no different than the last time I'd been in his office.

"Charles really seemed eager to impress me, didn't he?" Craig wheeled straight toward the plant and stuck his finger into the soil. "This needs triage."

"You're his boss. Of course he wants to make a good impression." I filled a paper cup with water and handed it to Craig. "Excuse me for a minute." I went across the hall and tapped on Kirk's door.

"Enter."

Poking my head in, I gave him my most brilliant smile. If he knew about Naomi, I didn't want him feeling sorry for Craig once again ending up with the old, haggy wife. "Hey, stranger. Why aren't you behind Craig's desk like last time?"

Was I flirting? Ew.

"Well . . ." Kirk turned his head to one side and gave me a peculiar look. "It seemed weird, so I moved all the necessary things in here. Are you feeling all right?"

"I'm fine." I dropped the syrupy tone. He'd known me for years. I'd never been the flirty type. "Did the night crew stop cleaning? The desk is filthy."

"Craig never wanted them touching his documents or moving

his files around. Guess I forgot to tell them to add his room back to the schedule."

I crossed my arms and rubbed my hands along them. "Why do you think he didn't want the cleaning crew in his office?"

"I just told you." Kirk motioned for me to come farther into his office. "Denise, what's going on with you? Do you need a day away? Go off somewhere and relax. Relieve some stress."

"Do you think he had something to hide, Kirk? Is that why no one was ever allowed to be near his desk?"

He folded his hands together and narrowed his yes. "Have you seen anyone to help with the psychological aspect of Craig almost dying?"

"Stop!" I snapped my fingers. "Quit asking me more questions and answer the ones I'm asking you."

"Craig has trust issues, Denise. You know that. The only person he'd let clean up after him was Naomi. Was he hiding something?" Kirk spread his hands. "She'd be the person to ask."

I stood on a modern area rug. Tracing the outline of a cubist design with my toe, I weighed how far I should push. "I'm sorry. You're right. I'm under a ton of stress. Craig's in his office right now, trying to look for clues to his life and career."

"He's here?" Standing, Kirk rubbed his hands together. "I've got to give him a hard time about taking such an extended vacation to stay home with his pretty wife."

His

I CRUMPLED the philodendron leaf in my hand and dropped the remains into the trash can. Not only had I worked in this building before, I worked in this very room. *Dr. Craig Littleton.* Pulling open a drawer of the desk, I came face-to-face with the biggest mess I'd ever seen. Candy bar wrappers, coffee-stained papers, receipts, scraps, old lunch bags . . . all stuffed into one drawer. The difference between the sanitary desk of my home and the EPA super-site pollution of my work desk astounded me.

Did I compartmentalize that well? Keep Denise at home in nice, tidy surroundings with a good reputation in the community and church? Mess up my office and mess around with Naomi at work? Dr. "Jekyll" Littleton and Mr. "Hide"?

"Craig!" A deep voice boomed behind me. "Got new wheels, huh?"

What is it with people? They know I've lost my memory, but they still expect me to remember them. Before I could maneuver to face the mystery person, he jumped in front of me. "Hello." I stuck out my hand. "Kirk, right?"

He pumped it quickly, let go, and pounded his fist into my knuckles. "Good to see you, man. Let me see your smile."

I raised my eyebrows. "Are you going to paint my portrait?"

"Quiet, Moaning Lisa. Show me your pearly whites."

Curling back my lips, I smiled.

"Lucky you didn't lose any of your teeth in the accident."

"Is that what we do? Look in each other's mouths?"

"All day long." The man clapped his hands, turning serious. "It's been crazy here without you. How long 'til you'll be back to work?"

"I really appreciate you taking up the slack."

He leaned against the edge of my desk, looking down at me. "I take it that means you still don't know when you're returning?"

I craned my neck to keep staring up at him. "I'm not sure how I'd be able to work from this wheelchair, so that's the first goal. Get out of this contraption and onto my own two feet."

"Ah." Kirk waved a hand off to the side. "There are plenty of handicapped dentists, I'm sure. It's what's in your noggin that counts."

"The sum total of my noggin's contents isn't too impressive." I shoved the messy drawer closed.

"We've had some problems. I don't know exactly what Denise has told you, but Naomi quit, Jennie's been temperamental, Diane's in and out on sick leave, and we're starting to lose clients."

I judged his tone of voice when he spoke about Naomi, but he didn't seem to put more emphasis on her name than on any other. Good. I didn't want to come in as the clueless half of a good-old-boys partnership. Elbow nudging and innuendos. Crass jokes. Slurs against Denise.

Kirk seemed like an upstanding young guy.

I should have been more like him.

Denise came in the door, a file folder in her hand. "Craig, do you want to go over William Rodain's file while we're here? If you see any inconsistencies, or it brings anything to mind, we might have a lead for the police to pursue."

I frowned. "The police?"

Kirk patted my back dramatically. "Yeah, Craig, the police are people we pay to keep us all in line. They wear uniforms and have shiny emblems called badges pinned on their chest."

"No way." I played right along with him, as if I could remember our friendship. "And does it hurt when they pin the badges to their chest?"

"No, dork." Kirk laughed. "They have drugs for that, which they filch from the property they've impounded."

"Wow." I made my eyes grow wide. "You sure know a lot about the police. Have you been to jail?"

Denise waved the file in front of my face. "If you guys have a minute to take a break from your fun little game, I can explain the whole thing to Craig."

"Kirk, you've been outranked. What my wife says, I do."

"Well, that's a first." He pushed off the desk and shook out his pant legs. A triangular mark in the dust showed where he'd rested. "I'm happy to see you in the flesh. Let me know when I should start sending people your way again."

"Keep up the good work," I said again, waving as he left. "Nice guy," I said to Denise. "Now what's this about the police?"

She opened the folder and laid it on my desk. "You were unconscious for so long at the beginning of this ordeal. We really haven't talked about all the specifics of what happened before you came to. I met with a detective a few times about your involvement in the accident. At first, they wanted to know who the man who died was. Once they identified William Rodain and determined that nothing criminal seemed to be going on, they became less interested. The last time I talked to the detective, they were trying to figure out why you two were arguing that day."

"So I'm not in legal trouble?"

"Nope." She looked at me with a sparkle in her eye. "Luckily."

"I won't be serving twenty years in a maximum security joint after the judge doesn't believe I don't remember a single detail about my crime?"

"We should talk more often, Craig. Really talk. There's so much I still haven't discussed with you." Her voice trailed off and her eyes dulled.

"What?"

"In my heart of hearts, I don't think you've done anything illegal. . . ."

"What haven't you told me?"

She shook her head. "Never mind, we can talk about it some other time. Let's get through this file."

"No." I reached for her hand. "Is there something you should tell the police that you haven't? To protect me?"

"I'm not hiding information from them." She ran her fingers through her hair. "But I'm not sure it's their business that you were having an affair or that our money is gone."

"Our money is gone?"

"Almost all of it."

"How much are we talking?"

"Thousands. Tens of thousands."

I raised an eyebrow.

"Almost a hundred thousand, actually . . . that I know about."

"Where did it go?" I searched her face. If she kept holding information back to shelter me, I would never solve the mystery of my life.

"You took it. Our financial guy said you withdrew the bulk of our liquid savings, but no one is sure why. Or knows where you put the money. At least we still have our real estate investments . . . if you didn't sell them off without telling me."

My mind whirled. Why would I need so much money? Where would I have stashed it? Was it in a dingy locker at a bus station like in the movies? Did I gamble it all away? Trouble with the mob? Blackmail?

"Craig, my gut says the money is connected to William Rodain. If we put our brains together on this, maybe we can figure things out before the police come to our door and drop another bomb onto our life."

Chapter Twenty-Two

Hers

A WEEK AFTER OUR VISIT to the office, the Fourth of July passed with no more fireworks in our family. A quiet Sunday night a few days later found us playing Yahtzee. Two fours rolled out of the red plastic cup to join the other one I already had. As I scooted the matching dice together and swooped up the remaining dice, the phone rang. "Jamie, can you get that? I'd like to finish this turn while the luck is good."

He left Craig, Nicolas, and me at the table and grabbed the phone off the counter. "Hello. Littleton residence. Jamie speaking."

I gave him a thumbs-up. My phone manner lessons had paid off. I almost hoped it was my old aunt on the phone so she could hear what a gentleman of the current generation sounded like.

"Hello?"

Jiggling the cup, I readied a new roll.

"Hello?"

The tone of his voice stilled my hand. When he stopped craning his neck, I knew the caller had finally spoken. Maybe it *was* Great-Aunt Elma. Sometimes it took her awhile to get going.

"Yep, she's here." Jamie held the phone out toward me. "Some girl. She sounds upset."

"You guys go on without me." I headed to the office and drew the doors closed behind me. Wondering who was calling, I examined the phone for a moment before I put it to my ear. "Hello?"

"This is Samantha Rodain. I—" Her next words were undecipherable, strangled by audible emotion.

"Oh, I'm so glad you called. Are you all moved in with Mrs. Van Horn?"

"Why didn't you tell me?" Now her words were clipped, as though she mastered the emotion and stuffed it down inside.

"Tell you what?"

"Did you hear what your son said when he answered the phone?"

I replayed Jamie's words and my pride at his manners. I couldn't find anything wrong with it, especially nothing big enough to bring on Samantha's ruckus. "What was wrong with what he said?"

"It's not what he said. It's what you didn't. I thought you were my friend. I thought you really cared about me. I mean, you prayed for me!"

"I do care about you, Samantha. What would make you think that I stopped?"

"Your last name is Littleton."

Teenage girl emotion crescendoed to a much higher pitch than boy outrage. I blinked, and the truth steamrollered over me. I groaned.

"Oh, yeah. Your husband is in the hospital. You just happened to start volunteering in *my* room. And never mentioned that your husband killed my dad!"

I held the phone away from my ear as she grew louder and louder. Drawing a deep breath, I steadied myself. "Craig didn't kill your daddy, honey. If you'd give me just a second to talk, I'll tell you what we know."

"I don't want to talk to you. You lied to me!"

"Samantha . . . you're right. I started out by deceiving you. I was still in shock, trying to wrap my mind around my husband's injuries. I didn't know about you until the police told me you were in the same hospital. I felt responsible for what happened, so I wanted to see you."

Why didn't I tell her before? I hit my forehead. By the ragged breathing on the line, I knew she was listening. "Your dad didn't have any identification with him. They were interviewing me, hoping I could tell them who he was."

"So why didn't you introduce yourself as Denise Littleton? If you had nothing to hide, why didn't you just tell me?"

"I'm sorry. No one knew how Craig and your dad connected that day. They still don't. I hoped to find that out by talking to you. Once I figured out that you didn't know any more about their relationship than I did, I felt awkward about bringing it up."

"Have you lied to me about anything else?"

A chink in her armor, a sign of possible forgiveness. "No, honey, and I won't again. If you remember, when I visited with my friend, I told you I had something to say after surgery. And I thought about telling you last time we talked, but the little girls were there and I wasn't sure how you'd take the news." I waited for her response.

A moment later, Samantha spoke. "Why do you think Dad was on the road that day?"

"Well . . ." I sat in the office chair and spun. "Craig was your father's dentist. We can be sure they knew each other that way."

"Can I talk to your husband?"

That caught me off guard. In the hospital, she and I talked. She never spoke to Craig. If she started having conversations with him, would he be quick to shift his attention from our boys to focus on what she needed? He did it before. A teenage girl who was recovering from cancer and recently lost her only living parent made for quite a sympathetic character. "Um, why do you want to talk to him?"

"He was the last person in this world to be with my dad. I want to know what happened that day."

"Samantha, there's no reason for you to talk to Craig. He can't recall a thing. He thought he relived a memory the other day, but what he described never happened."

She drew in a breath. "I'm sorry, Denise. I thought everything was better with him since you were home."

"I'll make you a deal."

"What?"

"As soon as Craig remembers your dad, you can come over and spend a few hours asking him questions."

"Actually, that's why I was calling. Mrs. Van Horn needs to go visit her sister over the weekend, and I was . . . well . . . now, I'm not so sure."

"Would you like to stay with us? I understand why you might not be comfortable around me, but I'd still love to have you."

"Are you sure I wouldn't be any trouble? You probably have other plans."

"No, no. Should I stop by and meet Mrs. Van Horn?"

"When would be good for you?"

I checked my watch, as if it might remind me of my plans for the next few days. "Tomorrow at ten I have to take Craig to a physical therapy appointment. If you want to give me directions to your house from the hospital, I can come over while he has his appointment."

"Sure." She gave me her information and we hung up.

I sat back and closed my eyes. *Lord, that was hard. I'm sorry for lying to her. Thank You that she's giving me a second chance. Don't let me mess it up. Please help Craig remember soon, so she can have more information about how and why her father died. Please let it be a great, heroic thing that Craig and William were doing.*

I never tried to think of all the good reasons the men could have been together. They could have been teaming up to do a run for charity, or to fix up someone's house, or . . . anything. But Craig hadn't mentioned anything other than a hike in the gorge. And they were fighting.

The phone rang in my hand. I pressed the answer button. "Hello?"

"Mrs. Littleton, sorry to be calling so late."

"Samantha, you just hung up. It's definitely not too late. Did you forget to tell me something?"

"Uh . . . Mrs. Littleton, this is Heather McCallister."

"Oh, Heather, hi. I just got off the phone with someone else and your voice sounded like hers."

"Samantha, you said. She's a teenager?"

"You might meet her this weekend. She'll be staying with us."

"Oh." She didn't sound excited about another teenage girl spending the night at her boyfriend's house. "Is she Nick's cousin or whatever?"

"No, she's not related. Would you like to speak with Nicolas?"

"So he's not grounded anymore, right?"

"Right. Today is his first day of freedom."

"He promised he'd call as soon as he was allowed."

I stood up and walked to the kitchen. "Maybe he got busy and didn't realize he was off restriction."

Nicolas heard me and mouthed, *Is it Heather?*

I nodded. "Here he is."

He took the phone and disappeared, much as I had.

Jamie stared at me. "I hope you don't talk to my girlfriends on the phone that long when they call for me. I'll never get a date."

"Good strategy for me to keep in mind, but I was talking to someone else before Heather called."

Jamie rolled a Yahtzee and the rest of my explanation was no longer needed.

After the boys went up to bed, I lounged in the living room. With the lights low and Craig sprawled on the far end of the couch, I had to look carefully to see his scars.

"During the game, who were you talking to?" His voice was still so foreign, so rough.

I turned so my back lay against the armrest and stretched out my legs. "Samantha Rodain called."

Craig perked up. "Why did she call?" Upon my pointed look, he relaxed. "I'm not getting obsessed with her, Denise. I'm just making conversation. Like a normal husband asking his wife about what's going on in her life."

"She'd like to spend this weekend here. The woman she's staying with is going out of town."

"I'd love to meet her."

"You'll get that chance soon."

He touched my foot with his warm hands, pulled it into his lap, and rubbed his thumb along the arch.

"Mmm." I lay back and slid down so both feet were reachable. "That feels amazing." Closing my eyes, I let the comfort and love soak into my body, up to my soul. I no longer carried the burden of hiding my identity from Samantha. Really, that had gone better than I feared. How nice it would be to have her sweet presence at our house.

My mind switched gears into reverse. Why did I tell Heather about Samantha coming? I wasn't so old that I forgot how confusing and insecure teenage relationships were. I caused her needless jealousy. Nicolas's feelings had been focused on Heather—and only Heather—for quite a while. Meeting a girl who was recovering from leukemia, who was really only spending the weekend because of her relationship with his mother, wouldn't be enough to sway his affections.

Craig's fingers crept up to my calves. He massaged with short, sure circles.

Also, I wasn't hiding the revelations of the missing money or the police involvement from Craig anymore. He had recovered to the point where I saw him as more of an equal, not a weakling who needed protection from the tough facts of our life.

When his circling hands reached my lower thighs, I opened my eyes. His hooded gaze spoke of offering me more than just comfort or relaxation. Bending my legs, I scooted close to him. We stared into each other's eyes, moving together slowly. His lips parted and mine tingled. As we met, his stubble scratched my chin. Eyes drifting shut, I fell into his kiss. My mind swam as I wove my fingers around his neck and snuggled closer, drinking in his taste.

We had kissed since the accident. My brain realized this, but my heart felt as though I had never been kissed before. His hands ran through my hair, traced the outline of my back. As soon as his touch left a spot, it cried out for more attention. He planted small kisses over my face and returned to my mouth. I struggled to keep a foothold in reality. We were on a very public couch in the center of our home. An impressionable young man could enter at any time and have a picture branded into his mind that he would not want to see.

"Oh, Denise." Craig nibbled at my ear lobe. "I do love you. I love everything about you. Your smile and your laugh. The way you walk, and the way you look when you're mad. The way you talk to the boys, and how you take care of me."

His words swept me into the ocean of desire, away from my tenuous grasp on propriety. I didn't know where his hands would go next and I didn't care. I wanted them all over me. "Do you remember?" I whispered in his ear. "Do you remember being with me? Do you remember the night on the beach?"

"No, but you can tell me about it."

"It was the second night of our honeymoon."

"Wait." Craig pulled back and smiled at me. "Was the second night better than the first?"

"Oh, yes." I giggled at his horrified expression. "The first night, the hotel left a complimentary bottle of champagne, but I never drink. After one glass, my moods were swinging more than Tarzan in the jungle. You spilled a bottle of perfume I left on the bathroom counter, and I cried and cried. We never got around to what we had planned and waited so long for."

He wiggled his eyebrows. "But the second night?"

"It was magical." I ran a finger along his eyebrow, drew a heart on his disfigured cheek.

He kissed my fingertip. "I think it will be again."

"You can't make it up the stairs. What are we going to do? There are no doors off this room, if you haven't noticed."

"Who cares about that?"

I froze. "The boys are home."

"Tell them to stay upstairs." He left a trail of kisses along the tender spot of my neck.

"Craig." But his caresses erased the outrage and his plan gained validity. The doctor said familiar situations could bring back Craig's memory, and we had done this for years and years. Could he be recalling those times? "Does it feel right when you kiss me?"

"So right, sweetie." He pulled me closer.

"But you're not remembering?"

"I can discover you. It'll be like our honeymoon all over again."

Something in my spirit checked me. I pushed against his chest, seeking some room, fresh air to cool my head.

He groaned.

His ribs. Too late, I thought of how hard I pushed. "I'm sorry. That hurt you, didn't it? I wasn't thinking."

"I'm fine." He tugged my hand. "Let's get back to where we were."

Blowing my hair out of my face, I resisted. "I don't think I can do this."

"Maybe I *can* make it upstairs. I could sit backwards and use my arms to—"

"No." I swung my legs off of his lap and stood. "There's something not right about it."

"We're married. You're my wife. I'm your husband. It's a blessed union." He used a funny pious tone.

"But, Craig." I wrung my hands. "What about Naomi? What about what you've done with someone else? We've just skipped over the fact that you were unfaithful. I'm not jumping back into bed with you just because my hormones are screaming to. I don't even have the results of my testing back yet."

The passion disappeared from Craig's gaze. "I didn't realize I was forcing you to kiss me."

"Don't be like that. Don't pout." I softened my tone. "You've always had this effect on me. Even when I'm not interested in romance, one touch of your hand and I lose my mind."

"You're punishing me for something I have no knowledge of."

"Come on." I crossed my arms over my chest. "I'm not 'punishing' you. It just doesn't seem right."

"But it is right."

"You say you love me. Can't you show me by listening to me?" I implored him with my eyes. "Until you've remembered being married to me, it'd be like loving a familiar stranger. I don't ever want to be with anyone else. I want to know that you *know* who I am." Without looking back, I fled to my room.

Chapter Twenty-Three

His

WE DIDN'T TALK about the night before. Denise took me to therapy and left me in the waiting room with a chaste peck on the cheek.

"Where are you going?"

"To meet Samantha's guardian. If I pass inspection, she'll be able to come over."

"And if you don't?"

"Never fear. I have an excellent touch with older people. For some reason, they all love me." She wiggled her fingers at me and left.

Thumbing through an outdated copy of *People* gave me a crash course in semi-recent world happenings. How odd it felt to think about the world continuing to revolve while I had lain in a hospital bed. New political alliances formed, old ones crumbled. Natural disasters occurred, babies were born, and celebrities championed new causes. My life was such a small, insignificant note in the rhythm of humankind. *But, Lord, You gave me a reason to live, a purpose. I just have to remember what it is.*

"Craig Littleton?" A man waited, clad in University of Oregon green and gold. "How are you today, sir?"

"Fine," I said automatically. He must have been new. "Yourself?"

"Enjoying the sun." He rolled me toward the back of the room.

Bunny, my therapist, glanced up from adjusting the tension on a machine. "Craig, you're looking well. Ready to get to work?"

"I was just thinking that what I've been missing the last few days are some really sore, stiff muscles. Can you help me out?"

Laughing, she moved behind me and wheeled my chair into position. Before me stretched two long bars, placed parallel to each other. "We're trying a few new things today, starting with some walking. I've been in contact with your doctor. He wants new X-rays taken of your legs. If the bones have knit back together, he'd like to take the casts off. We'll really kick it into gear when that happens."

"Great. All the torture you've dished out so far has been so much fun." I reached out and gripped the bars. Pulling myself up out of the chair, I managed to get into a standing position with most of my weight held up by my arms.

"Okay. Step with your left leg. Now your right." Bunny talked me over the short distance with calm, encouraging words.

By the time I reached the end of the bars, my arms wobbled and sweat moistened my shirt.

"Excellent, Craig, excellent." She slid a chair next to me. "Now let's do the isometric exercises."

I sank onto the seat and let my arms hang loose. The walking was difficult, no doubt about it, but the isometrics were just as intense. Muscle by muscle, Bunny instructed me to tighten, hold, and release without actually moving the limb.

"Why do you start physical therapy while patients are still in casts?" I flexed my calf.

"If we waited until you were all healed up, you would lose most of your muscle tone. Plus, exercise lowers your chance of blood clots, keeps your blood flowing well, and prevents your bones from stiffening up."

"What you're saying is that I'll thank you later?"

"Absolutely."

Thinking about my legs made the skin inside the cast itch. I dug at the edge for relief. "The less time with these things on, the better."

"That attitude is what makes you a great client. And that you actually do your homework." She ran me through the remainder of my exercises. At five minutes to eleven o'clock, she allowed me to climb back into the wheelchair. "Physically, you're excelling, Craig. The extent of your injuries should have kept you in the hospital for at least another week."

"It was the hospital food."

She did a double take. "Hospital food helped you get better faster?"

"No." I rolled my eyes. "I couldn't handle any more of it. I had to get home."

Pointing a pen at me, she nodded. "A good sense of humor can heal, too. Has your memory returned? Any breakthroughs?"

"I thought so, but I apparently made it up."

"What do you mean?"

"According to my wife, it was impossible. Never happened."

"In a situation like that, do you feel stressed? Are you able to communicate your feelings to your wife?" Bunny sat on a padded table, crossing her legs at the ankles.

"She listens. Whether she understands or not, I couldn't say." I cleared my throat. "But she really tries."

"Your mental health might benefit from some counseling. Here you are, a grown man, having to relearn the pattern of your life. You're probably going to need some vocational rehab. That can feel pretty discouraging."

Denise and I kept putting off calling the psychiatrist Dr. Rossing referred me to. "I'm not afraid of a challenge, Bunny. I'll relearn whatever I need to. Underneath it all, I'm aware of a deep faith in the Lord of the Bible. Even if I don't know who I am, He does."

"Spirituality and a sense of humor. Double the healing, double the fun." Leaning forward, Bunny said, "I've seen patients beat enormous odds if they're backed by prayer." She stood and stretched. "My next client will be waiting, so our fabulous time together must come to a close. See you next appointment."

"All right. See ya. Thanks for the workout." I wheeled toward the waiting area, imagining how terrific it would feel to walk out on my own two feet. Bunny didn't seem to think it would be very long.

I would have loved to wait outside in the sunshine until Denise came back, but the glass doors were heavy and awkward. "Excuse me," I said to a woman thumbing through a magazine. "Could I have some help with the door?" My helplessness drove home the fact that I had given up a huge amount of freedom when I was injured. Yet I was luckier than some. I would be getting out of the wheelchair.

"Sure." She jumped up as if walking were easy and propped the door open with her foot as I rolled out onto the sidewalk.

"Thank you." How many doors had Denise opened for me? She did so much, with such grace. I failed to appreciate how my accident had transformed her life, as well.

And had she ever complained? Whined about how much trouble I caused? An uncomfortable conviction about last night darted around my mind. She'd given so much and asked for so little in return . . . and I had to give her a hard time about wanting to move slowly in our romance. What a pig.

Hers

I PULLED UP TO an old cottage, crumbling brick separating from its facing. Instead of a driveway, two strips of concrete ran up the small hill to the house. Grass grew between the tire tracks, and pink and yellow rosebushes lined the front. As I got out of the car, I examined the house across the street from the address I'd been given.

It was a bungalow, just as Samantha had described to the girls at the hospital. Lattice leaned against the side of the house, climbing roses entwining to the top. A short hedge edged the property. What was it like for Samantha? To wake up every morning and see her childhood home across the street? Its emptiness surely reminded her of her father's death.

Maybe the weekend at our house could be a reprieve, an escape from being surrounded by all the signs of her dad. I strode up the hill and knocked on the door.

The mission-style door cracked open, a tiny chain crossing the space near the top. A voice spoke through the crack. "Who is it?"

"I'm Denise Littleton. Samantha told me to come by today to meet you."

"Give me just a moment." She closed the door, the chain clinked, and the door came ajar. "Please, come on in."

In the hazy, dark interior of the house, my eyes took a moment to adjust enough to see Mrs. Van Horn. She moved farther into the house and took a seat in a brown rocker with a soft-looking, crocheted, multicolored throw hanging over the arm. Her steely white hair cropped in a precise wedge, she perched black, square-framed glasses on her nose, and studied me head to toe. "So you're the lady who lied to my Samantha?"

What a start. If I had told the truth in the first place, I wouldn't have to deal with the embarrassment. "Yes, well . . . It wasn't something I meant to do, and I was relieved to tell Samantha the truth."

"I knew her father for years."

"William? What was he like?" I settled, unasked, into the chair next to hers.

She stared off into the distance for a moment. "He tried to be a good father. His job took him away quite often. After her mother died, Samantha would stay with me for weeks at a time. But when he was home, he loved to garden and dreamed of writing a book."

"What did he do?" The obituary hadn't mentioned his occupation.

"He was a regional sales manager for a lumber company. It was a struggle to make ends meet, though, the last few months. Seems only weeks had passed from when he was laid off to when they found Samantha's cancer."

"So you've taken care of Samantha for years?"

"Off and on." The woman nodded solemnly. "She even has a bedroom here, which made it easier when bringing her home from the hospital."

"Where is she?"

"Out back. I asked her to give us some time to ourselves."

I crossed my legs and pushed with the grounded heel, setting the rocker into motion. "How is she doing?"

"As well as can be expected."

"And how are you?"

Mrs. Van Horn crooked her neck and looked at me. "You are the very first person who's asked me that since William died. You're a sensitive one, aren't you? Sensitive to others?"

I tsked. "You didn't answer my question."

"Insightful, too." She rubbed her hand along the armrest. A mark in the varnish declared her movement habitual. "He was like a son to me. Next to Samantha, I believe I loved him more than anyone else."

"What was your favorite thing about him?" I rested my cheek on my hand.

"His devotion to Samantha. He really hated to be gone from her so much, but it was the only job he knew how to do. He wanted to provide for her. When he failed at that, well . . ." She shrugged. "Why don't you poke your head out the door and call Samantha in?"

"Sure." I walked between the eating area and the cramped kitchen to the back door. Warped panes of glass framed Samantha. She sat on a wrought-iron bench, engrossed in a book, fuzzy head glowing in the sunshine.

As soon as the latch clicked, she jumped up, sliding a bookmark into place. "Denise!"

Her obvious excitement soothed my guilt. I reached out to hug her. "Thanks for forgiving me, Samantha. I won't lie to you again."

She squeezed her arms tightly around my shoulders and stepped back. "The longer I thought about it, the more sense your decision made to me."

"But I was wrong."

"You were. But I can sympathize with you. What's a good way to introduce yourself if your husband . . ." Samantha grimaced. "Anyway, that's all old news."

"Yes, let's talk about what you'd like to do, make some new plans."

"Plans for what?"

"Plans for during your visit. Like . . . do you want to go to the movies?"

Samantha shook her head. "Too many germs floating around in a public place."

I racked my brain for a fun, teenage activity that didn't involve a public place. Bowling? No, still too many people. A restaurant? I'd have to get takeout. "Well, we could—"

"Really, Denise, I'd like to hang out at your house and get to know your family. Maybe talk to your husband a little, if he's remembering any of the accident."

"There's been no sudden, overnight change, Samantha. He won't be able to help you."

"A girl can always hope." She fiddled with an earring. "Want a piece of apple pie? Mrs. Van Horn and I made it last night with apples from our tree." She pointed to a corner of the small yard where an aged apple tree twisted up from the ground.

"Sounds delicious." We walked back to the house. "Do you like to bake? Because we could cook up a storm this weekend."

"Could you teach me to make a soufflé? I love all things French and have always wanted to make one, but Mrs. Van Horn just doesn't do soufflés." She hushed as we went into the kitchen. "She prefers low-maintenance food."

"I've never baked a soufflé, but I'm willing to try. The worst that could happen is a total collapse and utter failure."

Bouncing, she clapped her hands. "We're going to have *so* much fun." She dished up three pieces of pie, handed me one, and carried the other plate to Mrs. Van Horn.

I cut off a bite-sized tidbit from the tip of the slice. The crust flaked apart. The aroma of cinnamon and nutmeg wafted up. My first taste impressed me. "Girl, you'll be doing all our cooking. If you feel comfortable with her coming to our house, of course, Mrs. Van Horn."

"Samantha's a good judge of character." Mrs. Van Horn winked. "I'll give a number you can reach me at in case of emergency."

"Do you have any special instructions?"

"Just take good care of her. She's practically a grown girl, very responsible. If anything needs doing, she can handle it."

"Mrs. Van Horn, don't you worry." I balanced my plate on my knees. "Her stay will be quiet and relaxing. Probably even boring."

Chapter Twenty-Four

His

FROM DENISE'S CLEANING, if I hadn't known who was coming to spend the weekend, I would have thought the president was stopping by. Why did she bristle at my interest in Samantha? Denise also must have felt connected to the girl to expend so much effort for such a short visit.

Of course, I didn't remember ever seeing her prepare for anyone else's visit.

"Craig, can you unload the dishwasher onto the counter?"

"I'll do my best." At least she'd found a job at my level. I flipped down the door of the dishwasher and took the linen towel she held toward me.

"The silverware all needs to be dried, even if it looks like it already is. I hate pulling a spoon out of the drawer only to see water spots, okay?"

I bit my tongue, refusing to ask why she didn't use the drying cycle on the dishwasher. She had a reason, I was sure, but I could also guarantee it wouldn't make sense to me. "Are you going to be able to relax before Samantha gets here?"

"Why would I need to relax? I'm doing fine." She rubbed a damp strand of hair back off her forehead with her arm. Jabbing the mop into the bucket and wringing it out, she proceeded to clean the floor, even shoving the handle underneath my wheelchair as I dried the dishes I could reach without my ribs spitefully reminding what an invalid I was.

Nicolas, who'd been out mowing the lawn, came into the kitchen from the garage door. Blades of grass fell from his shoes as he walked across the tile.

"Nicolas. Go back to the door and take your shoes off." Denise threatened him with the mop. "Can't you see what I'm doing?"

He shrugged, but returned to the edge of the kitchen to remove his shoes. "I didn't want to get my socks wet."

"Stinker." Denise wielded the mop handle at him as he passed her. "Go take a quick shower so you don't smell."

He sniffed at his armpits. "Like a rose."

"And tell your brother I'm going to check his room in five minutes. He better not have moved the mess into his closet or under his bed because I'm going to look there." Ripping a paper towel from the roll, she scowled at the grassy footprints still on the floor as Nicolas left.

The phone rang.

Denise whirled and grabbed it. "Hello?" Tucking the phone under her ear, she dunked the mop in the bucket. "Oh, really?" Rivulets of dirty water drained when she wrung the strands. "Okay, we'll see you then." She hung up and turned to me. "Samantha will be about an hour late. She ran out of one of her meds so they have to stop by the pharmacy to refill the prescription."

I stacked the last dish from the upper tray onto the counter. "Why don't you take your own advice and soak in the tub?"

She glared at me, but a smile played at the corners of her mouth. "Are you saying I smell like a teenage boy?"

"Just go."

"After I get these dishes in the cupboards."

I backed out of the kitchen before she could give me a new assignment. "Will you send Jamie down if he passes inspection?"

Denise glanced over her shoulder at me as she stretched on tiptoe to put a glass bowl into the top cabinet. "Sure. Why?"

The way her body elongated, I didn't complain about the view. "We haven't spent father-son time alone lately. Since we've got an hour to kill, I want to see if he'll hang out with me."

Ten minutes later, he found me in the office. "Dad? Mom said you wanted to see me?"

"How'd your room look?"

"All right." He grinned. "When Nicolas gave me the five-minute warning, I stuffed everything else into my hamper."

"Let me guess." I raised my eyebrows. "It's not just dirty clothes in there."

"A few dishes, some books . . . nothing glass."

"Hey." Leaning back, I gripped the wheels of my chair. "Want to bring your board to the park and show off your moves?"

His eyes lit up. "You want to watch me skate?"

"I haven't seen you in action yet."

"Awesome!" Jamie dashed out of the room and was back with his skateboard and helmet before I made it to the front door.

"Leave a note for your mom on the whiteboard. I've got the cell, so she can call if she needs us back earlier."

Getting down the small steps proved a challenge, but the sidewalk stretched smoothly all the way to the park. At the slight downward slope to the skateboarding section, Jamie jumped on his board and held on to the handles of my chair. We arrived in style.

A pod of young boys, caps turned backward, cruised up and down the ramps, constantly grabbing their loose pants and hiking them up.

"Have they not heard of belts? Or of shopping for clothes that actually fit?"

"Whatever, Dad." Shaking his head, Jamie thrust his board forward, ran after it, and leapt on. Over the next half hour, he barely stopped to breathe. I'd heard him talk about "grinding," and I could figure out which trick that was, but the rest of his acrobatics blew my mind.

This was the same boy who could melt into the sofa cushions and not move any muscle except for his thumbs as he played video games for hours on end. I made a mental note to spend more time with him outside, encouraging him to hone his skill.

Panting, he flopped on the grass in front of me. "Water. Dying. Need drink."

Scanning the park, I pointed out the closest drinking fountain. "There's water about fifty feet that way."

"I know. Too far." Jamie grasped his throat. "Please, Dad, save me. Mom always makes me bring a water bottle."

"I'll pay you a buck if you can ride the handrail on the steps right next to the fountain."

Jamie popped up. "Sweet."

"Get a drink while you're there."

A lesson impressed itself upon me right then. My youngest boy could seem spent and worn-out, but all he needed to get going was the right motivation.

Wiping his mouth with the bottom of his T-shirt, he cruised back to me, mission completed.

I tapped the arm of the wheelchair. "Ready to go, bud?"

"Yeah." Jamie's head bobbed. "I've conquered the biggest and the best. I'm okay to head home." He copied a victory dance we saw in a football movie we rented a few days ago.

"At least your mother hasn't called, so we're not in any trouble." I turned up the sidewalk. "You were amazing out there, Jamie. I'm really proud of you."

"Why would you be proud of me for skateboarding? You've always made fun of it." He pushed with a toe and raised his hands to balance as he matched my pace.

"I have?"

"Every time I brought it up."

I braked and Jamie slowed also. "Jamie, I'm sorry for the times I've hurt you with negative comments about your skating. I can tell it's very important to you and you put your heart into it."

He leaned down and hugged me, apparently not caring if his friends could still see us. "I love you, Dad."

"I love you, too, son." I'm pretty sure I smiled the whole way home. Jamie opened the door and I called out, "Hi, honey . . . we're home!"

Hers

AS I DESCENDED the stairs, bathed and dressed, I thought the house sounded far too quiet. Scribbled words covered the whiteboard: *Dad's taking me to the park to skate. Have phone. Back soon. ~J*

"Nicolas?" I wasn't sure if he went with Craig and Jamie or if he took off somewhere else. Over the few days of his being off restriction, he had proven to be the normal trustworthy, reliable Nicolas I missed from before the accident. Craig spent massive quantities of time with both boys lately. Proportionally, their disrespect reached record lows and their chores were completed on time and with good attitudes.

The effects of giving his attention to them now merely highlighted how shortchanged they had been for years. Though glaringly obvious with hindsight, his neglect had been invisible to me at the time. Same as his treatment of our relationship. He worked long hours, sometimes coming home after I was asleep and leaving before I awoke. At least, that was what the old Craig had claimed. Frankly—and I had brought this up with my therapist—I wondered if he used to stay out some nights. Half the time he either traveled to various conferences and conventions or worked such long days that I never saw him.

The doorbell rang, and I padded over to answer the door. Samantha and Mrs. Van Horn stood on the stoop, a duffel bag at their feet. "Come in, come in." I swept my hand toward the living room.

"I'm so sorry we're late." Mrs. Van Horn stepped in and gave the room a glance.

"Not a problem. I'm just glad you noticed while there was still time to do something about it." I smiled at Samantha, who was wearing her wig.

Mrs. Van Horn chucked the girl and gave her a lipsticky kiss on the nose. "Have everything you need, sweetie?"

"Yes, thank you."

"If she's missing anything," I said, "I'd be happy to run to the store for it."

Mrs. Van Horn stared into Samantha's eyes. "You be good." She turned and pressed a twenty-dollar bill into my hand. "Just in case."

I took it only because I planned to have Samantha put it into her bag the instant Mrs. Van Horn left.

"I'm sorry, but I must be off. I've got to hit the road right away if I'm to make it to my sister's while it's still light."

I ushered her out the door. "Drive safely, Mrs. Van Horn. Be careful."

"I will." She marched down the sidewalk and climbed into an ancient Oldsmobile.

There didn't seem to be any limit on what this lady could do. Already, she had impressed me by taking in a teenager. I hoped when I got older I'd be as active as she was. If she had energy left over after caring for Samantha, God bless her.

"Well, Samantha, I'll show you where you'll be sleeping." I led the way up the stairs. "We furnished the extra room as a guest room. It's tucked between our master suite and the bonus room. The boys' rooms are at the other end of the house."

"You have a beautiful home."

Drawing back and pointing to her door, I let her pass me in the hallway. "Right in there."

She took small steps until she crossed the room. "It's so pretty." She fingered the sage green drapery before running her hand over the embroidered white bedspread.

"The dresser's empty, so you can unpack if you'd like." I walked past the bed. "You have your own bathroom here, too."

She spun around and fell back on the bed. "I could live here forever."

"I've always wanted a daughter." I wiggled my eyebrows. "Should we go start dinner?"

"Are we making a soufflé?"

"If it collapses, we'll order takeout." Laughing, I led her downstairs and into the kitchen.

"Where's the rest of your family?" She donned the apron I held out to her.

"I'm not sure where Nicolas is, but Jamie and my husband will be back in a few minutes. Jamie loves skateboarding, so Craig took him to the park."

Samantha picked at a nail. "Oh. That's nice they can spend time together."

Too late to change the subject, I realized that talking about what a great father Craig had turned into might cause Samantha to miss her own father. "Sorry. I wasn't thinking."

She shrugged, but I wondered how the weekend would go with Craig around the whole time. Maybe I could get him out of the house with the boys again tomorrow so Samantha and I could have more time together. Though it had been only a short time since losing her father, she must miss her mother, too.

The front door squeaked open and Craig's voice found us. "Hi, honey . . . we're home!"

Samantha's eyes lit up. "You sound like an old sitcom! Dad and I used to watch reruns all the time."

I hadn't recognized the reference.

Pulling Samantha behind me, I took her to meet them. Nerves balled up my stomach at the thought of introducing Samantha to the man who might be responsible for her dad's death. It felt riskier than attempting a soufflé, that was for sure. But if I didn't acknowledge the nerves, then maybe nobody else would notice.

We rounded the corner of the entryway arch and I opened my mouth to begin the introductions. Gasping, Samantha stopped so quickly I wrenched her arm. "What?" I peered over my shoulder.

Her face was as white as a full moon in a drenched night sky. She clasped her hands over her heart.

Following her gaze, I came to Craig. "What's the matter, Samantha?"

Her hands rose from her chest and covered her mouth as she fell to her knees. Jamie stared at her as if he just laid eyes on the strangest specimen of the female species. How could I fault him? I had no idea why Samantha freaked out. "Craig, this is Samantha." Awkwardly, my gaze bounced back and forth between the two of them.

His wheelchair on Samantha's level, Craig reached out a hand. "Hello, Samantha."

Instead of shaking his hand, she scuttled back across the hardwood floor until she ran into the wall behind her. "Dad? Is it you?"

Craig glanced at me, then back at Samantha. "You can call me 'Craig.' "

"No." She stretched a trembling arm toward him. "Dad, don't you recognize me?"

Dad? Why was she calling him that?

Nicolas burst through the front door, stopping right behind Craig. He scanned the scene before him: all of us gathered in the entryway, his brother's weirded-out look, aproned Samantha crying on the floor with her wig askew, and my surely shocked face. "Um, I'm going upstairs."

"How can you be alive?" Samantha crawled toward Craig. "They all . . . they all said you were dead." She dropped her head onto his knee and sobbed, wrapping her arms around his legs, casts and all.

Nicolas froze, wrinkling his face. "What's going on here?"

"Denise." Craig gestured at the girl. "What's she talking about?"

Ignoring the panic in his voice, I knelt down and stroked her back. What did I really know about Samantha? She'd been through a lot in her short years. Had she lost her ability to separate fantasy from reality? Did she really think Craig was her father?

Why would she think such a thing?

Chapter Twenty-Five

Hers

"SAMANTHA, WHY are you calling Craig your dad?" I pulled her hair back from her tear-streaked face and tipped my head to look her in the eye.

"He *is*. He is my dad." She jerked her head up. "Daddy, why didn't you come see me in the hospital? Have you been here the whole time?"

Confusion and compassion warring in his eyes, Craig put his hands on each side of her cheeks. "I'm not your dad," he said tenderly. "I don't even remember your father. I'm sorry."

Tears tumbled from the edges of Samantha's eyes and rolled over Craig's fingers. "But you look like him and you talk like him. You *are* my dad." She sucked in a ragged breath. "Maybe . . . maybe you just don't remember that you are. Denise said you have amnesia."

"This is absurd." The words blurted out of me. I wasn't sure whether I was referring to Samantha's idea or the emotional tornado that had touched down around us. "Let's go sit and talk this out.

Nicolas, grab the tissue box for Samantha." I moved the group into the living room, pulled the sheers to keep the sun from blinding us, and perched on the couch next to Samantha. "You say that Craig looks like your dad?"

"No." She raised her voice. "He is my dad." Another tear squeezed from her eye.

I considered the best course of action. She would be staying with us for a few days, and I needed to minimize her embarrassment when she realized her mistake. "Grief is a powerful emotion, Samantha. It can blind us, or make us see things differently than they are. I can understand how, if Craig resembles your father, your first glimpse of him would bring up conflicting emotions."

"I can prove it." She stood and raced toward the door. Was she running away? But she turned and clambered up the stairs.

Blowing out a sigh, I took stock of my family. Jamie and Nicolas stood by the eating bar with shocked expressions on their faces.

"Mom?" Jamie met my questioning gaze. "Does she really think our dad is her dad? That would make her, like . . . our sister."

Craig cradled his head in his hands and rubbed his temples. "I'm not her father, boys. It's sad, really, that she could make herself believe it's even possible."

Nicolas plopped down on the hide-a-bed. "It's not possible, right, Dad?"

"How could I be?" Craig tossed out a dry laugh. "For her to be telling the truth, your mother and you both would have to be crazy. I'm in the family portrait. I've seen for myself that this is my home."

Why hadn't Samantha reacted to the portrait at the top of the stairs? We walked right past it when I showed her to her room. *No, she was looking the other way, over the landing to the entryway below.*

Craig's comment penetrated my haze. For Samantha to be right, I had to be wrong. What woman didn't know her own husband? And I knew, for a fact, that Samantha's father had been killed in the accident. The police told me before she even knew, though the cops hadn't discerned his identity by then.

Samantha pounded back down the stairs and appeared, breathless, in front of us. "Here." She held out a photo to me. "It's a picture of my dad. He gave it to me when I first was diagnosed with leukemia, and I've never been without it since."

The picture showed a middle-aged guy with dark hair. Creased, a corner torn, the finish worn off, the picture reminded me of Craig, but didn't match him exactly.

"See?"

"Samantha, it's really hard to tell what this man looks like."

She stared at the photo as if seeing it anew. "I have better ones at the house. That's just from being tucked underneath my pillow at the hospital and stuffed in my bag."

"I'd like to see them sometime." I patted the cushion next to me, hoping she would relax. I promised Mrs. Van Horn we would create a calm, restful mini-vacation for Samantha. Instead, I'd worked her into a frenzy.

"Take me now, please." The tremble disappeared from her voice, and I recognized the sound of stubbornness pounding a tent stake in, planning to take up residence.

I glanced at Craig's worried face. "I don't think that's wise. We've got a lot planned, like making the soufflé, and I didn't ask Mrs. Van Horn about you stopping by home."

Samantha stuffed her hand into her back jean pocket and pulled out a key. "I'd really like to go to my house, Denise."

I had two choices: keep talking to her or give in. If I kept talking, she would dig in her heels and get more agitated. If I capitulated and took her by her house, at least I would get her away from Craig for a while, giving him a chance to think of what we should do.

My imagination conjured up her refusing to leave once we got there. "Promise you'll just find the pictures and come back with me?"

She jerked her chin down and thrust it up in what I interpreted as a nod.

"All right."

Her shoulders relaxed an inch or two. "And you'll all look at the pictures and be honest about what you see?"

"Sure." I bent over to hug Craig before leaving and whispered, "Have a plan by the time I get back."

During the drive, Samantha didn't speak to me. Lips moving without making sound, she stared out the passenger side window.

At a stoplight, I watched out of the corner of my eye and thought she was saying, "He's alive."

I parked in front of Mrs. Van Horn's and started up the hill. Samantha headed in the opposite direction, toward her old home. Jogging after her, I reached for her arm. "Where do you think you're going?"

She drew back. "To get the pictures."

"I thought you meant at Mrs. Van Horn's house."

"I said *my* house." She crossed the street, passed the hedges, and turned the key in the lock.

Hanging back, I yelled, "Are you sure this is all right? Are you supposed to go in by yourself?"

She slipped into the house.

The sun beat down, glinting off the windows of the bungalow. I shaded my eyes and waited for her to reappear. *Lord, how did we get here? This is not what I expected our time together to be like.*

Five minutes passed before I ventured up the sidewalk. "Samantha?" I stuck my head in the house. The front room held nothing but sheet-covered furniture. Many of the patterns were boldly flowered and out-of-date. Mrs. Van Horn must have used her collection of old linens. The silhouette of one piece suggested a piano.

Creeping forward, I felt as if I were walking on hallowed ground. Sunshine sneaked around the roll-down shades on the windows. Dust floated in the vertical beams and a hush permeated the house. "Samantha?"

"Back here."

Following the sound of her voice, I found her in a small bedroom, sitting on a sheet-draped bed, an album open on her lap. Silent tears dripped from her chin.

I settled on the bed beside her. "May I?"

She nodded.

Lord, give me the right words. Let me help her accept her father's death. I slid the album from her lap to my own. Craig bent over a dark-haired little girl, pushing her on a red tricycle. Heart speeding, I flipped to the next page. And the next. Most of the pictures were of Samantha, but every now and then, Craig made an appearance. I closed my eyes, rubbed them, and refocused on the pictures. *Craig? How can this be?*

"It's him," I whispered. His hair was shaggier then I remembered, but all the men wore it that way back then.

An idea buzzed into my brain. More followed until a full swarm droned in my thoughts.

Slow down. Think of what you know.

First, I knew the man at my house definitely was my husband of nineteen years. But even I had to admit that the man in the pictures with Samantha was also Craig. He might have called himself William, but he was the same man. No doubt.

Which meant Craig was Samantha's father.

Mrs. Van Horn's words echoed in my memory. *"He tried to be a good father. His job took him away quite often. Samantha would stay with me for weeks at a time."* I thought of Craig's frequent business trips, the long workdays when I was sure he hadn't been at the office all the time, and the nights he hadn't come home. Had he been able to pull it off? Lead a double life without either of his "families" finding out?

I rebelled at the notion I could have been fooled for all those years. Yet Craig's intense interest in Samantha the second he heard her name in the hospital, how Samantha's hospital bills had been covered, how the money disappeared from our account . . .

Samantha's age fell between Nicolas and Jamie's. Craig had already proved himself to be unfaithful to our wedding vows. Who was to say that Naomi had been the only woman? Maybe he entertained a long string of mistresses over the course of our marriage. Maybe

Samantha's mother had been one of his lovers. Could he have had a daughter between his two sons? Were there, possibly, more children out there?

Widows sometimes opened their doors to find illegitimate sons or daughters on their steps, staking claims on the estates. Usually, the "children" were running a scam, searching obituaries for their next victims, targeting those who sounded financially well-off and vulnerable to lies. But every now and then there had to be real undiscovered children coming out of the woodwork. From the doorstep to the courtroom to the bank.

I flipped back to a picture of Samantha and her mother. The woman had a heart-shaped face and a genuine smile. I memorized her image, sure I would obsess over it later if . . .

"Denise?" Samantha broke through my contemplations, her voice soft. "What are you thinking?"

I turned to her. Her eyes reminded me of Craig's. Didn't I latch on to her as quickly as Craig? Could half of her genes have come from the man I married?

Are you going to stay married to him?

I shoved the question aside and answered Samantha. "You might be right . . . *and* I might be right."

"How?"

"Mrs. Van Horn said your dad was gone a lot for work."

"He didn't want to leave me."

"I'm sure he didn't." I pushed my hair from my face. "My husband was away from home quite often, too. I think he came here, to be with you, when I thought he was at conferences or working late." The words hung in the air like itchy, starched shirts pinned to a clothesline.

Samantha closed the album and rubbed her hand over it. "You think my dad and your husband are the same person?" Her words seem to unpin mine from the clothesline and draw in their scent, feel the fabric to see if it was dry and ready to be dropped into the woven basket at her feet.

"You're sure he's your dad, right?"

She nodded emphatically.

"And I'm sure that he's my husband. What other explanation can there be?"

Side by side, we sat on the bed and stared across the room at the old plaster wall. She couldn't have liked my deduction, but she considered it. "It . . . that would mean my dad lied to me."

"Will you still come stay the night with us?" With Mrs. Van Horn out of town, there didn't seem to be any other options, yet it would be awkward. What would we tell the boys? How could I broach the subject with Craig if Samantha were there with us?

Wait a minute . . . if Craig was William, or William was Craig, who had died in the accident? The police had found a body there, right? *A severely burned body,* I reminded myself. Hadn't I wondered from the start if the police knew any more than I did about what happened? They must have confused something in the identification of the dead person.

Samantha rose and walked to the doorway. "I want to talk to Dad. I want to show him these pictures and see if he remembers them."

Samantha wanted to talk to him as much as, if not more than, me. But I needed to talk one-on-one with him, without us having to censor our emotions and their impact on Samantha.

I stood and straightened the sheet. "Can I discuss the situation with him first? I'd like to give him some warning and let him have time to think about it. Afterward, I promise, you can talk with him alone."

"Okay." She followed me out of the house, clutching the album to her chest as if it were her most precious possession.

His

WHEN DENISE AND SAMANTHA left, the boys and I stood around looking at each other. Well, they stood, and I sat in my wheelchair.

"That was weird." Jamie kicked off his skater shoes, their huge white laces still tied.

"Extremely." Shaking his head, Nicolas scratched his chin. "Dad, is she mental?"

"She's experienced a lot of loss lately. I'm sure it'd do her good to see a counselor, someone who can help her sort out everything."

"Do counselors make house calls on weekends?" Jamie smirked.

Denise wanted me to come up with a plan. Could I get a counselor? Probably not. After an hour of contemplating the situation, the best plan I came up with was to act natural and ignore the issue. The boys were easily convinced to do the same. Male DNA came in two varieties: those who thrived on conflict and those who avoided it at all costs. Thankfully, we all shared the avoidance type.

By the expression on Denise's face when she and Samantha came home, I doubted my plan was going to be instituted. Samantha flashed me an inscrutable look and ran directly upstairs, presumably to the guest room.

"Craig, will you come into the office?"

I wheeled my way in. She closed the doors behind us, positioned the office chair next to me, and sank onto the leather.

Shaking her head, she toyed with a strand of hair. "Things are not looking good."

"Do you think it's safe to have her in our home, Denise? If her delusions are so strong, she might be capable of anything."

"She's not crazy, Craig." Her head still shook.

Dread pumped from my heart, radiated to the rest of my body. "What are you talking about? I'm not her father. Her father is dead."

"Don't you think it's just a little bit weird that she looks like you?"

"She doesn't look like me. The boys look like me, like us, like the two of us mixed together. Yesterday I was noticing how Nicolas has my face shape, but your nose. Why would you say she looks like me? It's as if you're saying she really is my daughter."

She fiddled with her wedding ring.

"Are you kidding me? How could I be her father?" I threw my

arms out, exasperated. "Ever since I woke up in the hospital, you've been telling me who I am. Now you're going to add in another child?"

"I've been telling you who I knew you to be. It's not my problem that your dirty past is catching up with you."

"I'm not capable of that, Denise. I'm a loyal man. I feel it in my gut. And how would I have had a daughter that you didn't know about?"

"Family sharing." Denise clapped her hands. "You know? Like job sharing? A couple nights at one house, the rest of the week at another."

"Stop it! Stop acting so calm!" I shouted. "Stop holding your emotions inside!"

"You want me to tell you how I feel?" snarled Denise. She jumped up from the chair and shoved it back. With a thud, it bounced off the wall. "I loved you. I loved you even when you didn't love me. For years, I've tried to make you fall back in love with me. I have wrestled tooth and nail to save our marriage."

She wagged a finger in my face. "But you don't remember that. Oh, no, you can't remember a thing. How convenient that is for you while all this junk is surfacing. At each new revelation, I've chosen to stand by your side. You had an affair with Naomi? I'm still here. You drained our bank account? I'm still here. You can't work now and don't know if you ever will be able to? I'm still here. But—" She broke into tears, choking sobs pulsing from her body.

"Honey . . ." I reached for her. "Come here."

"No." She backed toward the door. "If I let you close, you make my brain go mushy. I'm tired of following my heart. I need to start making intelligent decisions."

"Denise." Why did I tell her to stop holding her emotions inside?

"What's next, Craig? What secret grenade will explode in my lap next? We both know you were unfaithful. Then here comes a girl you latch on to the second you hear her name, even though you—" she made quote marks in the air "—can't remember anything. And she's got your eyes and a photo album full of proof that you're her father. I can't handle any more shocks to my system." She opened the door and lowered her voice. "Now, I promised Samantha she could speak to you alone. I'll send her down. Try to think of someone other than yourself when you talk with her."

Mind reeling, I wished I could run after Denise. Did she think I was faking my amnesia? No matter what skeletons hung in my closet, didn't she understand that not knowing what they were was more horrendous than knowing and dealing with the consequences?

My current identity had been formed with her words. Her memories had become my own. Without her by my side to guide me through, I was lost, adrift without an anchor. Yes, unexpected waves kept swamping our boat as soon as we bailed out the water from the last. I knew it was asking a lot to want her by my side after an affair. Yes, a new daughter suddenly turning up added tons of dead weight to our floundering vessel.

But I couldn't remember any of it! This short taste of a life with Denise and the boys made me hungry for a lifetime with them, yet Denise didn't seem able to handle any more.

"Hello?" Samantha paused at the doorway. "Can I come in?"

"Yes, yes." I recalled Denise's admonition to think about others before myself. What if Samantha were my daughter? Most likely, she wasn't. Either way, she deserved to be treated with kindness and respect. "Come and sit."

With small steps, she came forward. "Would you look at these pictures with me?"

"Sure." I reached for the book. Instead of sitting in the office chair Denise vacated, she stood by the wheelchair, looking over my shoulder.

Was there any way to describe it? I had opened the album I found in the hall closet and seen myself with my children. When I opened Samantha's album and saw myself with my child, a child I hadn't known existed, my universe expanded in a painful, yet joyful, way. My brain couldn't process all the implications. "Is that us?" I thumbed a picture of me raising a little girl high in the air.

"I think I was about two there." She sniffed.

I'd seen my fill of tears for the day. What could I do to make her feel better? I didn't turn around. She joined the list of children I had let down. She'd gone through chemotherapy and a bone marrow transplant without me, believing I was dead. Now, I turned up alive and still failed to be there when she needed me.

When I finished going through the pictures, I knew I was her father. That was definitely me holding her furry hand on Halloween night with her in a lion costume, dropping leaves on her as she lay in a pile I had raked, and smiling down at a crookedly held camera, which I guessed Samantha held. Me standing between Samantha and Snoopy . . . at Knott's Berry Farm.

An ache formed in my heart as I scrutinized my daughter. Our similarities went further than our eyes. Her hand rested on my shoulder. Our nails were shaped the same. Her earlobes hung free like mine, while the boys and Denise's connected to the bottom of their ear. Yes, the boys were mine, but she even more so. How could I have left my daughter to face the world alone for so long? The pressure behind my eyes increased to such a degree, I allowed a few tears to escape.

I raised my arms.

She fell into them and we sobbed together. I kissed her cheek and squeezed her closer. "I'm sorry, I'm so sorry. I didn't know. I can't remember anything, Sam."

"You remembered that you used to call me that, didn't you?" Her chest shuddered and her crying slowed as if my nickname gave her comfort.

"Honestly, I don't know if I remember or not, but it felt right to say it."

Someone knocked on the door. "Dinner's ready," Jamie called.

Samantha climbed off my lap. "We'd better go eat."

"Tell Denise I'll be there in a moment." I rubbed my face. It felt so right to believe Samantha was my daughter, but with all the confusion, I planned on getting a DNA test to confirm it.

What a miracle, Lord. If Denise hadn't met her in the hospital, we might never have found each other. Thank You for bringing us together.

I would thank Denise, too, though I knew it was a horrible surprise for her to discover. Her curiosity over William—my other identity—led to my reunion with Samantha.

The name William niggled at my mind. What was it about me using two names? Deceitful. How could I have led a double life? Baffling. But something more . . .

My heart seized. The police had identified the body found at the accident scene as William Rodain. Where had that body come from? What other unspeakable thing had I done?

Chapter Twenty-Six

Hers

"WELL, DENISE, what a surprise." Pastor Miles threw the door open in a gesture of welcome. Never mind it was nearing ten o'clock on a Saturday night and I hadn't called first. He grinned as if he couldn't have been happier to see me.

"I'm so sorry. Is it too late? I saw the lights on as I drove past and I . . ."

"No, no, never too late for you. Come on in. I'll have Sheryl make you up a cup of tea." He ushered me down the hall and into his cozy study. "Sheryl?" he called out the door. "Can you bring some of your delicious hot stuff into the office?"

He winked at me, and waited until her trilling laugh echoed down the hallway before adding, "Get your mind out of the gutter, woman. Denise Littleton is here and I promised her some tea."

Weren't they so cute in love? Disgustingly cute. I plopped onto a burgundy love seat and heaved a sigh.

Settling into a worn brown leather recliner, he turned his attention my way. "How's Craig doing?"

I couldn't think of a thing to say.

"I'm guessing this is about your husband? Is he back in the hospital?"

Mutely, I stared at the stitching of my purse.

A moment later, Sheryl stepped in with a steaming mug and set it on a cup holder near my elbow. "I hope chai is okay, Denise. Holler if you want more."

"Thanks. This will be fine."

She left and quiet drifted in her wake.

Pastor studied me. "Denise, I can't help if I don't know what I'm supposed to help with. *Is* it about Craig?"

"No," I blurted. "It's about William."

He scratched his eyebrow with the back of his thumb. "Who's William?"

"That's what I'd like to know." I huffed, crossing my legs. "Apparently, *Craig* is William."

"I'm not sure I'm following this."

A manic laugh erupted from the pit of my belly. I roared like an insane woman until I could barely breathe and tears ran down my cheeks.

With a cocked head and a crinkled brow, the poor guy looked ready to call the mental hospital. He reached toward me.

"I'm sorry, I'm sorry." I held up a hand until I regained my composure. "It's so crazy, you won't even believe it."

"I've heard some strange things in my years."

"Craig had an affair."

He didn't even blink. "I know. I'm so sorry."

"What?" I scratched my forehead. "How do you already know?"

"Craig told me when I visited him in the hospital."

"I'm pretty sure you don't know he fathered a child with another woman. That he pretended he was a whole other guy, lived a separate life in Portland when he wasn't with us."

His eyebrows shot up so high, they almost flew away. "Are you sure? That seems so unlikely."

"We just figured it out tonight. He called himself William. His 'daughter' Samantha is staying with us for the weekend, a bizarre coincidence that I won't take the time to explain. She recognized him, even though he still didn't remember her."

"So whose body was discovered at the accident site?"

"We don't know yet, but obviously the police were confused. Whoever it was, he was arguing with Craig right before the car got hit. I'll call the detective next week, when things have calmed down."

"Hmm . . . this is definitely not a normal occurrence. Never seen anything like it before." He tapped his lip for a few moments.

"What am I supposed to do?"

"Denise, I have three questions for you."

After an uncomfortable pause, I bit. "Okay?"

He leaned back heavily, forming a steeple with his fingers over his mouth. "Are you angry?"

"Of course I am. Who wouldn't be?" I tightened, waiting for a rebuke. "Don't I have a right to be?"

"Sometimes we choose to give up our right to be angry." Pastor's voice gentled, deepened. "Do you love him?" The word *love* vibrated with emotion.

My shoulders fell. There was no denying the truth. "I do. He's been so different since the accident."

"Here's the hardest yet. Are you going to forgive him?" Pastor sat back, having thrown down the gauntlet.

"Forgive him *again*, you mean. How can I? Look what's he's done to me. Every time I think we're on track for a new life, another secret jumps out and slams me back into reality." I took a sip of the creamy chai and dared him with my gaze to give a pat answer, like "seventy times seven" or "the log in your own eye."

"Has he apologized and taken responsibility for the past?"

"Does it even count if he doesn't remember what he's apologizing for?"

"Ah." He pressed his lips together and nodded several times in a row. "I've seen women who've been hurt in a similar way. Want to hear where you're headed?"

"Not really." What could he possibly foresee in the insanity?

"Yes, you do or you wouldn't be here." He chuckled and nodded. "You came to me because you want me to give it to you straight, right?"

I shrugged. He was on to me. What could I do?

"Let's look at it if you let your bitterness lead the way. You end up alone. Or you end up with a husband who constantly grovels at your feet. Who pays penance for what he's done. Always indebted to you for taking him back." He nodded again. "Then you come to enjoy the power that brings. You take joy in lording his sins over him." His eyes burned into my soul. "Is that what you want?"

I scoffed. "Of course not."

"Then you can't forgive halfway. You have to trust him fully. Let him be a real man again."

I rubbed my thumb along the etched pattern on the mug. "Wouldn't I be a fool to stay with him?"

He shook his head. "We're all fools in love. Look at Christ's love for us. Makes no sense. It's foolishness to those who won't accept it."

"But He's God. He never runs out of forgiveness. I'm just petty, little Denise. How can I forget the hurt and betrayal?"

"I once counseled a woman whose husband's unfaithfulness would play out like X-rated movies in her mind. He was genuine in his repentance, but she couldn't move toward reconciliation until those movies were erased. The trouble with a human mind is that it can store nasty stuff in deep vaults for years and protect it more vigilantly than a dragon guards his cave filled with stolen treasure."

"What did the woman do? The one who couldn't forget?"

Pastor raised his hand in a fist. "The movie would begin and she would mentally stamp the word FORGIVEN across the film." He bounced it against the padded arm of the chair. "Each time it popped up—" his fist fell again "—she labeled it. Soon, the letters covered all the screen and she'd rid it from her mind."

I set the mug back into the cup holder. "I should go. Everybody else is playing a video game and they think I'm taking a shower. If I get back before they finish, they'll never know I left." But I didn't rise. Somehow, I hoped Pastor would give my crammed brain yet another thing to think about.

He shifted his weight. "Right now you're acting like the judge, stamping GUILTY on each page of Craig's life. Maybe it's time you change your stamp."

His

WE MADE IT THROUGH the weekend, mainly by ignoring the emotional uproar. Because Denise avoided being alone with me, I had no opportunity to talk with her. Samantha patted my back or squeezed my hand every now and then when the boys or Denise weren't looking. We developed an unspoken agreement not to flaunt our father-daughter relationship—no matter that I couldn't reconcile how I was the father of two families—in front of the rest of them. I appreciated her sensitivity.

About an hour before Mrs. Van Horn was due, Samantha and I found ourselves in the kitchen with no one else around.

"Samantha, would you be comfortable having your blood drawn for a DNA test? To conclusively show you're my daughter?"

She dipped an apple slice in caramel. "I'll do whatever it takes, Daddy, to be with you."

I resisted a huge sigh. If I knew with one hundred percent certainty she was my daughter, I would never let her go back with Mrs. Van Horn. The DNA test would prove our relationship. Not to Denise or Mrs. Van Horn or Nicolas or Jamie. Not even to Samantha. I was the one who needed proof of who I was. I could only take Denise's or Samantha's word for so long without wanting to know for myself.

Breaking an apple slice in half, I stared at my hands. "Here's the thing, Sam . . . I don't think it's a good idea to spring this on Mrs. Van Horn the second she gets here."

"I totally agree. She might have a heart attack and keel over." Samantha's eyes grew wide with mock horror.

"Samantha!" I shot her a warning look. "I'm not asking you to keep it a secret from her forever. Obviously, she's going to need to know as soon as we can figure out where you're going to live."

"You're my dad. I'm going to live with you." Tipping her head, she stared at me. "Right?"

"Of course, but there are complications. You're living with Mrs. Van Horn because she's your legal guardian. Denise and I haven't had a chance to discuss bringing you here to live."

Her face fell. "But we have our own house. I've been taking care of the garden. I can cook and clean. We don't need anybody else."

"I know this is hard." I reached for her hand. "We'll figure it out. Mrs. Van Horn will have to give her permission for the DNA test. If I stopped by her house to discuss it, it'd be like seeing a ghost, so Denise will have to be the one to let her in on it. Hold on a little longer."

"I trust you, Dad." She leaned forward and kissed my cheek. "But hurry. I don't want to be apart any longer than we have to."

"I'm proud of you, Sam. You've done so well on your own."

A bittersweet smile hung on her face.

The doorbell rang.

"She must be early." I scooted back to allow Samantha to pass in front of me. "Grab your bags and meet her at the door. I'll hide back here."

"Love you, Dad." One quick peck later she ran out of the kitchen.

"Love you, too, Sam," I whispered.

Rumblings of three voices echoed back to me. Denise had told me the house belonged to Samantha as William's—or my—sole heir. What would be involved in making a dead man come alive again? We needed the DNA results before we approached the courts. I would have to be named her guardian. I didn't know if I had life insurance or not. If they paid out, I would return the money. And hope they didn't question my amnesia and accuse me of fraud.

Again, how did I cover the tracks that led to my double life? And why hadn't the police shown more suspicion about the other body?

The phone rang.

Knowing Denise was busy at the door, I moved to answer it. Since the wheelchair didn't maneuver easily and I was usually holed up on the hide-a-bed, I hadn't yet answered my own phone. "Hello?"

Click.

Pulling the receiver from my ear, I checked to see if I still had a connection. Maybe I pushed a button without knowing it. Shrugging, I put it down on the counter. Denise had been getting a lot of hang-up calls lately, but she joked that the caller just liked hearing her voice. I guess they didn't want to talk to me either.

I needed to speak with the boys, feel out whether one of their friends was hanging up if they didn't answer.

The phone rang again.

I clicked it on and answered with an over-the-top drawl. "Hellllll-ooooo."

"Craig? Is that you?"

Was this a trick question? Could I answer honestly and say, "I don't know. Ask me when we get the DNA tests back because quite possibly I'm William, too." I opted for a noncommittal, "Uh-huh."

Her words rushed out in a torrent. "I've missed you. I'm sorry I hung up on you, but she always answers the phone so it's become a habit to disconnect right away. Can you talk?"

It took me a moment to place the voice. "Naomi?"

"Oh, good! You've given up this 'can't remember' charade."

I swallowed. My mistress was on the phone. She, out of all the women I met since the accident, probably knew the most about my life. The real things, not the double life I hid from Denise or the sham with Samantha. If I played it right, perhaps I could get some true information. "Did you visit me in the hospital?"

"Oh, baby." She practically purred. "You're not still holding that against me, are you?"

"You caused me intense pain. You also said you were through with me, yet here you are calling."

"I tried to stay away, but I missed you too much. I've been by the house a few times, even used my key to get in once, but she's always there or you leave with her. It's not fair. Can you get away for an hour or two tonight?"

Was that how I set up my trysts in the past? Bile rose in the back of my throat. I never wanted to talk to the woman again, but I couldn't gain information if I let her know how I felt. "Have you forgotten about the accident? I'm still in a wheelchair, two broken legs, broken ribs, torn-up face."

"Are you, like, permanently scarred? I mean, is your face totally messed up?" Disgust tinged her voice.

"Denise doesn't seem to mind it."

Naomi harrumphed. "Who cares what she thinks?"

I do. "So tonight won't work."

"When do I get to see you again?"

Never. "What happened the day I was in the accident?"

"I got angry, then I was worried, but once I heard you were in the hospital, I cried my eyes out."

"Why were you mad?"

"You know I hate it when you show up late. I figured you changed your mind and went to church with your family."

"I was supposed to meet you?" Where? And how late had I been?

"Is this a new game or are you back to the amnesia story?"

You're losing her. Go for the information you want the most. "Tell me about William Rodain."

"Are you taping this? Are the police there or something?" Her voice shook.

"No way." I forced a confident tone. "Just tell me about William."

"Listen, Craig, if you really don't remember . . . maybe it's better that way."

"Who was with me that day? Why were you waiting for me? What did I tell you about Samantha?"

She sucked in a breath. "I'm not ready to throw away what we have, but I'm also not going to fill you in on your own life and your psycho plans. I warned you about this. You should have kept that all separate from me."

"Wait, Naomi, if you—"

"We both swore never to talk about William, and I'm keeping my promise. Call me when you want to get together. Bye."

As I slammed the phone on the counter, Denise walked in. "What's the matter?"

I shook my head. "Phone call."

"Who was it? Why are you so upset?" She crossed her arms and leaned against the counter.

How could I tell her I'd been talking to Naomi? Both of us viewed her as an enemy. I would look guilty, dumb, unfaithful. . . . "Hang up," I muttered. Which was partly true. The first time I'd answered the phone, Naomi *had* hung up. Consumed with aligning the facts, I could not bear the idea of an argument with Denise or any more distance coming between us.

And lying about the phone call? Doesn't that put distance between you?

"Whew." Denise stretched her neck to one side. "A crazy couple of days, huh? Did you ask Samantha to keep it mum, like we'd talked about?"

I climbed the change of subject as if it were a rescue rope dropped to me in a pit of hungry alligators. "You're right. It was nuts. Crazy. Insane. Unforgettable. Yes, Samantha's fine with waiting to tell Mrs. Van Horn. I also brought up the DNA testing. Went well, I think." I nodded and zoomed ahead. "I'd like to get the boys tested, too. When we go to court, I'd like proof they're all my children."

She frowned. "Saying you want the boys tested makes me feel like you don't believe they're yours. Do you think I don't know who their father is?"

"No, honey." I forced my speech to slow. "I wasn't trying to insinuate anything negative against you. Judging from my past, I think it'd be valuable to show the judge confirmation of the facts on paper. In case I haven't recovered my memory yet, I'll be testifying about what I've been told, not what I've experienced. Plus, Samantha wouldn't feel as singled out."

"It would make it easier on her, wouldn't it?" Denise bit her lip and stared out the kitchen window into the garden.

From my lower level, I peered out the sliding glass doors. A robin bounced along the lawn, scrutinizing the grass with a tipped head and roving eye. "The upper roots of the clematis are showing. Can you remind me to tell Jamie to cover them with a big rock?"

A dishtowel flew passed me. "I can't believe you remember the name of a plant and not the day we married." Denise rolled her eyes.

"Sorry." I snagged the towel from the ground and tossed it back at her.

She smirked and yanked the sprayer from the kitchen faucet, pointing it my way.

"Don't you dare."

"Try to stop me."

I rolled forward, hoping to reach her before the water squirted.

She jumped on the counter and swung her legs up, still threatening me with the sprayer. "Come closer, sweetie."

Braking, I tried to make puppy eyes. "Please get down and talk like a civilized person. I've already had a shower today."

"No, you didn't." She smiled.

"Okay, I had a very thorough sponge bath today and I don't need to get wet again." I shook my finger at her. "You can't get my casts wet anyway."

"Aw." She jumped off the counter and pushed the hose back into the faucet. "You win, poor baby."

I pulled her close to me and pressed my cheek to her side. "I love you." My grip tightened as desperation sparked. What if I lost her?

Despite my driving need to be independent, I doubted I could succeed without her next to me.

"Love you, too." She swayed back and forth for a moment. "Craig, we haven't talked about what will happen with Samantha when the DNA tests show she's your daughter."

"Sam asked about that."

"She did?"

"In a way. She took it for granted that I'd live in the house she was brought up in with her."

Denise stiffened. "What did you say to that?"

"What every good husband says: that I need to talk to my wife. But not to worry, though, because we would figure something out."

She twirled her finger around a lock of my longish hair, uneven from the shaving in the hospital. "I think she should move in here."

"Are you serious?"

"She deserves a father, doesn't she? It'd be easy to convert the guest room into a permanent room for her. We have the space. Mostly, though, after almost losing you, no way would I want you to be anywhere but right here."

Denise loved me. Really and truly. Wanted me to be with her. Even to the point of accepting an unexpected daughter into the family. "Until we get the blood test back, no decisions need to be made, but I appreciate your offer."

"It's not a business deal, Craig, it's a child we're talking about. Anyone with a heart would say the same."

"I'd like to go see the house."

"Samantha's?"

"Yes."

She tucked her hands into her pockets.

"It might be powerful enough, fresh enough, to make me remember."

"Can it wait until you have your casts off? You'd be able to get around better. Her old home is definitely not handicapped accessible."

I didn't miss the slight put-down to "my" old house compared to the new beauty I lived in with Denise. Why was there such disparity between the lives of my children? Couldn't I find a way to provide fine things for Samantha, too?

Denise stared down at her feet, waiting for my response.

"If I have to wait, I will."

❍❍❍

That night I rolled to my side, stuffed a pillow under my head, and fought with God.

Yes, I lied. It's for Denise's good, Lord. Naomi doesn't attract me. I'll never be involved with her again. Denise would only be hurt if she knew Naomi was still calling.

Silence.

I'll tell her to stop calling as soon as I get some answers.

Silence.

You have all the answers, but You're not sharing them with me. What else am I supposed to do?

Silence.

I rolled to the other side.

Chapter Twenty-Seven

Hers

I HAD TROUBLE meeting Mrs. Van Horn's eyes at the door. So much had transpired since she dropped Samantha off, but none of it could be discussed. "How was your trip?"

Samantha slipped out the door, set her duffel on the porch, and hugged the woman.

"Oh, fine, fine. I missed my girl here too much, though."

"And the long drive didn't bother you?"

"Ach." She waved her hand in the air. "My husband and I used to drive a truck for years and years."

"Really?" I couldn't imagine her petite frame behind the wheel of a semi.

"Best vacations of our life. Course that was before Samantha and her dad moved across from us. By the time Samantha needed me, I was home all the time."

"Would you like to come in?" I opened the door farther. As long as she didn't see Craig, everything should be all right.

"No, thank you. We really should be going."

Samantha slung her bag onto her shoulder. "I thought your husband died years ago."

"My first husband, God rest his soul."

I smiled at her expression. "How many times have you been married, Mrs. Van Horn?"

"Just twice. Had enough love for two husbands, but not enough for three." She grinned, perfectly shaped dentures showing. "I had such a good visit with my sister. Thank you so much for keeping Samantha, but next time I'd like to take her with me and show her off."

We visited a few minutes more before they left. I stood on the sidewalk, waving good-bye as they pulled away.

Meandering to the kitchen, I thought of how Samantha must feel. She found her dad, whom she believed was dead, and had to leave him in three short days. Good thing Mrs. Van Horn loved her so much.

Craig couldn't care for her from a wheelchair anyway, and I wasn't sure if she'd let me. To her, I was the other woman. To me, her mother was. Though I doubted her thought processes had progressed that far yet.

I glanced at the calendar as I passed it. On Tuesday, the doctor planned to remove the casts. Soon, Craig would be able to move around again on his own, climb the stairs, and sleep in his own bed. He could start his vocational rehabilitation. Now he had more than himself to figure out, though. He needed to figure out how to gain custody of Samantha. And then what we would do with her.

Ask her to live with you.

Of course. What else could I do? I liked her. A lot. Even though she represented another hidden side of Craig, I could foster my protective instinct and grow to love her. She didn't deserve to be punished for what her father had done.

I shook my head. It was still difficult to conceive of the double life Craig had led. But I had seen the pictures for myself, the similarities of Craig and Samantha. The DNA results would only confirm what I already knew in my heart, that he was her father. Maybe that explained why I wanted to know Samantha better. Because she reminded me of Craig.

Coming around the corner of the kitchen, I saw Craig bang the phone on the granite counter. "What's the matter?"

"Phone call."

The doctor warned me that Craig's recovery might include mood swings. As of yet, I hadn't seen one, but this could have been the first. "Who was it? Why are you so upset?"

"Another hang-up call." Anger steamed from his body.

A disproportionate reaction to the circumstance. Maybe the stress of the weekend was getting to him. When I asked, words poured from him. I never heard him speak so quickly. After we talked for a few minutes, he suddenly changed the topic to gardening, though his anger still simmered under the surface.

A spray from the kitchen faucet should cool him down.

He persuaded me not to, but his mood lifted during our playfulness. I wrapped my arms around him and swayed, thinking of how many times in our early marriage we had danced to the radio in the dinky kitchen of our first apartment. We never danced in this house.

When the topic turned to Samantha, I said, "I think she should move in here."

He didn't express the excitement I thought he would, but I felt better to have said it aloud.

I went upstairs to the guest room and dissected the weekend and my conversation with Craig. He had played along with me, but I didn't feel as connected to him. Our closeness was fading and I wasn't sure why.

Stripping the sheets off the bed, I prayed for Samantha, for Craig, for the boys, for Mrs. Van Horn, and finally for myself.

I pictured him banging the phone against the counter so violently. Over a hang up? I prayed he would not become an angry man.

Hadn't I dimly heard him talking when I was chatting with Mrs. Van Horn? An unsettling doubt crept up my spine. Did he lie to me?

No. He promised to tell you the truth. You're just digging up the past.

But another voice piped up. *Wrong. You're a fool to believe him. He's done nothing but hurt you for years. Once a cheater, always a cheater.*

Holding the corners of the pillowcase, I shook the fabric until the pillow fell out onto the unmade bed. Why shouldn't I trust him? He hadn't done anything since his memory loss to make me suspicious of his current actions.

See? That's your problem. You've relegated his bad behavior to the past and disconnected it from who he is, but he's the same man who lied to you.

Gritting my teeth, I threw the pillowcase onto the pile. No one had called since the hang up. I could ask the phone company to redial the last number that called us. Of course Craig was telling the truth, but evidence would prove it. He wanted to put such faith in the DNA tests. What was the difference in searching out information to confirm my belief?

I did know he was telling the truth, didn't I? Why would he lie about such a dumb thing? It'd probably been a telemarketer, or the library calling to say a book was on hold, or a charitable organization asking for a pledge. Maybe their machines were slow to start playing after someone answered. Maybe Craig suffered undiagnosed hearing loss from the accident.

I tiptoed downstairs and sneaked into the kitchen. The phone was gone. Why had I put up such a fuss about only having one family phone so the boys' calls would be easier to monitor?

"Mom?"

I spun around. "Yes?"

Jamie stood behind me. "Bulldog's on the phone. He wants to know if I can go rafting with his family tomorrow."

Gulping, I steadied myself with a hand against the wall. "When did he call?"

"Just a second ago." Jamie waved the phone in my face. "So can I go?"

"What day?"

"Tomorrow. I already told you."

"Don't sass me, young man."

Jamie covered the mouthpiece before muttering, "Sorry."

"Where do they go rafting?"

"Down in Beaver Falls. We'd stay overnight at his aunt's house."

"Promise to stay out of trouble?"

"Mom! No, I'm going to get in as much trouble as I possibly can." He rolled his eyes.

"Fine. You can go."

"Thanks." He ambled away. "Yeah, she says I can. What do I need to bring?"

So much for getting proof of who called. Future hang ups would not be so lucky. We could spare the few cents the phone company charged for caller ID.

In a way, I was relieved to have the choice taken away from me. If Craig had caught me, what would I have told him? "I trust you, but I'm checking up on you."

No paradox there.

❍❍❍

I woke the next morning feeling out of sorts. After Bulldog and his parents picked up Jamie, I lounged around in my pajamas, reading the paper.

Craig rolled out of the guest bath, wiping his chin with a towel. Even though we still called it a guest bath, I had moved all of Craig's toiletries into it. Between his sponge baths—which he managed himself—and shaving, the little room created its fair share of laundry.

"What's the matter with you?" he asked.

"Nothing." I held the paper up to hide my face. "Why?"

"You don't usually laze around all morning. Are you feeling okay?"

I slapped the paper down and tossed my head. "Can't I just relax for once without the Spanish Inquisition?"

Craig held up his hands. "Sorry. Didn't mean to make you mad."

"I'm not mad." I stalked out of the breakfast nook. "I'm getting dressed and going to Sarah's."

Sarah and I hadn't made any plans. All I knew was I needed out of the house and away from Craig for a few hours. A few hours to be myself and not worry about whether trusting him was a smart choice or not.

"Can I come along?" Nicolas chased after me. "I just learned a new pool trick and I want to try it on their table. The ones at the arcade are in pretty bad shape."

Maybe he needed out of the stifling atmosphere, too. "Why not?"

I didn't tell Craig good-bye when we left.

❍❍❍

"Denise! What a surprise!" Sarah yanked me in for a powerful hug before turning herself on Nicolas. "Were you guys just in the neighborhood?"

"Something like that." I huffed into her house. At the edge of my peripheral vision, I caught her and Nicolas exchanging curious glances. "Is it okay if Nicolas plays some pool while we talk?"

Sarah nodded, and Nicolas scurried down to the basement, probably grateful to get away from his crazy mom.

"I'm going to fix you a cup of calming tea. You go sit." Sarah pushed me toward the contemporary microfiber couch.

Not a minute passed before she came out with two steaming mugs. White squares dangled from the strings of the tea bags, twisting in the air with the speed of her movement.

"Did you already have the kettle on?" I reached for the mug she held out to me.

"No. Ethan had an instant hot water faucet added for my—" She settled into a side chair and tucked her legs under her. "Oh, I guess it must have been a week or so ago."

"What were you going to say?"

"Nothing." She shook her head. "Doesn't matter."

The gears clicked in my brain. "I missed your birthday! Oh,

Sarah, I'm sorry. I've been so caught up in myself and my drama I forgot. Maybe I can make it up to you and take you out for—"

Sarah cut me off. "It doesn't matter, Denise. Our friendship is strong enough to withstand a little hiccup, I'm pretty sure. Just tell me —why are you here?"

Despite wanting to kick myself if it were humanly possible to reach my tush with my foot, I had to admit she asked the right question of me. "Craig is driving me bonkers. I couldn't handle being around him a single second more."

"What's the old trickster up to now?"

"That's just it. I can't tell." I moaned and set my mug on the side table. "I don't know if he's telling me the truth all the time or feeding me yet another line."

"Last time we really got to talk, you were raving about how different he seemed and how in love you were. What happened?"

I gathered my hair at the nape of my neck and stared down at the cream carpet. "There's so much junk in his past, Sarah. He had an affair, he took the money, and who knows what else."

"But you knew all that before."

I scoffed. "I have a fuller context now."

Sarah waited.

"I mean, how many affairs did he have?" A tear skated from my eye to the tip of my nose and hung there, quivering, before dropping into the plush carpet.

"Are you finding out about more women?" Joining me on the couch, she put an arm around my shoulder.

"Remember Samantha, the girl you met in the hospital?"

"Sure."

I faced Sarah so I could see the shock in her eyes, to know I wasn't making more out of this than a sane person would. "She's Craig's daughter."

Sarah gasped and dropped her arm. "But how could that be? You were told her father died in the accident, right? Who died, then?"

Shaking my head, I shrugged one shoulder. "Police make mistakes.

They mixed up the identification, I guess. There is no doubt in my mind she's Craig's daughter. When you see them next to each other, you'll believe it, too."

"I'm confused."

"Join the club."

"No, not that. When did you see them together?"

I grimaced. "I've really got to talk to you more. She spent the past weekend with us while her guardian was out of town. The second she saw Craig she started wailing about how he was her dad. She showed me pictures of her and Craig as she was growing up."

"But he was with your kids while they were growing up. I don't see how—"

"Samantha's dad was gone a lot. I think Craig was with her while I thought he was traveling or working late. He would have been with her mother while I was pregnant with Nicolas."

"No." Sarah's jaw fell open.

"We're going to have a DNA test done to prove it, which Craig also wants the boys to take."

"Why them too?"

"Maybe he doesn't think they're his."

Nicolas's head popped around the stairs. "Sarah, can I have a soda, please?"

"Help yourself." Sarah gestured toward the fridge.

Had he heard what I was saying? He didn't walk fast, or blush, or display any clue that he had, but I wasn't so sure. The boy could keep a lot hidden beneath the surface. He tromped back downstairs.

Once he disappeared from sight, I turned back to Sarah. "The silly thing is . . . that's not what's bothering me."

"There's more?" Sarah's eyebrows drew so close together they made a single line.

I laughed. "It's so dumb, but I think he lied to me about a hang-up call."

"Have you thought of talking to a professional? Because you need real help."

"You don't think he's lying to me? I'm not crazy for staying with him?" I stood and walked to the window. A blue jay chased some sparrows from a bird feeder. "He seems so honest and caring. I can't think of the last time he was sarcastic. And instead of attacking me, he's always complimenting me and looking at me with these lovey-dovey eyes."

"And what's wrong with that?"

"Nothing, if he weren't a liar and a cheat and a thief." I clutched my arms to my chest.

"You're right. He sounds horrible." Sarah slapped the armrest. "Kick him to the curb."

"I can't do it."

"Why not?" She came over to the window, stepped in front of me, and almost touched me nose-to-nose. Well, nose-to-sternum, really, because of our height differences, but she looked me straight in the eyes. "Because you love him. That's why. You're mad at the guy you knew before, you love this new man, and you need to reconcile the two."

"I know." Not moving, we stood for a moment.

My purse rang. The memory of that long-ago—at least it seemed like long ago—morning when I disrupted the church service stung my cheeks. What would I give to go back to that day? Would I beg Craig not to go hiking, declare my undying love, try to undo Craig's accident? Or would I allow it to happen, for him to suffer such pain, so I could get the new husband I loved even more?

"Excuse me." I dropped down on my haunches, fumbled for my phone, and flipped it open. "Hello?"

"May I speak with Denise Littleton, please?"

"Yes?"

"This is Dr. Brewster's office calling. We have the results of your tests back. Actually we've had them for a while. They were misplaced and we do apologize for the long wait."

Falling forward on my knees, I closed my eyes. "Yes?"

"Everything came back clean."

"I'm okay?"

"Yes, ma'am. Dr. Brewster would like to see you in a few months for your annual exam and he'll run another HIV test. Sometimes, if the sexual exposure was very recent, the test can show a false negative, but we don't expect your test result to change. Do you have any questions?"

"Uh . . . none I can think of."

"Call us back later if you do."

"Thank you." I held a fisted hand to my mouth. "Thank you so much."

"Have a nice day."

Lord God, how do I say thank You? How can I count all the blessings You have laid in my lap?

Sarah touched my shoulder. "Who was that?"

"My doctor." I tossed my hair back and smiled. "My STD tests came back and the whole panel was clean."

She grasped my hands and jumped up and down. "Oh, Denise, that's great!"

"I have to get home." I scrambled up, grabbed my purse, and yelled down the stairs. "Nicolas, come on. We've got to go." I spun round. "Sarah, thank you. You are so wise."

"I am?"

"Of course. I've been holding myself back from Craig. I've been punishing him for everything he's done in the past. Is that what God does?" I wagged my head from left to right. "No way. He believes in us when we turn over a new leaf. He stamps FORGIVEN on our record." I kissed her cheek. "I've got to go see my husband!"

Chapter Twenty-Eight

His

DENISE SLID the take-and-bake pizza in the oven and set the timer. “Nicolas, check this when the timer beeps, pop any big bubbles, and give it a few more minutes.”

“Okay, Mom.” He dribbled a basketball on the tile.

She put her hands on her hips. “How many times have I asked you not to do that in the house?”

“Sorry.” He tucked it under an arm.

I shot my arm out and punched the ball away, sending both of us on a mad scramble to get it. Of course my wheelchair couldn’t compete with a sixteen-year-old’s speed or agility, and he easily recovered possession.

“Craig!” My wife was not amused, though her voice seemed to have lost an edge lately, to have softened and warmed.

“I’ll show you the trick to a great jump shot as soon as I get out of these casts.” I thrust a finger at Nicolas.

"If you can get the ball from me." Smiling, he held it just out of my reach.

Denise ran a hand through her hair. "I guess we're ready to go, Craig."

"Be good." I stretched up and pulled on Nicolas's ear. "See you later."

"Can I call Heather while you're gone?"

"You can call her, but don't bend the rules." Denise kissed him on the cheek. "No friends over."

"Yes, Mom." He followed us out the door and helped me into the Denali.

As we pulled onto the street, I waved to him until he went back into the house. "Where are you taking me?"

"I want it to be a surprise."

"Everything is a surprise to me, sweetie."

Laughing, she nodded. "I guess it is, so I'm safe to tell you it's your favorite restaurant."

"Taco Bell?"

"A little more upscale."

"Wendy's?"

"You're getting a teeny, tiny bit warmer."

"Japanese?"

She stuck out her tongue. "I hate the smell of fish."

We ended up at a fancy steakhouse. I ordered a pasta dish and didn't explain why when Denise shot a questioning look my way. I didn't want to dampen her enthusiasm by reminding her how difficult it was for me to chew some foods still, how gnawing on a steak would be pure torture.

Over dessert, a nice soft bread pudding, she took my hand. "Honey, I need to apologize." She clutched her cloth napkin with her other hand. "When I'm with you, I feel cherished and honored and loved. But then these mind games start where I convince myself I'm falling for another lie. I argue with myself, yet I always pull back from you."

"It's understandable. I've put you through a lot."

"Not really. See . . ." She stroked her thumb over the back of my hand. "The memories of how you used to be are what haunt me, not who you are now. I need to forgive you for the past and move on."

"Move on?"

"I want to date."

I jerked my hand back. "Who? I thought you just said you want to be with me."

Her eyes grew wide. "I do." A grin burst over her face. "I meant I'd like to date you. Like this, tonight. Giving you a memory of our courtship, falling in love all over again."

"Oh." Fanning my hot face, I shoved my fears aside. "Sounds good. Let's date."

"This isn't normally a first-date discussion—or at least I hope it isn't. I got my test results back."

"And?" She wouldn't be talking about romantic dates if she were sick. If I had made her sick.

"Nothing bad."

The server brought the bill and put it on the end of the booth. Neither of us made a move to take it. I was content to hold Denise's hand and stare into her eyes for the rest of my life.

"One of the traits I love best about you is how you treat me." Denise's gaze fell to my mouth, and I itched to kiss her. "You're sweet and honest, which makes me feel safe."

Honest. Me, the man who'd spoken with his ex-lover and hidden it from his wife. Denise blurred as my eyes lost focus. A movie played against the backdrop of my mind.

Naomi, dressed in scrubs, bumping playfully against me as I made notes in a patient's chart. The scene repeated, the film looping together. In the short clip, I didn't see myself react to her flirtatiousness. Motionless, except for the pen in my hand, I kept making the note.

"Craig?"

I shook my head, and Denise appeared in the center of a black tunnel in front of me. The colored portion of the world expanded until the blackness faded away. My stomach rolled. "I'm sorry. All of a sudden, I'm not feeling so good. Could we go home?"

"Sure." Denise laid the bill on my lap and touched my forehead with the back of her hand. "You do feel a little hot."

Tell her.

"I'd like to lie down."

After paying the bill, she rolled me out of the restaurant and up the concrete ramp from the lower entrance. The mental projector kicked on again and I saw myself vaulting over a concrete divider. I smelled diesel, the fumes of passing cars, and a fetid human odor. Whooshes and whizzes signaled the traffic passing. The movie played at a tilted angle. As I tipped my head to straighten the frame, it stopped.

Denise was waiting to help me into my seat. "Are you about to faint?"

"No." I tried to sound offended and manly. "I'm fine."

"You're pasty and sweaty, Craig. Whatever's coming on is coming on fast." She drove me home, gave me a sleeping pill, and tucked me in. "See you in the morning. Call my cell if you need me during the night." Denise set Nicolas's phone down, which he was letting us borrow at night to use as a walkie-talkie system. "Or I could sleep on the couch? Be closer to you?"

Swallowing hard, I shook my head and closed my eyes. How would I keep these visions from her if she were not even ten feet away? I promised to tell her when my memory returned, but these were not images I could share. How did they play out? What was I doing at the side of the road? Until I knew the context for these images, I wouldn't share them.

Yes, the context of the scene involving Naomi and me was clear. But that was the very reason why Denise didn't need to hear about it. She knew I'd been having an affair with Naomi, but she didn't want a play-by-play of it, did she?

Shouldn't you let her decide?

Denise kissed my cheek, and I heard her creep away. The screen lit up again and the whirl of the past filled my ears. Zooming along a highway, the wind whistling past my ears. A dragon of dread breathing fire into my belly. My fate waiting for me to grab hold of it.

Of what? What was just round the next bend in the road?

And I was driving, but I was in the passenger seat, too. *God, I can't make sense of how I could be both Craig and William. And if I am, who died in the accident?*

Still questioning, I fell asleep.

❍❍❍

Heavy footsteps down the stairs woke me. The sun lit the room brighter than I believed I could have slept through.

"Morning, Dad." Nicolas waved from the kitchen, leaned into the refrigerator, and emerged with an orange. "You excited?"

Yawning, I rubbed the remainders of sleep from my eyes. "Huh?"

"About today? Getting your casts off?"

Today? With Denise and Nicolas running off to Sarah's house, my wife's change of heart and promise . . . and the glimpses playing in my mind, I had forgotten this was the day.

Nicolas ripped a section of peel from the orange and broke into a paraphrased, falsetto song. "They say that waking up is ha-ard to do."

"What are you doing up so early anyway? And why are you so happy?"

Tossing a slice of orange into his mouth, he winked. "Mom's letting me see Heather today. She's picking me up and we're going to hang out at the mall, but I gotta be back by one o'clock."

A horn honked and Nicolas bolted toward the door.

"Have fun," I called after him.

A faint, "Bye, Dad," echoed back to me.

I spun ninety degrees and let my legs slip to the floor. After today, the weight of the casts would be gone. My therapist cautioned me that I would need more PT to regain my strength, but I couldn't wait to walk on my own. Later, as I rubbed shaving cream over my chin, sitting in the wheelchair with a hand mirror propped on my lap, I thought of how I would stand and lean into the mirror the next time I shaved. How I'd be able to reach my own glass in the kitchen. How I'd put an Andrea Bocelli CD in the surround sound and slow dance with Denise. How I'd climb the stairs and open the doors to our room—that part got a little hazy because I still didn't know what it looked like—and guide my wife to the bed.

By the time Denise wheeled me into the doctor's office, I was rubbing my hands together with excitement. "Do you want to come back with me and watch?" I waggled my eyebrows.

She wrinkled her nose. "I don't do well with smells."

"You think they're going to stink?"

"Honey, Jamie broke his arm trying to keep up with some older boys at the park about two years ago. When they took off his cast, it stunk worse than his gym bag."

"I'm offended." I crossed my arms, trying to scowl. "I'm no preteen boy, sweating and getting dirt and grime down my casts."

"Five dollars if you detect an unpleasant odor." She stuck her hand out.

"Deal." I shook it. "You'd better come in to make sure I don't lie."

"Don't need to." Denise smiled. "I told you last night, I trust you."

A needle pricked the balloon of happiness inside my chest.

The nurse called me into the back and helped me into a room. The doctor appeared soon after with a small electric saw in his hand. "Good morning, Dr. Littleton. Good to see you. Are you happy these things will be coming off today?"

"Depends. Is that an evil glint in your eye?"

Raising the saw above his head, he cackled. "Don't you worry. It's just a leg or two."

I shrunk back, then thrust my chest forward. "I'm a man. I can take it."

Dr. Rossing grinned. "When I compare you to that broken man I first saw at the hospital, it's a miracle."

"I feel like a miracle." More than just my physical health had been given back to me. My marriage, my emotions, my ability to function in a memory-recalling world . . . all threaded into the cord of my life. My spiritual aspect seemed to have weakened, though. Understandable, since I hadn't been seeking God's will lately. I let lies come between not only Denise and me, but between God and me, as well. The only glaring empty spot was my vocational abilities.

Soon enough. I'll figure that out when the time comes.

"Your therapist says you've been doing a great job, and your X-rays looked terrific."

"So the casts get to go?"

He flashed me two thumbs-up, and I whooped.

The doctor made quick work of the job, and soon I sat in the passenger side of the van with a peculiar smell stuck in my nose. The flesh on my legs had shrunk, leaving two aspen-white twigs. The hair had darkened and curled tightly in its moist atmosphere. Even though I strictly followed the doctor's orders about not getting the casts wet, I couldn't stop the natural sweat that formed beneath the plaster molds.

"Are you going to pay with cash or by check?" Denise laughed.

"Can you smell it right now?"

In response, she tapped two switches and both windows opened.

"Do you still love me?" Reaching over, I slipped my hand onto the nape of her neck and massaged.

"Always." She moaned. "That feels incredible."

"I can't pay off my debt because I don't have any money."

"I'll pay it off for you." Flipping the turn signal on, she pulled into a Dairy Queen drive-thru. "You can buy us both a huge Blizzard."

My mouth watered at the thought of a peanut butter cup smashed into creamy vanilla ice cream. "I haven't had one in ages."

Denise slapped her thigh. "Yet another random piece of Americana you remember. You have such a firm grasp on all the details except what's really important, don't you?" Shaking her head, she inched up on the car in front of us in line.

"Sacrilege. Ice cream is supremely important." I squeezed her neck more tightly. "Apologize at once."

"Uncle, uncle!"

"And now you're telling me I'm your uncle. Which is it, Denise, am I your husband or your uncle?"

She snorted with laughter, and the car ahead of us pulled forward. Drawing up to the speaker, she turned to me. "You want your usual Nerds with cookie dough?"

"You're kidding."

"Nope. Want something else?"

"Peanut butter cup."

She smiled, ordered two, and put her hand on my leg. "That's my favorite. You never used to touch it because you said peanut butter made your throat itch."

Chapter Twenty-Nine

Hers

TEASING ONE SECOND, quiet the next. I couldn't predict Craig's behavior when it followed no reasonable pattern. *Funny. That's what he used to say about me.* I paid for our treats at the first window and stopped at the second.

"Here you are." The employee handed me two cups and slid the window closed.

I drove to the top of the hill and parked on the street in the shade of a huge elm. The city spread out before us, heat waves distorting the view. Up above it all, I felt peaceful seeing the crawl of traffic and knowing we were almost home. We sat, hearing nothing but the scrape of our spoons against our cups or a smack of enjoyment.

Craig put his half-empty Blizzard in the cup holder and scratched at his leg. Much of his tan had worn off during his hospital stay, but the stark whiteness of his calves revealed how dark the rest of his skin still was.

"Are you okay?"

He nodded, gazing out at the world below.

"Do you want to do anything else?"

"We've done enough celebrating. Let's go home." He rested his elbow on the master console, dropping his head to his hand.

That was fine for him to think ice cream was the extent of our celebration. How was he supposed to know I was planning a party to celebrate his recovery? Many of his friends from church and the country club had stayed away, unsure how to treat him if he didn't remember them. Which he wouldn't. But I'd found a way to bypass the awkwardness and still bring people who cared about him together.

A takeoff of *This Is Your Life.* Instead of everyone worrying about what to talk about, how to adjust their view of Craig without treating him differently, they were going to put on a little show—a speech, skit, song, or picture show—to explain who they were and why they cared about Craig.

Maybe the barrage of information would jump-start Craig's memories. I grinned even thinking about it. Sarah, who'd been thrilled when I called her with the idea the night before, was taking care of all the invitations and setting up the catering. I needed to finalize the guest list when I got home.

I turned the key in the ignition and the Denali purred. It was my baby, my favorite gift from Craig. When the car sensed my key, it knew my preferences: which areas to heat on the seat, what radio station to tune in, and how far the seat should be from the pedals.

The car knew me better than Craig ever had.

When we got home, Craig crutched his way up the steps and in the front door. From the living room came gunshots and the sound of breaking glass.

"Can we move the video games back upstairs?" I begged Craig with my eyes. "Now that you're not confined to bed you can play them in the bonus room again, right?"

Nicolas wasn't playing alone, as I had thought. Jamie sprawled across the open hide-a-bed.

"Jamie! You're home." I rushed over and pressed a kiss into his hair.

Bumping my knee into the metal corner of the bed frame, I yelped. Tomorrow, I was taking back my living room. No more messy sheets always in view, no more awkward shuffle around the coffee table, and no more sleeping alone. I savored the last thought. Was I ready for that? Did Craig know who I was enough for it to mean what it should? I thought so.

"Mom! The alien almost got me 'cause you were in the way."

"Did you have a good time?" I sat down next to him and scratched his back. As a toddler, he would only nap if I scratched until he fell asleep.

He winced and pulled away.

"Did you get a sunburn?" I yanked his shirt up in the back to display a fiery, cherry-red patch of skin. "I thought I told you to use sunscreen."

"I put it on everywhere I could reach, but the middle of my back was too hard."

"Jamie, you should have asked someone else to do your back."

"Yeah. Like, 'Bulldog, can you rub lotion all over me?' Or better yet, ask his mother." He made a face.

"Hey, Mom." Nicolas stretched out his legs and crossed his ankles. "Someone called. We let the machine get it."

"Why?" I stood.

Jamie spoke as quickly as he could. "This ginormous monster was chasing us and we couldn't pause or we'd lose our fighting momentum."

Craig limped his way to a recliner and rubbed his legs. "Look, boys. I got my casts off."

They both turned toward him for a millisecond.

"Cool."

"Awesome."

I walked to the answering machine, punched the play button, and leaned over to hear the message over the game.

"Call me."

Click.

Sounded like Sarah. I dialed her number and walked to the office.

"Hello?"

"Sorry no one answered. The boys were too involved in their video game to pick up the phone." I whispered, "Were you calling about Craig's party?"

"It's a surprise party, Denise. Why would I call you when I know Craig's always around? But I was hoping to talk to you. Should I go with the beef or chicken dish?"

"Um . . . chicken. You sure you didn't call?"

"Positive."

"Okay, I'd better go. Bye."

"Bye." A question rang in her voice. We'd never had such a short discussion, but now all I could think about was who had called.

Back in the kitchen, I listened to the message twice more and couldn't figure it out. "Boys, pause the game. Listen to this and tell me if you know who it is."

Jamie dropped his head back until all I saw was a lot of neck.

"It won't kill you."

He jerked his head up. "Mom, you know nothing about this game. We probably *are* going to die."

"It'll just take a minute."

I played it again.

"Some woman," Nicolas said.

"Thanks a lot. Go on with your game."

As I turned, I caught the expression on Craig's face. Ashen and as pale as his legs, he looked nauseated.

My stomach seized into a gristly ball. "You know what, boys?" My words were tightly clipped. "I'm tired of hearing the sounds of death. Just unplug the whole thing and go upstairs."

They obeyed without speaking and filed passed me. Rarely did I use such a tone of voice, and they knew I demanded instant obedience when I did. I never broke off staring at their father, who gazed at his hands.

As soon as they were out of earshot, I stuck my hands on my hips.

"Craig, do you know who the woman is on the message?"

Rubbing his hands together, blinking, he opened and closed his mouth as if trying to say something.

"Your silence is incriminating you." I clenched my jaw. "Who is she? Were you talking to her as Samantha left?"

"It's not what it looks like," he mumbled.

"Of course it's not." I pointed to my face. "Do I look stupid? Because I'm not. I can clearly see what's happening here, what my gut has been trying to tell me all along."

"No, Denise." He shook his head. "Naomi called, but—"

"Naomi?" I shrieked. "You liar!" And here I thought we'd been building a new life together when all he'd been up to was his old tricks.

"All I wanted was information from her."

Pure, righteous anger seared through me. "Lies, lies, lies. You're full of them!"

"She can tell us why I was parked on the side of the road. She knows where I was going. She knows about William."

"I'm sure she knows more than I'll ever know about you because I don't care anymore." I stomped my foot. "I don't want you here."

"Please, Denise. If you'll calm down, I can explain it all, and you'll know I wasn't doing anything with her. There's no reason for me to leave."

"Go to Naomi, for all I care. I'm done with you." I slashed my hands in front of me. "Done."

"Come on, Denise. I don't have anywhere to go. I don't even have a car."

"I'll drop you off. You remember where she lives, don't you?" I stabbed a finger in the air. "In fact, I think you remember it all. This whole amnesia deal has been a charade. You faked it."

"Why?" Craig stood and used his crutches to wobble toward me. "Why would I do that? I have nothing to gain by losing you."

"Maybe you thought you wouldn't lose me if you lied. Then you wouldn't have to tell me about Naomi or Samantha." I gaped at him for a second. "I bet Samantha's mother isn't really dead. You probably have her hidden away and bribed to keep it all secret. That's where the money is, isn't it?"

"I don't remember anything, Denise! That's the only reason I talked to Naomi. Because I *want* to remember, and she might have the missing piece."

"It doesn't matter anymore. You lied." I spoke through clenched teeth. "Your lies are poison in my bones. I refuse to be with someone I can't trust."

"It was one lie. Are you going to throw me out because I lied to you once? Our marriage can disappear because of one lie?"

"Our marriage disappeared a long time ago, Craig; it's just been a pleasant diversion the past month or two pretending we could save it. You undermined everything I've been discovering about you. You acted like the old Craig."

"I will never cheat on you. I promise." His eyes pleaded with me.

"Your words aren't worth a penny. I want a separation."

"I don't, Denise." He choked back tears. "I want to be with you for the rest of my life."

I sneered. "It's no life when there's no trust, no genuine love. You've used me as a housekeeper, a nanny, a business partner, a prostitute for too long. I was beginning to think you really loved me, but—"

"I do love you." He came forward, brushed my hair from my face.

I stepped back. "I'll let you stay for tonight. By tomorrow, you need to have something figured out because I'm not going to let this drag on and on for days."

"And then what? Can't we talk about this?"

"I'll set up a meeting with Pastor Miles early next week. We'll get his perspective on the best plan from here on out."

"Denise." He reached out again, stroked my lower lip with his thumb. "Please, I beg you, don't do this. Let's talk after you cool down, and I can tell you the whole story."

Luckily for him, I was a mature woman or I would have bitten off his thumb.

Chapter Thirty

His

ELBOWS ON KNEES, I hunched on the edge of the hide-a-bed. The house was quiet and dark, everyone else having gone to sleep a long time ago. I swallowed back a wave of emotion. Fear danced in the shadows of the drapes, springing out and spinning me in a dizzying whirlwind of desperation, then dropping back into hiding, leaving me breathless.

I had lost her. I lied about Naomi and lost Denise.

What a stupid thing to do! Why didn't I consider how fragile our new bond was? What would it have hurt to tell her the truth? We could have staged another phone call with Naomi and arranged it so Denise could listen in. We could have scripted questions designed to uproot the hidden truth. *We*. But, because *I* had kept it secret and deceived Denise, *I* would be alone.

What was I going to do? What kind of job could I find? Where would I stay? I didn't know anyone in the world that Denise hadn't introduced me to. Pastor Miles might have been able to line up a spare room for me to sleep in, but how would I pay for it?

My body still felt broken and battered. I had months of physical therapy ahead of me until I'd feel healthy and strong. My leg bones ached fiercely from carrying unaccustomed weight. With my tongue, I pushed on the inside of my cheek. The scarring stretched and pulled, zinging pain across my face.

When would I see the kids? Jamie and Nicolas had to have heard parts of the argument. Did they agree with Denise's decision? Did they hold the lie against me, too?

It didn't really matter. I wasn't a good role model for them anyway. Did I really want them to end up like me? Cheating on their wives, lying to their families? I let them down as well. The less time I spent with them, the better.

And Samantha? She was better off without me, too. I had nothing to offer her.

I should just walk out of their lives forever. I had lost their trust and knew no way to regain it.

What about my *trust? Where have I been putting it?*

Not in the Lord, that much was sure. In Denise, probably. Trusting her to lead me to who I was, to care for me, to stand by me. And in medicine. Trusting it to heal me, bring back my memory, strengthen my body.

What of my soul? Didn't it need strengthened?

My deceit, bad choices, and wrongly placed trust . . . all led to ruin. Debris and destruction surrounded me: the remnants of marriage and fathering, dreams of the future.

Take me to the past, Lord. I've failed, trying to do this on my own. I don't want to be weak anymore. Please make me strong. I don't want to lie to myself or anyone else. Please make a truth teller out of me. I don't want to feel alone. Please, please let me feel Your presence.

Darkness pervaded the house, but a glimmer of hope floated in my heart. I was never truly alone. God was by my side. He could work the whole situation out in a way to bring glory to Him, but I needed to walk the narrow path, not jump off into the thicket of dishonesty I was so used to tramping through.

Lord, take me through the darkness. Let those visions from last night return, but make them clear and true. Show me who I was, then show me who I am, who You want me to be.

I lay back against the propped-up pillows and closed my eyes, focusing on the memory of diesel smells and the sound of traffic. *Let me remember the day I almost died and show me the reason I lived.*

The convertible materialized on the screen of my mind, sunlight bouncing off its glossy finish. I held a clump of wildflowers in my hand, wrapping string around the stems. Throwing the bundle into the car, I walked to the front. At the same time, cement crumbled beneath my hand and a queer taste filled my mouth. I staggered toward myself, gripping my belly.

"Back on the road, man. We're almost there." I throw the flowers into the car.

I wiped my mouth on the back of my hand. "Give me another minute."

I jerked upright on the mattress, the last picture freeze-framed in my memory. How could I talk to myself? How could I watch myself walk? Distinctly, I felt the grit of the cement, tasted the residue of my vomit. Clearly, I spoke to myself.

Were there two of me? Not really two bodies, but two selves?

Samantha said my name was William and I was her father. That I lived with her in a little home one town away where I gardened and traveled for work. I saw those pictures. I remembered her hugs.

Denise said my name was Craig and I was her husband. That I lived with my family in an upscale neighborhood where I worked as a dentist. When I wasn't running around with other women, that is. I saw those pictures, too. I had fallen in love with my boys and my wife all over again.

I was two people, two separate personalities. Could it be? Did I have a split in my psyche? Had I been Craig one week and William the next? When my memory returned, would both of me come tagging along?

Denise would think it was just another ploy to explain my behavior, to excuse my actions.

I threw off the sheet and shuffled on crutches to the sliding glass door. The sculpted bushes, the lawn meandering between the raised flower beds. Peaceful and tamed. Unlocking the latch, I slid the door open and stepped onto the limestone patio. My bare feet recoiled from the cold rock. They had been encased in plaster for so long that the mere sensations of the outside world threatened to overwhelm them. Stepping into the prickly grass, I paused. The heat of the day radiated from the earth. The bellied call of a bullfrog punctuated the crickets' song.

Loamy air filled my lungs, freshened my mind. A bistro table stood on a bricked platform near the back of the yard. I made my way toward it. A gust of wind raced through the leaves, rustling them above my head, then died away.

If I closed my eyes and listened, it was almost as if I could hear the plants growing around me, the buds forming, the roots tunneling.

The chair screeched on the brick as I dragged it back from the table. An appreciation for nature: both Craig and William seemed to share that. After all, long ago, we were formed for a garden.

Until man lost the garden by his deceit.

My deceit. Being both Craig and William. But the police identified the dead body as William. There had been two people by the car that day. Who was the extra body? Why didn't I see the other man in my flashes?

Maybe I made up the policeman. Maybe I conjured up Denise and Samantha and Pastor Miles, too. The entire world as I knew it could be in my tiny, messed-up brain. Maybe I wasn't sitting on a wrought-iron chair in the middle of my backyard under an oak tree in the dead of the night. Maybe I was curled in a fetal position on a bed of a psychiatric hospital, sedated, dreaming, imagining, living without living.

But You are real, God. Even if You are the only One who is.

Digging my fingers through the grass, I fumbled around until I brought up a smooth acorn. I rolled it in the palm of my hand, pricked the stem of the cap against the pad of my thumb.

Tell me what I need to hear, Lord Jesus. I trust You to let me know what I need to know. And I trust You to bring me through it, no matter what the truth is. Show me what is real and what is false. Take me into the darkness. Be my light.

Nothing happened.

I stayed in the garden for an hour or so, gauging time by the movement of the moon. The white orb looked uniform, but closer inspection revealed dark patches, the very texture of the land visible across the deep darkness of space. What secrets lurked in the cracks and crevices of the surface? Who would have the resources, the courage, to explore them all?

I limped back inside and locked the door, determined to get some sleep. Tomorrow would be a hard day. If I didn't get any rest, it would be even harder.

The refrigerator kicked on, humming, and the ice maker dumped a new load of ice into the bin. After so many nights of sleeping in the living room, the sound became a sort of comfort, a lullaby. Heaviness cloaked my mind and a dream crept toward me.

The dental office. Naomi bumping her hip against me. A bright light above me. The light morphed into a longer fluorescent. I wandered the aisle of a convenience store, between M&Ms and Doritos, fountain drinks and beer. Flicked a lighter and dropped it back into the bin of blue, red, and gold cylinders. Stepped out into the hot sun, stagnant air clutching my throat.

Blowing, loosening the grip, wind grazing through my hair. Driving along the freeway, stomach empty, soul hurting. And my denying it. Telling myself what I was doing was right. Unable to think of those I would be hurting. Focusing on what lay ahead. Resolving to move forward. Ignoring God's prodding to slam on the brakes, jerk the wheel around.

I woke enough to throw the blanket off my sweaty body and fell back into the dream.

Body bracing against the swerve of the car as it pulled to the edge of the freeway. Standing in front of the car. Tires screeching, metal crunching. My arms flailing. The crunch of my legs. Screams piercing the air. Skidding, bouncing along the asphalt. Slamming doors. Hands pulling me along the ground. Despair clawing at my heart.

I bolted upright, chest heaving.

I knew.

I remembered it all, every disgusting detail, every confusing choice. How trapped I felt, desperate for any option. How weak and manipulated by my situation I had become.

Denise was right. I didn't belong with her and the kids, didn't deserve a stunning home or a second chance. I had to leave, to let her have a life without me.

In the morning, I'd pack up, try to put into words how sorry I was, say good-bye, and walk out the door.

It was the only choice, now that I knew.

Chapter Thirty-One

Hers

THE PATIO DOOR clinked open. Was a burglar sneaking in? I checked the doors every night before I went upstairs—which used to be Craig's habit—but not tonight. If I had slipped into the living room, I might have had to speak to Craig.

I'd rather let the house be broken into.

With a fingertip, I pulled the curtain away from the window. A man stood on the grass. I gasped and tried to remember where my cell phone was. He limped toward the back of the yard, and I realized it was Craig. Of course. He couldn't sleep any more than I could.

His white T-shirt glowed in the moonlight, as did the white stripes on his boxer shorts. He slumped down in the chair, laying his crutches on the grass by his side. After a while, he reached into the grass and studied something in his hand.

He looked so lonesome, so forlorn. Was he thinking about me?

Probably. Though it could just be a selfish slant of where he would go and what he would do since I was kicking him out.

Nicolas had asked me to come into his room when I told him good night.

"What's going on with you and Dad?"

"I'm not sure." I told him as I picked up a dirty glass to take to the kitchen. But I thought of Craig, and put it down.

"Jamie and I could hear you screaming at him. You've never yelled like that before."

"I shouldn't have done that. Between the accident and your father's amnesia, I've been under a lot of stress." I sighed. "We're still sorting things out."

"Are you getting divorced?" He fiddled with his headphones.

"Can we talk about this tomorrow, Nicolas? I'm so tired."

He nodded, a quick, barely perceptible movement.

"Thanks, baby boy." I kissed his head. "I promise, I'll sit down with you and Jamie tomorrow and explain as much as I know."

I had been so grateful to escape that conversation a few hours ago. Now, as I looked down from the window at Craig in the backyard, I struggled with asking him to leave. The boys needed their dad. Would he still want to see them if I threw him out? Or would it be easier for him to take Samantha and go create a new world with just the two of them as a family?

Maybe he could stay. The office could be turned into another bedroom without too much work. Samantha could still come and live in the upstairs room. All of the children would have their father with them.

When he ogled me and said he loved me, I believed him. *Idiot!* The man was having secret phone calls with a lover. Or ex-lover, if he was telling the truth.

Do you really think he wants to be with other women?

A part of me wanted to believe his denial. To sit down with Pastor Miles and work through the conflict. To see why Craig lied. To discover what he had lied about.

Yes, I accused him of faking the amnesia. Honestly, though, I didn't think he was capable of fooling the medical community and keeping up such a charade for so long.

Lord, please help his memory come back. Show me when he's telling the truth and when he's lying. Make him transparent. If there's any way, make our marriage work. Forgive me for deciding to make him leave without asking You first. And I'm sorry for letting my temper take over. Palm flat, I placed my hand on the glass. *Comfort Craig.*

After he came in, I crawled under my sheets and stared up at the ceiling until the sky lightened and darkness melted back into early morning shadows. My stomach churned the whole time. A showdown seemed inevitable, as if Craig and I were two cowboys, placed back-to-back, counting off paces for each year of marriage, knowing we were about to spin around and fire a shot.

I slid on my slippers and padded downstairs to start the coffee. If Craig were awake, we could talk before the boys got up.

Dressed in a polo shirt and khakis, he was already pouring a mug of coffee when I entered the kitchen. He glanced up. "Hope you don't mind."

I shrugged and took the mug he offered to me.

"Can we talk?"

"Before we do that . . ." I poured some creamer and stirred its whiteness into the dark brown until the liquid changed to a uniform tan. "I need to say how sorry I am for how I treated you yesterday. No matter what you've done, I shouldn't have screamed at you and cut you off."

"It's okay, Denise. You've been amazingly strong and kind despite all the circumstances. I don't blame you for blowing your top."

I led the way to the nook, slid onto the window seat, and curled my legs up underneath me.

Craig propped his crutches against the wall, took a kitchen chair, and turned it to face me. "After all you've been through . . ." He rubbed a hand over his face. "I have more to tell you. It's going to be very, very difficult to hear."

The clock on the western town's tower struck high noon.

"I've remembered."

He spun and pointed his gun at my heart. I waited, suspended in time, for the shot to burst out of the muzzle of the gun.

"I'm not Craig."

As the hammer hit the gunpowder, a cloud of smoke exploded. The bullet pierced my body. I jerked back and slumped against the window. "What?"

He stared at me, compassion in his gaze.

I cleared my throat. "What are you talking about?"

"My memory came back to me. I'm not your husband. I'm not Craig."

"Yes, you are."

"My name is William Rodain."

"No." I shook my head violently. "We've talked about this. Somehow, you're both of them. When we get the DNA tests done, it will all get sorted out."

"I wondered about that, Denise. I tried to figure out how I could be both Craig and William, to lead a double life. But there were two huge problems with that idea."

"The only problem I see is what you chose to do with your life, our marriage. That's the problem."

He continued as if he didn't hear me. "The first problem is that I remember talking to myself. In some visions I saw myself walking, interacting with Naomi, driving a car. But most of my memories came from inside of me, where I couldn't see myself, but heard and felt what happened around me instead."

"Imaginations can tweak memories." I sipped my sweetened coffee, trying to rid my mouth of the bitter taste coating the back of my throat. "I remember events I never attended because Sarah described them so well, I felt like I was there. It makes perfect sense for you to remember yourself in different ways."

"Before I remembered everything about myself, I was trying to make the pieces fit together, too. Because I wanted to be with you. So

I wondered if I had multiple personalities, or some kind of mental disorder."

I straightened. "It would explain how you could have been so different with Samantha than you were with us."

"But there's the other problem. Two men were by that car. I can't be both men. One of us died in the accident. The police found a man's body, and I'm the one who lived."

I followed the train of thought. If only one man lived and he claimed to be William, then . . . "No!" Strength left my limbs, and my wrist collapsed, spilling hot coffee over my nightgown. "If you're William, then Craig is dead." The liquid spread, burning my thighs.

"That's what I'm trying to say in the kindest way possible." He snatched a napkin off the table and dabbed at my lap.

I grabbed the napkin. "A woman knows her own husband," I huffed. "It would be ridiculous to think I would bring you home from the hospital if you weren't my husband."

"It's not as far-fetched as it sounds, Denise. You were supposed to believe—you were led to believe—I was Craig."

"Okay." I smoothed my hair back and stood. "I'm calling your doctor. He didn't mention delusions, but a brain injury could spark them, I'm sure."

"Let me tell you everything. If you still think I'm loony, I'll call the doctor myself."

Was he safe? Should I give him a few minutes to talk crazy, or would that put my life in his hands? He didn't seem like he was about to go psycho with a kitchen knife. In fact, he looked calm. Calm . . . and sad.

Gathering the wet section of material away from my skin, I sat back down. "I guess it can wait a minute or two."

Craig-who-said-he-was-William closed his eyes and spoke in a monotone. "I met your husband at the dentist's office. I'd lost my job, my wife had died only a short time before, and my innocent little girl had been diagnosed with cancer. During the night, I ground my teeth so badly my jaw ached all day long."

My tongue ran along my molars, imaging the grinding I'd done lately. I filed the random facts of his wife's death in my mind. It matched what Samantha said, but he could have found that out from her and worked it into his crazy story.

"When I gave my name to the receptionist and told her I was there to see Dr. Littleton, she laughed. I just stood in front of the desk until she settled down. Finally, she said, 'Okay, I'll play along, Mr. Rodain.' She even winked at me before she took me back to a room."

I held up a hand. "Craig, I hope your appointment was lovely, but we already know William was your 'patient' no one except Naomi ever saw. You've just created this scenario to fit your newest version of your life."

"Not Craig. William." He put his hand on his chest. "This is where the story starts, so this is where I'm beginning. The receptionist was Naomi, of course."

"I figured." I crossed my legs.

"She was still giggling when the dentist knocked on the door. A double take later, she met him and they whispered behind me. When Dr. Littleton introduced himself to me, he already had his mask on."

"Can I tell you how strange it is to hear you talk about yourself in third person?"

"I'm not talking about myself. I'm talking about your husband."

"Craig." I shook my head.

He leaned forward. "Humor me. Call me William. What harm could it do to indulge me?"

"If I encourage you, what will you come up with next?" I stood up. "Is this going to take much longer? Because I'm hungry."

He gestured toward the kitchen. "Make yourself at home."

I harrumphed, slammed a frying pan onto the stovetop, and turned it on high. "I'll make you breakfast before I call the doctor."

His voice was as soft as fleece. "Like I said, you've been so kind to me."

For a few moments, I stood motionless. His tone of voice undid me. I knifed a blob of bacon grease into the hot pan. A tear fell, sizzling in the grease. "Why are you doing this to me? After everything else, why make more up?"

"I don't want to hurt you, Denise. It's the last thing I want to do on this earth. And I don't expect you to believe this right away. But there's one thing I've realized in this mess. I'm not going to be weak. I'm not going to take the easy way out. The Lord will make a better way for me if I am faithful to the truth."

Sniffing back more tears, I cracked half a dozen eggs into a glass bowl. "I'd give every cent you left to our name to know what the truth is."

"I didn't see your husband again for a few months, but his office was closer to home, so I switched to him. Plus, he helped me manage the grinding."

I jammed the whisk into the eggs. "Yes, you're a great dentist."

"So your husband and I talked the first day. Or I made guttural sounds when he asked questions. They must offer a course at dental school on how to interpret people whose mouths are stuffed full of hands."

I shrugged. Craig really could decipher an amazing amount from what his patients told him. Back in the early days of our marriage, I would test him. I'd lie back on the old ratty, flowered couch we found on the curbside during one of our garbage day drive-arounds. I'd take a huge bite of apple and tell him a story. Afterward, I quizzed him and he always aced it.

I splashed some milk into the eggs and beat them some more. "Just your natural talent."

"He remembered it all, too, Denise. Months after that first appointment. The week before I saw Craig for the first time, Samantha had been diagnosed with leukemia. Being at the forefront of my mind, it was a subject I discussed with the dentist, like a woman talks to her hairdresser or something."

"Ah, yes. The dentist as therapist."

"So when he called me back in, he asked how she was doing. Which was normal. But here's the weird thing."

"What could be more weird?" I poured the eggs into the hot pan, but a thread of mystery entangled my mind.

"Denise, he knew things about Samantha's condition that I found out only days before."

Looking up, I squinted. "What do you mean?"

"The doctor had just told Samantha the chemotherapy wasn't sufficient and she would need a bone marrow transplant. Craig already knew about it. He emphasized how much money that would take. He knew I didn't have insurance—having lost my job—because I paid up front for the other dental work. 'You can't afford to take care of your little girl,' he told me. And on and on, the whole time looking at my teeth, he talked about how someone with enough money could find a match for Samantha's bone marrow or pay for a new treatment where they use the patient's own stem cells."

I gaped at him. "He didn't." *He?* Was I falling for this nonsense?

"The last thing he told me was how someone with money, like a dentist with a thriving practice in an upscale neighborhood, could take care of Samantha forever. He asked me how much I thought my daughter's life was worth."

"What did you say?"

"He left the room, and I lay shaking in the chair, the bright light still blinding me. A coldness seeped into my bones, as if evil pervaded the room."

Making breakfast in my kitchen, listening to a lunatic, a chill crept over me, too.

"I should have run right out of there, never given him a second thought. Instead, I played his conversation over and over in my head, asking myself what he was getting at. I mean, my daughter is priceless. Did he want me to sell her to him? Nothing made sense, but my bones shook with the fear he'd evoked."

"So you went back to the office?"

Call-Me-William shook his head. "The phone rang twenty-four hours to the minute after my appointment. I recognized Dr. Littleton's voice immediately. He asked the same question, word for word. 'How much is your daughter's life worth?' "

I scraped the cooked egg off the bottom of the pan and turned the heat down one notch.

"Somehow, I felt trapped into answering. So I told the truth. She was worth everything and anything. Her life was the only thing I cared about. Then, as if we were spies or something, he set up a clandestine meeting at the park. When I arrived, he waited on a bench, holding a newspaper up in front of his face. I realized then, though I had been around him twice, I *never* really saw his face."

"You're kidding me." Dusting the eggs with salt and pepper, I shook my head. "I have to give you extra points for creativity."

"I sat down next to him. From behind the paper he asked me what I'd do to make sure Samantha lived. This time I was ready. I said, 'Anything, absolutely anything.' He responded, 'I'm glad to hear you say that,' put down the paper, and looked at me."

"And?" I popped four pieces of bread into the toaster.

He held his hand up in front of his face. "It was like looking into a mirror."

"So my husband was your identical twin, is that what you're saying?"

"I know it sounds crazy, but near enough. Maybe not twins, but we looked like brothers. Craig told me he could guarantee a donor for Samantha, her hospital bills would be taken care of, and her college education paid for."

I scooped some of the eggs onto a plate and set it before him. "In exchange for what?"

"My life."

Chapter Thirty-Two

His

I SHOULDN'T HAVE BEEN able to eat while recounting the biggest mistake of my life for the first time, but the eggs smelled so good I couldn't resist. Digging a fork in, I took a bite and talked around it. "I didn't think about the other choices I had. I only thought of the benefits to Samantha's life, how I had failed her because I couldn't provide what your husband could promise her." I shoved another bite into my mouth. "Especially, I thought about how I couldn't live with myself if I didn't take the deal and she died. I'd die in her place in a second. And here was the opportunity to do that."

Denise finally stepped away from the stove and rested on a bar stool. "Why would he want you to die?"

Eggs caught in my throat. Choking, I took a swig of coffee. In all of my rehearsing before Denise awoke, I knew I would tell Denise just as soon as I could, but I had not really thought through the ramifications of my words to her life. I'd gotten caught up in the joy of remembering, of discovering who I was. And forgotten that the truth meant her husband was dead. Forgotten the reasons behind the arrangement. I couldn't meet her gaze. "He was leaving you."

She stood so quickly the stool teetered behind her. "I'm getting tired of this, Craig. I'm calling your doctor."

"I'm sorry. He wanted to run off, but he said he couldn't leave you and the boys without a good reason or you'd get all his money in alimony and child support. Instead, he decided to fake his death."

"So Craig had to die, too?"

"He would pretend to. I would in reality."

"And just because you guys looked alike, I would think he was dead?"

"Craig assured me he had more of a plan than that, but he wouldn't let me in on it."

She reached for the phone. "Enough."

"Please." I wanted to stand and wrap my arms around her. Comforting her had become a pleasant habit, but I wasn't who she thought I was. I didn't belong in her embrace, or in her house, or even in her life.

I knew I would lose her with my admission. I had toyed with the thought of continuing to be Craig more than once. Denise could keep teaching me who I was. Samantha could move in with us as Denise suggested, and we could live as a happy family forever.

But my whole life would be a lie. No matter how much I'd grown to care about Denise, living a falsehood would be torture. I would be stepping out of God's will for my life again, and surely I would end up with equally disastrous results.

Her fingers hovered over the touch pad.

"Call the detective instead. Let me explain the whole thing to him, and he can take me to the nuthouse in the back of the patrol car."

Shaking like a marsh reed in a hurricane, Denise handed me the phone. "Call him yourself. Number's on the fridge." She walked into the living room and curled up in a recliner.

I dialed the number and waited for him to pick up. "Detective Marshall?"

"Yes. Who is this?"

"That's a more complicated question than you meant it to be, sir. My name is William Rodain. If you could come to Denise Littleton's house, I have new information about her husband's accident."

At his prompt, I reminded him of the address.

"I'll be there in about half an hour."

I hung up.

Denise was still curled up in the chair.

"He'll be here in thirty minutes." I heated up her own plate of eggs and set it next to her on the side table. "Eat something."

"I can't." Staring into space, she didn't visibly move a muscle the whole time. Even when the doorbell rang, she didn't react.

"Be right back." I glanced over my shoulder as I hobbled to the door. I couldn't even tell if she heard me. I opened the door to a man near my age, a couple of days worth of scruff blurring his features. "Come on in."

He stuck out his hand. "Detective Marshall."

I put as much strength into my handshake as I could manage. "William Rodain."

"Name rang a bell, so I checked my records. I know you're not Mr. Rodain. I saw his dead body. I may be losing my touch as I grow older, but I don't think I've confused dead and alive yet."

"That's what I want to talk to you about, sir." I ushered him in.

Denise's gaze followed him as he entered the room, but she stayed silent.

"Excuse her, Detective. I just unloaded a ton of information on Denise and I think she's in shock." I sank onto the couch and clasped my hands. "You see, I was brought to the hospital, as you know, from the accident. When I came out of the coma, I couldn't remember who I was. My identity seemed to hover right out of reach. Denise told me everything I knew about myself. Until the last few days, I believed her version of who I am."

Detective Marshall took out a notepad. "Has your memory returned?"

"It has. I'm not Craig Littleton. I'm William Rodain."

His eyebrows scrunched together. "And what makes you believe that?"

"Flashes of my old life, at first. Now I have complete memory of what led up to the day of the accident. I'd like to fill you in."

He dipped his head in acquiescence. "Go ahead."

"I met Dr. Littleton when I was his patient. I told him about my daughter's leukemia. Later, he contacted me and asked me how much her life was worth. We met and he offered me a deal."

The detective scribbled in his book. "The deal was . . . ?"

"He would ensure Samantha received the very best care money could buy, bribe her way to the top of the transplant list, and help her through college in exchange for . . . for my life."

His eyebrows popped up.

"Craig offered all of that if, when he faked his own death, I would be the one to really die."

"Why was he planning to fake his death?"

Denise turned her head toward the wall as she spoke. "He wanted out of his family without any financial consequence."

Detective Marshall stared at Denise for a few seconds before giving his attention to me. "How would that happen? How would you be able to take his place?"

"Craig was a very thorough man." Denise cringed as I said *was*. "He said he would take care of the details. All I had to do was follow his directions. Over the next month or so, he called quite often, giving me the next thing to do."

"Like what?"

"Like which salon I should go to and which haircut I should request so we'd have the same hairstyle. Which store had clothes on the hold rack or layaway for me. Where I had athletic shoes waiting for me. I joined a gym to lose ten pounds to get down to Craig's weight. Everywhere I went, everything I did, it was already paid for."

"He was grooming you to look like him?"

"Exactly."

The detective cleared his throat. "I'm sorry, sir. None of those things would actually matter when we determine your identity. We don't look at hairstyles or clothing or exact weight because those things can change every other day."

"I understand. These were just some of the details Craig wanted to make sure of so that when Denise identified his body, I would be convincing enough."

"What happened the day of the accident?"

"Samantha—my daughter—had been in the hospital for so long, I'd grown accustomed to waking up in an empty house. But I woke up that day feeling more alone than ever. Let me be clear in this, Detective. I was not suicidal. I did not look forward to dying that day, but I saw no other way to save my daughter."

He rubbed his chin. "What did you do next?"

"I dressed in black shorts and a blue shirt, same as Craig. He even coordinated our underwear, so there would be no question we matched. My stomach rumbled so much, I skipped breakfast and walked a few blocks to the bus stop."

"Was it normal for you to take the bus?"

"No. Usually I drove my car, but Craig didn't want to have my vehicle left anywhere but at home. He didn't want the police to trace the car to me."

Marshall nodded and made a note.

"I got off near a convenience store right by the highway, which was the spot where Craig and I arranged to meet."

"Was he already there when you arrived?"

I shook my head. "I was running early. Nerves, I think. So I wandered around the store, looking at the candy and chips and drinks and asking what was the last thing I wanted to indulge in while still on this earth. But I got scared and went outside."

"Why did you get scared?"

"As I said, Craig was very thorough in planning this out. He did not tell me to go into the store. If he pulled up and I wasn't where I was supposed to be, maybe he wouldn't go through with it. Samantha wouldn't get the care she deserved and I would have failed her again."

"So you left the store?"

"I did. I went around to the side and waited by the Dumpster like Craig told me to. A few minutes later, he pulled up, jumped out of the car, and went into the store."

"He was dressed the same as you?"

"Yes. Which made me worry if the clerk might say something about him just having been in there. I dropped low, ran to the car, and crouched down in the passenger side."

"All right. You can get up now."

I unroll from the ball I'd made on the floor of the car and slide into the seat.

"Don't forget to buckle up," he says. "I don't need some note on a police log that my license plate was stopped and an unbelted passenger was ticketed. Denise would think, What passenger?"

"Yes, gotta keep myself nice and safe." I bring the seat belt around my middle. As the buckle clicks into place, I dryly chuckle and stare out the open top of the car. My hands tremble.

Denise pulled her legs closer to her body and closed her eyes.

"When Craig came back, he drove onto the highway, and I sat up in the seat."

The detective's expression was not as full of doubt as Denise's had been. "What went wrong? How did Dr. Littleton die instead of you?"

"I used to rock Samantha to sleep sometimes. I'd feed her formula so Victoria could sleep in on the weekends." I cough, covering the emotion in my voice. "One night, though, I fell asleep, her little head on my shoulder, and I had the strangest dream."

Craig doesn't prompt me for more.

"I dreamed a fierce angel held a blazing sword to my neck, but I wouldn't let go of Sam. When I jolted awake, my neck burned and had a little line across it for a few days. Victoria asked about it, but I never told her how it came to be."

"What's your point?"

I wipe my eyes. "When Samantha woke and lay in my arms, staring up at me, I knew I would die for her if I ever needed to. I made a pact in that dream. My life for hers."

"We were on our way to the Columbia Gorge. Craig told his family he was going hiking there. When we arrived, he was going to park the car, put on sweatpants and a hooded sweatshirt, and take off in a cab that was supposed to be waiting. I was to climb up to the top of Multnomah Falls." I swallowed hard.

"And?" His pen waited over the notepad.

"Are you sure about this? Making deals with God carries big risks."

I scowl, disbelief at his question bringing my eyebrows together. "Are you giving me any choice, Craig? Does your offer stand no matter what I do?"

He gazes out at the traffic. "You're my ticket to freedom, man. I have what you want, and you can provide me with what I need. I'm not claiming it's a great deal for you, but it's what we agreed upon."

How horrible to say this aloud. Denise would never be able to look at me as anything but a weakling. Yes, I had been trying to save my daughter, but I'd taken the coward's way to do so. Daring to glance at Denise, I forced the words out. "I was supposed to *accidentally* fall over the edge. My body would be brought out of the pool at the bottom, I would have his ID on me, and Dr. Craig Littleton would be dead."

Denise dropped her head into her hands. I thought I heard her groan, "Why?"

"How did you end up on the side of the road instead?" Marshall asked.

"As we were driving, my stomach ached more and more. Craig could tell I was getting nervous, having second thoughts, so he reminded me that he had taken care of Samantha already."

"Did you trust him? How did you know he would really do what he said after you were dead?"

"I never really questioned him."

Denise jerked her head up. "You trusted him even though you knew he was lying to his family and faking his death?"

Wondering the same thing, I narrowed my eyes. "It doesn't make logical sense, but I wasn't thinking well anyway. I did confirm the money transfer."

Craig rips open a pack of Dentyne and pops a stick in his mouth. "Gum?" He offers a piece to me. "I've already made the transfer."

I shove his hand back to his side of the car. "Why don't I take you at your word? You don't think of me as a person. I'm just a pawn in your little game."

"It's the last call dialed." Craig tosses his cell phone in my lap. "Push the green button twice and enter the code you gave me."

"That should be fairly easy for us to prove," Marshall said. "I'll have to get a warrant to trace his money. Unless you want to give permission for us to have access to your financial information, Mrs. Littleton."

She nodded.

He made another note. "We'll also send someone over to the store to get a copy of the surveillance camera tape from that morning. If you're telling the truth, we should see both of you in the store."

I spread my hands wide. "Why would I lie about this? I'm telling you this crazy story because it's what happened. If I'd remembered it sooner, I would have told it sooner."

"But you still haven't explained why you were parked at the edge of the road."

Sweat beads on my brow. "Pull over, Craig."

"Why? You really want out this late in the game? What's going to happen to Samantha if you don't go through with this?"

My stomach gives a giant heave. "Pull over!"

Before the car comes to a complete stop, I jump out and retch over the concrete barrier into a grassy field.

"I felt sick and demanded he stop immediately. Though he wasn't happy about screwing up his plan in any way, he really didn't want me puking in his car. How would that look to the authorities when they found it in the parking lot?" I scratched my head, trying to stay in the present, to not fall back into the memory of that day too deeply. "Craig was annoyed with me, but he tromped out to the field and left me alone for a few minutes."

I heave again and my legs shake. Cars whiz by and I think of how dangerous it is to be parked so close to rushing traffic. It won't do to get in an accident on the way to one.

Craig returns, carrying a small bundle of wildflowers, and tosses them onto the dash. "Back on the road, man. We're almost there."

I wiped my mouth on the back of my hand. "Give me another minute."

"Remember," he said, "you're doing it out of love."

Another heave.

He hands me a bottle of water.

I rinse my mouth, splash water on my face, and use my shirt to dry it.

Anger flashes over Craig's features. "We don't have time for this. Suck it up and get in the car."

"Then he started pressuring me to get back in the car. The whole time he treated me like a commodity, someone who could be bought and sold, not like a person."

"That's how he treated everyone." Denise's voice was as cold and sharp as an icicle.

"As weird as it may sound, that bothered me the most about the whole deal. I wanted him to look me in the eye and call me by my name. I needed him to acknowledge that I was a person, too. And that's when it happened."

I clench my fists. "Know this, Craig Littleton. I will do anything to save her life, but this is not right. There has to be a better way."

He lunges at me. "Get in the car. You're not backing out on me now." His elbow locks around my neck.

"I'm not going to do it." I roar, spinning to break loose.

"What happened?"

"I told him I was changing my mind. We scuffled. I'm sure it distracted the drivers on the road. I heard tires screeching, and Craig's car hit me. That's the last thing I really remember until I came to in the hospital."

Tapping his pen on his leg, Marshall leaned forward. "Is there anyone able to collaborate your story?"

Denise coughed, spoke in a strangled voice. "Talk to Naomi Porter. She'll have the answers to all your questions."

Chapter Thirty-Three

Hers

"MA'AM? WE'RE BRINGING Naomi Porter in for questioning right now."

"Thank you, Detective Marshall." I hung up the phone. Only three hours since the detective left my house, and they had already found her.

The boys were awake and lounging upstairs, unshowered, playing a skateboarding game borrowed from Bulldog. Neither of them acted as if anything had happened yesterday. They were so blasé, I almost wondered if I really had a late-night chat with Nicolas or not.

A yawn affirmed my lost sleep. "Craig?" I caught myself. "I mean, William?"

My husband wasn't my husband. My husband was really dead. The past months had been a farce. These things were true, but they had not yet solidified in my mind. The ingredients swirled around without forming an identifiable dish. Soon, I'd have to turn my attention to the new facts of my life, but I couldn't handle it yet.

He laid down the newspaper he'd been scanning. "They've got her?"

"Yep."

He stood, using a crutch for leverage, at once. "Let's go."

We shouted up to the boys that we would be back soon and headed for the police station. I glanced over at Craig—at William—who made it to car on his own. *Is this the last time we'll drive anywhere together? How can I look at him, see Craig, and it not really be him?*

Once we arrived, we were shown to a stuffy, dark room. On the other side of a glass partition stood a table, a rolling office chair, and a metal folding chair.

Detective Marshall entered our small room and shook our hands. "I'll be interviewing her. Is there anything specific you'd like me to ask about?"

"Why?" The word burst out of me. "I want to know why Craig planned all this."

The detective dipped his head. "She won't be able to see or hear you." He ducked out the door and reappeared in the other room.

Naomi followed him. The last time I saw her had been the chance meeting at the office when I found out she was moving. Though she seemed nervous then, I hadn't noticed any physical changes.

The woman sitting on the folding chair looked far different from the Naomi I'd known for years. Her normally sleek hair frizzed from her head in irregular waves. Even from our hiding place, I could see an uncertainty in her stride. Her faded skin. Her gaunt, sunken eyes.

I smiled. She deserved to age as much as I had through the entire trauma.

As soon as the thought passed through my consciousness, I knew it displeased God. Did I become prettier if she grew less attractive? No. So why did I think it mattered? Jesus died for her just as surely as He died for me. I was no better than she. I sinned just as often.

I want the truth, Lord. Make her speak the truth.

Craig—William—patted my hand and stared through the glass. "She looks awful, doesn't she?"

I nodded.

We fell silent as Detective Marshall began his interview. "Ms. Porter, as we indicated when we first contacted you, we'd like to know more about your relationship with Dr. Littleton."

She crossed her long legs, tugging her cotton miniskirt up to an indecent level. "He was my boss."

"Wasn't he also your lover?" Detective Marshall sounded like he was discussing the weather, not the sordid details of my failed marriage.

"I really don't think my personal life is any of your concern." Naomi ran a hand through her hair. Instead of calming the mane, her action caused more strands to pop out.

"Sure. Then let's talk about the death of William Rodain."

"Who?" Her voice quavered.

"Or should I say . . . murder?"

"I didn't have anything to do with that." She rolled her head on her neck, punctuated her statement with a finger jabbed in the air.

"With what?"

"With Will—" Her face tightened and she clapped a hand over her mouth.

The detective kicked back in his comfy chair. "Tell me what you didn't have anything to do with."

"I'd like to speak with my lawyer."

"Of course." The detective straightened. "But you're not being charged with any crime, so why don't you just sit and talk a little longer. Unless you're hiding something." He raised his eyebrows.

"I didn't do anything wrong. It was all Craig's idea."

"He set you up, did he?"

"No. I wasn't even involved. I told him, from the very beginning, I wanted left out of it." Her shoulders heaved from her vehemence.

"I believe you, Ms. Porter. I really do. And I think you feel horrible about what was done, don't you?"

"I do."

"So you can help us hold Dr. Littleton responsible for what he did."

"I don't . . ." Naomi squirmed in her seat. "It's just that . . ."

"Would you feel disloyal? Is that what you mean?"

She nodded curtly. "I don't think it's my place to talk about his business."

"Let me be clear about one thing, Ms. Porter. We already know more than you think we do about this case. The better you cooperate with us, the better things will go for you." He crossed his legs slowly; I admired the way he made himself look comfortable, making Naomi wait for him to say more. "I spoke with Dr. Littleton this morning. He said he's done with you, so don't feel like you're betraying a confidence. He's already spilled the beans."

"No, he didn't." Naomi clasped her necklace in her hand.

Instinctively, I knew Craig had given it to her. Odd to watch her react to feeling betrayed by Craig when they had both betrayed me.

"We know about the meeting that morning at the convenience store, the matching outfits, the waiting taxi. We want to know why. Why was Dr. Littleton leaving his family, Ms. Porter? Why did he go to such lengths?"

She ran the pendant back and forth on the silver chain. "She can't make him stay. I know he's hurt from the accident and she's got her claws stuck in him again, but he'll find me once he's better. We'll run off just like we had planned."

"Where were you going?"

"Craig bought me a place down on the Mexican coast. We were going to stay there the rest of our lives."

"Why draw William Rodain into the plot? Plenty of men leave their wives every year without blackmailing a man into killing himself."

She looked away. "Craig can tell you that if he decides to."

"Craig Littleton is dead."

She gasped. "What happened? What do you mean?"

Detective Marshall leaned over the table. "He died the day of the accident. At least according to William Rodain. The man taken to the hospital, who came out of the coma with amnesia, is now claiming to be Mr. Rodain."

"No, no, no." Naomi moaned. Tears sprang up, and she wiped her face with her fingertips. "That can't be true."

As she cried, I realized I'd been cheated out of yet another normalcy. I hadn't cried since the revelation. The wife should have been the first to cry after hearing about her husband's death, not the mistress.

The detective leaned back in his chair. "Why not? It's true that the men were switching identities. One of them was supposed to die." He opened his hands wide. "Guess the wrong one did."

"No, we were going to run away together. I was supposed to go back to my apartment for a few days, go to the funeral, tell Denise how sorry I was for her loss, that I couldn't finish my two-week notice, and meet Craig in Mexico. That's why he wanted a real dead body. He didn't want anyone getting suspicious. We wanted to have a peaceful life, without his wife always coming after us."

Detective Marshall shook his head. "I don't buy it. He could have had the same thing with a divorce. Why did he really need to turn up dead?"

"There was some money."

"Yes, we've heard he didn't want Mrs. Littleton to get her hands on it. Is that right?"

"She's always been after him for his money."

I couldn't help rolling my eyes at that statement. Yep. All eight years of dental school, I stood by him only for the money.

If I were able to go into the room, I would have throttled Naomi for the way she talked about me. But, I reminded myself, to hear her out was the only way to learn what Craig had been thinking.

"Because there was so much of it." The detective's tone didn't change, but I could tell he was fishing. For what, I wasn't sure.

"You know about the offshore accounts?" Naomi looked up with alarm.

Detective Marshall didn't skip a beat. "And how much money is in them."

"So Denise is going to end up with two million dollars, and I'll have nothing!" Naomi wailed.

I sank back against the nearest wall. Had I ever really known my husband?

"How did he acquire so much wealth?"

She dropped her head and sobbed.

"You don't need to protect him, Ms. Porter. A dead man is beyond the reach of the law."

"He did something with prescription drugs, but I didn't want to know the details of that either."

"It would be hard to sleep at night, wouldn't it? If you knew everything Dr. Littleton was doing?"

"He wasn't like that." Naomi spit the words out. "He was trapped, and he had to find a way out."

"Do you have anything else you'd like to share, Ms. Porter? Maybe you can enlighten us on some other aspect of the case?"

"How could you have been wrong? I talked to him. I watched him inside his house pretending with his family. Why did all the papers say William died if Craig was the one in the hospital?"

"Because, Ms. Porter, they had already switched identities."

"It still doesn't make sense. Both of them were hurt. There should have been questions over who was who."

"Ma'am, we don't rely on description to identify bodies."

"Then how did you mix them up?"

The haziness in my mind cleared as she asked the question. Craig's blueprint unfurled before me in neon color. "Oh, Craig," I whispered. His arms came around me. But no, if anyone held me, it would be William.

William Rodain. The man who had gone along with the horrible plan to make me believe my husband was dead.

I listened for the detective to confirm my revelation.

"Ms. Porter, we rely on science. We identified them based on medical records."

Naomi's eyes closed. I knew what she was going to say next.

"He switched them. He switched the dental records."

Chapter Thirty-Four

His

"IT'S TRUE," Denise murmured. "It's all true." She collapsed against my side.

Grabbing under her arms, I hoisted her upright. "Denise, are you okay?" Despite my grasp, she slipped lower. I supported her weight and leaned back to compensate.

Her head fell against my chest. "I'll never be okay. Those times I felt like I was being watched, the phone calls, the footprints on the carpet . . . all of that was her trying to be close to you. To him."

Propped on crutches, I drew her closer and stroked her back. She didn't pull away from me.

The detective came through our door. "She's provided us with a lot of missing information."

His entrance seemed to break through Denise's shock, reminding her that I was holding her. She slipped her arms up and pushed back from me.

I nodded. "Naomi knows more about the plans than I did."

"So you weren't aware the dental records had been swapped?"

For the first time it struck me that, in a way, I had been part of an identity theft. I hadn't been trying to steal from Craig by becoming him, but I was sure we broken many, many laws with our plan.

"No, sir." I vehemently shook my head. "I never thought about anything but saving Samantha's life. It seems so obvious, but I didn't consider . . .We didn't want . . ." Wimping out brought me to this dark place.

Be a man. Face your consequences.

I squared my shoulders. "Am I going to be arrested?"

Detective Marshall scratched the back of his head. "Well, I'm not sure who we're going to charge with what. Ms. Porter aided and abetted the scheme. She lied to us when we first spoke with all the office staff, and she withheld crucial information. But you, Mr. Rodain, actually participated in the identity exchange." He held up a finger. "However, your choices were made under duress, with the threat of your daughter's life hanging over your head."

"I deserve whatever comes my way. My grief and confusion and fear clouded my mind, but I should have known better."

"It wasn't smart, what you did. That's for sure." He raised his eyebrows at me. "I'm sure we'll have more questions for you and Mrs. Littleton, but you both are free to go for now."

"Really?" I slid my hands into my pockets so he wouldn't see the way they trembled.

"You just make sure we know how to contact you." He glanced at Denise and left the room.

"I've got to get home." Denise brushed past me.

I caught her arm. "You can't drive like this."

She shoved her keys into my hand. "Fine. You drive."

Metal clinked as the keys smashed into my palm. How long had it been since I drove? Could I navigate through all those cars without panicking at the remembrance of the screech of brakes, the searing pain? I had been on the road since, but not as the one in control of the car.

The room was empty. Clearly, Denise wasn't going to wait while I stared at the car keys and explored my self-doubt. I could either drive her, or she would drive herself. An automatic should be doable. I hurried out the door and saw her turning the hallway corner. Rushing after her—the best I could—I tried to put aside my fears and focus on keeping her safe, being there for her as much as she would let me.

When I reached the parking lot, I found her sitting on the curb beside the Denali. I limped over and unlocked her side, waited for her to climb in, and closed the door behind her. I whispered a prayer for strength, courage, and safe travel to Denise's house as I slid the crutches into the backseat.

She stared straight ahead, uncommonly pale.

"I'll need you to direct me. I don't quite know all the turns yet." I felt like a fool admitting it.

She gave a quick nod, braced her elbow on the armrest, and shielded her face from me with a hand. "Get on the freeway going south."

We made it home with the minimal amount of communication.

Home. The fancy bricked façade that held a crumbling family. It wasn't my home and I couldn't pretend it was anymore.

Ignoring the boys' questions of where we had been and—once they'd seen her face—what was wrong, Denise plodded up the stairs and closed herself in the master bedroom.

"Dad? What's going on?" Jamie asked.

Scowling, Nicolas flexed his shoulders. "Tell us. What did you do to her?"

I pinched my top lip and studied them. Jamie. Wacky, loud, daring, tenderhearted. Nicolas. Quiet, unsure, angry, struggling to find his place in the world of men. This was the last time they would look at me as their father. Any minute, they would hear that their real father had been dead for almost two months.

No blood of mine ran through their veins, yet my new world had been built on the premise that they were my flesh. Knowing they weren't, that I would have no part in their lives, tore at my gut.

"I'm sorry, boys. It's not my place to tell you." I herded them into the kitchen. "Let's give your mom a few minutes on her own, okay? I'm sure she'll want to talk to you soon."

Scanning the phone list on the side of the refrigerator, I found Sarah's number and dialed. "Sarah? This is Craig." No, I wasn't, but the explanation couldn't be done over the phone or in front of the boys.

"Oh, I don't know that you've ever called me before." She held back any questions she might have wanted to ask.

"Denise needs you to come over."

"Is she okay?"

"She's not hurt. I mean, physically, she's all right." I cleared my throat. "I think she needs your support right now. She doesn't know I'm calling you, but I know she'd be glad if you came over."

"Craig." The phone dropped twenty degrees from the coolness in her voice. "If you have hurt her, so help me—"

"I did, Sarah. But I didn't mean to." I choked up and could barely get the next words out. "Please, could you tell her that? I never meant to do this to her."

"I'm coming." She hung up.

Rubbing the back of my neck, I made another call. "Pastor Miles, this is Craig Littleton. Is there any way you could come pick me up this afternoon?"

We set plans to meet in an hour. The man sounded curious, but he didn't pry. I figured he probably was privy to quite a few secrets in his profession. Bet he could toss around a thousand different scenarios and never come close to the truth on this one.

Sarah arrived a few minutes later. She let herself in, shot daggers at me with her eyes, and went up to Denise's room.

Both boys had taken seats at the kitchen bar. With bewildered looks, they seemed to understand intuitively that their life was changing. Again.

Lord, they're such good kids. I wish they were mine. Can I have a last connection with them?

"Hey." My word jarred the glass silence. "Want to teach me how to play that skateboarding game?"

I might as well have said, "Let's pretend nothing is wrong and ignore what's happening," considering the way they seized the suggestion. Nicolas even grabbed a bag of Doritos and a six-pack of cokes to take into the bonus room with us.

We closed the door and kept our voices low. I tried to forget what Denise must have been telling Sarah, tried not to picture Sarah's expression when she understood. By making someone else believe it, the truth would become that much more real to Denise. I knew, because it had seemed so abstractly impossible until I said it aloud first to Denise, then to the detective. Once they believed me, I couldn't go back. I couldn't undo it.

Sarah poked her head in the door. Mascara smudged beneath her eyes. "Can I talk to you?" Instead of calling me by name, she pointed at me.

"Keep playing," I told the boys. I followed Sarah.

She sat down on the top stair.

I sank down beside her. We both stared straight forward, down the flight of stairs.

"So you're not Craig?"

"No."

"How can that be?" She snapped her head to look at me, scrutinized my face.

"The resemblance is uncanny, isn't it?"

She narrowed her eyes. "Are you making this up? Another cheap trick to throw Denise off what you're really up to?"

Closing my eyes, I dropped my head into my hands. "Sarah, if I could, I would take it all back. I wouldn't consider his offer. I wouldn't tell him about Samantha. I wouldn't even go to Craig's office if I could go back in time and change the past."

A sharp intake of breath. "No, you wouldn't take it back." Sarah touched my arm. "You love her."

"What?" I jerked myself up by the banister and dropped my voice to a stern whisper. "The whole time I've known her, I've been a lie. Her husband was a lie. I'm part of the reason her husband is dead. What kind of a man do you think I am?"

She just stared at me.

"I wouldn't take advantage of a woman who was hurting so badly!"

"William, right?"

"Yeah."

"I'm not saying anything about your character, I'm talking about your heart."

I shook my head. "She doesn't need me. All I am is a mirror of her husband, a constant reminder of what she's lost."

The doorbell rang.

"I've got to get that." I wanted to stomp down the stairs, get some aggression out, but the first step sent splinters of pain up my leg. I gingerly picked my way down, supremely conscious of Sarah's calm gaze on my back.

The nerve of that woman. I couldn't possibly love Denise. She didn't know me. In fact, we had never really met. Our interactions had all been based on my being Craig Littleton, not William Rodain.

No matter that I thought she was beautiful. No matter that I couldn't fathom the forgiveness she offered me after discovering an affair. No matter her steadiness under all the pressure.

I swung the door open. "Pastor Miles, thanks for coming."

"My pleasure." He started to move forward.

"I'd ask you in, but now's not really a good time. Could I meet you in the car in a few minutes?" I kept my arm across the doorway just in case he didn't get what I was saying.

"Sure, sure." He backed up. "I'll be in the car."

I closed the door and climbed my way back up the stairs, overruling my legs' complaints and ignoring Sarah. Feet, crutches, feet, crutches.

The boys paused the game when I came back into the room.

"We started over with two players," Jamie said. "You want in again, Dad?"

Tears hazed my view of his freckled face. "Guys, I've got to go. Pastor Miles is waiting to talk with me."

Nicolas stood. "When are you coming back?"

"I don't know." The tears came faster now, rolling down my cheeks. Before I could wipe them away, the boys were hugging me, begging me to stay.

"It's best if I go." I squeezed them as hard as I could. The pain in my ribs felt almost refreshingly normal. "Your mom can explain it all." I drew back and gazed at each of them. "I want you to remember this, boys. You can always count on your heavenly Father. He will never let you down." I broke away, stumbled down the stairs, grabbed the bags I packed last night, and headed out to the waiting car.

Chapter Thirty-Five

Hers

"WHAT WAS THAT NOISE?" I asked Sarah as she walked back into my room.

"He left."

"Who?" Wiping my nose, I tried to think if one of the boys had something planned.

"Your fake husband. William."

I laughed through my tears. "Did he say when he'd be back?"

She plopped down on the bed next to me. "Sweetie, I don't think he's coming back."

"What?" Panic froze my stomach.

"Pastor Miles picked him and all his bags up. He said good-bye to the boys."

"No, he didn't." I darted off the bed. "Where are they?"

"Crying their eyes out in the bonus room." She looked over her shoulder. "Might be smarter for you to go talk to them instead of grieving in separate rooms."

"Quit telling me what to do." But I stopped at the door, drew in a deep breath, and composed myself. I started to go out . . . and spun, my back against the door, arms pressing behind me. "What am I going to say to them, Sarah?"

She gazed at me with helpless compassion.

"Am I really supposed to tell them their dad is dead? It's insane. They just said good-bye to their dad. How does that seem right?"

"Tell them the truth."

"How much? That he had an affair? That he tried to fake his death and it didn't work—or it worked too well—and he died? That William was never their father?" I clutched my heart. "Do you know what that will do to them? To think they could love someone like they loved Craig, and it all turn out to be fake? How embarrassing to be so fooled, to be so mistaken about the person you love most in the world."

"You don't need to be embarrassed, Denise." Sarah offered her arms to me.

I fell keening into them.

"You loved a hurt man when he needed to be loved. You helped him when he needed to be helped. You shouldn't be embarrassed about that."

"I kissed him!" Covering my mouth, I recalled all the hours I spent at his bedside in the hospital. "I kissed him when my husband's body wasn't even cold."

"You didn't know." She smoothed my hair. "How could you have known?"

"Shouldn't a good wife know?"

Sarah shook my shoulders. "You were a great wife. You forgave Craig everything. Everything. You thought he was alive, and you forgave him for everything he did to you."

"He's dead, though, Sarah. Craig is dead." I accepted her comfort then, allowing my stiffness to relax into a quivering mass of sorrow.

I cried until I could cry no more.

Finally, Sarah took my face in her hands. "You need to talk to Nicolas and Jamie. This confusion might be worse than knowing what's going on."

I shook my head. "Not worse, but more painful."

"I'll be right beside you."

We made the long journey down the hallway. The shades were drawn in the bonus room. Most times, the boys did that to see the television screen better, but they sat in the dark, doing nothing. Neither one would look at me as I came in. Sarah took a spot in the corner of the room, out of the way.

What do I say, Lord God? Why is their father gone? Why do I have to be the bearer of the bad news?

The only answer I heard was an affirmation that I was the only one who could take such horrible truth to them. Even though Sarah loved them as if they were her own, I had to be the one to say the words, to destroy their world, because I loved them more than anyone else. I would be the one beside them, picking up the pieces, sharing my fears and listening to theirs.

I perched on the coffee table in front of them. "Nicolas, Jamie, there's something really terrible I need to tell you both."

"We already know, Mom." Nicolas slouched farther into the couch. "Dad told us he was leaving."

"I'm afraid it's worse than that." I sat between them, glancing back and forth.

"What's worse than you kicking Dad out of the house?" he snapped.

"I understand that you're upset. Just hear me out." I touched my hands together, fingers spread wide. "After the accident, hearing that your dad didn't remember us, our family, our life . . . that tore me up."

"But he's remembering, Mom," Jamie said. "Can't you let him stay? Give him more time?"

I touched his arm. "There's a deeper reason besides amnesia for why he didn't remember us. The man in the hospital bed . . . the police thought he was your dad because he had your dad's ID on him." Their expressions held nothing by disbelief. "We accepted it because he looked like your dad, but it was really another man. A man named William Rodain."

"That's stupid." Nicolas jumped up. "Just 'cause you're mad at Dad, you're making up some dumb story so we won't care that you kicked him out of the house. Well, it's not going to work!"

"I didn't believe it at first, either. I don't blame you for doubting me, but William's memory came back last night. He remembers being with your dad right before the accident. He's not your father. He's Samantha's."

Nicolas released a primal scream. "No, he's not!"

I reached for his hands, but he yanked them away. "He and I went down to the police department earlier. There's a witness who filled in the other details of how we all were led to believe William was your father. She collaborated William's claim."

"Some woman, huh? Was it the one he'd been sneaking around with?"

My jaw dropped. "What are you talking about, Nicolas? How would you know?"

"Everyone knew, Mom. Everyone but you. My friends told me. They saw them together."

I ran a hand through my hair. "I'm not ready to talk about that right now. I'm trying to tell you about your dad."

Jamie's bottom lip trembled. "If that guy wasn't Dad, then where is he?"

"He's dead, you twerp." Nicolas bolted out the door and clumped down the stairs.

I sprang up and ran to the doorway. "Get back here, Nicolas! I'm trying to talk to you."

The house shook as he slammed the door. A rumble of a car starting drifted through the windowpanes. I ran over, pulled up the shades, and groaned as I saw the Denali backing out of the driveway. It headed straight for Sarah's car, screeching to a stop mere inches from hitting it. "Sarah, he almost hit your car."

She joined me at the window. "He's too upset to be driving."

"But what do I do about it? Call the police?"

"Mom, you can't sic the cops on Nicolas." Jamie pulled me away from the window. "He's just mad. He'll come back as soon as he cools off."

"Maybe that's best." Sarah shrugged. "He has his license. Let's give him a little while."

"It'll work," Jamie said.

"How do you know what your brother's going to do, Jamie?" I shook my head. "He's dealing with more than he ever has before."

"'Cause you always said Dad was cooling off when he drove away. He always came back, didn't he?"

Did he? I let him drive off to skip church and go hiking. He didn't come back from that. But Jamie's insight made me think of how often Craig left angry over our latest tiff. Nicolas was just dealing with his anger the way his father had taught him to.

"Okay." My shoulders fell. "I'll wait, if that's all I can do."

Sarah raised her eyebrows. "We can pray."

My first reaction was to argue that it wasn't enough, but I knew she was right. We formed a prayer triangle, Jamie and I on the couch, Sarah sitting on the coffee table facing us. The three of us made me think of the three persons of my God. I knew my Father heard Sarah ask for protection over Nicolas, for safety, for wisdom as we dealt with Craig's death. The Holy Spirit was with us, but He was also in the car with Nicolas, speaking to his heart. And Jesus . . . He put down His carpentry work to carry Sarah's words to the foot of the throne.

Sometime during the prayer, Jamie lifted my arm and crawled onto my lap. Which took me right back to the last time he needed my closeness so much that it overrode his growing independence. That day in the hospital, when we heard how badly Craig was hurt.

But it wasn't Craig.

It had been my reality for so long that I couldn't stop thinking about the last seven weeks without framing them in that context. My mind comprehended Craig's death, but it hadn't translated yet to my heart.

After Sarah finished praying and left us alone, I whispered, "How you doing, baby?"

He didn't answer.

"Too much to take in all at once, huh?"

Jamie shrugged. "I don't know how to feel. It doesn't seem like Dad's really . . . dead. I just hugged him. Am I supposed to cry like you or get mad like Nicolas?"

Didn't I feel the same way? *Tell me what to do, how to feel, and I won't let you down.* But it was never that easy. Whichever direction our emotions veered, we always feared we were doing it wrong.

"Feel whatever you want to feel, Jamie. I won't think any less of you for crying or blame you for getting mad. You can always talk to me about it, though. And God. He knows your heart better than I ever could."

"He liked my new trick."

It took me a moment to figure out he was referring to William, not God. "Did he?"

"And he played with me a lot. More than Dad ever did."

Instinctively, I made an excuse for Craig. "Well, your dad was always working, and Mr. Rodain was always here at home because he needed to get better. That's two different circumstances to compare."

"Samantha said she was my sister."

She talked to the boys about it? *Of course, she did. She called him Dad in front of them.*

"She showed me the pictures of her and her dad. He was really nice to you, Mom. I heard him say you were pretty one time. Did Dad think you were pretty?" He turned his head to look at me.

"Your daddy told me I was pretty the first day we first met. Did I ever tell you about that?"

When Jamie shook his head, his hair tickled my chin.

"I was already late to class one day when this guy ran past me and bumped my books out of my arms."

"Dad ran into you?"

"No, he was the one who stopped and help me gather my papers after the jerk kept going."

Jamie relaxed against me.

I hugged him close and kept telling the story.

His

PASTOR MILES didn't really know what to say, but he promised he would check on Denise and the boys. As great as my reunion with Samantha would be, their pain would go profoundly deeper.

Bags hanging from my shoulders, I waved as his car drove off. Across the street from me stood my house. Dark, empty windows gaped back at me. Rogue growths of roses threatened to pull down the trellises. The grass had turned straw yellow in the absence of faithful watering. All in all, it looked uncared for, unloved.

This is just what I notice on the outside of a building, God. How much damage did my neglect do to the inside of my daughter?

Behind me, a ruckus arose. I turned to see the door flung open.

Samantha flew toward me, arms wide. "Dad! I heard the car pull up, but I couldn't tell who was in it." She reached me and almost pulled me to the ground with the ferocity of her hug.

"Sammie-sam!" I wanted to lift her off the ground and swing her round, but I wasn't strong enough yet. "You can't believe how glad I am to see you."

"You're not in the wheelchair anymore."

"I got the casts off yesterday."

"Why'd you come here, though?" She pulled back and stared up at me. "I haven't told Mrs. Van Horn yet, but she can look out her window as easily as I did and see you."

"Things have changed a lot in a very short time, sweetie. Let's go inside and I can tell you and Mrs. Van Horn together."

She grabbed a bag and started up the walk. "I can't believe you're here."

"I'm not leaving you again."

"What about Denise? Are they moving here?"

"Wait." I stopped her at the door. "Should you go in and warn Mrs. Van Horn?"

A quiet voice reached me from behind the screen door. "What would she warn me about? That the dead are walking and talking? Thank You, Lord almighty! It's true!"

Yanking the screen open, I met the gaze of the woman who had always been there for our family, caring for Samantha when I had to work, giving her the motherly talks I couldn't even think about without turning beet red, and most important—hardest to believe—taking in my daughter when everyone thought I was dead.

I couldn't stop the grin from spreading over my face. "There's been a huge mistake, Mrs. Van Horn. I was in a car accident at the beginning of June, the police misidentified the dead man's body as mine, and I had amnesia. Last night, I remembered who I was. Who I am."

"Lord above, it's a miracle." She fanned her face. "Is it really you?"

"In the flesh." I nodded and stepped into the house. Wrapping my arms around her little body, I said, "Thank you so much for what you've done for Samantha."

"Do you remember everything, Daddy?" Samantha came in and closed the door. "Do you remember me?"

Letting go of Mrs. Van Horn, I turned to Samantha. "Everything, honey. Like . . . when your first tooth fell out, the tooth fairy didn't come. I forgot all about the tradition and your kindergarten friends made fun of you, so the next day the fairy brought twice as much as they all got under their pillow, apologized for being late, and gave some excuse about a hurt wing."

Samantha giggled and her eyes welled up. "You do remember."

"All of it. Every glorious second of being your father."

"Samantha, can you get me a glass of water?" Mrs. Van Horn worked her way over to a chair and sat, still fanning herself. Glancing at me, she smiled. "Don't worry. I'll be fine in a moment and then I want to hear all about where you've been and who took care of you and what made you remember."

As soon as Samantha came back, I settled onto the threadbare couch with her and laid out the whole sorry tale.

Chapter Thirty-Six

His

I SLID THE ORANGE and green flowered sheet off the piano, lifted the key cover, and hit a chord.

"Play something, Dad." Samantha scooted the piano bench back.

Sinking onto it, I fingered the keys. "Any requests?"

She clasped her hands together. "Play 'I Could Have Danced All Night.'"

From memory, I stroked the melody onto the smooth keys. Singing in her sweet soprano voice, Samantha lifted the sheet, held it open with both arms, and twirled around the room.

Laughing, I embellished the tune, adding a slide and a trill. Unaccustomed to the motion of playing the piano for so long, my fingers stiffened and cramped. But my daughter still danced, so I played on.

Her shadow skipped from wall to wall as she spun around the candles burning in the room. Nothing, not even the power being turned off, would keep the two of us from spending the night in our own house. Mrs. Van Horn insisted on cooking our dinner and sending fresh bedding over, but now, as the sun sank into the horizon, it was just my daughter and me, celebrating our reunion.

The song came to an end. I held the last note, drinking in Samantha's pure song. After I lifted my fingers from the keys, a hush fell over us.

She slid onto the bench beside me. "What was the hardest part for you, Dad?"

I stroked a B flat, my hand pale against its blackness. "There was a lot of pain at the beginning and not knowing who I was frustrated me incredibly, but the very worst of all of it was last night when I realized you had been alone." I cupped her cheek. "I'm so sorry, Samantha. I made a very wrong choice. I thought money would save you. You needed the doctors and the transplant and a future, and I thought giving those to you would make up for losing me."

She blinked away a tear. "I forgive you, Dad. But you never needed to give your life to save me. Jesus already did that."

The truth. Again.

I thought of what might have been. We would have managed to pay the hospital bills. Worst case, Samantha would have fought the leukemia and lost. But I would have been by her side through it all, and even loss would turn to gain as she went to the place she was created for. A paradise with no sickness.

I wrapped an arm around her. "I'm sorry I tried to play God, picking who should live and who should die."

Samantha shook her head. "I don't want to talk about what you tried to do anymore, Dad."

I kissed her forehead. "What was the worst part for you?"

"Either your memorial service or when I saw you at Denise's and you didn't know who I was." She rubbed the tip of her nose. "She and her boys made me doubt myself. Even you made me question it for a while. And I hate that I believed you might have lied to me, hidden them from me. But once you saw the pictures, I knew you were really my dad. I didn't like having to leave you there with another family, but I knew you'd take care of it soon."

I would ask more about the memorial service later. I didn't want to bring more mention of death into the peace of the moment. "Denise wanted you to live with us. She forgave me for keeping you a secret. I mean, she forgave who she thought I was."

"She wanted me to live in that house?" Samantha gaped at me. "I can't believe she wanted me."

"It's pretty gorgeous compared to this old place, isn't it?" I saw the old slat and plaster walls, the low ceilings, and simple square rooms with new eyes.

"I love this home, Dad." She leaned sideways against me. "Denise is awesome, though. Is she going to be okay?"

"She's really strong, Sam, like you are. And she loves Jesus, too. Maybe that's why I liked her so much."

"Why?"

"Because she reminded me of you." I tilted my head to rest on Samantha's. Picturing Denise walking onto the patio of the hospital, hefting my wheelchair into the back of the car, stirring a pot of chili on the stove . . . my heart ached to think I would never be with her again.

Sarah could extrapolate whatever she wanted to from my feelings for Denise, but they didn't mean anything. I'd fallen in love with a woman I believed was my wife. The only reason she opened her heart to me was because she thought I was her husband.

But you do love her.

I sighed at the thought. If it were true, my heart was even worse off. If my love proved real and hers was based on a lie, mine was useless. And my love didn't matter now anyway. She had just started grieving the loss of her husband.

I nuzzled my daughter's hair. Samantha was all the family I needed.

Hers

"WHERE DO YOU THINK he might be?" Pastor Miles rubbed both temples as he leaned against the kitchen counter.

I paced the kitchen again, shaking my head. "Have any ideas, Jamie?" Glancing at my watch, I counted the hours Nicolas had been gone. Seven. Seven hours! I chose not to involve the police once I discovered that I would have to tell them Nicolas didn't have my permission to take the car—as in, report the car stolen and fill in the first line on my son's permanent record. No way. He was a legal driver and I understood why he was upset.

"They say history repeats itself, but you never learn, Mom." Jamie slumped in his chair and yawned. "I bet he's with Heather again."

I could have popped myself in the head. What a no-brainer. "I'll call her parents and see if he's there." I checked my watch again. "Though I doubt they'd let him be there for this long without calling me."

The church directory showed their home phone as unlisted. I chose her father's cell number and dialed. "Mr. McCallister?" Though he was Sarah's brother-in-law, we had not made it to first-name basis. "This is Denise Littleton. Is Nicolas at your house?"

"He's not, I'm afraid."

"Oh, okay. I'll call some of his other friends. We had some hard news today and I'm not quite sure where he—"

"I said he's not at our house, but I know exactly where he is. And if he's laid a hand on my little girl, he's going to regret it."

"What are you talking about?" I tightened my grip on the phone, pressing it harder against my ear. "Where is he?"

"We're driving to a motel right now, Mrs. Littleton. Heather just called and asked us to pick her up there."

I gasped. "Why is she at a motel?"

"I couldn't understand everything she was saying because she was crying so hard."

No, Lord. How much do You think I can handle?

"Please." I grabbed a pen and a scrap of paper. "Please tell me where you're headed. And don't let Nicolas leave until I get there."

"I wouldn't be worried about me letting him out of there. You should be more concerned with me leaving him alive." But he gave me the name of the motel and the room number before hanging up.

Both Pastor Miles and Jamie stared at me.

"Nicolas is at a motel with Heather McCallister." I focused my words toward Pastor Miles. "Can you drive me?"

"Sure." He pulled his keys from his pocket faster than I could grab my purse.

"Jamie, you stay here. Call me if he happens to comes home before me." I ran out the door after the pastor.

Tension crackled during the whole ride. As we pulled into the motel's parking lot beneath the flashing red neon light advertising VACANCY, I gripped the door handle, ready to jump out as soon as we stopped.

"Now, Denise," Pastor Miles intoned as he shifted into park. "The most important thing is to remain calm. Listen to Nicolas and really hear what he says. Don't let your anger scare him out of being honest."

"You'd better be the one who does the talking, then." I darted across the pool of light from the streetlamp and, following room signs, I made my way to the right number, Pastor Miles close behind.

The door was half open. Heather and her parents stood against the far wall, Heather sobbing in her mother's embrace. Nicolas sat on the edge of the bed, tears dripping from his face, his head downcast.

I rushed to him, dropped to my knees. "What were you thinking?" I demanded even as I gently wiped his cheek. "How could you bring Heather here?"

He didn't act as though he'd heard me.

"Now that you're here," Mr. McCallister said, "we'll be going. And keep your boy away from Heather. I don't want him ever talking to her again."

Jumping to my feet, I spun and got right in his face. "Nicolas is a good kid. I'm not saying he made a great choice today, but he just found out his father is dead. So cut him a little slack, all right?"

He stepped back.

Pastor Miles tapped the man's arm. "Come talk to me in the hall for a second before you take your family home."

The three McCallisters trickled out into the hallway. I knew Pastor Miles would explain the whole situation to them.

I dropped back down in front of Nicolas. "Oh, honey, why? Why did you bring Heather to a motel?"

"Isn't it obvious?" He snorted. "I'm just like my dad. All I care about is getting a girl into bed."

"What's gotten into you, Nicolas?" I shook his shoulders.

"Or my mom, too. You slept with someone you weren't married to."

Indignant, I rocked back on my heels. "I did not."

"I'm not naïve, Mom. I saw you and him kissing. You thought he was your husband, and I know what happens when you're married."

"Nicolas Littleton, you will shut your mouth this instant. How dare you!" My body shook. I steadied myself with my hands. "We never did a thing."

"Well, Dad did."

"Do you want to make the same choices your dad did? Do you want to hurt others the same way?" Sobs overwhelmed me. "Nicolas, I loved your father. I'm devastated he's gone. But I'm angry that he left us with such a mess to sort through. You can learn from his mistakes and be a better man. Taking your girlfriend to a motel is not the way to start being a better man."

"I'm sorry!" Nicolas tumbled off the bed onto the floor. "Nothing happened, Mom, I swear. I just wanted to be in a place where I could talk to her without anyone interrupting us. She understands me so well. And then she was hugging me and things started to get out of hand, and I think I scared her because I wasn't stopping when I should have. But she stopped me, Mom. Heather stopped me." He crawled into my arms and hung on as if I were a buoy in a stormy ocean and his boat had just capsized.

Thank You, God, that Heather stopped him. He was looking for comfort and put himself in a tempting place, but You saved him, Lord. You saved me, too, from worrying about a grandchild coming way too soon, or the emotional and spiritual toll on my son.

"Don't run away from me like that again, you hear me?" I pressed my lips into his hair.

"Yes, ma'am." He wiped his eyes on my sleeve.

I cradled his head against me.

Chapter Thirty-Seven

Hers

SLIDING MY FEET into black heels, I smoothed my dress and studied my reflection in the full-length mirror. I left my hair down around my shoulders so if I needed to hide my teary face, all I had to do was lean forward.

"Denise?" Sarah knocked on the door. "Time to go. The car's here."

Sighing, I left the bedroom and followed her down the stairs. "Where are the boys?"

"They've already gone out."

We stepped out on the porch. A cardboard box sat in the corner of the railing. "What's this?"

"I don't know."

I bent to lift it.

"Don't do that." Sarah tsked. "You'll get dust on your dress. I'll just put it inside."

"No, I want to see what's in it." I straightened and locked the door. "Bring it to the car for me, please."

She regarded me with a weird expression but did it anyway.

As I strode toward the black limousine, I wondered which neighbors peered out their windows, pitying me. When the story broke, it had been a heyday for the media. A news crew set up across the street and filmed me even now. I held my head high and climbed into the back of the car, sliding onto the seat opposite the boys.

Despite the circumstances, I knew they were excited to be in a limo for the first time. I didn't stop them from exploring the little gadgets tucked here and there in the massive car. Sarah slid in next to me, putting the box at my feet.

As the car started toward the church, I pulled open the folded flaps of cardboard. A sheet of notepaper lay on top of the contents. I drew it out stealthily and shifted into the corner of the seat.

Dear Denise,

Here are all of Craig's clothes back. Samantha insisted on ironing the pants, even though I was putting them right into this box. It was her way of saying thank you, I think, for helping me. Sometimes I wonder how I would have done if you hadn't believed I was Craig. How I would have recovered without you. As dubious as it sounds, God blessed me with you caring for me in the hospital and in your home.

I can never repay you for all that you did, but I'm starting a job next week, a management position in an office. Pastor Miles set me up. Turns out he's got connections with people who are high up. I will send you as much as I can each month to pay off the money that was spent for Samantha's hospital bill and my own. I'm still making my way through the legal maze of "resurrecting," but will return the money in Samantha's "college fund" as soon as I can access it.

The police have decided not to charge me with any crime, so at least I'm all right legally.

I read in the paper that Craig's funeral will be held today. Please know that Samantha and I are praying for you and the boys. I wish I could be there for you, but I know it's not my place. I know you were never really my family, but I miss you.

William

Under his name, he had scrawled his phone number.

I dabbed my eyes with a tissue. He missed me. He wanted to hear from me, or he wouldn't have included his phone number.

I had thought of calling Mrs. Van Horn's number. Once, I even picked up the phone and started dialing. I wanted to tell him about Nicolas, the motel room, and his emotional breakthrough with the counselor. I wanted to ask how Samantha was doing, or if William needed any follow-up surgeries. But I lost my nerve, talked myself out of it.

I stared at the numbers on the bottom of the note.

I wouldn't call him today.

But someday I would.

Epilogue

His

WHETHER IT WAS a good idea or not, I wasn't sure. All I knew was that I had to face it. In the months since leaving Denise and the boys, I probed my life as never before. Obviously, I had been an easy target for Craig. Since my wife's death, life had been an act, me only pretending to live. A deep vein of depression ran through those long days, even if I had been able to hide it from my daughter. Once cancer threatened Samantha's life, the option of leaving this world while at the same time taking care of her physically and financially tempted me beyond rationality. That was the old me.

I was done being weak. The Lord made me strong. He gave me back my family, restored me to my home, and gave me new hope to love again. So I was facing it—what had become my greatest fear, my most recurring nightmare.

Or I would be facing it as soon as I could make myself let go of the steering wheel.

Samantha, bouncing from one foot to the other, knocked on the driver's side window. "Come on, Dad. It's cold standing out here."

Open the door, I told my hand. Surprisingly it obeyed.

"Why were you staring off into space like that?" She shoved the door shut behind me.

"You can see the falls from here." I pointed across the asphalt parking lot. Water tumbled over Multnomah Falls, cascading down the rock-hewn path in the cliff. Fir trees framed the peak of the falls, broken up by the bright yellow of the changing oaks. One pine blocked the lower half of the waterfall.

Perspective, a crazy thing. In reality the tree barely rose as high as the pools at the bottom. It was an obstacle that looked a lot bigger than it truly was.

"Wow, that's cool." She appreciated the massive beauty for all of three seconds. "Can we start now?"

I ambled past the bulletin boards on the metal-roofed kiosk. The Columbia River peeked through the windbreak of trees lining the parking lot. For October, the air was warm, the sky clear. Patches of fog clung to the mountains.

Samantha skipped ahead. Her hair had grown out a few inches to where a stranger wouldn't guess the style came from chemotherapy loss, but might peg her as a fashion-forward teen. Looking the picture of health and vivacity, she turned and skipped backward. "Can't you go any faster?"

"I was just thinking of how nice your hair looks."

She fluffed the ends. "It's coming back with a little wave in it."

The sidewalk sloped down into a white-tiled tunnel, taking us under the eastbound lane of I-84. Voices echoed in the passageway. The black line of tile accenting the walls drew my gaze toward the rectangle of greenery at the other end.

A creek ran to our right. Ahead, train tracks spanned the path and water. I wished a train would pass just as we went under the steel girders. I imagined the screech and thunder of the machine passing overhead.

"Slow down," I hollered as Samantha reached the bridge.

"Look, Dad." She pointed down at the water when I caught up. "There are minnows in the stream."

For a moment, we watched the tiny fish fight the current.

I bent over and massaged my shin. "Should we check the gift shop for a map of the trails?"

Samantha shook her head. "I want to explore. We won't get lost if we follow the signs." She took my hand in hers and we worked our way through the crowds to the bottom platform. An ache pulsed through my legs as we climbed the long shallow stairs to the landing. How was I going to make it all the way up the trail?

"Doing okay, Dad?"

I squeezed her hand. "I'm always fine if I'm with my favorite girl in the whole world." Maybe if she hadn't fought leukemia, maybe if I hadn't been lost to her for so long, she wouldn't let me get away with talking mushy to her. Forty days. A long time to be without my memory, but a longer time for her to be without a father.

Reaching the railing, I leaned forward, putting most of my weight on my arms and stretching my legs. A huge log floated at the edge of the pool, pinned against a graveled bar. Water drifted down from a little ridge on the pool above. An arcing cement bridge stood guard over the upper pool. I could at least make it that far.

"Ready?" I released the railing, allowing my legs to carry the full weight of my body once more. A sign at the first turn of the Larch Mountain trail informed us that it was two-tenths of a mile to the Multnomah Falls bridge and one mile to the top of the falls.

No problem. I had covered far greater distances than that on the treadmill in physical therapy.

Rainwater pooled in hollowed-out joints of older trees, leaves floating between moss-coated trunks. Flat, square rocks piled upon each other, forming a retaining wall on the high side of the trail. My pace slowed as the grade steepened. A group of Japanese tourists bustled by, forcing me to brush against the netting strung overhead to catch falling rocks.

Just ahead I spied a wooden bench. "Sam, let's take a little rest."

She turned back with a frown, but her expression changed as soon as she caught sight of me. "You're already sweating."

"I'm an old, old man." A huff escaped my lungs as I sank to the bench. Oh, blessed relief! My shins burned from the effort. Apparently, a real-life uphill slope was far different from an artificial stroll on an inclined treadmill.

Cold from a metal plaque seeped through my sweatshirt, but I didn't want to read it. "In Memory of . . ." I had enough of those in my own life. I didn't need someone else's loss weighing on me, too.

When my breathing returned to normal, I stood, ignoring the pricks of pain. "Let's get to that bridge."

Samantha stopped kicking at a decaying fallen tree and joined me back on the trail. She slowed her pace considerably, and I tried to distract myself from the pain by taking in the beauty around me. At least the pain kept me too busy to think about why I was putting myself through such torture. Samantha knew I was supposed to have died for Craig, but she had never been told the details. She had no idea what our outing really meant to me.

The columned railing of the cement bridge came into sight. This time I laid my stomach over the broad strip and leaned over, facing straight on to the water.

Samantha put a hand on my back, as if scared I might tip.

"Don't worry, honey."

She rubbed along my spine but kept her hand there as she gazed at the falls.

The slender stream of water bounced off ridges of rock, fanning into fine mist that blew onto our faces. The constant erosive force of the water had carved a shallow cave into the lowest portion of rock. A few boulders sat randomly along the edge. How far they must have fallen!

Following the flow of the stream from the pool to the lower fall, I scanned the platform where we first stopped and the stone lodge at the entrance to the path. A line of people snaked out from a coffee cart.

Another bench, set back against a curved wall of stone, beckoned from the other end of the bridge. "I'll be over there," I said. "Take your time."

Hopefully, a lot of time.

She gave me fifteen sympathy minutes before yanking me up off the bench. "Let's make it to the top before winter arrives."

At least she wasn't too old to explore the body-sized crevices in the rock that came next along the path.

I made a big show of taking pictures, conserving my energy, as she shoved her small frame into the gaps and posed. Making it to the next bench became my single-minded goal. The ground on the hillside of the path dropped farther away. I concentrated on keeping to the inside of the path. "Samantha, don't go near the edge."

"Don't worry, I'm fine." But she moved from the center.

A gang of teenagers slipped by us at the next switchback, jostling each other. Didn't they realize this wasn't a game? People accidentally slipped off the path each year. I couldn't stomach the thought of seeing it happen.

The early morning fog burned off and sunshine warmed the soil, summoning a woodsy aroma of moss, decomposing leaves, and pine. An older couple excused themselves around us, the gentleman using a walking stick. Why hadn't I thought of that?

Between two trees, I caught a glimpse of a pond, a strip of trees, and the Columbia River beyond. We came to a safer spot in the trail. A field of boulders rose on the right. Samantha leaned against a tilted rock and relaxed before I could even suggest another break. An oak leaf larger than my hand lay between us. I picked it up and rested it over her closed eyes.

"Dad!" She brushed it away, giggling.

Soon we reached a meadow of ferns. I snapped another shot of Samantha with the backdrop of the feathery stalks. Would the hike go on for eternity? It seemed we'd been on the trail for hours. Surrounded by some of the most beautiful land God created, but still . . . how could one mile drag on for so long? Maybe I read the sign wrong. Maybe I wouldn't be able to make it to the top.

We hit another switchback and the trail pitched forward. My feet tingled as they slapped against the asphalt-paved path, each step jarring my body.

A short distance later, a small trail peeled off to the left, leading to a bridge over a stream. Trees grew on the banks, undergrowth spilling over logs. We followed the main trail, picked our way over a patchy repair of a washed-out section, and a small fall came into sight. Most of the water rushed into the shaded pool beneath, but a few trickles meandered down the sides of the rock and mingled with the calmer water.

Samantha took the lead as the trail narrowed and merged into a walled path of descending stone steps. The steps deposited us into a circle with a steel railing.

I made it. I had climbed to the top of Multnomah Falls. I stumbled to the outer edge, gripped the railing, and surveyed below. The white water fell, fell, fell an incomprehensible distance. I shuddered. *Lord God, how can I ever thank You for saving me from that?* One hop over a waist-high railing was all it would have taken for *me* to fall, fall, fall. . . .

"Dad." Samantha rested her head on my shoulder. "Isn't this awesome?"

Overcome by the Lord's mercy, I couldn't speak. "Mmm."

"Thanks for bringing me here." She pulled a water bottle out of her backpack and handed it to me.

"I can't imagine being here without you." I broke the seal and tipped the bottle into my mouth. Lifting my gaze, I took in the panoramic view. The mighty Columbia spread out to the east and the west. A sandbar broke the calm surface, paralleling the mountains on the Washington side. Far below, cars in the parking lot looked like grains of colored rice.

"Pardon me?" The older man who had passed us held out a camera. "Would you mind taking a picture of me and the missus?"

I had always been a sucker for an English accent. "Point and click?" I took the camera, framed the shot, and captured a memory.

As they turned and headed back up the steps, I closed my eyes and drew a deep breath. I had conquered my fear. I climbed to the spot where I was supposed to have died and I wanted nothing more than to live. To live for Samantha. To live for myself. To live for God.

Whatever You have planned, Lord, I'm so grateful for the life You've given back to me.

My cell rang. I opened my eyes in time to catch the glares of the nature lovers around me. I wouldn't take the call now, but I wanted to see who was calling. I slipped the phone into the palm of my hand and read the screen.

Denise. I blinked. Her name remained.

The phone rang again.

We hadn't talked since the day I left her house. Could she really be calling me? I had entered her number into the phone contact info mainly as a precaution so I wouldn't forget it if I ever needed to get hold of her. I had sent two large checks so far, to cover my expenses, and gotten no response.

It rang once more.

Did the boys miss me? Maybe one of them had asked to speak with me. Maybe they wanted to ream me out for pretending to be their father.

I flipped open the phone and brought it to my ear. My throat dried. "Hello?

Silence. Then, "William?" Her warm, mellow voice spoke my name without the doubt or sarcasm that permeated it the day we discovered the truth.

"Denise? Is it you?"

"Sorry it's been so long." Her voice quavered.

"Have you been crying?"

"A little. Today would have been our twentieth anniversary."

She was sad over Craig? So she called me? After all those hours of secretly hoping the phone would ring and I could talk to her again, she only wanted to talk about missing Craig? It sucker punched me.

I leaned against the rail. "I'm sorry."

And I was. Of course she should be sad. Of course she was thinking of Craig on such an important day. Did I think her world should revolve around me? A fraud who'd done nothing but bring her pain?

"He's only been gone four months."

"It seems like all that happened a lifetime ago."

"That's just it, William. He may have only been dead since June, but he left us emotionally long before." Her words came more quickly. "Jamie learned a new skateboard trick and he keeps begging me to get you to come watch it. Even Nicolas mentions how quiet the house seems without you here."

I held my breath. "And you?"

"I . . . I've missed you. I've missed our talks. Obviously my life is still a huge mess right now, but . . ."

"But what?"

She sighed. "You're probably moving on with life, getting everything back to normal with Samantha. I don't want to ruin that. I shouldn't have called. Just forget—"

"No." My sharp statement drew Samantha away from admiring the view.

"Who is it?" she whispered.

I held up a finger. "No. Please don't hang up. Are you saying you want to see us?" My stomach twisted as I waited for her answer.

"I . . . I would love to."

My heart lifted, unlocked all the dreams I had stuffed into storage.

I whooped. "Anywhere, anytime you want. I promise I'll be there."

My thanks to

Chris Ginocchio, M.D., who answered numerous questions regarding the medical aspects of the story with unceasing patience. Jeffrey Johnson, M.D., Lisa Vanden, M.D., and Jon Caulley, P.T., who also helped with medical details. Any inaccuracies are mine and mine alone.

My mentors, whether through personal contact or inspiration: Randall Ingermanson, Jane Kirkpatrick, Sandra Glahn, Bonnie Leon, James Scott Bell, Deborah Raney, Jill Elizabeth Nelson, Eva Marie Everson, Bette Nordberg, Patricia Rushford, Randy Alcorn, Nancy E. Turner, Francine Rivers, Lauraine Snelling, Karen Ball, and Roxanne Henke.

Donna Fleisher, my freelance editor, for your keen eye, generous heart, and ruthless hand. This book would still be making the rounds at publishing houses if not for you.

Kim Moore and her partner in crime, Nick Harrison, who rejected my manuscripts again and again, but never stopped supporting me.

Andy McGuire, for recognizing potential and pushing the acquisition through before your departure. You made my lifelong dream a reality.

Paul Santhouse, Randall Payleitner, Laura Lentz, Pam Pugh, and the rest of the wonderful team at Moody. You cared for both this book and me in a marvelous way, making my debut experience a joy. Your prayers held me up when I might otherwise have fallen.

Redeemed Writers Critique group, both past and present members: Sherrie Ashcraft, Miriam Cheney, Debbie McMillin, Kristen Johnson, Laurie Boyd, Ernie Wenk, and Angella Diehl. Each of you contributed to this book in untold ways. May the years strengthen our bonds and yield many contracts.

Nikki Raichart and my grandmother, Shirley Smith, for being "reading" guinea pigs and providing valuable feedback.

Sarah and David van Diest, my agents, for tirelessly seeking a home for my writing and guiding my career. God brought you into my life at just the right time.

Angela Meuser, my comrade in the trenches of writing and life. May everything you touch bear plentiful fruit.

My children, Andrea and Joshua, for putting up with a mom who's attached at the hip to her laptop. Your unfailing confidence in my writing abilities is nothing short of childlike faith!

Sherrie and John Ashcraft, my parents. For always being there, through the worst times and the best. Mom, you planted the seed. Dad, you proofed and polished. Your encouragement has pushed me higher than I ever hoped to fly.

And my Lord Jesus, who knows every plot twist of my life and works it all together into a far better story than I can imagine.

Discussion Questions

1. How do Denise and Craig relate to their children? In what ways does their relationship with each other influence how they relate to their kids?
2. Why would an adult choose a behavior that places his or her marriage, children, job, and reputation at risk? What rationalizations does Craig make for his behavior?
3. Have you ever had to apologize for something you didn't do? Can such an apology be heartfelt?
4. How does Denise come to the point of forgiveness? In her mind, how are forgiving and forgetting different?
5. Which character did you most identify with? Why?
6. Was Sarah a good friend to Denise? How would you be a friend to someone in similar circumstances?
7. Did their church support them enough? What role should a church play in helping families survive painful or destructive situations?
8. Describe a time when you witnessed a marriage not only survive, but thrive, after working through betrayal? What made it possible for the couple to accomplish that?
9. In what ways did Denise change as the story progressed?
10. Identify the lies each primary character believed, and describe how those lies led to harm.
11. Discuss your experience with anger in marriage, and tell how you resolved the issue. Do the same with forgiveness.
12. Have you ever kept secrets from your spouse? How did it turn out?
13. How would you counsel a husband or wife to rekindle love for a spouse?
14. What would you say to a friend who has given up hope or run out of options?